YELLOW STONEFLY

A NOVEL

TIM POLAND

Swallow Press  Athens

Swallow Press
An imprint of Ohio University Press, Athens, Ohio 45701
ohioswallow.com

Printed in the United States of America
Swallow Press / Ohio University Press books are printed on acid-free paper ∞ ™

28 27 26 25 24 23 22 21 20 19 18 5 4 3 2 1

Library of Congress Cataloging-in-Publication Data
Names: Poland, Tim, author.
Title: Yellow stonefly : a novel / Tim Poland.
Description: Athens, Ohio : Swallow Press, 2018.
Identifiers: LCCN 2018032215| ISBN 9780804012072 (hardback) | ISBN 9780804040952 (pdf)
Subjects: | BISAC: FICTION / General.
Classification: LCC PS3566.O419 Y45 2018 | DDC 813/.54--dc23
LC record available at https://lccn.loc.gov/2018032215

for gerri

Prologue

Randy Mullins knew full well just how lucky he was to have a stable job. As human resources director for the Old Dominion Furniture Company plant east of Sherwood, Virginia, he'd been reminded of his good fortune too many times to take it for granted. He was the one who reviewed the job applications and conducted the interviews with men and women hoping desperately for employment that might at last provide some sort of dependable livelihood. He was the one who filled out the paperwork and conducted the compulsory exit interviews with workers being laid off or let go because a line was being shut down or a portion of production outsourced overseas. His memory was heavy with their faces. He knew how well he had it, with a job he could count on to provide for him, his wife, and their two children. And he knew as well as anyone how quickly that could change. Randy Mullins wasn't about to take any chances.

So when his wife took the kids over to Kentucky for a few days to visit with their grandparents, he pursued this particular episode of his occasional faithlessness with the same caution and appreciation he brought to the other aspects of his life. He kept his car a notch below the speed limit all the way to Bluestone Bottoms Adult Superstore, across the state line in West Virginia. Randy Mullins knew, of course, that a world of pornography was readily available online with a few clicks of the mouse, but that would involve credit cards, receipts, a digital trail on the home computer he shared with his wife and children, and the threat of suspect spam in the email inbox of that computer, of a stack of lurid junk mail in the mailbox at the end of their driveway. Thirty-five miles away in Bluestone Bottoms, he wasn't apt to be recognized, and he paid cash for the three DVDs he selected. He decided against a fourth DVD, entitled *Totally Rampant*. Three should be more than adequate.

Halfway home it began to rain, so he drove still more cautiously, decreasing his speed and training his vision directly on the wet pavement unrolling ahead of his low beams. The road shimmered before him in the damp night. The straightaway two-lane now began its shift into the tighter curves of the final twelve miles of the road that would feed eventually into the backside of the subdivision where he and his family lived on the outskirts of Sherwood. Before leaving for Kentucky, his wife had stocked the refrigerator with prepared food, so he'd be properly fed in her absence, including a chicken casserole and Randy's favorite, her special sausage lasagna. As he slowed further into the curves through the close hemlocks and pines that fed down the adjacent slopes nearly to the road's edge, something approaching a beatific smile teased the corners of Randy Mullins's mouth at the thought of his steadfast wife's casseroles. He'd have some of the lasagna tonight, maybe with a beer, before slipping into his terrycloth bathrobe and settling in with his new DVDs.

What leapt across the road in front of his car appeared so suddenly, disappeared so quickly, that Randy had no time even to register what in the world it might be before he mashed his brakes. A muscular, tawny flank flashed across the watery blur of his windshield for a split second. Not a deer. Perhaps a large dog, a massive coyote? Before whatever it was vanished into the night, he could see only enough of it to know it was there. And that it had a very long tail.

The car bucked. Its wheels turned into the curve and fell into a skid across the slick pavement. Randy Mullins's knuckles grew white wrestling the steering wheel as his car slid over the outer edge of the curve, rasped over the gravel of the road's berm, collapsed into the two-foot-deep drainage ditch beside the road, and stalled out. He gasped frantically, trying to catch his breath. He seemed to be uninjured, save for a crease of soreness across his chest from the seatbelt harness. The air bags had not deployed. His breathing, shallow and rapid, began to slow gradually. The three DVDs on the seat next to him had flown out of their blue plastic bag and lay scattered on the floor of the passenger side. It was raining harder now. The interior of the car resonated from the rain pelting the roof. What had it been?

Randy collected the DVDs from the floor, returned them to their bag, and stuffed them under his seat. He released his seatbelt, held his door open with his right hand, and struggled to push himself up and out of the car with his left hand. His foot slipped on the wet vegetation in the ditch, and he fell to his knees on the gravel berm, yanking his right arm out of the way just as his door slammed back down on the tilted vehicle. His smooth-soled shoes slid over the wet gravel and grass and slipped from under him again as he stumbled around to the front of his car to view the damage. All things considered, it certainly could have been worse, but it was bad enough. In the reflected glow of his headlights, fortunately still on, he could see well enough the right front wheel buckled in on a broken axle.

The rain had soaked through his jacket and shirt to the skin, and he began to shiver as he tried to bumble his way up out of the ditch to retrieve his phone from the car. The odds were slim he'd be able to pick up a signal for his cell phone in this ravine the road snaked through. The damp quiet of the night along the road was broken by the rumble of an engine, then the waxing glow of headlights rapidly approaching the curve behind him. In his rush to be seen and hopefully helped in his moment of distress, he again stumbled to his knees on the gravel at the edge of the road. Groping for the left front fender of his car for support, Randy Mullins pushed himself upright and began to raise his arms to flag the vehicle down. The large, extended side-view mirror of the pickup caught him squarely in the ribs and knocked him to the ground on the edge of the wet road.

THE truck stopped, promptly but with precision, giving no sign of panic by the driver. For a few seconds, nothing moved in the night along the road but the rain falling through headlight beams. A few seconds further and the truck shifted into reverse, the back-up lights came on, and the pickup rolled calmly backward and off to the side of the road by the man down on the pavement. A man stepped slowly from the cab of the truck and paused, drawing in a long, slow, deep breath, as if to scent the night. Moving without haste, he reached behind the seat in the cab, withdrew a rain slicker, and put it on over his work shirt. He flipped the hood of the slicker up over his head. His face, within the hood of the slicker, remained shaded from any view. Like a shadow, he walked with steady, composed steps to the man down on the road.

Shoulders steady, his hooded head bent forward, the man from the truck looked down at the man on the road. After a few motionless moments, the hooded head turned to the side and spat casually onto the pavement. The man on the pavement lay on his back, crumpled in a heap, gasping for air, his lips trying to form the words he would speak if only he could draw a breath.

"Heh . . . heh . . . help me."

The hooded head cocked to the side for a moment, considering the subject on the ground, and then the man from the truck pushed his glasses up his nose, squatted, and looked into the eyes of the man on the ground. The fallen man's eyes fluttered, trying to focus on the image leaning over him.

"Puh . . . puh . . . please."

The man from the truck rose and turned his hooded head up, into the night, and sniffed. Once. Twice. Three, four, five times. He found the scent of something recently passed. Something fresh, yet ancient. Something indescribably wild. The man from the truck drew one long inhale through his nose, held it, then exhaled slowly as he squatted again, slid his arms under the neck and knees of the fallen man, and lifted him from the pavement. The man on the pavement found his voice and howled in pain.

"Shhhhhh," said the hooded man.

The hooded man slid the other man lengthwise into the bed of his pickup beside two battered plastic coolers, something covered with a muddy blue tarp, and a dog kennel. Save for its pink tongue, the dog was invisible within the dark hollow of its kennel. A mild, eager whimper issued from the kennel as the man in the slicker settled the other man's body into the truck bed.

"Shhhhhh," he said softly to the dog.

The hooded man lifted the blue tarp, revealing a gas generator and two red plastic fuel cans. He spread the tarp over the other man and gently tucked it around his injured body. The other man groaned and whimpered. After a long look in each direction along the road, the hooded man climbed back into the truck cab and turned the ignition. As the truck idled, he leaned across the seat, opened the glove box, and felt among its contents until he located what he sought. The rear window glass of the truck cab was missing, and he leaned his hooded face through the opening to look down on the man gasping in his truck bed. After a moment he reached his right arm through the open window. In his hand he held a small-caliber pistol. He held it to the top of the other man's head and fired one round into his brain. The head of the man under the tarp jerked slightly, then his body fell limp. The kenneled dog yipped briefly at the report of the gun.

"Shhhhhh," the hooded man said to the dog, then pulled the hem of the tarp over the man's face, settled back inside the truck cab, returned the pistol to the glove box, and drove his truck back out onto the road leading south toward Sherwood.

Spring

1

HER SHIFT WAS OVER, BUT SHE WASN'T DONE FOR THE day. Not quite yet. Sandy Holston initialed the last of the day charts she'd been reviewing and dropped it into the appropriate hanging folder in the rack by the desk behind the nurse's station. She scooped her purse from the floor under the desk and slid the strap over her shoulder. The purse was small in comparison to the bags carried by most of the other nurses and nurses' aides. Sandy carried little in it, only the essentials—wallet and checkbook, of course, keys, a small hairbrush, an old tube of lip balm, a four-inch case knife, and a plastic case containing two tampons, in case of emergency. She carried no makeup—never wore it. More recently she had added the cell phone that, as a birthday present, her friend Margie Callander had bought for her and insisted she carry because it was high time she at least pretended to live in the twenty-first century. Sandy had tried to explain to Margie that, as kind and generous as the gift was, it wouldn't be of much use. After all, she spent the vast majority of her time either at work or home, both equipped with landline phones, or up at James Keefe's little bungalow wedged in the ravine along the upper Ripshin River, where Margie knew full well a cell signal didn't have a prayer of ever reaching. "Indulge me, honey," Margie had said.

Sandy's purse also contained a thin spool of 6X tippet and a small plastic case of flies. Just a few of the basic patterns—a couple of prince nymphs, two Adamses, three yellow stoneflies, and a woolly bugger. The tippet and flies were for the spare fly rod she kept lodged behind the seat of her truck—in case of emergency. And the purse itself, a thing of olive-drab canvas, complemented its more curious contents. Sandy had fashioned it herself, recycling pieces of an old fishing vest. She'd cut away one of the compartmented storage pouches and stitched one of the shoulder straps back onto it so she could sling it over her shoulder. The purse served a practical function and was crafted accordingly. The shifting intricacies of women's fashion were for women other than Sandy Holston. "I like it, it's cute," Margie had said when she first saw it. "And so you, that's for sure."

Sandy notched her thumb under the shoulder strap of her purse and stepped out from behind the nurses' station as Joyce, her replacement, arrived for her shift. Joyce Malden, one of the other supervising nurses for this wing of the Ripshin River Valley Nursing Home and Rehabilitation Center, thrived on whatever gossip happened to be winding its way through the Ripshin River Valley, gossip she seemed compelled to share whenever possible.

Older and heavier than Sandy, Joyce Malden let out a huffing, heavy sigh as she slung her huge shoulder bag to the floor beneath the desk. "Sorry I'm late," she said.

"Not a problem. Right on time, pretty much. Have a good night." Sandy turned to leave the nurses' station, but she was too slow to escape Joyce's newest bit of news.

"You know the man who went missing up in Sherwood?"

Sandy was caught in place, her body leaning toward the long hallway leading away from the nurses' station, her head turned to Joyce's insistent voice. She nodded, her body straining away from Joyce's enthusiasm. She'd heard a bit about the story a few days ago while driving to work, listening to the local news and weather on the radio in her truck. A car found abandoned on one of the county roads leading into Sherwood. A man reported missing by his wife, who was out of town visiting family and couldn't raise him on the phone. The man's absence confirmed by his employer, who said he hadn't been to work for two days. No apparent signs of foul play. No significant clues forthcoming at this time. Investigation continuing.

"Well, the missing guy is the husband of Rhonda Mullins. Can you believe it?"

Sandy knitted her brow.

"You now, the woman who volunteers here? Does the crafts class for the residents on Monday afternoons, beading and all that stuff? Always brings a big tray of cupcakes?"

Sandy shook her head slowly. "Don't think I ever met her."

"Oh, that's right. You're usually off on Mondays."

Sandy usually worked weekends and took her days off during the week. And did so gladly. Far fewer other anglers plodding up and down the trout streams of the Ripshin Valley during the work week. A much better chance on those days of having the streams to herself.

"Anyway, the missing guy is her husband, and do you know what I heard?"

Sandy could feel her body leaning further away from Joyce.

"They say they found pornography in his car. And not some girlie magazines, but movies. DVDs. The really nasty sort. A bunch of them. And Rhonda always seemed such a nice woman, bless her heart."

Sandy was released from having to conjure any sort of response to Joyce's climactic tidbit when the phone at the nurses' station rang and Joyce turned to answer it. Sandy slipped quickly away down the hallway. She wanted to bring Edith back into her room before she left for the day.

While she walked down the hallway toward the exit that led out into the courtyard, Sandy couldn't avoid thinking how giddy Joyce must have been over the details of Sandy's own tale. When Sandy was hired at the nursing home, Joyce Malden had already been working there for a few years. Sandy could imagine a cadre of nurses and aides gathered around the nurses' station, intent and focused on Joyce at the center of the group for days after it all happened five years ago. Uncomfortable as it made Sandy to be the focus of anyone's attention, she couldn't have blamed Joyce or any of them all that much. It was a good story. Good enough for the publicly known facts to be ample grist for the imaginative embellishments inevitably added to the mix by the likes of a Joyce Malden.

Those publicly known facts had been transmitted by local newspapers, regional television news, and reports from the county sheriff's office and the state police. Most anyone in the area would have known that in the late spring of that year Sandy Holston, a woman in her early thirties then, had moved into the Ripshin Valley from over the ridge in Dalton's Ferry, taken a job as an LPN in the nursing home north of Damascus, and subsequently done her best to attract as little attention as possible. When asked officially, those she worked with said they hadn't given her all that much thought, really, that she did her job efficiently and dependably, that she was quiet, a bit aloof, and seemed to keep to herself.

Afterwards it came out, of course, that her ex-husband, one Vernon Adams, had been serving a prison sentence for manslaughter, for beating a man to death in a bar fight. He'd served the full sentence, plus additional time for a failed escape attempt. Upon his release in the fall of that year, he'd tracked down his ex-wife at her new home on Willard Road near Damascus. Apparently bent on some manner of revenge, the ex-husband had pursued Sandy Holston into the waters of the lower Ripshin River, across the road from her home, where he found her trout fishing with her friend, one Margie Callander. The two women had fled across the river and downstream. Before he could reach his intended victims, the ex-convict ex-husband was caught unaware by the sudden and dramatic rise in the water level of the river, the result of a huge release of water from the hydroelectric dam upstream at Willard Lake. The assailant was swept up in the sudden surge of water, his head smashed into one of the many large boulders projecting from the riverbed, and drowned. His body was eventually recovered over a mile downstream. The two women had made it to the far riverbank just in time. Once the high waters of the dam release receded, they were able to return safely to the other bank. Authorities questioned the two women, their stories were confirmed, and no charges were filed.

As the public facts came out, they fed directly into the more fluid and variable versions of events narrated and amplified by the voices of the Joyce Maldens of the Ripshin River Valley. Most of these versions made it to Sandy's ears in one form or another. She paid them little mind, but they were out there, nonetheless, vibrating in the air around her. There must have been an ill-advised affair with a married doctor or something like that because, really, why else would a nurse leave a good-paying job at the big medical center near Dalton's Ferry to work in a nursing home in a little backwater like this? She'd moved into old Calvin Linkous's house out on Willard Road, rented to her by his greedy little daughter not even a month yet after poor Calvin had dropped dead next to that big pile of old tires out behind the place. The daughter had even let this outsider take in Calvin's dog, Stink, without even a how-do-you-do about how much Calvin loved that damn mutt. Some things just weren't decent. Of course, who else would want that old mutt, smelling like he did of all the skunks he'd killed over the years?

When her husband killed that man, do you know, she was sitting right there at the bar, right in the middle of all that mess. Saw the whole thing happen right in front of her eyes and never said a thing. Never shed tear one. And the husband killed that man, someone said, because she must have been having an affair with him, and he was coming for her to do the same to her, and would have, except that other folks in the bar wrestled him to the ground until the police got there. Horrible as all that is, could you really blame him, bless his heart, her sitting right there, the hussy, with some other fellow for all the world to see? And just why is it she don't have the same last name as her ex-husband? Someone knew someone who knew the deceased ex-convict ex-husband's mother, and that woman was not at all shy to let it out what a lousy whore her ex-daughter-in-law had always been. Now, don't you know, they say she's taken up with that strange old widower, what's his name, Keefe, lives in that little shack up on the fire road above the lake. Nurse up at the hospital emergency room in Sherwood said she brought him in with some sort of injury once. You have to wonder what she might have done to him. Now there's a marriage made in heaven. Hard to tell which one's more strange of the two. She acts more like a man than a woman, standing right out in the middle of the river, fishing all the time. Not normal for a woman, carrying on like that. And just what do you suppose was going on when her ex-husband came for her, her and that other woman, just the two of them, out there in the river, doing what? Fishing? Call it what you want, but looks more like those two gals are likely, well, you know, *that way*. Bless their hearts.

Sandy left these imagined facts and the known facts of her life to whirl and shift as they would. Walking down the long hallway, away from Joyce, in search of Edith, she held the private facts of her life close, to be shared partially with only a select few, to be shared fully with no one. She had no point to prove. She was who she was, at home in her skin with no more apologies to make.

She was Sandy Holston, that woman from over the ridge for whom not one but two men had died. And yet they hadn't died for her, neither Vernon nor the drunken red-haired man Vernon killed at the bar, the red-haired man she'd never met before and whose name she still couldn't recall. Both had died for a version of her—the beloved wife, the good-looking woman ripe for the picking on the adjacent barstool—versions of Sandy they had each fabricated themselves and attempted to drape over her. Neither version had ever fit her. She wondered if any of these other women ever understood that, the women she would still catch looking furtively at her from time to time, their quick glances revealing a mixture of envy, awe, and fear of the woman for whom men had actually died.

She was Sandy Holston, "a cold fish, that one," some had said. And perhaps she was. She had finned her way into the world as a late "surprise" to her middle-aged, childless parents, both of whom had by that time long since settled comfortably into a life crafted for only two. Other than the shrine of old photographs on her mother's bedside table, she had no memory of the father who died in a foundry explosion while she was still a toddler, leaving her with a mother entrenched in the life of a grieving widow and who seemed startled by the presence of a daughter who might intrude upon that grief. When her mother died, she closed up her mother's house and married Vernon Adams because he had professed what he called love and his proposal had seemed reasonable and she could think of no reason not to accept. She stepped out of the shadow of the life her parents had shaped for themselves and into the one planned out by Vernon and felt no recognizable sense of loss. Nothing had yet presented itself that might sink a barb into the heart pumping blood through her flesh.

She was Sandy Holston, and yes, she had agreed to participate in her imprisoned husband's ill-fated escape attempt. She could think of no simple way to refuse, and she doubted he would ever actually enact his plan—to wait for the right moment, then flee the prison work detail, escape into the national forest land nearby, run over the ridge and down to the clearing by Dismal Creek, where Sandy would be waiting with the car. And she did wait, as agreed, one day a week for months, while Vernon waited for his opportunity on the other side of the ridge. And while she waited, she learned to fish. Other nurses at work had told her how awful it must be to be married to an imprisoned killer. More sympathetic ones had told her they knew just how much she must miss him, gone for all those years. Sandy dug through her husband's things, searching for some touch, some scent, some sensation that would indicate she did miss her husband's presence. She found nothing to ignite longing in her except an old abandoned fly rod, one thing never used by her husband. So while she waited, in the clearing by Dismal Creek, a respectable trout stream, she fished. And in her long waiting, she became a fly fisher, wading gracefully through the current of the stream, taking the stocked rainbow trout easily, learning to stalk with increased precision and skill for the cagey, more elusive native brook trout. Over the months she came gradually to the realization that it was as if she had not been born, not felt lashed to the world around her in any way, until that first day she stepped into a trout stream. A first barb had at last managed to lodge itself in her heart. She loved something.

When Vernon finally did make his escape attempt, Sandy now had something to protect and preserve. The man who burst into the clearing where she was stalking a particularly large brook trout was no longer anyone she could recognize as a husband—he was now a dangerous man coming in between her and a good fish. She fled the stream to her car and escaped the approach of the desperate convict just as the pursuing guards emerged from the creek into the clearing and locked him in their gun sights.

She was Sandy Holston, who moved over the ridge to the Ripshin River Valley, at the far edge of the Rogers Ridge watershed, to wait out the impending release of her ex-husband from prison. She'd waited out half of that first summer along the Ripshin until old Calvin Linkous's heartbroken, skunk-killing dog, Stink, finally accepted her presence in his home and hobbled up to her, nestled his snout in her lap, and allowed her to pick off the army of ticks attached to his mottled hide. By the end of that summer, she was more glad than she could ever let on that her only friend, irascible, salty-tongued Margie Callander, refused to allow Sandy to flee from her as she had most everything else in her old life. And yes, as they said, she had taken up with that eccentric widower, James Keefe, a man far older than she. She had been drawn to him because of the rhythm of the river in his voice, because of his little bungalow on the banks of the upper Ripshin, and because neither of them could ever care for the other as much as each cared for the river that ran through their lives and the fish in it. Never effusive in their affection, they had grown comfortable with one another, though it hadn't come easily, and they shared a sense of obligation, in their own odd ways, to the river as they knew and loved it.

And as the public facts had stated, after his release from prison, the ex-husband had come for one Sandy Holston, bent on killing her for reasons unspecified. He had pursued her into the river, where he was subsequently overwhelmed and drowned by the discharge of water from the upstream hydroelectric dam. What the public facts did not contain, what was contained in the private facts Sandy held so close, was that as Vernon had pursued her, she had retreated downstream with intent and purpose, with precise design, leading him into position at the head of the deepest hole on that stretch of the river just as the wall of discharged water arrived downstream. She'd lured her ex-husband into position just as she would have played a fish. She was a killer, too.

She was Sandy Holston, a woman with a questionable past and a smelly old dog, whose life played out along a tight line between herself and a fish on the other end. She was, admittedly, a "cold fish," living largely on her own terms, but in this place, this watershed, this river valley, she was also a woman who might, in her own way, love.

AFTERNOON sunlight poured through the glass doors at the end of the hallway. It was the first fully warm day of spring, and Edith had asked to spend as much of it as possible outside, in the courtyard. Sandy was on her way to retrieve Edith, but before she could reach the exit, she was stopped by the exasperated voice of one of the nurses' aides issuing from the room to her left.

"Now be a good boy for mama," the nurses' aide said. Sandy walked to the open door of the room and saw the aide was bent forward, wagging her finger in an old man's sunken face while her other hand tugged at the fingers of one of the man's hands, which were clutched tightly to the hem of the blanket covering him. "We have to get you cleaned up and changed. We don't want to lie there all icky with poo-poo diapers, now do we? Come on, now, let's be a good boy."

"Stop that." Sandy set her purse on a straight-backed chair by the door and stepped to the aide's side.

"What?" The nurses' aide turned, startled only slightly, the look of exasperation clear on her face.

"I said stop that." The aide straightened up, took a step back, and her face went flat as Sandy removed her hand from the old man's. Sandy recognized the look shifting across the aide's face. It was, in part, a response to Sandy's nominal authority over her, but more so it was the face of one of those women, the ones who still regarded Sandy with awe and a bit of fear as the woman for whom men had died.

"But I was just—" Sandy held up her hand, stopping the aide in midsentence.

Sandy drew the curtain around his bed, then took two latex gloves from the aide's cart, drew them on, and leaned toward the old man in the bed. His head tilted to the side and his mouth hung halfway open, his tongue protruding slightly as it worked hopelessly with the twitch of his lips to form words. His left hand still clung desperately to his blanket, the right lay limp at his side, the fingers curled and immobile. Sandy finished snapping on the gloves and turned to the man, her voice firm and even.

"We're going to change you now, Mr. Rankin." His eyes flitted back and forth while the left hand struggled to clutch the blanket tighter. "I'm sorry to disturb you, but it has to be done. Just look at Edie, and she'll hold your hand. We'll be done in just a moment."

Sandy glanced at Edie and nodded toward Mr. Rankin's hand. "Just hold it," she said softly. The aide did as instructed, and the man turned his frantic eyes to her. While he was momentarily distracted, Sandy flipped the lower portion of his blanket aside, slid off the soiled incontinence pants, disposed of them, wiped his crotch clean, and slid on a fresh pair of pants. The old man was barely able to turn his eyes back to Sandy by the time she had finished.

"There now," Sandy said as she pulled off the used gloves and dropped them in the waste container hanging from the aide's cart. "You'll rest better now, Mr. Rankin." She held her hand briefly over his limp one, then slid the curtain aside, scooped her purse from the chair, and motioned for Edie to follow her out into the hallway.

The nurses' aide rolled her cart out of the room to where Sandy waited.

"Don't ever do that again." Sandy slung the strap of her purse over her shoulder.

"Why? You saw what a mess he was. I was just—" Sandy cut her off again.

"That's not what I'm talking about." Edie's brows pinched together in confusion. "Don't ever talk down to a resident that way again. He lacks mobility and speech, but you can see he has some awareness of what's going on. He's frightened and embarrassed. He's a grown man. Don't talk to him like he's a child."

"Yes, ma'am."

"And pull the curtain for privacy. He's a person, and something like this can be humiliating."

"I'm sorry," Edie said, the look on her face a mixture of mild regret and genuine fear.

Sandy nodded and walked to the glass doors leading to the courtyard.

Early in her time at the nursing home, Sandy would have given little if any consideration to the emotional frailty at play in custodial care such as that just performed for Mr. Rankin. It was a necessary task to be completed, nothing more. Sandy knew her professional approach was different now, and more than anyone or anything else, Sandy knew this change had come about because of Edith Moser.

EDITH was alone in the courtyard in her wheelchair, her eyes closed, her face turned up to the afternoon sun. The courtyard was an alcove of sorts, a concrete patio enclosed on three sides by the exterior of the building. An arbor extending from the nursing-home roof covered half the courtyard and an assortment of patio furniture. Spaced intermittently around the patio were a few large flowerpots, newly planted with petunias and pansies that had yet to take hold. Two other flowerpots were without flowers, containing instead sand with a variety of cigarette butts speared into it. The open side of the courtyard faced west to the lawn behind the structure, which rolled out to an adjacent pasture where a few spotted cattle could be seen grazing behind their wire fence. The far side of the pasture swept up a slope and into a thick stand of hardwoods and pine. Edith's chair sat at the far open edge of the patio, the wheels locked in place, exactly as Sandy had positioned her a few hours ago. Sandy stepped quietly to her side and squatted by the wheelchair.

Edith's face caught and held the afternoon light as if it were emanating from her to the sun. Her lips turned up in just the hint of a smile, more like a grin, as if she knew something no one else would ever have the insight to perceive. The skin of her face was loose, hanging slightly, but still soft and largely unwrinkled. Her legs, stick-thin and virtually useless, were propped on the foot supports of the chair, covered by the robe and blanket Sandy had wrapped her in before bringing her outside. Edith's hands lay folded in her lap, webbed in thick blue veins under waxy skin as soft as that of her face. Her arms were only slightly more useful than her legs.

Sandy looked at her face, then reached out to gently touch one of Edith's hands in hopes of not waking her too suddenly. Her hand still hovered just above the old woman's when Edith spoke.

"I know you're there, you. Come to take me away from this glorious spring day and drag me back inside my little cave, haven't you?" Edith's eyes remained closed, her face still held out to the sunlight. She lifted one hand, found Sandy's, took it in her own, then lifted the other hand and began softly to pet the hand of the younger woman beside her.

"You have to go in at some point, Edith." Sandy relaxed under the touch of the old woman. "Thought I'd get you settled before I leave."

"Just until the sun reaches the ridge, please, dear? Won't be but a few minutes longer. Please."

"Of course, Edith."

"Thank you, dear. You've made an old pagan so happy." A grin etched itself onto the old woman's face.

Edith Moser was a marvel to Sandy. When she became a resident of the nursing home, shortly after Sandy started working there, she was very old then, close to ninety. Now she was physically capable of little more than drawing air into lungs, pumping blood through veins, and holding her face up to the sun. As Edith's body grew more frail, her mind and voice, in direct proportion, seemed to Sandy to increase in sharpness and clarity. Edith had spent her childhood in her family's home by the lower Ripshin on the old river road. When Edith was a child the river had, in fact, been just the Ripshin River, there being no hydroelectric dam yet in place, no Willard Lake to divide the upper from the lower. The house was a rickety old two-story thing propped up on a foundation of river stones. It was a "rough and mean" place, she told Sandy. As soon as she was old enough, Edith left that house on the river. She hired on at the furniture plant in Sherwood and worked her way up to line supervisor at a time when women were rarely in charge of anything. Never married, she eventually built a little four-room cottage on the riverside land that was transferred to her after a chimney fire consumed the old house with both her parents in it. She lived along the river and worked in the furniture plant until she was forced to retire on a union pension, which she could still count on in those days. She'd known all along the risks of loneliness that a solitary life could leave her with, especially now, in her old age. But, as she told Sandy, the risks that came with being "stuffed into a life" of someone else's choosing were far worse. "A steep price," she told Sandy, but worth it. When she realized she'd grown too old and "tattered" to physically care for herself much longer, she gave away her modest possessions, sold the little house on the river, sold her car, and made preparations to move into the nursing home. She'd made all the arrangements. She drove herself to the nursing home near Damascus, where she met the boy who bought her old Ford, gave him the keys and title to the car, and, leaning on her cane, walked into her last home.

It had been a bit slow at first, but soon enough Edith had broken through Sandy's rigid clinical shell, demanded that she recognize that Edith, like the other residents, was more than a regimen of clinical tasks to be tended to, was still a person inside this "raggedy sack of bones" and that "you'd better get that through your head right now if you and I are ever gonna be friends." Sandy had felt a layer of herself peeled away and found Edith, another woman who refused to live inside the lines someone else had drawn around her.

When Vernon had returned that autumn and it had all happened, Edith had, of course, heard the story, the public facts, as well as the flurry of gossip that got stirred up around it all. She had taken in what she needed to know and winnowed out the rest. While others whispered and speculated, Edith left judgment and insinuation to "those other fools." During those first afternoons, so much like this one, Sandy found herself beside Edith's chair, watching the sunset while the old woman patted her hand, stroked her hair, and demanded nothing of her. With Keefe there was something like love, for certain, but they kept each other at arm's length, that affection sustaining but never reaching fully into their separate selves. Margie was a mother duck, nudging her fledgling out into deeper water. But Edith understood. Understood her. Understood it all.

Sandy dropped to her knees and sat back on her heels. Edith's patting ceased, but she kept Sandy's hand held lightly between both of hers. Her eyes opened slowly, and the grin broadened across her face. The sun was now close to pressing onto the ridge across the pasture.

"You see, sun's almost touching it now. Told you it wouldn't be but a bit longer."

"I'm guessing you enjoyed your day outside," Sandy said.

"Oh my, yes, dear. Certainly better than being in there with all those smelly old people." The grin returned, more impish than before, and Sandy had to chuckle along with Edith. "Actually, things got a bit exciting at one point."

"What happened?" Sandy asked.

"Big old red-tailed hawk sailed right in over the pasture and landed just up there on the roof." Edith's eyes trailed up to the roof to their left. "Such a beautiful bird. I do so admire such creatures. Not a lick of nonsense about them. All business."

"Yes, so beautiful and powerful," Sandy said.

"She just sat there, taking it all in for a moment. And then she turned her eye on me. Gave me such a look, I swear, as if she was giving serious thought to carrying me off for a little lunchtime snack. Though I don't know that this old carcass could have provided much of a meal."

Sandy chuckled again and gave a soft squeeze to Edith's hand.

"Really now, dear. When you think about it, it wouldn't be such a bad way to go. At least be of some use to something. Sort of like being recycled, don't you think?"

Sandy smiled and leaned her head to the side of Edith's leg. The old woman lifted one hand and began to stroke the younger woman's hair. "What happened then?" Sandy asked.

"You see those little sparrows over there?" A half dozen house sparrows hopped about the courtyard, searching for edible morsels. "Well, there's one less of them than there was before. Guess that hawk decided there just wasn't enough flesh left on these old bones and went for something a bit meatier."

The rim of the sun began to bite into the ridge.

"There now," Edith said. "Sun's made it to the ridge, and I'm a woman of my word. Time to roll me on back in there."

Sandy stood and gripped the handles of Edith's wheelchair.

"Besides, if I know you," Edith said, "you're on your way to get a little fishing in before the day's all gone."

"Hope to," Sandy said. Keefe might be expecting her, and if she wasn't too long in getting there, she might make it while the yellow stoneflies were still hatching on the upper Ripshin.

"It's been such a lovely day, dear. Thank you for indulging me."

"Of course, Edith."

"Well, come on now. I've held you up long enough. Let's get this show on the road."

Sandy turned the wheelchair toward the glass doors and rolled Edith across the courtyard.

"One thing, dear," Edith said as they came to the doors. "I'm afraid I've made a goodly mess in my drawers. Guess you'll need to get someone in to clean me up a bit. Pitiful being this helpless."

"I'll take care of you, Edith."

With all of her professional precision and efficiency, Sandy settled Edith back into the bed in her room. She cleaned her, changed the soiled pants, and propped Edith comfortably up in bed. She took a hairbrush from the drawer in the bedside table, brushed the old woman's thin, wind-tousled gray hair, and reaffixed the clip that held it in place.

"Thank you, dear," Edith said. "Now, you shoo and go catch some fish."

"I'll see you tomorrow." Sandy leaned over and pressed her lips to Edith's forehead. The old woman's eyes closed, and the grin eased back onto her face under the younger woman's kiss.

2

STINK SAT BESIDE HER IN THE TRUCK CAB, GAZING PENSIVELY out the rear window, his muzzle resting on the back of the seat near Sandy's shoulder. She'd lived with this dog for five years now but didn't know exactly how old he was. She guessed about twelve or thirteen years, and the veterinarian in Sherwood had said that, given his history, he was in pretty good shape for a dog his age. He'd walked with a slight limp since before Sandy came to Willard Road, when Stink was still the devoted sidekick of Calvin Linkous, but that was the result of a barrel full of birdshot Sandy's neighbor Tommy Akers had put in the "damn dog's butt" one time for running Tommy's small herd of black Angus down the road. "He was still a pretty young pup then," Tommy had told her. The cyst around the bit of birdshot still in one of his rear legs had grown to the size of a golf ball, though the vet said not to worry about it, and a little arthritis had added to his limp, but he still managed to waddle around pretty well, all in all. The odd mixture of tawny hues that composed Stink's coat shifted with changes in the light. Sandy still couldn't decide what color he was.

Sandy had stopped at her house after work to pick up her dog and gear before heading up to Keefe's. There were still a few hours of daylight left, and if she was lucky, she might yet be able to get in on the tail end of the yellow stonefly hatch. Stink wobbled a bit on the seat as they bumped their way up the fire road, but he kept his chin firmly on the back of the seat.

"Looking very thoughtful today, darling." Sandy reached over and scratched briefly behind his ears. Stink's eyes shifted slowly to Sandy. He took her in for a moment, then drew in a long breath and expelled a deep, wistful sigh that made his jowls flap slightly. His eyes returned to the rear window.

"Weight of the world, buddy. Weight of the world." Sandy's nose wrinkled a bit. She rolled her window down a few inches further and waved her hand in front of her face.

For most of his life, Stink's primary mission had apparently been to kill every skunk in his part of the Ripshin River Valley. Thus the name Calvin Linkous had given him. It seemed too appropriate not to keep. His gait was too shaky now for him to be much of a hunter, but every once in a while an unsuspecting skunk would wander too close to the dog for its own good. No matter the various mixtures of soda water, peroxide, and unscented douche that Sandy applied to neutralize the stench, a certain whiff of the acrid smell would linger. Not even time and the sloughing off of old skin and hair ever made the dog fully free of the aroma. Stink's most recent slaughter had been only about a month ago. A young skunk, newly emerged into the world from its den, had made the deadly mistake of carelessly waddling by the old tractor tire behind Sandy's house where Stink often curled up.

"A little ripe today, you old killer."

They appeared suddenly, leaping up the bank from the stream below and pausing, startled for a moment, in the middle of the road. Sandy, however, had been driving slowly up the rough fire road and was easily able to stop a good thirty feet from the doe and her fawn standing in front of the truck. The fawn's white spots stood out clear and distinct on its sorrel flanks. The doe's ears were erect and alert, her deep brown eyes locked on the threatening vehicle. Sandy could see the muscles in the doe's tensed thigh twitching. Stink turned to look for the reason for stopping and spotted the two deer. His bent tail thumped slightly against the seat back, and his mouth cracked open, exposing his pink and purple tongue. Sandy looked at her dog, then back to the deer, cupping her hand over the dog's neck.

"On a good day, you couldn't catch them. You'll have to stick to skunks."

The doe whistled a snort, and she and her fawn fled up the slope. They disappeared through the dense growth of rhododendron lining the fire road as easily as if they were taking flight across open prairie. Sandy lifted her foot from the brake and continued up the road to Keefe's bungalow.

She pulled her pickup in beside Keefe's on the fan of gravel at the end of the cottage and let Stink out. He toddled to the wooden steps leading up to the plank porch of the bungalow, sniffed around for a moment, lifted his leg on the bottom step, then walked up to the front door and waited for Sandy.

Set at the back edge of the clearing that opened down to the stream, Keefe's bungalow fit the space it occupied. Rather than an attempt to force some preconceived structure into the space, it had been built in keeping with the small clearing, the modest Appalachian trout stream pitching down the slope before it, and the forest surrounding it. The bungalow was a decidedly humble affair, a small rectangular structure of well-weathered cedar planks with a mossy cedar-shake roof extending over the wooden porch that ran the short length of the front of the cottage. The porch, where Stink now waited, was enclosed by a railing and the posts that supported the roof canopy. It could not have been more architecturally ordinary, yet each time Sandy looked at it, she couldn't imagine it actually being constructed. For her, it inhabited the clearing like a creature that had emanated from the soil beneath it, the forest around it.

Stink's bent tail wagged as Sandy carried her gear up the steps and tried the doorknob. Locked. Keefe wasn't there. She dug into her little canvas purse, extracted her keys, and unlocked Keefe's door with her own key. Inside, the bungalow was a two-room affair, the interior space given over to the living area Sandy and her dog entered, with a kitchenette at one end of the open room and a river-stone fireplace at the other. The fireplace was open through to a small, sparsely furnished bedroom on the other side of the chimney stone. A nondescript bathroom opened off of the tiny hallway passage between the main living area and the sleeping quarters.

Sandy dropped her gear on the floor and went to the kitchenette to fill a bowl of water for her dog. Stink amused himself sniffing amongst the more interesting clutter on the heavy pine coffee table sitting in front of the fireplace. The table contained its usual sort of mess—several books, an open fly box containing a variety of different flies, an ashtray, and assorted shreds of material Keefe sometimes used for tying flies. Today there were two crow feathers, one striped belly feather from a wild turkey, and three desiccated squirrel tails. Stink was most intrigued by the squirrel tails. Sandy set the water bowl on the kitchenette floor and walked back into the main living area to get her gear out.

"And stay off the sofa," she said. Stink looked up at her, wagged his tail a few strokes, took one of the squirrel tails on the coffee table into his teeth, and promptly tugged himself up onto the sofa, where he lay down with a huff and began to lick the dried fur, holding the tail between his front paws. "Such a good, obedient boy. You make me so proud."

Sandy stepped into her waders and slipped on her fishing vest. The room wrapped around her as she got her gear ready. While the other areas of the bungalow were slight and spare, this room was cluttered and densely packed. At its center sat the coffee table, along with the sofa where Stink now lay and an armchair, both of dark brown leather, both equally cracked and well worn. On the shelves that covered the walls from floor to ceiling all round, books were stuffed with little concern for organization: some set askew, some upright and spine out, others in careless stacks, and all well coated with a layer of dust. What space remained in the room was filled with fishing gear—old waders and fishing vests; an assortment of fly rods, some old, some newer; an old wicker creel hung from a small set of discarded deer antlers mounted on the wall near the front door. In the back corner of the room sat Keefe's fly-tying bench with a straight-backed chair in front of it. The workbench was in fact an old desk, with a magnifying lamp attached to the left side and a brace of small drawers rising up from its back side. On the desktop and spilling from the drawers, the tools of the craft Keefe plied here—hooks of many sizes, a vise, scissors and pliers, bobbins, spools of various colors of thread, and shocks of feathers and fur in an array of textures, types, and colors, both drab and vibrant. Keefe was a skillful artisan, deftly producing all the standard fly patterns effective on the fish in the waters of the Ripshin River, patterns intended to imitate specific insects at various stages of development as well as those designed simply to attract and excite the eye of a hungry trout. But to Sandy he was also an artist, occasionally creating fly patterns defined more by their fanciful beauty than by any practical application in the catching of fish. He'd made the earrings that now dangled from Sandy's ears—a fairly conventional woolly bugger pattern, with the hooks clipped off but with strands of aquamarine peacock herl woven through the black fluff. Each time she stood in the midst of the bungalow's clutter, she felt what she could only explain as an embrace, one infused with a warmth she still craved after these past five years.

Keefe had never been overly forthcoming with details of his past. He had not, at first, even been inclined to permit Sandy much in the way of admittance to his little hermitage. Only as a result of the random happenstance of two anglers along the same river occasionally intersecting did their two very separate lives begin to become intertwined. Though they had grown comfortable and intimate with one another over the years, their relationship remained one very much situated in the present, shaped by a shared love and respect for the waters of the Ripshin and the fish in those waters. About all Sandy knew of Keefe's past was that he had been for many years a professor at the community college in Sherwood. His credentials could have landed him a more prestigious, higher-paid academic position, but he had chosen Sherwood to be close to the trout waters of the Ripshin Valley. Eventually, Sherwood had not been close enough and he and his wife, Alice, had moved into the little bungalow nestled in the midst of national forest land here along the headwaters of the Ripshin. When his wife died in an auto accident only three months after the move, Keefe retreated into a private world of guilt and grief along the banks of the waters he loved still more. They each had traded a past life, at great cost, for a life along the Ripshin. And this had been a fair trade and enough for each of them. Their lives together thus far were of this place and this time, and neither clamored for more.

Sandy strung her rod and tied on the last yellow stonefly pattern in the fly box she carried in her vest. This one fly would likely be all she required for the evening's fishing, but if she'd made it in time for the hatch and the brook trout were hitting, it would only be foolish not to have a few extras of this deadly fly pattern. She had a few yellow stoneflies in the emergency case in her purse, but it was simpler to step to Keefe's tying bench and grab a couple. She knew he'd been tying this pattern in preparation for the season.

On Keefe's tying bench she found an ample supply of newly tied yellow stoneflies, hooked in neat rows into a square of tattered foam board, at least a dozen of them. Sandy pinched one from the foam board, placed it in her fly box, and reached for one more. The second fly was tied with the same degree of expertise and identical to the first. But it was tied backward. The yellow dubbing was wrapped around the wrong end of the hook shank, making it impossible to thread the tippet through the hook's eye, and the tinted squirrel-hair hackle swept away from, not over, the hook itself.

Sandy examined the small placard of flies more closely. Three neat rows of yellow stonefly patterns. At first glance they all seemed tied with Keefe's usual precision. On closer inspection she found one more, perfect, except that it also was backward. Sandy set the card of flies back on the bench and dropped onto the chair. Keefe had always been prone to moments of reverie and distraction. And he'd certainly tied this particular pattern so often that he could do it almost automatically. That, combined with one of those moments of distraction, could easily be responsible for the faulty flies. After all, it was only a couple of them. Then again, it could signal something more. Sandy, scrolling back through her memory, couldn't think of any other signs that might, with this incident, begin to shape a pattern. This was simply a fluke, something that could be reasonably explained. Then again, so much of their time was spent apart, when a telling moment would be unnoticed by her. And there was that one time. She had tried to push it to the back of her mind, but it pushed its way forward nonetheless. About a month or so ago, as she was getting ready to leave Keefe's place, he'd offered her the key to the fire-road gate, so she could let herself through. The entrance to the fire road was barricaded by a pipe-rail gate. To pass onto the fire road required a key to the huge, rusting padlock that held the gate closed. Aside from forest service personnel and game wardens, the only ones with a key were Keefe and whoever owned the other house along the fire road, a weathered, crumbling structure of brown-painted cinder block and plywood a half mile downstream from Keefe's. "Some fellow from down in North Carolina, I think," Keefe had told her. "Never seen him."

That time a month past, Keefe had dug the key out of the clutter on the coffee table and held it up for her. She'd had her own key to the gate for nearly four years by then.

When, with some uncertainty in her voice, she had reminded Keefe of this, he shook his head, chuckled, and tossed the key back onto the coffee table.

"Of course. Wasn't thinking, I guess. What do they call it? A senior moment?"

They'd both laughed it off and thought no more of it. It could be nothing. Nothing at all. A moment of distraction. Could happen to anyone of Keefe's age. Anyone of any age, for that matter. But she'd keep a closer eye on him now, watch for the signs.

Sandy put the defective flies in her fly box, along with one more of the good ones. Stink continued to lick the squirrel tail as she gave his ruff a quick scratch, picked up her rod, and left the bungalow. She crossed the clearing to the streamside footpath and turned upstream, in search of the yellow stonefly hatch, brook trout, and Keefe, in that order.

Keefe at His Workbench: Yellow Stonefly

Unwinding from the spool, each turn of the yellow drubbing thread tight and contiguous with the turn it follows. Turn after turn along the shank, beginning to hint at a body, accumulating into a simulation of the thorax of *Suwallia pallidula,* so favored by *Salvelinus fontinalis.* Tiny shock of hair from a squirrel tail, bleached and dried, every bit as good as elk hair, more fitting for being native to this place. The strands are bound to the body, ragged and unshaped, then tufted and trimmed to the swept-back likeness of the translucent double wings. Different strands, divergent shapes, various textures, wrought into an alternative configuration. A believable shape to tell a truthful tale in a fraudulent form. A practical beauty. A beautiful lie. An aggregate woven around that which gives it reason and function, woven around the . . . around the . . . the thing . . . What is the name? Must it have a name? Did it ever have a name? Woven around the thing that carries the shape yet is at the same time the core and purpose of the shape. The thing . . . it must have a name, somewhere in its delicate curve. The thing that anchors the design crafted to duplicate and deceive.

3

THOUGH THE SUN WAS WELL BEHIND THE RIDGE, THERE remained more than enough light filtering through the newly leafing trees, and the cooling air still held much of the day's warmth. The stonefly hatch was largely spent. Here and there, a few stragglers remained on exposed rocks or flitted through the air around Sandy, their tiny yellow bodies floating within the blur of their four translucent wings. She'd made it just in time to cast her simulated yellow stonefly into the dissipating flurry of real stoneflies. The trout would still be stirred up.

Sandy moved from her observation blind behind one of the larger boulders along the stream and stepped in a half crouch into the shallower water at the edge of the pool. She waded in with a seamless grace her gait could never match on land, barely stirring the water from its natural course. Stripping only a few feet of line from her rod, all that was required, she targeted the back of the pool. A single slight flick of her wrist set the line in motion and dropped her fly on the tongue of current feeding into the tail of the pool. The tiny yellow fly rode the surface of the water for barely a second before the fish hit it. As brook trout will do, the fish took the fly hard and fought fiercely. Time and familiarity had not diminished Sandy's awe and respect for these small creatures. This degree of ferocity in a larger species of trout could have snapped her line handily, and Sandy never forgot that. Her rod bowed in a deep arc, and Sandy held it high, leading the scrappy fish quickly but smoothly into the shallower water around her legs. Cupping the fish in her hand, she slid her hook from the trout's bony upper lip. Its speckled back glistened a deep blue-green across her wet palm; the bright orange of its abdomen and ivory-tipped belly fins would be brighter still during the fall spawning season. Sandy released the fish back into the stream, where it disappeared instantly into the safety of deeper water.

The pool was alive and responsive. This she had learned, yet she limited her disturbance to the tail of the pool. Now she could move to the head of the pool, to the churning chute of water pouring in from the pool above, to the swirling back eddies under the overhanging rock ledges where the bigger fish waited.

Slowly, cautiously, keeping to the left of the current, she waded toward the head of the pool and set her sights on the back eddy to the right of the chute. The rushing water cut through the opening and fanned out through the pool. The back eddy formed behind the more agitated water. Beneath a huge hump of stone that bent to the water, the back eddy swirled around a circle of calmer water where a brook trout could hold outside the main current, saving its energy, protected by the ledge of rock above, while the river brought food to it. That small circle of water was Sandy's target. Here the bigger fish would be. She'd taken fish in this pool many times, but getting them out of the back eddy was always tricky. She'd have only one chance.

Gauging the distance across the seam of current, she fed a little more line from her reel. Success would count on two things. She would need to bounce the yellow stonefly off the rock hanging over the eddy, to make it act like an insect that had bumbled from its perch into the water. That she could do easily. The harder task would be to keep her line from collapsing into the current between her and the eddy, which would then jerk her fly suddenly downstream, startling her prey and sending it so deeply into hiding under the rock ledge that she'd never entice it back out today. Her gaze turned for a moment up the slope, following the cascading course of the stream from pool to pool, through forest and stone. In her enlivened flesh she felt the implacable heft of centuries that lifted these mountains and forged them into this watershed, spilling the rush of time and water down into this pool where she stalked her prey. She had learned the language of trout. She could speak with the waters of this pool, and the fish it held, in a tongue intelligible in the wild world of water and stone. Here, on this evening, she spoke fluently. Rod and arm, like a single thing, held high over the slicing current, she shot her fly out to the rock overhanging the eddy. It bounced from the stone and dropped into the eddy, barely disturbing the surface. The fly sat the surface of the eddy, hardly moving. For a moment it shone forth, a shimmering dot of blazing yellow on the dark, still water, before the fish struck.

Under the throbbing bow of her rod, the brook trout spun and dove into the depths of the pool under the churning current. The tension in her arm hummed with the song in her tight line as she knelt in the shallows and drew the fish to her. Freeing the hook from its lip, she cupped the big brook trout in her hand for only a moment, relishing the weight of this native fish that draped well over both sides of her palm. Among the descendants of the brown and rainbow trout stocked in the controlled waters of the lower Ripshin, a fish of this size would be typical, worthy of no special note. Here in the wild reaches of the Ripshin's headwaters, an indigenous brook trout such as this one was a prize beyond account. The fish slid smoothly from Sandy's hand, held for a moment to collect its senses, then vanished into the depths of the pool, in search of its haven under the hump of stone.

Sandy shook the water from her hand and reeled in her line. She'd arrived in time for the yellow stonefly hatch and made the most of it. The well-made fly had told the story it was intended to tell, and she had delivered the tale well. It was enough for the day. The late afternoon light in the ravine was growing dim. She waded around the tail of the pool, stepped out to the footpath, and followed the path a few yards to a break in the rhododendron. Ducking through the opening, she climbed up the embankment to where the fire road cut out of the forest and curved along the riverbed at this point. It was time to find Keefe. Sandy turned downstream.

A few hundred yards down the fire road it didn't surprise Sandy to find Keefe at the old Rasnake homestead. Old-timers in the valley called it that, and so did Keefe on occasion. Up a slight rise from the fire road, the dense trees opened out into a clearing. In the clearing were the tottering remains of three fieldstone chimneys, all that remained of three humble cabins that housed the extended Rasnake family when they first moved into the valley after the government ran the Cherokee out. The clearing was a regular retreat for Keefe, and Sandy found him there often, especially late in the afternoon when the sun had dropped behind the ridge. Keefe's rod leaned against one of the old chimneys, and he sat on the worn hearthstone, now caked with moss. He stared straight ahead at the other two chimneys across the clearing, his elbows on his knees, his hands hanging limp between his legs. He appeared startled when she walked up into the clearing, but immediately his face relaxed and he sat up from his slump and greeted her with the angler's standard salutation. "Do any good?"

"Little bit," Sandy replied, the angler's standard response.

Keefe looked up at her from under the brim of his battered brown fedora, a grin dimpling into his face.

"That answer may be adequate for some other fool you meet on the stream. I think I merit a bit more detail, my dear."

Sandy smiled, leaned her rod against the chimney next to Keefe's, and sat down beside him on the mossy hearthstone. She rubbed her hand a few quick strokes across his back, as if trying to warm him if she had done it more vigorously. She left her hand on his shoulder and leaned lightly into his side.

"Well?" he said.

"Upstream, the pool down from where the fire road cuts above it. The big hemlock down on the far bank."

Keefe nodded knowingly. "A few of the big ones in the back eddies there."

Sandy nodded as well. "Bounced my fly off the boulder to the right, couple feet above the cutaway. Got one of those big ones."

"Wonderful. On a yellow stonefly?"

"Yeah. I took a few from your bench. I was out." Sandy made no reference to the flawed flies, but she looked tentatively at the side of Keefe's face, searching for a readable sign.

"Good. That's what they're for," he said.

Sandy stood and stretched, arching her back. "I'm hungry. You have anything to eat back there?"

Keefe pushed himself up from the hearthstone, took his rod, and handed Sandy hers. "I think we may be able to stir up something."

Keefe walked a half step behind Sandy as they stepped out of the clearing onto the fire road. Sandy turned immediately downstream, and as she turned, she saw from the corner of her eye that Keefe seemed to hold back, for no more than a second, and that he expelled a shallow sigh before he turned down the fire road in step with her. Any other time she'd have noticed nothing in this moment, but now, after finding the botched stoneflies on his bench, she was on the alert. Had he found his haven in the clearing, but then not known how to return to the bungalow from there? In this place he had lived for over twenty years, this place he knew so intimately, had he been lost? For now, she would say nothing, only continue to watch for the signs that might form a pattern. Sandy took Keefe's hand, something she rarely did, and held it close as they walked the fire road back to the bungalow. Keefe's hand firmly returned the press of her grasp.

4

OPPORTUNITIES FOR SANDY TO GET TOGETHER WITH HER friend Margie Callander were occasional, at best, for all the usual reasons of work and family obligations. Margie worked as a nurse in the intensive care unit of the hospital up in Sherwood and did her best to manage two young sons from her first marriage, encroaching on their teenage years, and her husband of the last four years, J. D. Callander, the good-natured but overworked game and fish warden for the Ripshin Valley. That she and Sandy would both have a day off at the same time was rare, indeed. Margie agreed readily to Sandy's proposal of meeting for breakfast at the Damascus Diner, followed by a little fishing up in the headwaters afterward.

"Oh, hell yes," Margie had said when Sandy called. "I need a day away like you can't believe. J.D.'s been spitting piss and vinegar for days now, and these boys will be out of school for the summer in a couple of weeks, at which point they'll really start to drive me nuts."

Damascus was a tiny patch of human congregation collected at a bend of Route 16 along the lower Ripshin, the road most locals referred to as the old river road. Midway between Sherwood to the north and Willard Lake to the south, it survived as a point of convergence for people driving north to jobs in Sherwood, if they were lucky enough to have them, and for fishermen towing their bass boats south to Willard Lake. Other than a few modest houses and mobile homes stretched along the bend, the meager social and economic life of Damascus emanated from two places, the Citgo station and the Damascus Diner. The Citgo station was an amalgam of gas station, convenience store, and bait shop and managed to make a go of it selling fuel, beer and cigarettes, lottery tickets, and incidentals to the locals who inhabited the homes and farms in the fields and ravines spread through the hills around Damascus. It sold more fuel, more incidentals, and tubs of night crawlers to fishermen passing through. For anything not available at the Citgo, which was quite a lot, folks drove the twelve miles up the old river road to the Walmart in Sherwood.

The Damascus Diner, the other half of community life in Damascus, sat across the road from the Citgo. A refurbished squat cinder-block building that had once been a welding shop, the diner sat in the middle of a fan of asphalt that provided space for parking. An oversized glass window where the garage door of the welding shop had once been fronted the diner; the rear of the diner reached within a few feet of the bank of the river. A large plywood placard hung over the front door. On a background of dark green paint, in meticulously hand-painted white block letters, "Damascus Diner" was written above a rudimentary outline of a fish around an equally rudimentary cross. The diner was operated by the women from the commune tucked in the ravine off Wilson Hollow Road. Furnishings inside the diner were of a simplicity in keeping with the sign. Scarred, thickly painted wooden booths sat around tables covered with red and white checkered vinyl tablecloths. On the walls, generic watercolor prints of rustic scenes interspersed with varnished wooden plaques engraved with Bible verses. The food was oily and heavy, ample and inexpensive, making the diner a popular spot with both local residents and those just passing through. The women who cooked the food and waited on the tables all moved through the grease-heavy air of the diner in their informal uniforms of straight, modestly restrained hair nearly as long as their ankle-length denim skirts.

Margie thanked the waitress when she topped off her coffee. Sandy held her hand over her cup and shook her head gently. She rarely drank coffee and when she did, only a little of it.

"To tell you the truth," Margie said, "I have to wonder how a guy like that ever got through med school and residency. Such a priss. One of those, oh, what to call them? Sort of, the overgroomed type, if that makes sense. Every hair in place. Thin little beard, all so carefully trimmed. Always a tie on under his lab coat."

Sandy grinned, nodded, and dabbed at the pool of egg yolk on her plate with a half-eaten piece of toast as Margie continued.

"I don't know, there's just something off with someone who spends that much time and effort fussing with himself. One time he's in with a patient, and the woman's having a reaction to the antibiotics he's got her on. And while he's examining her, well, she hurls all over him. Oh god, he goes running out of the room, tearing his lab coat off, screaming for a towel, and gagging like he was going to barf too. All I could do to keep from laughing. If I hadn't been busy trying to take care of that woman, I'd have been rolling on the floor, howling. I swear, he shrieked like a little girl. Seriously, how does a weenie like that get through medical school?"

"I've come across a couple like that," Sandy said.

Margie slid a forkful of home fries into her mouth and pointed her fork at Sandy's plate. "You gonna eat that bacon?"

"It's for Stink," Sandy said, and glanced out the diner window to see Stink in the truck cab, his nose sticking through the three inches of open window. "But if you want it, go ahead."

"No, no. Wouldn't want to take food out of your child's mouth. Besides, I'm getting fat and stuffed enough as it is. Not used to these big, greasy diner breakfasts."

"Something to last you through a day of fishing."

"More like last me into next week."

Sandy smiled and wrapped Stink's bacon in her paper napkin.

"Really, honey," Margie said, "I'm so glad you called. Your timing was perfect. Not to mention it's been weeks since I've heard from you."

"Well, busy with work. The usual." Sandy shrugged, even winced with a bit of guilt in her face, knowing full well she shouldn't run the risk of falling out of touch with the only real friend, other than Edith, she had.

"We all have work and other shit to attend to. We do, if we're lucky these days. That's not what I worry about. I worry about you reverting to a wild state, spending so much of your life out there in the wilderness, just you and James and your smelly dog. I half expect to hear that you've been found wearing animal skins, living off raw meat you've killed with your bare hands, keeping house in a cave."

"Oh, stop it," Sandy said. She chuckled, but knew the image had a certain appeal to her as well.

Only rarely did Sandy ever see anyone other than herself and Keefe up along the headwaters. Perhaps an occasional pair of day hikers or particularly ardent bird-watchers, only once that she could recall, another fisherman willing to trek up the rugged slopes for such small fish. No practical place to park outside the fire-road gate. The fire road itself, steep and badly rutted. The trail along the river, little more than an old game trail, snarled with exposed tree roots and stone outcroppings. Forbidding terrain for the casual visitor. Margie was closer to the truth than she might have imagined.

"It's not a wilderness and you know it," Sandy said.

"Pretty close. Plus it can get a little weird out there in places. Some spaced-out back-to-nature hippie commune or these toothless fucks out there in their so-called hunting camps." Margie formed quotation marks in the air with her fingers. "J.D.'s told me about coming across that sort of kooky shit from time to time."

"Nothing like that up near us." Sandy startled herself by speaking of her and Keefe in the first person plural. She wondered if Margie had noticed and quickly moved the conversation on to cover her odd phrasing. "You afraid to go fishing up there in the wilds today?"

"Wild horses couldn't keep me from it, honey."

"How is J.D. these days?"

"Bless his heart, what an insufferable grouch he's been lately." Margie caught the eye of their waitress and pointed to her empty coffee cup. "Budget cuts are just giving him fits. Laid off a bunch of people, so there aren't enough wardens in the field. Poor baby, now he's responsible for the better part of three counties. And if that isn't enough, they're expecting him to be on the lookout for that guy that went missing a couple weeks ago. You hear about that?"

"Yeah, I heard about it. God, that's really too much to ask of one person." Sandy smeared a glob of the diner's homemade blueberry jam on her last bite of toast.

"No shit." Apparently caught off guard by Margie's language, the waitress paused abruptly before filling her coffee cup. "Thanks so much," Margie said to the waitress. "We can have the check now."

Margie took a sip from her fresh coffee and continued.

"So he's overworked, worn out, and cranky. Not that I can blame the poor guy, but he's been a royal pain to live with lately."

"I'm sorry he's in such a state," Sandy said. "He's such a good man. Doesn't deserve that."

"Oh, he's a sweetheart. Don't I know it," Margie said. "But sometimes lately, let me tell you, it can test a person. And now he's all worked up about bear poachers or some such."

"Bear poachers?" Sandy knit her brows and leaned back in the booth.

"Yeah. About a week ago someone found a dead bear. Guts cut open and its paws cut off. That just flat out made him furious. Says poachers sell the gall bladders and paws to Asia, for aphrodisiacs, of all things. That's about put him over the edge. The boy has an unnatural love for bears."

The waitress stopped at their booth and laid their checks face down on the tabletop, one in front of each of them. "Thank you. And have a blessed day," she said, and turned to another booth.

Margie leaned across the table, motioning Sandy closer, and whispered behind her cupped hand. "'Blessed,' my ass. I swear, these religious kooks work my last nerve. Surely not living in the same world I am. But I have to admit the food's good. Then again," Margie said, resuming a normal tone of voice, "my children are in school, wreaking their havoc on their teachers for the day, my loving but cranky husband is off doing his game warden thing, and I get to hang out all day in your wilderness with you. Maybe I am having a 'blessed' day after all."

After they each paid for their breakfasts, Margie laid a large tip on their table and followed Sandy out to the parking lot. Stink pushed himself up on all fours, and his tail thumped against the seat back in the truck cab as Sandy and Margie approached. Sandy had waited for close to two months before Stink finally accepted her presence and warmed to her. He had taken to Margie immediately and continued to be partial to her.

"How's the old skunk-killer doing today?" Margie's voice was high-pitched and cajoling as she opened the passenger side door and laid her hands to each side of the dog's face and scratched and petted him vigorously. His tail whacked against the seat faster as he extended his head and licked his pink and purple tongue across Margie's face. She indulged him a moment, then pulled her face out of his range and wiped her face on her sleeve.

"I'm touched, Stink. But believe it or not, I've already had a bath today."

Sandy handed her the greasy paper napkin containing the bacon. "Here, give him this. Ought to keep him off you for a while."

"Look what your mother brought you, you old thing," Margie cooed as she fed him the strips of bacon, which he gulped down instantly, hardly chewing at all. She dug in her purse for a wet wipe and cleaned her hands and face. "I'll ride with you, okay?" she said. "We can keep yakking."

Sandy would have liked nothing more. While Stink's eyes followed Margie, she stepped to her minivan, retrieved her waders from the back, and tossed them into the bed of Sandy's truck. Margie Callander was no angler. Fishing was not a passion, but rather something to do, only on rare occasions and only with Sandy, as an excuse to get away from it all for the day. A sort of girls' day out. About the only sort of girls' day out she could have with a woman like Sandy Holston. Margie had her own waders because, as she said, she had to have "something to fit over this ass of mine." Beyond that, she used Sandy's gear and didn't care one lick whether she caught a fish or not. When Vernon came for Sandy, it was Margie who was with her, Margie who had stuck by her, Margie who had actually taken a shot at Vernon with the little pistol she carried in her purse. It was into Margie's arms that Sandy had collapsed when it was over and Vernon's body was drifting downstream. Other than Keefe, Margie was the only other person Sandy would fish with.

Stink looked back and forth at Sandy and Margie, panting happily between them in the truck cab.

"Okay to leave my van here?" Margie asked.

"I'd think so," Sandy said.

"Suppose we'll have to trust to their Christian charity, eh?"

Both women grinned as Sandy pulled the truck out of the lot and headed south.

"So," Margie said, "I've been blabbing away about my life all morning so far. What's up with you and yours? How's James these days?"

"Oh, he's fine." A rote response, but Sandy paused involuntarily before saying it, and now she could feel her jaw muscles tense, could feel her fingers clutch more tightly around the steering wheel. She knew, at least in part, that this was why she had invited Margie to go fishing today, that this was the question she hoped Margie would ask. A simple question with a difficult answer that she didn't quite know how to begin to give. But she knew Margie would be the one to tease the first thread loose from the knot.

Margie turned toward Sandy and leaned her back against the cab door. Her hand rested on Stink's back, scratching at his spine. A glint shone in her eye and an irrepressible grin spread over her face. "Uh-hunh. Hell, girl, the dog didn't even believe that one. Now spill it. What gives?"

"Really, he's fine, Margie." Sandy stumbled over her tongue, trying to speak and not speak at the same time. "It's just that, well . . ."

"I'm still sitting here waiting, and that chick is still pecking pretty hard at the shell. Come on, honey. Let it out."

Sandy pursed her lips, inhaled, and tightened her grip on the steering wheel. "It's probably nothing, but, it's just that . . ."

"Keep going."

Sandy spoke in a halting, tentative voice, groping cautiously, slowly through her concerns as the truck followed its course along the old river road, up around Willard Lake, and down the county access road to the gate on the fire road that followed the headwaters up to Keefe's bungalow. She tried to play it down, admitting she had precious little evidence on which to found her fears. One minor mental slip about her gate key and a couple of faulty trout flies hardly amounted to proof of developing dementia. And yet, it was out of keeping. Keefe was focused, thought carefully about what he was going to say before he said it, and his flies were always tied with such precision and expertise. Working in a nursing home, she'd obviously become quite familiar with the various signs and symptoms of dementia, but then again, she wasn't a specialist, just an LPN, and residents in the home with serious forms of dementia were housed in another wing of the facility, one in which she'd never worked. Keefe was normally a withdrawn, introspective man, and even an expert would have found it difficult to catch signs of aberrant behavior. Still, she couldn't shake the feeling that on that day she'd met up with Keefe in the clearing, he'd been lost, unable to remember the way back to the bungalow. That he'd been sitting there, waiting, confused, hoping she'd come along to guide him home.

When they turned into the entrance of the fire road, Sandy stopped the truck and got out to open the gate. "Like I said, it's probably nothing. I'm probably just overthinking it all." Sandy stood by the open door of the truck, lightly shaking the ring of keys in her hand.

"Maybe. This stuff is tricky, you know. So, what do you want from me? A second opinion?" Margie leaned forward in the seat and looked past Stink as she spoke.

"I guess so." Sandy stepped around the open truck door and started toward the gate. "What I really want is for you to tell me I'm full of shit and to stop fretting about nothing."

Margie leaned her face out the open window on her side of the truck cab. "I can do that for you right now, without further investigation."

Sandy worked her key into the rusted padlock that fastened the link of heavy chain holding the gate closed. As was often the case, she struggled with the old lock, inching her key back and forth, seeking the right spot where the key would catch with the corroded tumblers.

"You sure you've got the right key for that lock?" Margie's head leaned all the way out her window, a wicked grin on her face.

Sandy scowled good-naturedly over her shoulder at her friend. "There's a trick to it. Gotta catch it just so. There," she said, as the lock finally gave way and she walked the gate open. Sandy moved her truck through the open gate, got out to relock the gate, and returned to the truck cab.

"All right," Margie said. "Let's go see what your aging boyfriend is up to." She lifted her hand from Stink's back and reached to Sandy's shoulder and squeezed it gently. "I'm sure it's nothing, honey," she said. "Really, now that I think of it, it shouldn't come as a surprise that you'd think too much about such things. Think about it. You spend almost all your time with the elderly, so to speak. James, not that he's really elderly, bless his heart. Your residents at the nursing home. And let's not forget about this old guy right here." Margie patted the top of Stink's head, causing his tail to slap back and forth between the two women beside him. "I think I may be the only person you know who's actually your own age."

As was his wont, when they arrived at the bungalow and let him out of the truck, Stink walked around to the front of the cottage, hiked his leg on the bottom step, then walked up the remaining steps to wait on the front porch. Keefe was fishing in the wide, gentle pool across the small clearing in front of the bungalow, but Stink didn't appear to have seen him. Neither did Sandy and Margie, until they retrieved their gear from the bed of Sandy's truck and followed Stink around to the front of the house. When she saw him, Margie froze in place, her arms limp at her side, and her mouth dropped open slightly. Sandy paused, ran her fingers over her forehead, and chuckled softly, before moving in beside Margie and dropping their gear to the ground.

Keefe stood in the middle of the pool, fly rod in his right hand, plying the seam of the current with his usual deft, efficient casts. As always when fishing, he wore his weathered brown fedora. Otherwise he was completely naked. His forearms, neck, and face showed only a slight tanning of the skin from limited spring sunlight; the rest of his body, surprisingly sinewy for a man his age, displayed a predictable winter pallor. No sooner had they spotted Keefe than a fish responded to his elegant cast with a strike. Sandy had always admired the graceful serenity in Keefe's retrieval of a caught fish—never rushed, never any undue strain, never a hint of excitement or uncertainty. Caught up in her appreciation for Keefe's technique, Sandy forgot for a moment they were watching a naked fisherman. Keefe squatted as he brought the fish to hand, the tension in his thigh muscles visible even from their distance as he did so.

As Keefe released the brook trout back into the pool and retrieved his loose line, a vague sound began to rumble up in Margie's throat. "Uh, much as I'd like to say otherwise right now, you're not overthinking it, honey."

Keefe emerged from the stream, revealing that, in addition to the brown fedora, he also wore a pair of old deck shoes. He started across the clearing toward the bungalow, and his pace remained steady when he saw Sandy and Margie there.

"Well, this actually is nothing, believe it or not," Sandy said to Margie, recalling her own awkward embarrassment the first time she encountered this particular eccentricity of Keefe's. "Does it from time to time. Has since I've known him. Says it's good for the soul to fish naked every now and then."

Keefe's stride continued evenly as he approached the two women. He raised his thumb and forefinger to the brim of his hat and tipped it slightly toward them.

"Ladies." His voice was as steady as his gait as he continued past them, up the steps, and opened the front door. As he did so, he looked down at Stink, whose bent tail had begun to wag vigorously when he noticed Keefe's approach.

"Come on, old fella," Keefe said to the dog as they both passed through the doorway. "Let's see if we can stir up a pot of coffee and make ourselves decent. It appears we have company."

Sandy sighed, shrugged, and knelt to her gear on the ground while Margie tried hopelessly to stifle a giggle behind her hand.

"And this is normal, you say?" Margie asked.

"Sort of," Sandy answered.

"Oh, honey. I'm sorry, but if this is normal, well, what you were talking about before is going to be even trickier than I thought."

Sandy began to assemble her fly rod.

"Yeah, that's what I was thinking."

Ain't Been No Mountain Lions in This Part of the Country for a Hundred Years

From over the crest of the ridge, wind sheared off down the slopes through the trees, pushing before it a wave of scent and sound, lush markers of survival in a season of plenty. Swept through the air over the mountain, the promise of a means to live.

The fawn had been taken easily enough. It and the doe had been grazing new shoots of foliage breaking from the duff under the forest canopy. Young enough to be erratic in its flight, small enough to be brought down without too much effort, large enough to carry sufficient meat, the fawn was the obvious prey. There was no moment lost to choice. Through the thicker brush around the small clearing, her crouch was low and slow, upwind, down across the slope. Front legs stretched out and pulled her forward, the longer hind legs pushed with taut, ready muscle. The thick tail twitched, whipped with anticipation. Around the teeth, the lobes of whiskered jowl and snout quivered. Just outside the hem of the clearing, her hind feet found the purchase of an outcropping of stone. She set and leapt, bursting from the brush in an impossibly high arc. The doe fluted once and bolted. Frozen for a second, the fawn darted frantically away, then spun with unfocused terror in the opposite direction, into the descending embrace of claws. The fawn collapsed under the long, tawny body, held down by the push of paws. She found the ridge of the neck, and her jaw drove the teeth deep and through the spine. Jaw and teeth locked in place, she pinned the hapless fawn. It did not struggle long.

She dragged the dead fawn out of the clearing, through the deeper brush, and up the slope a short way until she came to a humped outcropping. The fawn's head flopped on the end of the limp neck when she dropped the body. To the side of the ledge of stone, she scratched out her cache and tugged the carcass into the impression. With her front paws she clawed into the forest floor and buried her prey under a covering of leaves and loam. She was hungry, but she would eat later, ripping into the chest under the rib cage, starting with the heart and lungs.

But now she would rest. Though the fawn was small and the kill quick, she was tired. First, replenish the spent breath. Eat after. From this ledge she could see the approach of any threat to the meal that waited. Across the rock ledge, she stretched the length of her body. The hind legs and long tail draped casually over the lip of stone. She licked one front paw and ran it over her snout, cleaning herself of the drying blood.

A Country unto Himself

The dealer had been late for their appointment at the rest area on I-81 near Pepper's Fork, so he hadn't made it back until well after dark. If a man said he'd do something, then he should just do it. It should be that simple. And if a man said he'd meet you at 5:00 p.m., then he should damn well be there at 5:00 p.m. Time was the simplest of things to manage. Anger, on the other hand, though it was largely a pointless indulgence, could nonetheless be quite real and a more formidable animal to restrain. However, he'd managed that, too, as he did all things. In a perfect world, he would have mashed the dealer's throat beneath his boot and gutted him of the same sort of organs he traded in. But he'd held himself in check, waiting, the scowl sitting like a stone on his face. For now, he would still have to do business with people like that from time to time.

The fire he started in the pit when he returned had begun to flare up nicely by the time he emerged from the trailer. Twists of gray smoke from the new fire wound up through the smoke hole in the camouflaged tarpaulin stretched above the fire pit. After setting the fire, he'd gone into the trailer, stripped off his shirt, and washed in the water basin in the tiny kitchenette. Now, bare to the waist, he stepped under the tarpaulin and stood by the fire, drying off with a dingy, threadbare white towel while the fire warmed his torso in the cooling night. The trailer wasn't much—little more than a camper trailer, with a cramped sleeping cubicle and what amounted to the only other room, containing a table with two cushioned benches, and a kitchenette that was no more than a counter with the water basin, a small refrigerator, and a propane cooktop. No, not much of a trailer, but more than enough for a self-reliant man who was doctrine, society, law unto himself.

He ran his fingertips over his closely cropped hair, through his coarse, untrimmed beard, tossed the towel over his head and pulled on each end of it, pressing his neck against the sling the towel made around the back of his neck. The cords of his chest and arm muscles grew taut with the tension, and the firelight revealed the tattoos, one on the pale underside of each forearm. Simple in form and style, each tattoo was a string of precisely inked, dark blue block letters. On the left forearm, Every True Man is a Cause, a Country, and an Age; on the right forearm, Power is, in Nature, the Essential Measure of Right.

A single, throaty bark emanated from the bed of the pickup parked by the trailer behind him. He walked to the truck, reached over the side panel, and released the dog from its kennel. A mongrel redbone leapt from the truck bed and ran to the edge of the firelight, where she squatted in the brush. After relieving herself, she trotted past the fire to a water bucket sitting by the trailer, into which she sunk her snout and slurped noisily.

He looked down at the dog, then stepped up into the trailer.

When he came back out of the trailer, he wore dark-rimmed glasses and a heavy flannel shirt and carried a large chunk of marrowbone thickly coated with shreds of raw meat. The dog sat quickly before him, and he gave her the bone.

The dog took the offered meal gently in her jaws and crawled under the trailer to eat. He walked to the edge of the fire pit and knelt on one knee, added a length of wood carefully to the blaze, and stared into the fire.

There had been no choice other than to shoot the man he'd collected from the roadside north of Sherwood. To remain off their maps, here in his sovereign land, no careless track could be left behind. The man was badly injured but still conscious. He may have seen enough to recall something later. There was nothing admirable in killing such a puny, pitiful man. It was merely necessary. He suffered no doubt, lost no sleep over it.

He buried the body in the floor of the storage cellar he'd dug into the hillside behind the trailer, where he kept his other meat—bear mostly, some venison. In the deep cool of the cellar, the dead man's carcass would be secure, forgotten, protected from scavengers inclined to dig up the remains. There was nothing more to be considered. It was done. A thing of the past.

The payoff for the bear bladders and paws was good, as usual, so the business with the man's body was a minor disruption with no damaging effects. Inevitably, there would be occasional problems to solve in this life outside restraint. He would continue to learn. Nothing he couldn't manage.

He stepped to the seam at the farthest edge of firelight. From behind him, he could hear the dog gnawing at the bone under the trailer. He lifted his nose and breathed in the immensity of his solitude within the dark surround of the woods. Scenting the night, he drew in through his nose a series of staccato breaths. One. Two. Three, four, five. Yes, there would be the occasional adjustment to be made, irregularity to be dealt with, problem to solve. This grand solitude would not be among those problems.

5

RARELY, IF EVER, DID KEEFE FISH ANYWHERE AWAY FROM the headwaters of the upper Ripshin. For him, the quest for the fish was never a venture whose success could be calculated in pounds and inches, in the count of fish taken, in numbers of any kind. Keefe sought intimate contact with some sort of elemental condition he'd located in the headwaters, in the cascading streams and deep, glassy pools cradled in the stones boiled up out of and tumbling down the hillside. A fly rod, to him, was the language by which he could carry on a dialogue with that condition, and the native brook trout that had haunted these waters for centuries were his interlocutors. Over the past few years, Sandy had absorbed the nature of Keefe's relationship to the headwaters and made it her own as well. Not only had she embraced this bond, but she now saw in it the answer to something for which she hadn't, in fact, known she'd been searching. The answer had materialized before the question could be formed.

However, unlike Keefe, from time to time Sandy still felt the need for the heft and weight, the palpable thrill, of a big fish on the end of her line. She now knew something of what the headwaters could provide and how critical that provision had become to her. She could no longer survive without it. But one thing the headwaters could never provide was the thrashing leap of a large rainbow trout or the crafty, deepwater struggle of a big brown trout, both of which might shred her line and escape if she didn't play them exactly right. To feed this occasional craving, she went to the tailwaters, downstream from the hydroelectric dam that marked the beginning of the lower Ripshin, just across Willard Road from her house.

A respectable caddis fly hatch had been on in the late afternoon when she returned from work, and she'd taken good advantage of the trout feeding on it in the two hours she had before the dam would begin to release water for power generation. She'd taken one decent brown trout and two rainbows by working her way upstream along the seam of the current. One of the rainbows, a wild, stream-bred descendant of the rainbow trout stocked in the river over the years, had brought to the contest the sort of weight and ferocity she sought. It had bent her rod and whipped her line frantically, tail-dancing across nearly the entire width of the river and back before she could put the fish in tow and bring it to hand. She held the caught trout by the tail with one hand and cupped its belly in her other. Before letting it loose, she assessed her prey—close to a pound and a half, at least sixteen inches long. The calculation felt good, as did the weight in her hand, and she allowed herself to enjoy the size of her prize for a moment before releasing it back into the stream.

Wading further upstream, nearing the path that lead from the river up to the road and across to her house, Sandy heard the warning siren from the dam. The siren announced that the release of water from the bottom of Willard Lake through the turbines of the dam was about to commence. In another nine or ten minutes a three-foot wall of water would arrive suddenly at her location downstream, making it dangerous, in fact impossible, to wade through the waters where she now walked. If she cast well, she would have just enough time.

During the winter, a dead hemlock tree up the riverbank had fallen, and the top thirty feet of the dead tree now rested submerged in one of the deeper, richer spots in the river. A snag like this would give both angler and fish the cover they sought. Sandy had yet to fish around this new feature the winter had deposited in the river. She'd saved it for last today. She knew there'd be a lunker holding somewhere down around the sunken branches.

Working herself slowly into position, Sandy set her feet and began to feed out line, sending her false casts away from her target until she had the right amount of line in play. When her line fit the distance to the snag, she shifted direction and delivered her cast, dropping her fly onto the edge of the flow folding around the fallen hemlock. She held her breath and only barely managed to resist the instinct to react when she saw the faint shimmer of gold move and shift within the pool. That gold would be the belly of a brown trout, and, from what she could see from her casting position, a big one. Maintaining her patience, she let the fly drift well past the snag before lifting her line and casting again. Her second cast brought the fly down onto the same fold of current, and the fish hammered it. Sandy set the hook and immediately leaned deeper into her crouch, arching her rod as far out to her right as she could to draw the fish into the middle of the river and away from the submerged snag, where it would surely tangle her line and break off. With the trout now moving into open water, she began a slow retrieve of her line while wading into more shallow water where her footing would be more stable. When the fish ran, she let it. When it dove and held, she retrieved it further toward her. Back and forth they went until the fish fatigued and Sandy drew it to her hand in the shallows.

As she had seen, the heavy belly of the brown trout glowed bright yellow. The gills were ribbed with deep grooves, and a slight hooked curve had formed in the fish's lower jaw. A big one. An old one. A wise one. Easily three pounds. Twenty inches if it was a day. As the course of the fish had shifted during their contest, Sandy's yearning shifted. Holding the big trout at the tail and belly, having bested an experienced, well-tested veteran of the river, she longed to kill it. Slip her thumb into the jaw and snap its neck. A tooth-lined jaw like this would likely cut the flesh at the base of her thumb, but not much before she could dispatch it. She might have the fish stuffed and mounted. It was certainly a prize most fishermen would consider worthy of that minor vanity. Or she might take her trophy to Keefe's bungalow, gut it, and cook a trout dinner for two. A fish this size would provide a decidedly sumptuous meal. Her arms still quivered from the fight as she held the fish at the surface of the water, cradling it gently in the current to replenish the oxygen it had lost in the struggle. Her fingers unfurled from the trout's body. The fish held still for a second in the shallow water at her feet, then righted itself and rocketed away. Sandy's eyes followed as the shining yellow streak of its belly disappeared in the depths.

Sandy reeled in her expended line as she waded across the river and climbed the bank up to the path. She walked four or five paces up the path, stopped, and turned to watch as the increased water level sent from the dam arrived. The gentle, riffled current of the river turned in an instant to a churning, deadly torrent. The same torrent that had consumed Vernon five years ago, but the scene did not replay itself for her now. That was finished. She thought only of the magnificent trout, stunned but free, holding in the depths under the surging flood.

MUD and brush kicked up along the path still clung to her damp boots and waders as she passed through the band of pines separating her place from the road and followed her narrow gravel driveway up to her little house. At the far end of the driveway, beside Sandy's truck, lay the old tractor tire into which Stink often curled to sleep. He pulled himself out of the tire and sauntered a few steps toward Sandy to greet her.

"Such a fish I caught, sweetheart. Such a fish." Sandy gave Stink a quick scratch behind the ears, then turned to the sound of Tommy Akers's old red pickup emerging from the pines and rumbling up the driveway. She leaned her fly rod against the side of her truck and watched as her neighbor approached.

Tommy lumbered down from the cab of his truck, then reached back inside and retrieved a well-used plastic grocery bag. As he walked around his truck toward Sandy, Stink walked in a wide arc around him, stalking carefully back to his tractor tire, emitting a low, guttural growl as he moved. Once back inside the ring of his tire, Stink kept his eyes locked on Tommy Akers, his jowl flaps twitching with the growl he maintained.

"That damn dog just never has taken much of a shine to me." Tommy looked at Stink, spit a thin brown stream onto the ground, and rested the palm of one hand on the great, protruding hump of his belly.

"Can you really blame him, Tommy?" Sandy said. "After all, you did shoot him once."

"That much is true."

Tommy Akers lived just up Willard Road from Sandy's place on what he called the "skinniest" farm in the valley, an elongated stretch of land, somewhere less than sixty acres, wedged between Willard Road, the river, and what Tommy always called "that goddamned government dam." He kept a massive vegetable garden and a couple dozen head of Angus beef cattle on the slender plot of land that had been in the Akers family for five generations. Tommy was, as he often said, the latest, and likely the last, in that long family line. There had been a son who'd enlisted in the army immediately after high school and was promptly shipped off to the first Gulf War, where he was promptly killed. In addition to his more conventional grief, his son's death became yet one more proof to validate Tommy Akers's suspicion of anything to do with the government. There was a daughter, too, but Tommy heard little from her these days. She lived in South Carolina with problems of her own.

"Now that I think of it," Sandy said, "you took a shot at me once, too."

"Oh Lord," Tommy said, his round, stubble-covered, ruddy cheeks flushing still redder. "All these years, and I still feel just plumb awful about that." Sandy had first encountered Tommy while fishing the tailwaters adjacent to his farm. He'd taken a hasty, poorly aimed shot at a groundhog raiding his garden. The spray of misguided birdshot had torn through the trees and splattered across the river right in front of Sandy.

"Good thing for Stink and me both that your aim isn't better."

"Looks like you been fishing." Tommy nodded toward Sandy, still in her waders and fishing vest. "Do any good?"

"Little bit," Sandy said. Her prideful response to the big brown trout had receded to the standard response.

Tommy had kept the family farm going with a fence-building business. A little over a year ago, he'd sold the business, planning to settle into a sort of retirement, just him and the wife, their garden and the cattle. His wife was dead before the summer was out. Sandy's friendship with Tommy had most often been carried out away from his farm. Tommy would roll up the driveway in his red truck for one reason or another, or they'd talk window-to-window, their pickups stopped beside each other in the road, pointed in opposite directions. You could carry on a conversation from the cab of a pickup truck for a good long while on Willard

Road. Sandy'd had only the most cursory encounters with Tommy's wife. She was a quiet, retiring woman, marked, in Sandy's estimation, by a certain timidity. According to Tommy, she'd never really rebounded from their son's death, had withdrawn still further into the quiet of her house and garden. "Never could really dig out from under that one," Tommy had said. "Not sure that she wanted to." In keeping with her reticence, she'd kept whatever complaints she had to herself. By the time the cancer had been discovered, hospice was the only option. Sandy had come down to the farm to help from time to time, especially to tend to the delicate cleaning necessary for the failing body of a woman, which Tommy's sausage-like fingers and broken heart could barely manage. Sandy had even helped some around the house and garden. She'd been out in the garden, on her knees, pulling weeds from around the cabbages, when Tommy stepped out onto the porch of his house. Sandy had seen the look before. Brushing the dirt from her hands onto her jeans, she'd walked to him and folded her arms around as much of his rotund body as she could, but all she'd been able to muster to say was "I'm sorry, Tommy." She'd wished that Margie had been there then. At these moments, Margie knew exactly what to say. Always. At the funeral, Tommy had sat stunned, looking like a cow the moment after the maul strikes. Perhaps for the occasional help she'd given, perhaps because she'd been there at that moment, Tommy accorded Sandy a sort of reverential gratitude. Now and then, in his simple way, he brought her little offerings of that gratitude.

"What's in the bag?" Sandy asked.

"Strawberries are coming in. I got more than I know what to do with." Tommy held out the bag. Sandy took it and looked inside.

"Oh, they're beautiful. And so many. Thank you, Tommy."

"I got strawberries coming out my ears. Thought maybe you'd like some. Maybe bake a few pies. They're mighty good for that." Sandy had never baked a pie in her life.

"They look wonderful." Sandy motioned toward her back door. "Come on in. I'll get us something to drink."

"Just as soon sit out here, if it's okay with you." Tommy lowered his girth into the one flimsy lawn chair behind Sandy's house. "Spring's fading out, and summer's on the way in. Air's too sweet to go in just yet. Would like a cup of that herb tea of yours. Gotten kind of partial to it. If you don't mind."

"It'd be my pleasure. Let me get a kettle on and get out of this gear. I'll be right back."

"Don't take too long," Tommy said, "or that damned dog of yours is liable to chew me all up."

A few minutes later, Sandy returned, dressed in jeans and a dark green blouse with the sleeves rolled up to her elbows. She carried two mugs of chamomile tea. After giving a mug to Tommy, she settled onto the low concrete stoop at her back door. Tommy sipped at his tea and looked up the slope behind Sandy's house to the twilight sky above the ridge.

"This stuff tastes like grass. And damned if I don't like it. Spending too much time with them cattle. Starting to eat like them now."

Sandy smiled and dipped her lips to her mug of tea. They sat quietly for a few minutes, drinking their tea, watching the darkening light in the sky, and listening to the faint snarl of Stink in his tractor tire.

"Haven't seen you in a couple weeks," Sandy said. "How have you been?"

"Oh, I been plumb crazy. Still just don't know what to do with myself sometimes."

Tommy wore the weight of his grief like a second belly heaped onto the already prodigious one that pushed his T-shirt to its limits.

"I keep the garden going, but mostly because she set such store in it. Like it's, well, sort of part of her still there."

Sandy held her mug in both hands and nodded as she listened.

"When the strawberries come in, she always put up a load of them in preserves. Best you ever tasted." Tommy's chest heaved as he choked back a sob. He washed it down with a swallow of his chamomile. "Thought it might be better if I made her preserves for her, do the things she used to do. Well, what a hell of a mess I made of that. Thought I'd best bring you some of the berries before I ruined the whole lot."

Sandy reached out and softly squeezed Tommy's forearm, all she could think to do. Again, she wished Margie was there to say something, the right thing.

"I just can't get my head around it. She was always so quiet. Never made a fuss. Barely made a peep when she did talk." Tommy sucked down a huge gulp of tea. "Her such a quiet woman and all, so how come the place is so all-fired noisy now that she's gone?"

A hawk rode the air above the ridge behind the house, dipped into a wide spiral, then dropped behind the tree line. "There goes a red-tail," Tommy said. "Hope he's headed down to my place. Some days, seems I've got more rabbits and groundhogs than I do strawberries."

SOME nights, if the weather was good, Stink would still sleep outside inside his tractor tire. But most often these days, he preferred to be with Sandy. And since the cow ticks on Willard Road seemed to have a special preference for Stink's flesh and blood, Sandy had to check him regularly for the parasites. She hadn't examined him in over a week, and she was certainly going to do so before he climbed up into bed with her tonight. Under the bright fluorescent lights in the kitchen, Sandy sat cross-legged on the floor and placed a lit candle and a square of tinfoil beside her. In her hand she held the forceps from her fishing vest.

"Stink. Come here, baby." Sandy could hear a huff of expelled air from the dog's lungs as he slid from the sofa in the living room and walked slowly into the kitchen. "That's a good boy," she said, and patted her thigh. Stink took two more steps and lay down beside her, resting his head in her lap. Sandy set the forceps on the floor and began to run her fingers meticulously through the dog's fur, starting at the ruff of his neck. Right away, in the thick muscle and bone behind one of his ears, she found a particularly swollen tick. With her forceps, she pinched the tick at the head and tore it from Stink's skin. The tiny tips of the arachnid's legs wiggled around the edges of its distended, blood-sodden body. Sandy held the tick in the candle flame until the bloody bag of its body popped and shriveled to a charred nugget. She dropped it onto the square of tinfoil and turned back to her dog. "That's one," she said, and continued her examination.

Shortly after the hawk flew over, Tommy had finished his tea and followed it home, but the density of his grief had lingered with Sandy. Of course, as a nurse, she had seen the outpouring of grief on many occasions, but she'd always observed it from a well-schooled distance. The weight of loss that Tommy Akers toted around in his vast belly was nothing new to her. She'd seen his relentless pain before, felt genuine pity for him, but when she reached out to embrace him, to touch his forearm, she reached across an inviolable gulf. His loss was a private agony, and nothing of hers. Her own mother's death had left no recognizable track. Where nothing had been given enough to leave a mark, there had been no hurt to heal. Tonight, something was different. As her fingers raked through Stink's fur, Sandy felt that impassable gulf begin to shrink. She was afraid.

It had been a week since she and Margie had gone up to the headwaters for a day of fishing and intruded upon Keefe's occasional ritual of fishing in the nude. She'd been a bit embarrassed for unburdening her fears to Margie the way she had on their drive up to the bungalow. Keefe had been fine that day. More than fine. He'd carried himself with unflappable poise as he walked naked before two young women—young women on the cusp of middle age, in fact, but much younger than he, one of whom was giggling openly. After getting dressed, he'd asked them both inside, had been gracious and hospitable, charming even. He served coffee, for him and Margie, herb tea for Sandy. They had sat around the coffee table, which he cleared off for their cups, and chatted while he stroked Stink's head. Sandy's dog was particularly fond of Keefe and lay on the sofa between him and Margie, his head in Keefe's lap much the way he rested in Sandy's lap now. Sandy sat in the armchair. Keefe had asked about their fishing plans for the day, recommended certain pools, suggested certain fly patterns, gave them each a few newly tied flies from his bench. Margie wouldn't have known if the fly was properly tied or not, but she examined the offered flies closely and glanced surreptitiously at Sandy, who cautiously nodded confirmation. The new flies were perfect. Keefe asked after J.D., who had taken a class with him at the community college many years previous. He'd even shared with Margie anecdotes of her husband as an overly earnest young student. Noting with both affection and sympathy how disconcerted J.D. had become when Keefe suggested that he might try, in the essay he was laboring with, to be a bit more flexible with the rules of the five-paragraph essay, Margie laughed, almost snorted, and nodded in enthusiastic agreement. "Oh, don't you know it," she had said. "Some things never change, bless his heart."

Sandy ran her fingers over the lump of encysted birdshot in Stink's hind leg, checking to be certain that the cyst hadn't grown in size. The carcasses of four scorched ticks lay on the tinfoil beside her. She'd go over him once more and that should do it.

The fishing had been very good that day, the brook trout rising eagerly to yellow stoneflies and several other patterns they threw at them. Even Margie caught several good fish.

"They really are so beautiful, honey," she had said to Sandy. "Kind of little though, eh?"

Late in the morning, they'd taken a break, sitting on a flat seat of rock, their feet extended into the water. Margie lit a cigarette and smoked while Sandy tied on a new yellow stonefly. The one she'd had on previously had been chewed to shreds by the dozen or so fish she'd taken so far that day.

"You know, honey," Margie said, "if there's dementia setting in, I sure as hell couldn't see any sign of it today. Except maybe for the whole fishing in the buff thing."

Sandy nodded and clipped off the excess tippet from the newly replaced fly.

"You know how this sort of thing can come on," Margie said. "It can be really intermittent, take a long time to develop, and it can be so different for different people."

"I know. That's the problem."

"Sorry I can't help, honey, but he seemed fine to me today. Lovely, really. Only way to know for sure is get him in for an examination."

"Fat chance he'd ever agree to that," Sandy said.

"Then let's just hope you're full of shit, like you said." Margie draped her arm around Sandy and hugged her tightly to her side.

"Yeah, let's hope."

But the fly had been cast, and now it was riding on the current. Sandy would have to stay on the alert.

She had discovered only one additional tick in her final run over Stink's hide. She blew out the candle, crumpled the burned ticks into the foil, and tossed it into the trash.

"All better now?" Sandy said, and opened the back door. "Better go out once more before bed."

While Stink sniffed and peed around a few select spots behind the house, Sandy stood in the doorway, listening to the crickets, gazing into the black night.

The texture of Tommy's grief still clung to her. She had never known a fear like this. Before coming to the Ripshin Valley, and to the headwaters in particular, she'd never been connected to anything closely enough to fear its loss so deeply. Loving in this way was too new for her to understand it yet. For perhaps the first time in her life she was able to love enough to fear losing what she loved, and it galled her she couldn't take that fear into her hands and wring a straight answer out of it. And so much of this new loving, as Margie had said, had been wrapped around things so much older than herself. Keefe, Edith, even Stink, she thought, as she watched her old dog raise his leg against one of the trash cans behind her house, then waddle past her back into the house.

When she stood immersed to her knees in one of the crystalline pools and looked up the slope, taking in the exquisite cascade of the headwaters, she felt the thrust of time. The mountain, the stones, the water, they were all dying. One day the round world would be finished creating itself and shrivel to lifeless dust, but that followed according to the click of geologic time. Her brief, paltry life would not last to encounter a grief so crushing. But Keefe was a man, wrapped in aging flesh as vulnerable as any other man. Edith, like any other woman. Stink, like any other dog.

That day, after she'd taken Margie back to her car at the Damascus Diner, Sandy had returned to Keefe's and spent the night. When they shared a bed, their occasional lovemaking was generally gentle, even-tempered. Pedestrian, by most standards. But that night Sandy had been ardent in her desires, leaving Keefe exhausted and not a little taken aback. She had pressed herself into him with fierce abandon, as if she could draw a diagnosis, an answer to her fears, directly from his body through her fingers and mouth, her belly and thighs.

Stink walked back to the bedroom, and Sandy picked up the phone and dialed Keefe's number. She was grateful there'd been a telephone line already strung back to Keefe's bungalow and that he'd finally relented a couple years ago when she asked him to have it reactivated. When he picked up, Keefe sounded muddled and disoriented.

"James. It's me," Sandy said. "Are you all right?"

Keefe took a moment to respond, but then his voice came over the line with more clarity. "Fine, my dear, fine." Sandy always found herself oddly pleased by Keefe's quaint, almost formal tone when he addressed her with terms of endearment. "Appears I fell asleep reading on the sofa again. What did you need?"

"Nothing. I haven't been up there for a couple days, and I just wondered how you were doing."

"Quite fine, my dear, though it seems I need to select more stimulating reading."

Sandy smiled.

"Had a bit of excitement here earlier," Keefe continued. "Something was up on the roof. By the time I got outside, it had bolted. Only just caught a parting glimpse of it disappearing into the trees. Bobcat, probably."

"A bobcat? I haven't seen one up there for at least a year."

"Me either, but I can't imagine what else it might have been."

When Sandy hung up with Keefe, she breathed more easily. The weight of grief and fear that Tommy had left behind began to lift a little. Still, she would have to be vigilant. There was no other choice for her now.

Walking back to the bedroom, she stopped, returned to the kitchen, and picked up the phone again. Margie answered on the second ring. "Hey, honey. What's up?" Sandy thought she might never get used to caller ID.

"I was wondering," Sandy said.

"What? Shoot," Margie said.

"I was wondering. Do you think you could teach me to bake a pie?"

Sandy smirked and hung her head, holding the phone to her ear while she waited for Margie to stop laughing.

Summer

Keefe at His Workbench: Black Caddis

A few turns of iridescent yellow at the hook end of the shank, to imitate the egg sac. Not a crucial component of the pattern. More a fanciful conceit, perhaps even an indulgence. A strand of impracticality laced into the weave of practical beauty—deepening the beauty, possibly; adding nothing to the practicality, for certain. A simulation of an outline. A shadow of a shadow. Fabricated to fall on the rippled surface in the late afternoon light, presenting a palpable fraud intended to hint at something barely there. Lay the hackle to the shank and hold it down, but loosely. At this juncture, form is no matter—scissors and thread will impose that in a moment. Look only at the raw bundle of hair, dark, thick, and disheveled like Alice's in the wind on the cliffs that day the fog rolled in from the North Atlantic and enveloped us, dissolving us to shadowy outlines as the mist filled our mouths, coated our lips, her lips raised to my cheek. Hers was dark and thick like this hackle, not like . . . like her, this one who comes here so often now, at first an interloper but now . . . yes, now so welcome. Desired, even. She, this other one who fishes with such resolute elegance, her with the hungry eyes and starved heart, her hair is yellow and dun, not of this pattern. Call her yellow stonefly. Her hair is not so yellow as that, but it seems fitting to call her so. Until the name returns. Tie the hackle firmly to the shank, fluff it, clip off the excess at the tail and head. Form is executed. Finished. A bit whimsical with the tease of yellow glimpsed within the black, but perfectly practical. Beautiful.

6

SUMMERS IN THE RIPSHIN VALLEY, BECAUSE OF ELEVATION and the surrounding mountains, air temperatures rarely got much past eighty degrees. But most summers, usually somewhere during the first week or two of June, the valley would get hit by a brief heat wave, with several days of temperatures at ninety and above before the weather returned to its more moderate conditions. This heat wave was nothing out of the ordinary. Completely typical for this place at this time of year.

Sandy walked into the nursing home wearing a sleeveless yellow top, khaki cargo shorts, and a pair of wading sandals. Only midmorning, and it was already hot outside. The skin on her bare arms grew taut with goosebumps when she passed from the torrid heat of the parking lot into the air-conditioned lobby of the nursing home. Neither her house nor her truck had air conditioning, so the sudden shift of temperature sent a shock of chill through her.

Joyce Malden held court at the nurses' station, filling the ears of two nurses' aides. "Oh, I saw Rhonda Mullins up at the Walmart last week, and don't you know she looked a fright, poor thing. Hair every which way, bags under her eyes, what a mess. And can you blame her, bless her heart, given all they're saying about her husband now?"

Sandy gave Joyce Malden and the nurses' station a wide berth, not wanting to get drawn into the orbit of Joyce's gossip. She kept her eyes straight ahead, down the hallway. Edith would be waiting by now. Sandy had heard enough of the gossip here and there to know that the authorities and Randy Mullins's wife didn't have the first clue as to what happened to him. She had seen the flyers about the missing man, with photograph, phone numbers, and an offer of a reward for information. The flyers were plastered all over the Ripshin Valley, stapled to trees and utility poles, tacked up on public bulletin boards, taped in storefront windows and beside checkout counters. The flyers had grown tattered and faded with time and exposure to the elements. The ones on bulletin boards were being crowded out by more recent concerns and announcements. One man was missing, simply gone, and whether his absence was merely a curious news item or a loss that could etch its weight onto the face of a woman shopping for groceries at Walmart, the pulse of the valley beat on without him.

The lack of official clues and information in the case presented no obstacle to Joyce Malden. "No, really. His car was full of those awful movies. And it wasn't just that. He was selling them, too. Had a place down in Bristol where he produced that horrible smut. And now they're saying he was in cahoots with criminal types in Knoxville and owed them money. Well, doesn't take much imagination to know how that would turn out. Poor Rhonda."

Joyce's voice faded out behind Sandy as she made her way down the hallway. As she expected, when Sandy reached her room, she found Edith dressed and waiting in her wheelchair. Not often, but on occasion, Sandy and Edith had taken outings like this before, and Edith was always eager to get started. She wore a pair of brown, soft-soled shoes, dark slacks, and a purple cardigan sweater. Her gnarled hands were folded over one another in her lap.

"It's pretty hot out, Edith," Sandy said. "Sure you want to wear that sweater?"

"Freezing in here with this air conditioning," Edith said. "Besides, at my age, dear, the blood runs a good deal thinner than yours. I'll be fine. Can we go now?"

"Are you sure you're up for this today, Edith?"

"Of course I'm not up for it. I'm old as rope and can't walk on my own damned legs. A better question would be, are you up for it?"

"Always," Sandy said.

"Well then, good. Let's get going, shall we?"

As Sandy pushed Edith toward the lobby and the front doors, both she and Edith could clearly hear Joyce Malden still holding forth, retelling her latest to another nurses' aide and one of the maintenance men.

"Oh Lord, but that woman's a gasbag," Edith whispered over her shoulder to Sandy. "Get us out of here, please, dear. Don't think I could bear another word, bless her heart."

Sandy smiled and pushed the chair a bit faster as the two women passed out of the nursing home and rolled across the parking lot to Sandy's truck.

Older than rope, Edith had said of herself. In fact, she was likely older than most rope still in service. Ninety-four, pushing ninety-five. Though her body had been fading for some years, her mind remained sharp, her will firm, and her desires unabated. More than anything, as far as Sandy could tell, Edith longed to be out of doors, her thin, nearly translucent skin in direct contact with the unhoused, natural world. And so, from time to time, if the weather was good, if Sandy was off work, and if Edith was up to it, which she most always was, Sandy would collect Edith in her pickup truck and take the old woman out for a few hours. Early on, Sandy had proposed various destinations for these outings, but she had long since learned not to bother. Their destination was always the same. On these rare and precious days that Edith got to leave the nursing home, she wanted to go one place, and one place only. The river.

Sandy pulled the truck into a gravel turnout on a tight bend of the old river road, about three miles south of Damascus. About ten feet down the embankment from the road, the lower Ripshin fanned out into a wide pool, thirty feet across and twice as long. The pool was cut by twin currents produced by a boulder that split the flow of the river at the head of the pool. Gushing around the boulder, the two seams of current framed the deep, still center of the pool. At the base of the embankment a wide, flat ledge of rock bordered the river, jutting out over it slightly. It was no more than a quarter mile upstream from where Edith had grown up, from where she had lived most of her life.

"My special place," she had told Sandy on one of their first trips here. "Funny, isn't it? Called it that when I was a child, and now, old as I am, I can't think to call it anything else."

While Edith waited in the truck cab, Sandy began to unload their things and carry them down the embankment to the river. She slung her purse over her shoulder and slid her spare fly rod from behind the truck seat. On these days with Edith, her emergency gear was more than adequate. Edith's wheelchair lay folded in the bed of the truck, and folded by it was the aluminum lawn chair that usually sat behind Sandy's house. Along with the lawn chair, Sandy picked up a large tote bag that contained the lunch Sandy had prepared for them. Her load was light, and Sandy sidestepped down the slope of the embankment with ease. She set her rod and reel and the tote bag off to the side of the rock ledge, then opened the lawn chair and set it in the center of the ledge. Before heading back up the slope to get Edith, she gripped the arms of the chair and gave it a little shake to confirm it was situated securely.

The old woman draped her arms around Sandy's shoulders as she scooped Edith from the truck cab. With Edith cradled in her arms, Sandy shoved the truck door closed with her hip and began to inch her way back down the embankment, moving with far less speed and far greater caution than on her last descent.

"It'd save us all a lot of trouble if you'd just toss me in here and be done with it," Edith said.

"Whatever you want, Edith." Sandy grinned, but also tightened her grip on Edith and set her feet more firmly to the slope.

After she'd settled Edith in the lawn chair, Sandy knelt on the rock ledge and leaned down to the stream. With both hands cupped, she scooped cool river water onto her face and arms to wash off the sweat. Wiping her hands on her shorts, she turned back to Edith. From the tote bag Sandy retrieved a thermos bottle and screwed off the plastic cap that doubled as a cup. "Iced tea?"

"Oh, please, dear. Thank you," Edith said.

Sandy had prepared the tea in the way Edith preferred, a hint of lemon and thick with sugar. She couldn't stomach the sickeningly sweet southern staple, but Edith loved it. A day this hot, Sandy would drink water.

Sandy rigged her rod and dug the little plastic case of flies out of her purse. She selected an Adams, a common pattern that should work on trout anywhere, especially the simpleminded stocked trout in this part of the river. While she tied on her fly, Edith sipped from her cup of chilled tea and drank in the river before her.

"Oh yes, look there," Edith said. A kingfisher cruised along the surface of the stream, then turned into an upward swing, emitted a single metallic squawk, and alighted on a sycamore branch on the far side of the stream. "Always loved those birds. Made me laugh, for some reason. Must be that funny sound they make."

Sandy finished tying off her fly and stepped from the rock ledge down into the river. The chill water rose over her bare calves and drew off the heat of the day. Edith would begin to talk now. Whether she added something new to the pot or spoke of things Sandy had heard her talk of before, Sandy would listen intently. Something in the aged warble of the old woman's voice sustained her, provided sustenance as crucial as food. Edith would talk and Sandy would listen while she fished. She took a couple of steps further into the pool and began to feed out line into her cast. The seam of current closest to them, beginning at the head of the pool, would be her first target. Sandy would stay largely in this one pool by their place on the rock ledge. Occasionally, she'd move a bit upstream or down from this spot, but never far. For the hours they'd spend by the river, Sandy would never have Edith out of her sight or beyond earshot.

"Used to be a big hemlock tree, right there." Edith raised a bent finger and waggled it in the direction of the far side of the pool. "Branches so thick and low, it threw shade over near half the river here." Between casts, Sandy glanced at the snarl of pines and locust on the bank where Edith pointed. Most of the pool was in full sunlight.

The first fish of the day struck, and Sandy reeled it in quickly. A fish of common size, with the dark back and dull pinkish flanks of a stocked rainbow trout that had been raised in a hatchery pen. Still, she removed the fly from the fish's lip and held it up for Edith to see. No matter how large or small, how common the fish was, the old woman was always pleased and clapped her frail hands together to applaud Sandy's success. Given what easy fishing was offered in this part of the river, Sandy wondered if she wasn't guilty of a touch of vanity in these outings with Edith. Did she in some way require the old woman's praise, even for such a mundane accomplishment?

"I recall one day," Edith said. "A lot like today. Hot as blazes and the sun beating down. Thought I might explode if I didn't get cooled off."

Sandy reeled in her excess line and flicked the excess water from her fly. She held her rod to her side at ease and listened as Edith continued.

"Was a Sunday and we'd been to church. Don't know that the hellfire the preacher and all the faithful had been ranting about could've been any hotter than the air in that little church. When we got back to the homeplace, soon as no one was looking, I hightailed it right on down here. That old hemlock, one branch in particular hung so low it nearly touched the water."

Sandy glanced again at the place on the bank where the tree had been and leaned her rod against her shoulder.

"So hot, well, I didn't even care. Waded right on out into the water there, still wearing my go-to-meeting dress. Not that I was likely to do much damage to it. Was already pretty tattered at that point. Walked right on in there, a step or two past where you are now, and took hold of that low branch and just let myself float up. Held tight to the branch and the current lifted me up and washed right through me. My hair and that old dress floating all around me, swirling in the water."

For a few moments, Edith fell silent, staring across the river, through Sandy, to the low-hanging branch of a hemlock tree that wasn't there anymore.

"Held myself there for I don't know how long, it felt so good. Washed all the heat and preaching right out of me. Like I was flying above it all. Just closed my eyes and held tight to that branch, and after awhile, it was like the river and me was made of the same thing. To this day, I think that's about the most perfect I ever felt."

Edith grew quiet again, looking deep into the waters of another time. Sandy cast her fly onto the still surface of the pool, just inside the near seam of current. A fish hit before the ripples around the fly could even begin to subside. Unhooking her fish, she turned to show it to Edith. Just as a bubble of disappointment was about to pop within Sandy, Edith returned to the river of the present and applauded her catch in her usual way. Sandy released the fish and waded toward Edith on the bank.

"After I got out of the water that day," Edith continued, "I sat right here for I don't know how long, trying to get dried out some before I went home. Didn't do much good, though. I was still a pretty wrinkled and soggy mess when I got back home. As you might guess, there was hell to pay, but it was worth it. Oh yes, it was worth it."

Sandy laid her rod on the rock and climbed from the stream. She sat on the ledge next to Edith, and the warmth collected in the stone was delicious against the cold damp of her legs and wet shorts.

"Back then," Edith said, "Daddy went back and forth pretty regular between whiskey and religion. I couldn't much tell the difference between the two, though. The whippings stayed about the same. Was pretty much always hell to pay, one way or another."

Edith reached to Sandy's shoulder and patted it.

"You fished so beautifully there, dear. I do think you're getting even better at this. So pretty to watch."

Sandy gave Edith's hand a gentle squeeze, then pulled the tote bag to her. "Would you like some lunch now?" Sandy asked.

"Oh yes, dear. What did you bring today?"

Sandy placed a chicken salad sandwich, cut in half, on a paper plate and set it in Edith's lap, along with a paper napkin. The old woman raised the sandwich carefully to her mouth, took a substantial bite, and chewed with pleasure. "Just love chicken salad. What's the sweet taste in there?"

"Raisins," Sandy answered.

"Delicious, my dear."

"More tea?" Sandy held up the thermos.

"Certainly," Edith said, "unless you've got something with a little more spunk in there."

Sandy smiled and pulled a half-full bottle of red wine from the tote bag. She poured them each a small portion in plastic cups and handed one to Edith. They tapped the lips of their cups together and drank. Edith took a long, luxurious slurp.

"Oh, now we're living," Edith said.

The two women continued to eat and drink in relative silence for a while. From time to time, Sandy handed Edith's cup of wine to her, then set it back on the stone beside her until she was ready for another sip. After they finished their sandwiches, Sandy retrieved two small plastic containers from the bag.

"What's this now?" Edith asked as Sandy handed the container to her, along with a plastic fork.

"It was supposed to be strawberry pie. Didn't turn out very well." The candied berry filling had come out well enough, but the crust had been a disaster, crumbling to bits around the filling in the pan. "Might not look so bad if we called it strawberry cobbler or something like that."

"Still, what a treat. And you made this?"

"I tried."

"Well, aren't you just full of surprises today."

"A friend of mine tried to teach me." Sandy grinned, thinking of how inept she was at pie making, how much Margie had laughed as she attempted to walk Sandy through the mysteries of crust and filling.

"Well, whatever you call it, it's just lovely," Edith said as she chewed, her mouth forming a smile around the bite of botched pie. "My legs and arms aren't worth a hoot anymore, but something this sweet and good makes me damned glad I've still got some teeth in here."

When they'd finished their lunch and Sandy had packed things back into the tote bag, she scooted to the edge of the rock ledge and dangled her feet in the river. She'd grown hot again in the early afternoon heat. After another moment, she turned her face back toward Edith. "Was it worth it, Edith?"

"Was what worth it, dear? Oh, that day in the river? My, yes, but it was."

Sandy hesitated, watched Edith's face until it shifted, showing she could tell Sandy asked about something beyond that.

"But that's not all you're asking about, am I right? Was what worth it?"

Sandy hesitated still longer, but then took in a long breath and spoke. "Was it worth it? All those years, you know, living alone?"

Edith folded her hands in her lap and gazed again at the spot where the big hemlock tree had once stood. "It wasn't always so easy," she began, "but yes, for me, it was worth it. I'd seen too much of how bad it could go the other way, and I just couldn't, wouldn't, risk it. Not saying it'd be right or worth it for someone else, if you know what I mean."

Sandy looked back over her shoulder with a half grin. Edith tilted her head to the side and returned the grin.

"Lived on my own terms, as much as any woman could, as anyone can. No apologies. No regrets, when all is said and done."

"And you weren't ever lonely?" Sandy asked.

"Of course I got lonesome. Who doesn't from time to time? But dear, just because I lived on my own doesn't mean I was always *alone*."

Sandy pulled her legs from the water, turned toward Edith, and sat cross-legged before the old woman.

"I had friends, a few darn good friends. Folks I worked with at Old Dominion. They're all gone now, of course. Could I have a bit more tea, dear?"

Sandy lifted the thermos from the tote, poured Edith another cup, and handed it to her. The old woman took a generous sip, then held the cup in her lap.

"And there were men, too."

Sandy's attention perked up noticeably as she slipped the thermos back into the bag.

"There now, that got your attention, didn't it," Edith said. Her body shook visibly as she chuckled. The grin Sandy returned was decidedly sheepish.

"I saw pretty early on that if all a woman needed was a man, that is, *needed* a man, you know, in that way, well, that was about the easiest thing in the world to come by. Men's like dogs. If the scent's in the air, well, there's always a couple that'll come running."

"Edith." Sandy thought she might actually be blushing.

"Now, don't look at me as if you don't know what I'm talking about. There's things that just don't change that much over time."

Sandy looked down and did her best to repress her own chuckling.

"And I liked it. Liked it quite a lot sometimes. I enjoyed the feel of a man. Had some damned fine times pressed up against a man."

"Did you ever love any of them? Want to stay with them? Maybe get married?"

"There was a couple of them that wanted me to. And a couple others I was plenty fond of. But none that showed me they'd be any different in the long run. And my whole life I'd seen women settle for the same old thing and pay for it in the end. I had me all the good times I needed, but like I said, I wasn't willing to risk any more than that. And I don't suppose it would have been fair to those men, either. Some of them were pretty good fellows."

Edith took another sip from her cup of iced tea and patted at her lips with the sleeve of her sweater. "There was a woman once. Gal I knew for a while in the rooming house in Sherwood we both lived in back then."

Sandy's posture changed abruptly. Her back straightened, her shoulders went back, and her mouth involuntarily fell open a bit. "Edith? You were gay?" she asked.

"Wasn't no *gay* back then. Just two women who enjoyed the touch of one another, who felt at home with each other for a while. And who would've had a downright impossible row to hoe if they'd wanted to live a life together around these parts."

Sandy leaned back on her arms, her palms pressed into the hot stone, and gazed with wonder on the old woman.

"Her name was Evelyn. Last I heard of her, she'd gotten married and was expecting a fourth child. But that was so long ago. And really, all said and done, when it came to, you know, that sort of thing, well, I suppose I really preferred the feel of a man."

Edith handed her empty cup to Sandy, who groped behind herself to locate the tote bag and drop the cup into it. She couldn't take her eyes from Edith.

"I got some and I lost some. Got some of it right and some of it wrong. But I did what felt right to me at the time. Kept myself honest and never hurt anyone particularly, not that I know of. And I never let anyone down. Then again, there was never anyone counting on me to be let down. Suppose that was the hardest part of it all, no one depending on me enough that letting them down would have been a misery. But must have been the right road for me because I'm still drawing wind, despite being an old bag of bones, and here we are, in my special place, having a glorious day."

Edith's eyes followed the strands of current through the pool for a moment, then turned back to Sandy. "So now," Edith said, "I suppose you think I'm just a horrible old woman. One with a tainted past."

Sandy Holston, also a woman with a past, reached out to Edith's hand and took it in both of hers. "I think you're beautiful," she said.

"Well now, child, I know you've been out in the sun too long." Edith freed her hand and, with some difficulty, unbuttoned the top two buttons of her sweater. "And I think I've been out here too long, too. That bit of wine has gone to right to my head, babbling on like this. Maybe I'll have a little nap now, dear, okay?"

"Of course," Sandy said.

"And maybe you can get some fishing done without an old woman carrying on so and interrupting." Edith's head had slipped forward onto her chest and her eyes had closed before her last few words were uttered.

Sandy remained at her side for a few minutes to be sure Edith was dozing comfortably. Once the old woman's breathing settled into a steady rhythm, Sandy picked up her rod and stepped back into the river.

Two fish, one from each strand of current inscribing the pool, rose easily and willingly to Sandy's well-cast fly. With each catch she turned to show the trout to Edith, but the old woman continued to sleep, her head down on her chest, drooped to the side. Though she had no expectations of more challenging or satisfying fishing in this stretch of the river, Sandy found herself growing disappointed and bored. Reeling in her line, she thought she'd do as well to return to the rock ledge and take a bit of a nap along with Edith. She saw the rise just as she was about to turn and wade out of the pool.

The ring of the rise rippled outward from its center just at the fall line beneath a thick outcropping of rhododendron about ten yards upstream from Sandy. The downy hair on the back of her neck bristled up through the perspiration on her skin. Sandy took a quick glance at Edith to confirm she still slept, then fed out line from her rod and waded upstream into casting position. This rise was a disturbance of the stream's surface not made by the common stocked fish she'd been taking thus far. A rise like this was the track of a fish that, though bred in the same pens as these other trout, had entered these waters fitted with the resilience and luck to survive two or three seasons in the river, growing into a worthy catch.

Her casts cut the heavy afternoon air, and her fly dropped to the water with precision and delicacy just to the left of the shadow thrown by the rhododendron. The rainbow trout holding in the shadow hit her fly on the second cast. Just big enough that she had to play the fish a bit, Sandy let it run downstream. Rod held high above her head, she followed the fish back into the big pool adjacent to the rock ledge where Edith rested. Sandy led it back and forth across the pool a couple times before the fish tired and she brought it safely to hand. A good, hefty trout whose flanks showed the deep pink tones of its wild life in a trout stream. Sandy wished, as she released the fish, that Edith had been awake to see this one.

The big rainbow had been enough to cancel Sandy's disappointment. Satisfied, she climbed from the river back onto the rock ledge with Edith to wait for the sun to bake her dry. Sitting beside the old woman, she looked across the river and tried again to imagine the big hemlock that died and washed away long before she came to the Ripshin Valley, tried to imagine the vast swath of shade it would have spread over the pool, offering cover and respite for fish and human alike, extending Edith a handhold in a current that buoyed her up within a moment of perfect peace. Sandy's legs were dry and her shorts nearly so when she was started out of her reverie by the touch of Edith's hand, patting and lightly stroking the top of her head.

"I hadn't been back to that house, not once, since I left." Sandy turned and saw that Edith gazed off into the distance, drifting upstream in time. "After I got hired on at Old Dominion and was settled in town, saw what life might be like away from there and how rotten it was when I was there, well, I got angry. Must have inherited a bit of daddy's mean streak. Wanted to go out there one last time, give them one last go-to-hell." Edith looked down at her hands, folded in her lap, then raised her gaze back out across the river. "If I believed in such nonsense, I'd say it was like I was called there, drawn there, by some sort of power outside myself. Maybe I was. So I could be there, as a witness."

Sandy shifted her position so she looked directly at Edith. She drew her knees up to her chest, wrapped her arms around them, and listened.

"Truth be told, you'd have to say I was more than a witness. Truth be told."

As Edith unfurled her memory, Sandy heard in the words just that—a telling, something to be told. Nothing in the old woman's voice trembled with confession or catharsis.

"Smoke was already coming thick out of the chimney when I came up around the woodshed and looked in the window. Didn't take but one look to see how it was. Like it was most always. Daddy was passed out on the settee, his mouth all drooped open the way it did when he was good and pickled. Before he passed out, he must have walloped mama a good one because she was out cold, her head leaning up against the wall, her legs spread out in front of her. I could see in the firelight she was breathing."

Sandy pulled her legs tighter to her chest and leaned her head closer.

"Little bits of flame were already licking out the seam in the stovepipe, and the door to that old wood stove was hanging open with smoke coming out there, too. And then, just at that moment, the fire in the stove shifted and a chunk of burning stovewood fell out, right on that old braid rug."

"What'd you do?" Sandy asked, her voice barely above a whisper.

"Stood there for another minute, just to make sure the fire was taking. Then I turned around and walked right on out of there. Never looked back once."

Sandy couldn't be sure if her heart was beating or air was moving into and out of her lungs, but she thought she saw just the faintest glimmer of a grin at the corners of Edith's mouth. Not a grin of derision, but a grin of some manner of satisfaction, as with a job well done.

"Knew for a fact that the world would not be one speck worse off without those two, and there was a damned good chance it'd be a sight better without them."

Edith took a long breath and looked down at the younger woman beside her. In Sandy's vision, the old woman seemed to expand before her.

"Folks who fret about sin call that a sin of omission. You know what that is?"

Sandy remained silent, knowing that she may very well have known what it was.

"Not that you did something you shouldn't but that you didn't do something that you should. Heard about that from a traveling preacher who stayed at that rooming house in Sherwood for a while. He knew a lot about sin but, far as I could tell, not much about anything else. And I never felt sinful, not once, and that's the God's honest truth."

Sandy leaned forward, wrapped her arms around the old woman's stick-thin legs, laid her head against her knees, and held on as tightly as she dared. Edith set her hand on Sandy's head like a benediction.

"Enough now," Edith said. "Between this heat, that wine, and all this nonsense about sinfulness, I'm likely to burst into flames any minute. You'd best be taking me back now before we both regret it."

"Yes, Edith."

Sandy held the old woman in her arms with something like reverence as they walked up the embankment to the truck. When they were halfway up, Edith looked down at the pool by the rock ledge and nodded toward it. "There. Right there. My special place."

Sandy paused and followed Edith's line of sight. "What?" she asked.

"When I die, if I don't catch fire all on my own, I'll be cremated, and I'd surely like it if what's left could be tossed out there. In the water, right there. Maybe you could see to that, dear?"

"Yes, Edith." Both women stared into the pool for a moment longer before Sandy carried Edith back up the slope to the truck.

7

SANDY WRITHED AND KICKED IN HER BED, AS IF STRUGGLING against restraints that held her tethered in place, until she kicked herself free and awoke from a fitful sleep. Her legs were tangled in the single bedsheet she slept under during the summer heat, and one of her two pillows had been knocked to the floor. Stink, who'd been stretched out on the cool wooden floor at the foot of her bed when she went to sleep, had moved to the side of the bed and now lay with his head on Sandy's fallen pillow, snoring. She propped herself up on her elbows and blinked in the gray dark of the room. A light breeze blew through the open bedroom windows. After leaning over the edge of the bed to see Stink snoring happily on the floor, she lay back onto the mattress, her head sunken into the one pillow remaining to her. A week ago she was blaming her restless sleep on the heat wave, unable to get comfortable in the muggy night air, irritated by the film of perspiration covering her body despite the efforts of the little fan she trained on herself while she slept. But the heat wave had broken two days ago. The air tonight was lovely, carrying a slight scent of rain. Sandy could no longer deny it. She had, as a general rule, slept much better, far more soundly, before love had been stirred into the mix.

Sleep had always been a simple business. After a certain number of hours of work and wakefulness each day, the body had to shut down for a while to replenish itself. Nothing complicated about that. And since the mind was clearly one of the many parts of the body, it required the same degree of downtime. Simple. Sandy dreamed, as all humans must, but her dreams were ordinary, never disruptive, and always forgotten immediately upon waking. Never had she been tormented by dreams that even remotely qualified as nightmares. Until now.

Even the nightmares were simple enough in form, easily understood. Tonight there had been two nightmares, occurring simultaneously, like a split-screen effect in a movie. On the left, Keefe sat naked at his fly-tying bench in the midst of a vast and cartoonishly barren desert landscape. He was hunched over his vise, staring blankly at his fingers, which were hopelessly ensnared in a tangle of yellow thread. On the right, Edith sat in her wheelchair, on the rock ledge by her "special place," in the shade of a massive hemlock tree. When Sandy reached for her hand, the old woman exploded in flame. The architecture of these dreams was obvious to Sandy, readily explained. What she didn't have an easy explanation for was how such dreams had suddenly begun to rattle her awake at night, leaving her sweating and shaking with terror. Love was making a mess of things.

And Margie had been right. Except for Margie herself, when the barbs of love had finally sunken into Sandy, they'd all been attached to someone or something much older than her, all of whom she was more than likely to outlive. The watershed, and the headwaters in particular, were dying, as all living things were. But they were perishing at such a glacial pace that her stunted human sense of time could never comprehend it. At least the watershed would outlive her. Keefe and Edith were another issue entirely. Why now and why them?

Sandy looked at the red, glowing numbers of the clock by her bed. Four-thirty in the morning.

"Goddamn it." She kicked the sheets off, swung her legs over the side of the bed, and sat up. Her feet grazed Stink's back as they came down. He emitted a faint grunt and continued snoring.

And Stink, too. In dog years, a calibration Sandy found ridiculous but still succumbed to, he was well into his eighties, older than Keefe and not much younger than Edith. She'd outlive her smelly old dog as well.

Love was, apparently, a condition reckoned in direct proportion to imminence of the demise of the beloved. Of course it was. And it was getting to be a damned nuisance.

Edith was safely tucked away in the nursing home. If she was ever in dire need, there would be someone there for her, twenty-four hours of every day. Still, Sandy would look in on her first thing when she got to work that day. Keefe, on the other hand, was all alone in his little bungalow. If she was so worried about him, why didn't she stay overnight with him more often than the once or twice a week she normally did? True, she wasn't at all certain there was anything medically wrong with him in the first place. Also true, it was a far shorter drive to work from her house on Willard Road than from Keefe's. Also true, Keefe didn't always want her there.

If she got going now, she could drive up to Keefe's and look in on him before going on to work that morning. She tapped Stink on his backside with her toes and rose up from her bed. "Get up, you lazy old thing. Leaving early today." After a night like this one, the dog was going with her, whether he wanted to or not. He could stay with Keefe for the day. Just now, she couldn't bear the thought of either of them alone. "Come on, get up," she said as she walked to the bathroom.

Stink raised his head, scowled after her a moment, yawned, and flopped his head back on the pillow.

THE rain was light, little more than a mist. It glittered like dust motes in the headlight beams from Sandy's truck as she struggled with the old padlock on the fire-road gate. Her fingers and hands, coated with the mist, glowed in the glare of her high beams. The lock was being stubborn this morning. Sandy wiggled her key gently, sliding it back and forth in the lock, her movements calibrated in millimeters. As she fought with the rusted old contraption, she wondered why in the hell they continued to battle this old lock when it would be so easy to replace it with a new one. Then again, something so seemingly simple would have to be coordinated with J.D. and the fish-and-game office, as well as the people with the forest service, who all needed keys for access. In all the years she'd fiddled with this lock, old and rusted when she first faced off with it, the idea of a new lock had never occurred to her. Not until this morning, when her lack of sound sleep and recurring nightmares had worked her into an uncharacteristic state of anxiety, convinced somehow that Keefe, at this very moment, wandered helplessly lost in dementia, desperately in need of aid only she could provide.

A curse was beginning to form on Sandy's lips when the padlock finally gave and popped open. She spit out a gruff sigh of exasperation and walked the long pipe-rail gate open. After pulling her truck through, she got out of the cab and closed and locked the gate, grumbling that she'd have to go through the same process again in another hour or so.

As she clicked the old padlock shut on the gate, she could just hear behind her the sound of footsteps rushing across the fire road, in front of her truck. Feet, hooves, paws—she couldn't tell. By the time she turned from the gate and walked back to the truck cab, whatever it was had fully disappeared through the thick stand of roadside rhododendron. In the headlight beams she could see the stiff, glistening leaves still shaking and dripping water at the point where whatever it was had run through. And whatever it was, it had roused Stink's attention. He stood on the seat in the cab, his bent tail not so much wagging as quivering, as was his entire body. His eyes were wide, frantically alert, trained on the spot in front of the truck where whatever it was had passed. The hair on his back had risen in a fine, bristled ridge the length of his spine, and a low, incessant growl rumbled deep in his chest.

"Shhhhhh," Sandy said as she slid into the cab and closed the door. "A deer?" She ran her hand once along Stink's ruffled spine, then shifted the truck into gear. "Probably just a deer. Nothing to get so worked up about." Her dog ignored her completely.

When Sandy pulled in beside Keefe's truck on the gravel apron beside the bungalow, the gray sky above the ravine had only begun to show a hint of diffused morning light. Here in the ravine it remained fully night-dark. The light was on in the kitchenette, spreading an elongated rectangle of light from the window onto the ground of the clearing in front of the bungalow. Stink nearly leapt from the truck cab and trotted a few steps into the clearing, raising his snout into the air and scenting heavily. Satisfied that what had so aroused his fur a mile back down the fire road was no longer in the vicinity, he resumed his usual routine for their arrival at Keefe's. He peed on the bottom step, toddled up to the porch, and waited for Sandy.

Coffee was in the pot on the counter, its aroma permeating the bungalow's interior, but Keefe was nowhere to be seen. Nothing whatsoever was unusual or suspect in the scene Sandy walked into. Nothing whatsoever out of place or out of keeping. This was exactly what she could have found any morning at this hour in Keefe's bungalow, and she damn well knew that. And yet, today, it spoke to her only of catastrophe. Her heart pounded frantically, her lungs heaved her breath in and out in bursts. Leaving Stink already curled on the sofa, she rushed back out the door, desperate to locate Keefe, certain he was in distress. No sooner had the bungalow door swung shut behind her than she saw Keefe's flashlight cut through the dark on the far side of the stream. He'd been in the cave.

WEDGED into the base of the slope on the side of the upper Ripshin opposite Keefe's clearing, the cave sat nearly even with the tail of the pool. In fact, the cave wasn't so much cut into the slope as it protruded from it. The persistent rush of ancient waters, the innumerable centuries of primeval shifting and buckling of the hardening earth's crust that shaped the headwaters, had at this spot folded and split a massive slice of the granite shelf. Thick, unimaginably heavy, the shelf here had broken, collapsed, and settled into a roughly triangular formation, with a nearly flat base under the two overhanging sheets of dense rock. At the rear of the cave, decades of the collected sediment of leaves, branches, and soil had plugged a small opening that led into a little cavern, no more than a few feet across, buried behind the visible portion of the cave. Rather than a cave, in any conventional sense, it formed a sort of lean-to of immense stone. Keefe had once suggested to Sandy that the cave's shape was not unlike a hollowed-out pyramid. "Of course, our little pyramid here is far older than the ones in Egypt," he'd said. "Nor did it require slave labor to be built. And every bit as grand, in my estimation."

The flat base within the canopy of stone made for a snug, sheltered enclosure in which to sit, to observe the fluid procession of the stream just below. Whether to monitor the movements of brook trout or simply because he was in a contemplative mood, the cave, Sandy knew, was a favorite and regular retreat for Keefe. "A good place to get away from it all for a bit," he had once said.

Incredulous, unable to imagine a life more "away from it all" than Keefe's, Sandy had been on the brink of pointing out this ironic fact to him when she was stopped short by the grin curling up the corners of his mouth.

At any other time, the cave would have been one of the first options to occur to her when finding Keefe absent from home. This morning, not until she saw his flashlight beam bobbing across the stream and up the bank into the clearing did her heart and respiration rate begin to subside.

Keefe began to come into focus as he stepped through the slash of light thrown by the kitchen window. He wore a threadbare gray sweat-shirt and baggy khaki trousers, rolled up to the knees, exposing his pale, slender legs. His legs were still wet up to the calves from wading back across the shallow shoal at the tail of the pool, and his feet squished inside his soggy old deck shoes. In one hand he held a flashlight, in the other, a coffee mug. On his head, as always, the old brown fedora. On his face, a smile of pleasant surprise. To the outsider, he looked the picture of exactly what those who knew of Keefe considered him to be—an eccentric old widower who lived alone in an old shack up along the headwaters, the kind of old kook who would have his morning coffee sitting in a cave in the dark. To Sandy, as he walked through the light toward where she now stood at the bottom of the porch steps, he looked to be the very thing she longed to find here this gray, misty morning—a water-weathered man, in full control of his faculties.

"I saw you pull in," Keefe said as he approached her. "To what do I owe the pleasure of this unexpected visit, my dear?"

Keefe kissed her lightly on the cheek as he passed, walked up to the porch, and sat on the top step. He clicked off the flashlight, set it and the coffee mug down, and removed his wet shoes and set them aside. His bare toes flexed, almost clutched at the lip of the step as he rolled his pant legs down. Thin, diluted light began to trickle into the ravine.

"Really," he said, "what brings you up to my little hovel in the wee hours? Is something wrong, dear?"

Sandy stood like a lump of mute stone, staring dumbly at Keefe. She had no idea what to say, no idea how to answer his simple question. She'd worked herself into such a snit, presuming disaster and having come prepared to triage the emergency she'd imagined, that finding Keefe at ease, utterly himself, she couldn't think of a single reasonable word to speak.

"My dear?" Keefe leaned forward, rested his forearms on his knees. "What is it?"

Sandy gained a moment's reprieve to collect herself when Stink began to whimper inside and paw at the door. She hopped up the steps and let the dog out onto the porch. Stink went immediately to Keefe, tail wagging, and eagerly ran his tongue over the man's face. She saw in her dog's unqualified affection for Keefe an indicator of some fundamental goodness in this man, despite his eccentricities and penchant for aloof melancholy. Stink had taken to Keefe immediately. There had to be something in that.

"There's the old guy," Keefe said as he draped his arm around the dog's neck and vigorously scratched his chin. "I suppose I should be flattered you got off the sofa just to see me."

Stink sat beside Keefe, and Sandy recognized a way to explain her presence here this morning. "I was wondering if, maybe, he could spend the day with you today while I'm at work."

"Of course. We can be old coots together, retired to our hermitage in the backwoods."

She hadn't expected him to agree so quickly. She went on explaining as if he hadn't. "Been some coyotes around below the dam lately. I don't want to leave him outside in his tire, and I can't leave him stuck inside the house all day."

There were coyotes everywhere these days. What could make today so especially dangerous? It was a lame explanation, but she'd have to stick with it now. She wondered if, perhaps, she was the one who might be losing her mental clarity.

"Coyotes up this way, too, but we'll look out for each other, won't we, old fella." Keefe tousled Stink's head and the dog licked him again.

"I could use some coffee," Sandy said, wanting to get past this topic as quickly as possible. "Do you want some more?" She turned to go inside.

"Love some," Keefe said. "There should be plenty of tea in there if you prefer."

"Feel like I need a little coffee today." Sandy disappeared inside the bungalow.

Keefe's coffee was rich, dark, and bitter. He drank his black. Sandy had sloshed a healthy portion of milk into hers. Back on the porch, sitting by Keefe as the clearing began to take shape in the morning light, she drank calmly from her mug, glad that fetching the coffee had provided the diversion she'd hoped it would. Stink and coyotes were no longer a topic of interest.

"Rain's let up now," Keefe said. "Feels good now that the heat has broken."

"Can sleep a lot better now that it's cooler." The ironic falsehood of Sandy's reply didn't faze her for a second. She was too happy in the moment. They were talking about the weather. The one topic everyone in a region had in common. The one subject about which they all shared the same information and experience. This was what old people talked about. "Hot enough for ya?" This was what two people comfortable with one another talked about. Weather. Sandy smiled, slipped her hand around Keefe's arm, sipped her coffee.

Sandy listened to the distant rush of river water spilling into the pool. The shapes and depth of the clearing were now visible in dim morning light. The ragged grass of the clearing, the leaves and branches encircling it, shimmered under the coating of morning mist. Several minutes of coffee and quiet passed before Keefe spoke. He held up his hand and pointed in the direction of the head of the pool.

"A new snag washed into the pool a couple days ago. Can you see it there?"

Sandy followed the line out from Keefe's finger and nodded her head to confirm she could see it. A small trunk, about eight inches in diameter, she guessed, had wedged into the pool and rose from it at an angle, cutting the current, tilted against one of the larger boulders on the far side of the stream.

"It's thrown a couple new twists into that back eddy. They're already starting to hold under its shadow."

Sandy nodded her head again.

"Breaking news from the heart of the headwaters," Keefe said.

She grinned, tightened her hold on his arm, pulled closer, and set her head to the side of his shoulder.

"Tiny scratches on the surface of time and the river," he said.

"I can tell you've been sitting in the cave," Sandy said.

"Forgive me, my dear. Sitting there, within the stones of a time so deep, well, I guess it makes me too philosophical. I'm sorry."

"Don't be. I like it when you're philosophical."

Keefe drained the last of his coffee and set his cup on the porch planks. "Curious how we humans seem to think eternity can't take shape until we happen onto the scene. Nonsense, of course."

"Definitely been in the cave," Sandy said. She leaned away from his side and set down her mug. "I'd better get going to work now," she said. "Thanks for watching Stink."

"My pleasure. Perhaps we'll take each other for a little hike today."

She set her hands to each side of his face, felt the press in her palms of the stubble on his jawline, the lines in his flesh. He was fine. Clearheaded as the waters in the clearing pool. She'd been a damned fool to twist herself into knots over two screwed-up yellow stoneflies. She pressed her lips to his and kissed him gently but long, then laid her face into his neck. When his arms found their way around her back to return her embrace, she knew he would be fine.

"I love you." She could feel the words vibrate in her throat, click over her tongue, but she didn't know now if she'd actually spoken them aloud. Neither of them had ever uttered these words to the other. She only just now, perhaps, realized that for her to say them would be to speak a truth. Whether or not Keefe would, could, say the words as well, to do so would send a shudder through the space compressed between their two bodies at this moment, and she wasn't ready for that. Not yet.

When she drew back and looked into Keefe's face, it showed the same calm, clear-eyed, unperturbed aspect it had when she kissed him. She hadn't given voice to the words humming in her throat. He was fine. They were fine.

A Country unto Himself

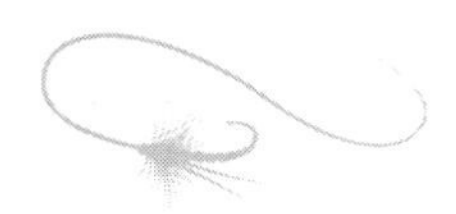

Seed corn and suet, Karo syrup and some berries, stirred into thick, pasty clumps. Good bait to attract any black bear. There was little room for mistakes at this point. He'd get it right this time, from start to finish.

Leaving the one carcass behind was a mistake. He'd fired too hastily. The shot had gone off mark and hit the bear in the rump. By the time he'd tracked it down and delivered the kill shot, the bear was far too deep in the ravine to haul it up to his truck on the fire road. The only road close enough was an access road to Willard Lake, sparsely traveled, but traveled enough to pose too great a risk of discovery. He'd taken the paws and bladder on the spot and left the carcass behind. No doubt it had been found weeks ago. They would be on the alert now. He'd have to be more careful and precise from here on in.

The heat weighed heavily on him, but he bore it, keeping himself gloved and covered to minimize his scent. His bait blind was far enough down from the fire road for cover but close enough to haul the body of a bear to his truck. In the hollow dug just deep enough to contain it, he dumped a bucketload of the sticky bait. Not too much—no need to waste it. He was only salting the hole right now. Get them used to coming around. Once they'd come to expect it, once they'd grown at ease with the spot, he'd wait for them, take three or four bears all at once, perhaps. He'd seen as many hanging around a food source together. If he shot with precision, and he would, he could dispatch them quickly. Once they were cached properly, he could hike out unseen and return with his truck. The long-abandoned logging road was barely visible or passable, but the truck could make it to where it met the national forest fire road. He would then drag each carcass up to his truck, drive out of this alien land, and arrive safely back at his own sovereign ground before anyone could possibly know. Three or four hides to sell or use. Three or four bladders, twelve or sixteen paws, all to sell. Enough meat to last him and the dog for many months. Enough of their money for ammunition and to keep the freezer running. That he'd be hunting out of season, taking well over the limit, of no consequence. The spoils of war. Their laws, their limits, did not apply to him. Their society was in conspiracy against manhood, but he was not part of their timid, puny mob. He was a society of one.

He dragged four heavy lengths of poplar over the baited hole and wedged them into place. Each length six or seven feet long, a good foot in diameter. Far too heavy to be moved by anything out here other than a bear. He'd return in a week or so to see if the bait had been found.

He slung the strap of the Winchester over his shoulder, pushed his glasses up his nose with his index finger, and climbed back up to his truck. The location was good. The ravine unfolded below him. A well-trained eye, alert and at the ready, could see what it needed to see, both prey and threat. He'd scouted this ravine and the next one over the ridge thoroughly. Nothing but forest and stream for at least three miles in any direction, save for the one old man in his fishing shack, and that was nearly two miles down the fire road. He'd watched him for a while one day, through the scope on the Winchester. The old man had been fishing when he first spotted him. He fished well, he had to give him that, but when he saw the old man release the fish he caught, any respect he might have mustered for him vanished instantly. As he watched a while longer, the old man waded from the stream, sat on a rock on the bank, and simply stared into the water. Just a moony old fool. He would pose no problem.

He sheathed the Winchester and tucked the case behind the cab seat. Before climbing into the truck, he raised his nose into the breeze and scented it in a series of short breaths. One. Two. Three, four, five. Yes, there it was again, something of what he'd sensed before. A new scent on the breeze.

8

THE SUMMER HAD UNFOLDED INTO EARLY AUGUST RATHER uneventfully, and Sandy was glad of it. The fishing had been good enough, considering the season. The low water levels of summer in the headwaters made already cagey brook trout even trickier to catch than usual. But if she adapted her approach, chose a fitting fly pattern, and delivered it with a little extra care, she could still take a good fish here and there. Most of the time, she and Keefe and Stink had strolled the fire road or sat on the bank and imagined how the fishing would be in early autumn when water levels increased and the brook trout grew more aggressive in preparation for their fall spawning. Once they even had a picnic together in the clearing at the old Rasnake homestead. And Keefe had been fine. Not once in the time she'd spent with him had she seen anything to rekindle the fears she'd experienced at the beginning of summer.

At work she'd had to recommend the firing of Edie, the nurses' aide, for her persistence in belittling or neglecting the residents. Such things happened from time to time in the nursing home, and no one was any worse off for it on this occasion. Edie hated her job and made it quite clear to Sandy on her way out that she "was gonna quit this shit job anyway, you bitch." Better for everyone involved, including Edie, that she was canned, and Sandy didn't give it a second thought afterward.

Margie called once or twice a week, mostly just to chat, and Sandy welcomed the calls, though she didn't share her friend's penchant for gabbing on the phone. Sandy listened, putting in her two cents here and there, while Margie held forth. Of late, Margie had been most focused on how work-worn J.D. was and on getting her sons, Luke and Matthew, clothing for the new school year that would begin soon. Luke was the older by two years and growing rapidly as he approached adolescence.

"Jesus, the child grows so fast, I've barely got him in one set of clothes before he outgrows it," Margie had said. "And now Matthew's whining about getting his brother's hand-me-downs. Insists on nothing but his own stuff. They keep this up, I may just let them both run around naked."

In particular, Margie was mystified by her elder son's recent interest in bird-watching after J.D. had given him an old field guide to North American birds. He spent hours watching the trees and keeping meticulous records of all the different species he'd seen.

"Suppose I should be glad he's not a video game junkie like most of these kids today," Margie said. "But geez. Latest thing, he's obsessed with finding, what is it? A perforated woodpecker, something like that?"

"Pileated woodpecker."

"Yeah, that's it. What in hell is so special about a woodpecker to an eleven-year-old boy?"

"They're big. And pretty secretive."

Another woman might have found the summer in the valley insufferably boring. Sandy found in the dull days a sort of soothing evenness and had settled into them gratefully.

OTHER than an occasional wave from the truck window as they drove past one another on the road, Sandy hadn't seen J.D. since she'd been up to their house for her futile pie-baking lesson. He was walking out of the Citgo station in Damascus, his cell phone to his ear, when Sandy pulled in to gas up after work. She pulled her truck into the pump island and stopped right behind J.D.'s dark green SUV.

"Fine, fine," J.D. said into the phone as he arrived where Sandy stood by the gas pumps. He raised his hand in recognition of her. "I'll be up there in a little bit." He switched his phone off with an irritated flourish and tossed it through the open window onto the seat of his SUV. "Damn it all. Like I have time for this foolishness. Hey, Sandy."

"Hello, J.D." Sandy set the clip on the pump nozzle and turned to him as her tank filled. "Long time. How've you been?"

"Same old same old," J.D. said. "Running around like a one-legged man at an ass-kicking contest."

"Sounds as if you just got another ass to kick."

J.D. smirked and sighed. "Yeah, definitely another one. Got to take a run up your way, actually. Tommy Akers is raising a ruckus about something again."

"What is it?"

"I'm not sure," J.D. said, and opened the door to his vehicle. "Claims something got into his cattle. Whatever it is, he's sure to be just as much of a nuisance as he usually is. I'd better get on up there."

J.D. plopped into the seat of his SUV and slammed the door. Sandy's gas pump shut off, and she set the nozzle back into its bracket. "Good to see you," she said. "Tell Margie I said hey."

"If I ever get back home tonight. Good to see you, too." J.D. extended his arm through his open window and waved as he pulled out of the Citgo and Sandy walked inside to pay.

AS Sandy slowed and turned into her driveway, a deputy from the county sheriff's office passed her in his patrol car going the opposite direction on Willard Road. Since Tommy's was the only other place between her house and the dam, she knew the deputy had been up there. She thought it would be good to drive down and see why Tommy had called in the local representatives of the government he held in such low regard and that he normally wanted nothing to do with. Sandy collected Stink from his tractor tire and drove back out onto Willard Road, curious as to what might be down the road to intrude upon this uneventful summer she'd come to appreciate.

Sandy pulled her truck in beside J.D.'s dark green SUV, the gold emblem of the state game and fisheries department imprinted on the front door. Tommy and J.D. stood in front of the vehicle, and Tommy's hand was raised, pointing to some distant spot across the pasture. In his other hand he held a shotgun.

"Hey there, neighbor," Tommy said as Sandy got out of her truck. "Always happy to see you, but you keep that dog of yours in that truck, okay? Got enough trouble with the cattle today."

It had been some time now since Stink had the agility to make the leap out of the truck's open window, but Sandy raised it halfway to appease Tommy. Stink sat calmly on the seat, his eyes fixed on Tommy and his shotgun, a low growl humming in his throat.

"Stay there, baby." Sandy closed the truck door and walked over to Tommy and J.D.

"You just come on out there with me, and I'll show you," Tommy said. His round, stubbled cheeks flushed red.

"Oh, come on, Tommy," J.D. said. "There ain't been any mountain lions in this part of the country for a hundred years."

"Tell that to the dead yearling I got out there." Tommy turned to Sandy. "Got a dead yearling at the far end of the pasture, and if it wasn't killed by a cat, then I don't even know my own name. And the government man here, well, suppose I shouldn't be surprised he don't believe me. Won't even go out there and see for himself."

"Damn it, Tommy. I'll go take a look with you. Of course I will. That's my job. I'm just saying it couldn't be a mountain lion."

"I know what I know," Tommy said.

"Why don't we just go take a look?" Sandy said.

"That's what I been saying. Now it's two against one. You coming, J.D.?" Tommy said.

"All right, all right," J.D. said. "Let's go. And it's not two against anything. This ain't a contest. Besides, what's she know about mountain lions, hunh?"

"Sandy here is a right smart little lady," Tommy said as they all began moving to get into J.D.'s vehicle. "She knows plenty, don't you?"

"Not about mountain lions," Sandy said. "I've never even seen one."

"And you don't need to bring the shotgun, Tommy," J.D. said as they settled into the SUV. Sandy had climbed into the rear seat, and Tommy took the passenger seat beside J.D. in the front. He held the shotgun upright between his legs, both hands wrapped around the barrel.

"I'll keep my shotgun right here with me, if you don't mind, government man."

"Stop calling me that." J.D. huffed, slammed his door, and fired the ignition.

J.D.'s government vehicle rolled and bumped over the embedded rocks and ruts in the cow pasture of the "skinniest" farm in the valley. Tommy directed J.D. to its farthest edge. Overhead, two turkey vultures spiraled in the air. Tommy pointed to a spot by the line of trees and brush that separated the pasture from the river, a short way past the pen where he kept his bull fenced off from the other cattle, and J.D. brought his vehicle to a stop there. A single tall oak tree stood solitary at the other side of the pasture. Most of the cattle were gathered under it in a bunch, and Sandy paused a moment as they got out of the SUV to notice how placidly the herd chewed at their cud, indifferent to the slaughter Tommy had brought them out here to witness.

Ten yards in front of them, just inside the tree line, a half dozen or so turkey vultures perched on an indeterminate hump of carcass. At the vehicle's approach, they had paused in their tugging and shredding of the remains to assess the threat. Tommy leaned his shotgun against his shoulder and took a step forward, waving his free hand to shoo the birds away. A couple of vultures hopped down from the carcass and strutted back and forth a pace or two.

"Why don't you just shoot them?" J.D. said.

"Why? They're just doing their job," Tommy shot back. "Which is more than I can say for some people."

As J.D. turned to Tommy with the beginnings of a snarl on his lips, Sandy stepped to his side and patted him gently on the shoulder. Tommy advanced further on the vultures, shouting and waving his arm. "Go on, you old buzzards. Scoot. Get on out of here."

Sandy could feel a slight breeze on her face from the flapping of their prodigious wings as the vultures took flight, sailing out over the pasture, then circling back to come to roost in the nearby tree line.

Tommy stomped to the carcass and pointed to it with the barrel of his shotgun. "There. See for yourself if you don't believe me."

"Geez, what a mess," J.D. said as he and Sandy joined Tommy at the side of the carcass.

"I don't know if you'll be wanting to look at this," Tommy said to Sandy.

"I'll be fine," she said.

And she would be, of course. After fifteen years as a nurse, in one capacity or another, she'd seen more variations of the world's assault on the flesh than either Tommy or J.D. would ever see. Sandy found no source for awe or astonishment in the human body—that animated bag of skin and hair, blood and bone—other than its remarkable frailty and vulnerability. She'd observed at close range the results of the vast array of means by which it could be beaten, broken, burned, punctured, gnawed, invaded, infested, infected, severed, and spent. If she ever saw any cause for wonder, it was only that any one body might make its transit over an average lifespan and remain relatively intact.

J.D. was right, though. It was a mess. The young steer's head was nearly severed. Its nostrils and snout were caked with dried blood and dirt, and its eyes had been pecked out by the vultures. The neck had been torn completely away, exposing a portion of the spinal column, festooned with shreds of tendon. Flesh had been torn out in chunks, and the wide, flat bones of the ribcage on the upside of the carcass were likewise exposed. Hide had been ripped away and lay shredded around the body, along with bits of entrails left from the steer's gutted chest cavity. Flies were everywhere.

"See. What'd I tell you," Tommy said, the shotgun barrel still pointing at the dead steer's remains. "Killed by a mountain lion or my name ain't Tommy Akers."

"Look, Tommy," J.D. said. "It's a damned shame, but there's no way this was a mountain lion. Probably coyotes. Could have fallen and been weakened. Easy prey. Was it sick?"

"Weren't sick. None of my cattle's sick. Couldn't nothing but a cat do this."

"Damn it, Tommy. There aren't any mountain lions around here. How many times do I have to say it?"

Tommy took a step closer to the carcass and poked with the shotgun at the frayed hide above the ribcage.

"Yeah? Well, just how do you explain that?"

Sandy and J.D. leaned in closer, squinting at the spot Tommy indicated.

"What?" J.D. said.

"That." Tommy poked at the spot again. "Claw marks."

Sandy could make out no mark distinct from the general shredding of the hide. Tommy was insistent.

"See there? That slice in the skin?"

"Geez," J.D. said. "The animal's been torn to bits. How in the world could you possibly see claw marks in this mess? And even if this mountain lion of yours did kill the steer, coyotes and buzzards have destroyed any sign of claw marks. You're seeing things."

Sandy leaned in closer still. On a flap of hide she thought she could just see a tear, a notch of sorts, no more than an inch in length. "This?" she asked, pointing.

"Yes, that," Tommy said. "Plain as day. You see, government man. I told you this little lady was smart."

"Just let it go, Tommy," J.D. said. "There's no way you can make that out as a claw mark."

"I know what I know. And that's a claw mark from a cat."

J.D. swatted at the flies around his head and stepped away from the carcass, walking back to his SUV. Sandy and Tommy followed.

"Tommy, I'm sorry. Probably coyotes, and vultures for sure, have made a mess of your stock. But it wasn't no mountain lion. State biologists have done studies. Eastern mountain lions have been extinct here for a hundred years. Proven science."

Sandy looked back across the pasture. She could just make out Stink's head protruding from the half-open window of her truck.

"Then how come you hear stories all the time about someone seeing a mountain cat?" Tommy dug a tin of snuff out of his back pocket and lodged a fat pinch into his lip. "I been hearing those stories all my life."

"And they're just that. Stories. Tall tales."

Tommy spat onto the ground. "Well, I heard tell a while back that you guys at fish and game are secretly releasing cats back into the mountains, to keep the deer down. What do you say to that, government man?"

J.D. threw up his arms, shook his head, and opened the door to his vehicle. "I say that's nonsense, Tommy. And I've had enough. I'm leaving. I'll put in the report."

Tommy kept hammering away at J.D. as the SUV bounced back across the pasture. By the time J.D. had brought the SUV to a stop between the house and barn, he'd had enough.

"Damn it, Tommy. Stop it. You know, I have a wife and kids I'd like to get home to, and I don't have time or energy for some old fool who thinks he sees mountain lions that aren't there."

Sandy was startled by this display of temper from J.D. She'd seen earnestness, consternation from him before, but never anger. Tommy's jaw locked. He stared at J.D., but didn't speak. Sandy wondered which prong of J.D.'s remark had pierced most deeply, being called a fool or the reference to a wife and kids Tommy no longer had.

Tommy opened his door, spat on the ground, and got out. Sandy climbed out, too, as Tommy walked slowly toward his house. Looking through the passenger window Sandy saw J.D. rubbing his forehead, clearly regretting the degree of his outburst.

"Look, Tommy," J.D. called after him. "I'm sorry."

Tommy turned, scowled at the game warden for a moment, and spat again. "You surely are." Tommy's shotgun dangled from his hand as he walked to his house and disappeared inside.

"You okay?" Sandy leaned into J.D.'s window.

"Doesn't seem so," J.D. said. "Tommy may be a fool sometimes, but I had no business calling him one. Just stretched so thin these days, and I, well, sort of been losing it from time to time. No excuse for that though. Ain't like me."

"No, it's not." Sandy reached into the vehicle and patted him on the shoulder again.

"I get short-tempered. Just so tired. It's a miracle Margie ain't thrown me out."

"Go home and give her a big hug and a kiss."

"I'd like nothing more."

Sandy stood back from the vehicle as J.D. shifted back into gear. "J.D.?" she said. "No chance at all it could be a mountain lion?"

Sandy realized that as they'd stood over the yearling's ransacked carcass, she'd become intrigued by the idea of a predator so formidable roaming somewhere through the mountains around her.

"None. Don't let Tommy's nonsense get to you."

Sandy stroked Stink's fur casually as she climbed into her truck and started the ignition. She wondered for a moment if she should look in on Tommy before leaving, but decided it would likely be best to leave him alone for now, in sole control of his version of events. Gravel spit from beneath the wheels and a plume of dust rose into the breeze as her truck rolled out onto Willard Road.

Ain't Been No Mountain Lions in This Part of the Country for a Hundred Years

The young steer had been heavy with meat, strangely so. Equally heavy laden with fat, as well. Not so lean and taut as a deer. It was far slower than a deer, simple to catch, but bigger, harder to drag down. The flesh was ample and would have fed and sustained her for days. She'd brought it down, torn out part of the neck, and ripped her way through the guts to the plump heart, but no further. By then coyotes had begun to close in. Only a few of them, a small pack, but too many to make a fight of it, so she abandoned her kill, not nearly finished with it yet.

Retreating through the thick brush at the edge of the open field, she followed the riverbank upstream to the dam. In the dim shadow of the dam, she crouched low at the river's edge for a moment and lapped a little water, to cut the thick tang of hot blood still on her tongue. The river ran in thin braids from the bottom of the dam, the water levels low enough for her to leap easily from rock to rock across to the other side and up the bank and into the trees. She had listened to the knowledge in her blood, had traced the course of the map inscribed in her flesh. She could not do otherwise. But her ancient range was now overlaid with the fledgling geography of human haunts. Lured by the scent of irresistible prey, she'd crossed these inscrutable lines into terrain that required enhanced caution.

She stalked carefully through the trees and arrived at another line, the access road around the lake that shone in the starlight off her right shoulder. She stepped onto the line. Her ears twitched at the rumble of the engine, and her eyes blinked back the lights piercing the dark as the vehicle rounded the curve. She crouched and leapt into the trees, the line safely crossed with only the fringe of the light beam catching her tail as she fled into the forest. The grinding of brakes and the squeal of tires on the road behind meant nothing to her. She ran freely through the trees, the venerable scent of the upland headwaters leading her as she moved, defining her stride.

With each leap further up the slope, deeper into the woods, her tread delineated the indelible lines of an indigenous territory, charted by sight, scent, and the reason in the blood. Here was the ineluctable cycle of seasons. Here the lean, wild flesh that nourished generations. Here the high ledges and deep cover. Here the caves in which to den securely. She ran on and on, rising through the night.

9

EDITH WAS DEAD. SANDY KNEW IT WITH CERTAINTY THE moment she held up the rainbow trout and turned to show it to the old woman. Clear to Sandy's experienced eye, there had been no spasm, no desperate, painful gasp, no frantic struggle to cling to the last breath. She had just slipped away, as they said, quietly, gently. Edith sat in the lawn chair as she had since they'd arrived at the riverbank. The only change, her head now lay slumped forward and onto her right shoulder. Her left hand remained in her lap, as it had been, her right dangled at her side, the gnarled fingers hovering a couple inches above the rock ledge.

The rainbow writhed from Sandy's distracted grip and flopped back into the stream. Calmly, she pulled it back to her, pinched the hook from its lip, and released it. Reeling in her line as she walked, Sandy waded toward the body.

Edith had been nearly insistent on going to the river this particular day when she learned Sandy had the same day off. Summer was drawing to a close, leaving few days remaining that would be warm enough for Edith to go on one of their outings.

"That, and they say there's a good lot of rain coming in at the end of the week," she had said when asking Sandy if they might go.

If Sandy had been completely honest with Edith, she would have told the old woman that she really wasn't up to it just then. She hadn't had a day off in nearly two weeks, not since a day or two after she'd been up to Tommy's and seen the mangled yearling. In the last week alone she'd worked two double shifts as well. She was tired and looking forward to a day off. In addition to that, she'd already agreed to join Margie and J.D. after work on the evening after her day off. They planned to take Margie's sons to see Sherwood's minor league baseball team play a game. Even Keefe was going. She wouldn't have a day to herself for over another week yet if she took Edith to the river, but all her hesitations felt petty and selfish. Sandy couldn't imagine offering any of it as an excuse to Edith, so she turned it in another direction.

"Are you sure you're up to it, Edith?" To Sandy's eye, Edith seemed more pale than usual. Not so pale that any other nurse on the staff would have noticed, but Sandy noticed. In truth, Edith had seemed to Sandy a bit slower and weaker of late.

"After all this time, you should know better than to even ask me that," Edith had answered.

Looking at the smile playing at the corners of the old woman's mouth as she lay propped up in her bed, Sandy could never have said no. "I'll pick you up in the morning."

As promised, Sandy had arrived at ten that morning and brought Edith to her special place on the river. A little before noon now, and the old woman was dead.

Sandy advanced through the water toward Edith's body with slow, graceful determination, having more to do with reverence than trepidation. She knew what waited. She stepped from the river, laid her rod down, and knelt beside the old woman's body. The nurse in Sandy lifted the dangling arm and laid two fingers to the wrist, confirming that the pulse had ceased. She laid the limp hand into the old woman's lap with the other and sat back on her heels.

"Edith." Two simple syllables, they slipped from her lips in a whisper and resonated over the waters of the pool, leaving Sandy empty of breath. As if fused to the rock ledge beneath them, she sat like a stone before the old woman's body.

The low sound of the current weaving through the rocks in the stream gathered behind Sandy as one minute passed. Two minutes. Three, four, five.

And then Sandy's shoulders broadened and pulled back as she drew a long breath into her lungs and exhaled slowly, the push of breath through her lips setting a counterpart of air to the rush of river water into the pool. She rose from her knees and removed her fishing vest, laying it on the rock next to her rod, the tote bag with their picnic lunch, and Sandy's little canvas purse.

Edith was dressed in a heavy cotton dress, dark blue with tiny white polka dots, and her shoulders were wrapped in a dark gray woolen shawl. Thick nylon support stockings on her legs. Her brown shoes on her feet. Sandy knelt, removed the shoes, and set them aside. She rolled each of the thick stockings down from the knee over the thin, purple-veined legs and stuffed one balled-up stocking into each of the brown shoes. From around Edith's shoulders, Sandy lifted the gray shawl, folded it carefully, and laid it onto the rock. With her right arm under the knees and her left encircling the shoulders, Sandy tilted Edith's head against her own shoulder and lifted the old woman from the lawn chair. Pillowing the head on the folded shawl, Sandy laid the body on the rock ledge, brushed a few strands of gray hair from the forehead, and straightened the skirt of the dress. Then, with gentle precision, she slid her hands under the old woman's dress and up the legs, detached the velcro straps, removed the soiled underpants, and tossed them aside.

Sandy heard the hum of a vehicle, not visible from the rock ledge, passing on the road above, followed almost instantly by the clacking call of a kingfisher flying upstream above the surface of the river. She turned to the call of the bird, catching sight of its wings as it vanished into the trees on the opposite bank. Sandy had dealt with dozens of such deaths, done her job of attending to the body's final needs, pronouncing the official time of death. Save for the locale, this death was no different. An aged heart had thumped out its allotted number of beats and stopped, leaving only the clinical routine of clearing away the inanimate corpse. There should have been nothing else to it. There should have been.

Sandy had lifted Edith's slight frame often enough to recognize the familiar touch of individual bones against the flesh of her arm when she carried the old woman. Sandy had always been able to carry the light and frail old woman with relative ease, but now the body felt heavier, more dense, as she lifted it again and carried it into the river.

With Edith's body pressed securely to her chest, Sandy waded into the deep center of the pool. This far in, the warm summer air couldn't counteract the cool temperatures of a trout stream. The exposed skin on Sandy's arms and legs grew tight and prickled as the cold water rose to the height of her abdomen and lapped at Edith's backside. Sandy shivered, she presumed from the water's chill, until the moan rose up in her own throat, so resonant and rasping it startled her, as if it had emanated from the earth beneath the river. She looked up to the patch of sky lining the opening where a massive hemlock had once stood. Imagining the low branches of the vanished tree, the band of shade it cast over the stream, Sandy turned Edith's head upstream and held her body out into the current. Her arms quivered but her stance was firm and sturdy. Edith's body lightened as the river lifted the weight. The skirt of the dress floated up and spread out over the surface of the water. Gray tendrils of wet hair clumped on the old woman's forehead, and Sandy pushed them away, smoothing them off the furrowed face. Sandy began to sway, in rhythm with the flow of the stream. Another moan rose in her throat, but it leveled off into a steady hum, vibrating in her chest as the river washed over and through the body she cradled before her: ". . . like the river and me was made of the same thing." Sandy released her grip, let the body begin to drift downstream for a second before she pulled it back to her. As she swayed in the current, she did this again and again, released Edith's body to follow its own course, then caught it and drew it back into her gentle grasp. The persistent humming in her throat pulsed down the length of her legs to her feet planted in the streambed, down the length of her arms to the tips of the fingers holding Edith's body afloat. The kingfisher clacked, emerged from its perch in the trees, and flew further upstream. Sandy's gaze shifted back and forth, searching the face and form of the dead woman in her arms and the river's surface for the ring of a trout's rise.

The sun had passed to early afternoon when Sandy carried the body from the river and laid it again on the rock ledge, the gray shawl carefully positioned under the head. She took one of Edith's cold, limp hands in her own. With her other hand, she reached to her little canvas purse and pulled it to her. Her eyes stayed on the old woman's body, drying in the sun, while her hand groped through her purse, among the fly box, case knife, and other few contents, until she found her cell phone. She would probably have no more than a fifty-fifty chance of getting a signal out here, but it didn't matter. Her battery was dead. She wouldn't be able to call for medical transport. She'd have to drive Edith's body back to the nursing home herself. Breach of protocol that it was, she was glad nonetheless. Who else might be fitting to transport this peculiar cargo? On the rock by the river, she claimed the right and responsibility. Sandy dropped the phone back into her purse and clasped the dead woman's hand in both of hers as the sun poured down on the two of them.

HER personal loss had been commemorated by Sandy's own impromptu private ceremony at the river. Now she had to turn Edith's remains over to the clinical practices of standard procedure. She wanted nothing more to do with it, wanted to be shut of it all as quickly as possible. Such business had nothing to do with the old woman for whom she grieved. She accorded no thought to matters of delicacy or discretion, but pursued her course with robotic efficiency.

Her shorts and top still damp from the river, her skin tightened again into goose bumps when she entered the starkly cooler temperature of the air-conditioned interior of the nursing home. The lobby was momentarily empty, and she passed through it without noticing. She commandeered an empty gurney, abandoned down one of the hallways, and pushed it back toward the entrance. At the nurses' station, Joyce Malden was holding forth, as usual, on the saga of the disappearance of Randy Mullins.

"Can you believe it? All these months now, and they still can't find him. Or I should say, can't find what's left of him, if you know what I mean. And poor Rhonda. They say she's selling their house and moving back to Kentucky with the kids. To live with her folks. Bless her heart, poor thing."

Sandy heard none of it, nor did she notice that Joyce, continuing to talk, was watching her passage out into the parking lot, where Edith's body was slung up by the seatbelt in the cab of her truck.

At the river she had handled Edith's body with care and devotion; here in the parking lot, there was a corpse in her truck, and she removed it, carefully but quickly, laid it on the gurney, latched the strap around the body, and rolled it toward the entrance.

By the time Sandy rolled the gurney back through the entrance, a small crowd had gathered. Joyce and the two nurses' aides she'd been regaling with her latest version of the Mullins family's woes stood just inside the entrance as Sandy rolled through the automatic doors. Death they had seen here, so the shock that registered on their faces was not from that. It was from death being wheeled into, not out of, the nursing home. Death being wheeled through the doors in a damp blue dress and a gray shawl. Sandy pushed directly past Joyce and the others. To her left stood two of the housekeeping staff—gray-haired, work-worn women. One stood with her eyes wide, a hand held over her mouth; the other stood with her head bowed, eyes closed, hands clasped, and her lips moving silently. To the other side of Sandy, the nursing-home manager stood with a middle-aged couple, the family of a prospective resident, apparently. All three watched Sandy pass with their jaws hanging open.

Sandy gave notice to none of it as she rolled Edith's body down the long hallway to her room. Joyce followed behind, the two nurses' aides a few steps behind her. The manager lingered in the lobby, trying to placate the couple. Joyce caught up with Sandy just in time to help her lift Edith's body from the gurney to the bed.

"My god, what happened?"

Sandy finished arranging Edith's body on the bed. She spread out the skirt of the dress, smoothed the gray hair back from the forehead, and laid each arm flat on the bed.

"Heart failure." Her voice was cold and thick, like a lump of lead in her throat. "Time of death . . . a little before noon."

"Oh, the poor dear," Joyce said. The two nurses' aides stood just outside the door to the room. The clack of the manager's high heels could be heard approaching in the hallway. Sandy couldn't bear another syllable of Joyce's particular version of empathy. She stared down at the old woman's face for one more moment, ran her hand over the forehead and hair, then turned away and left the room abruptly. She brushed past the nursing-home manager as she walked quickly back up the hallway, but didn't stop, didn't alter her stride in the slightest. Still startled and confused, the manager called after Sandy.

"Wait just one minute. You can't just waltz out—" She paused when Joyce grasped her arm.

"They were very close, poor thing," Joyce said, as if taking the manager into a special confidence.

Sandy paid heed to none of it.

IT struck Sandy as somehow odd, perhaps even inappropriate, that she could be so hungry at this particular time. She'd left her fishing gear and the lawn chair in the bed of her truck, tossed in on top of the wheelchair she'd rolled Edith out in that morning. Edith's shoes, with the stockings still stuffed into them, remained on the floor in the truck's cab. All she carried into the house was her canvas purse and the tote bag containing the uneaten picnic lunch. Stink rose out of his tractor tire to greet her when she got home, but she barely noticed him. The screen door nearly swung shut on his hindquarters when he slipped through into the kitchen, following at Sandy's heels.

Sandy emptied the contents of the tote bag onto the counter. Plates, forks, plastic cups, corkscrew, and paper napkins. A full bottle of red wine. Two chicken salad sandwiches, with the raisins Edith was so fond of. A small plastic container full of the little gherkin pickles of which Edith was equally fond. Two other plastic containers, each containing a homemade blueberry fry pie, which Sandy had purchased at the Citgo in Damascus. Sandy pushed the plates and forks aside and ate with her hands as she stared out the kitchen window into the waning afternoon light. She ate everything. All of it, ravenously. If there had been more, she would have eaten that, too. Still chewing the last chunks of fry pie, she wiped her hands and mouth on a paper napkin, unplugged the telephone on the kitchen counter, and took an old mug from the cupboard, dark green with a rising trout etched into the ceramic. With the corkscrew, she opened the bottle of wine and poured the mug full. She downed a large gulp of wine, topped off the mug again, and pushed through the screen door to the little concrete stoop outside. Stink held back, unsure if he'd been noticed yet, and the door slapped shut, leaving him inside. He watched Sandy through the screen as she sat down on the stoop and swallowed another gulp of wine.

The concrete stoop beneath her retained the heat of the day. Sunk only halfway behind the ridge that rose up from Sandy's little house, the sun cast long shadows down the slope. The air was flat, still, and warm. In her belly, the mass of food she'd wolfed down began to shift and grumble in her stomach as the wine worked its way through.

So this was grief. The occasion for such deep sorrow had certainly entered her life before, at least according to conventional standards. A mother whose passing seemed the fulfillment of her existence. A husband whose violent death she witnessed, in which she was, in fact, complicit. She had cried for both. And for both, what she had felt in the wake of each demise was something more like relief, perhaps release. A mother who had shaped her life around a private grief that offered scant space for Sandy. A husband whose greedy love for her offered scant space for anything but his private version of Sandy. Neither had pierced her skin to the pulpy center where the pain of loss might set its hook in the way the old woman had. Loss had transected Sandy's life, but never this palpable density of intractable absence, like a limb hacked away but still throbbing at the end of the stump. She thought, perhaps, she understood something of what Tommy had mentioned that day, of the deafening clamor generated by emptiness. She wanted Edith back.

The screen door rattled behind her. Stink sat on the other side of it, watching her, pawing at the door to be let out. She took another swallow of wine, leaned back, and pried the thin metal door open enough for her dog to slip out.

"Sorry, baby," she said. The dog sat on the stoop beside her, watching with her as the last of the sun slipped beneath the ridge. Sandy drained the rest of her wine, set the mug down, and slid her arm around the dog's shoulders. He turned toward her, looked into her eyes, thumped his tail twice on the stoop, then turned his gaze back to the deepening glow on the horizon.

It started as a churning in her belly, as if she might vomit, but her stomach clutched tight to the food it held. Straining against the stirring in her gut, the moan rose slowly in her throat, as it had earlier at the river.

But now, rather than leveling off into a hum, it continued to rise, until it exploded from her heaving lungs, rolling up the slope before her. She pulled Stink closer and sunk her face into his fur, sending the last of the moan into the flesh of his neck. And she wept.

10

THERE WOULD LIKELY BE HELL TO PAY. AND SHE COULDN'T blame anyone but herself if there was, given the way she'd run out yesterday after, for all intents and purposes, dumping a dead body. At the very least, she'd owe Joyce an apology. Then again, she would be amply compensated for her trouble, as Sandy would once again be providing grist for Joyce's gossip mill.

Sandy had sat on the stoop with Stink until well past dark, until she had exhausted herself with weeping, with navigating the deep channels of genuine grief for the first time in her life. By the time she dragged herself into bed, fully drained, she fell into a black, profound sleep and woke with barely enough time to make it to work. When she walked through the lobby to the nurses' station, pushing the empty wheelchair, only a couple minutes late, her hair was carelessly yanked into a ragged ponytail, her eyes were swollen, puffy, and red, and Joyce Malden was already standing behind the desk.

"Oh, you poor thing." Joyce strode out from behind the desk and consumed Sandy within her ample embrace. "I was so worried."

"I'm sorry." Sandy mumbled, struggling to speak against the press of Joyce's chest.

"We tried to call you all afternoon and couldn't get you."

Joyce released Sandy and looked into her swollen eyes. Despite what Joyce would inevitably do with this episode, Sandy could see that just now her sympathy was sincere.

"I think I unplugged the phone. Sorry."

"Poor thing. I know you thought the world of her." Joyce pulled her in close once more. Sandy's gratitude for Joyce's concern began to turn to embarrassment. She gently freed herself from the embrace, walked into the nurses' station, and set her purse on the counter, only then collecting herself enough to realize that Joyce's presence here at this time of day was out of the ordinary.

"Why are you here now, Joyce?," Sandy asked, but she didn't need to wait for an answer. There would indeed be hell to pay.

"What's-her-name told me to come in," Joyce said. "I'd guess to cover for you, just in case." Managers flowed fairly regularly in and out of the nursing home from the corporate offices in Roanoke and had little to do with the day-to-day operations, from a nurse's standpoint. The woman currently holding the position had been there only a week, and neither Sandy nor Joyce had yet had much contact with her. At least until yesterday.

"I really am sorry, Joyce. I owe you," Sandy said. "But I suppose you can leave. I'm here now."

"And a good thing you are, too," Joyce said. She walked in behind the desk of the nurses' station with Sandy, appearing not at all inclined to leave, and began her narration of the remainder of yesterday afternoon at the nursing home after Sandy had fled.

According to Joyce, not only was the manager new to the nursing home, but she was also new to the company, to the sorts of facilities it owned and operated, and certainly new to one of the more delicate aspects of managing such facilities. As it turned out, she had, in fact, never even seen a dead body before and most assuredly had never seen one wheeled by in front of her, newly deceased and damp with river water. After Sandy had rushed past her and Joyce had tried to calm her a bit, she'd stepped into Edith's room, taken one closer look at Edith's body laid out on the bed, and fainted dead away. Joyce said if she hadn't been there to catch her, she would have likely cracked her skull on the tile floor.

Once Joyce had revived her and walked her back to her office, she'd settled into a mix of anger over Sandy's behavior and anxiety about how to clean up the situation before contacting her dead resident's family. She had apparently found solace in the large three-ring binder containing the company's operations manual, then retrieved the file for one Edith Moser from one of the tall filing cabinets in her office. The new manager's face had shown a curious mix of confusion and relief when she discovered that Sandy Holston was herself listed as next of kin.

"Poor silly thing didn't know whether to shit or get off the pot," Joyce said.

"Me?" Sandy lowered herself slowly into the desk chair behind the nurses' station.

"Yes," Joyce said. "I was looking through the files with her. Form was dated almost three years ago. I assumed you knew."

"No."

Edith had apparently taken care of everything, well in advance, Joyce said. The file also contained the contact information for the lawyer who had drawn up her will and the funeral parlor where her remains should be taken, both up in Sherwood. Once transport had arrived and Edith's body was removed, the new manager slipped quickly back into prescribed procedures. She gave instructions for Edith's few things to be gathered up and for the room to be thoroughly cleaned. Then she checked her files again to see who was next in line. Edith had been living in one of the few private rooms in the nursing home, which came at a premium, and a few of the residents who could afford it were on a waiting list.

"Poor thing not even cold yet, and she's already looking at the bottom line," Joyce said. "Oh, speak of the devil."

The new manager had just rounded the corner from the lobby and approached the nurses' station. She wore a taupe pants suit with a satin sheen. Her hair was carefully styled and cut short. Across her shoulder, a bright paisley scarf, affixed at the shoulder with a gold brooch.

"Ms. Holston, would you come with me, please?" the manager said.

"About yesterday—" Sandy started.

"Just come with me." The manager turned and walked away toward her office.

Sandy scooped her canvas purse from the desk and rose from the chair. Here was the hell to pay, but whatever the tally, she would have, could have, done nothing differently yesterday.

"Thank you again, Joyce." Sandy patted her shoulder, gave it a brief squeeze, and followed the manager.

As Sandy approached the office door, she thought she recalled the new manager's name was Paulson. Something like that. She had no clue about the first name, and there was a perfectly good chance it had never been given. There was no name plate on the desk to help, and in the end, Sandy couldn't have cared less. She was empty, cored out, from Edith's death and the previous night's indoctrination to grief.

The manager sat at her desk, fingering two file folders that lay before her. She motioned Sandy toward an empty chair in front of the desk. Sandy slung the strap of her purse over the back of the chair and sat.

"I should think it would be rather obvious why I've called you in here this morning." From under her carefully styled hair, the manager looked directly at Sandy. Her fingers still played around the file folders on the desk.

"Got a pretty good idea," Sandy said.

"It's been explained to me that you had a close relationship with the Moser woman, so. . . ."

"Her name was Edith." Sandy felt the skin on the back of her neck tighten.

"Yes, yes. Edith, of course." The manager shifted in her seat, glanced down at the folders, then back at Sandy. "As I was saying, I can understand that you were close to Mrs. Moser."

"She was never married."

The manager visibly bristled and sat up rigidly.

"Ms. Holston." The manager deliberately drew out the Z sound at the end of the title before uttering Sandy's surname. "Such details hardly matter at this time."

"It mattered to Edith."

"If you don't mind."

Sandy guessed the new manager was at least five, maybe even eight or ten years younger than her. With the cut of her clothing and hair, it was hard to tell. Sandy kept quiet and looked knives through the younger woman.

"Given that we have a signed waiver on file for these times off the premises and given that you are designated as Ms. Moser's next of kin, the usual issues of liability that would be of concern here don't really apply, which is fortunate. However . . ."

The manager leaned back into her chair and brought her hands up in front of her, the fingertips of each hand steepled together.

"To bring a dead body right into the building in that fashion, to just roll it in, right in front of everyone, including potential customers, who were shocked and horrified, I might add, and whose business we've certainly lost, well . . . Your behavior displayed unbelievably poor judgment, an utter lack of professionalism."

"No, I don't suppose it was very professional," Sandy said.

"To say the least. Though I can understand you may have been upset, given your personal relationship with the woman, that in itself, excessive personal involvement with the residents, hardly falls in line with the professional standards our company requires."

Excessive. The word rubbed over the raw ache in the center of Sandy's chest like coarse sandpaper.

"Despite your relationship with Mrs. Moser, despite the fact that you've been on the staff here for several years, I simply can't run the risk of another lapse in judgment like this one. Irresponsible and unacceptable."

Sandy sat still in the chair, waiting for the payoff.

"I'm terminating your employment here, effective immediately. You'll leave the premises following this interview and not return. Your final paycheck will be mailed to the home address we have on file for you."

The manager removed a sheet of paper from one of the folders and slid it toward Sandy, along with a pen. "Initial that beside the mailing address listed there to indicate that it's current, and sign at the bottom to indicate that this situation has been explained to you."

Sandy leaned forward and picked up the pen. Her face showed no expression as she signed the form. This was, in the end, not a surprise to her.

The manager retrieved the signed form and placed it back in the folder. From the other folder, she removed a few other sheets of paper.

"I'll need your signature a couple more times, as next of kin." She slid the next form to Sandy. "This states that the resident died of natural causes and that the company is in no way responsible for her death."

Sandy signed without reading a word of it.

"This next is a receipt for the deceased's effects, that you've received them. Sign at the bottom right there. Her things are in the bag there behind you."

Sandy signed again, then turned in the chair. A large black garbage bag, which she hadn't noticed when she entered the office, leaned against the wall in the corner.

"And this is a copy of the contact information you'll need. The funeral home where the remains were taken and the lawyer in charge of the deceased's estate."

Sandy took the sheet of paper, scanned it, barely noting the information, and folded it away in the breast pocket of her scrubs.

"That concludes our business, Ms. Holston," the manager said. "You can leave now."

Sandy rose from the chair, but the manager continued as she gathered up from her desk the folders with the signed forms. "It would have served you well to keep in mind the realities of this business. We make our money, including your paycheck, not just from caring for the elderly, but by keeping residents living as long as possible. Live bodies in the beds, that's the baseline for our source of revenue. You might want to remember that."

Revenue. Edith, as *revenue*. The frail, treasured body she'd held up in the cleansing current of the Ripshin River, a source of *revenue*.

Sandy's arm rose from her side in a precise arc, as if it moved with the same practiced skill she applied to a sidearm cast that would drop her fly into place on the surface of the water under a tightly overhanging branch. Her arm swept across the desk, and the flat of her hand caught the side of the manager's face with full force. The folders flew from the woman's hand and she slumped in her chair, momentarily stunned, her hair knocked askew across her forehead.

Without pause, her movements decisive, Sandy turned from the dazed woman, grabbed her purse from the back of the chair, lifted the garbage bag with Edith's belongings from the corner where it sat, and walked out of the office.

Predictably, Joyce Malden was in position, pressed against the wall just beyond the office door. The garbage bag grazed Joyce's hip as Sandy strode past, not saying a word, barely noticing that Joyce stood there, her eyes wide, her mouth agape. Bless her heart.

EDITH had entrusted her with her last worldly business, and the first thing Sandy had done was flee into her own night of private sorrow. She would now tend to Edith's final affairs quickly, efficiently, with as little fuss as possible. The way Edith had wanted.

She tugged on a T-shirt and a pair of jeans and threw her work scrubs in the dirty laundry, not wondering when she might need them again. When she called Dawkins Funeral Home and Crematory in Sherwood, it was barely past 8:30 in the morning, but the funeral director picked up on the second ring. He had a funeral later that morning and a viewing in the evening but told her if she could be there no later than 10:00 he could meet with her for a few minutes, which would be all they'd need to take care of the paperwork. No answer at the lawyer's office, so she left a message. On her way to the funeral home, she would leave the garbage bag of Edith's clothing in the drop-off box at the clothing bank in Sherwood. The old woman's few garments no longer contained anything of value.

The funeral director led Sandy through the odor of flowers and formaldehyde to a small office crammed with dark, cherry-wood furniture. He was tall, his white hair meticulously groomed, with an odd shine to it. His white shirt was crisply starched, the cuffs affixed with gold cufflinks. A red silk tie was precisely knotted in place with a full Windsor knot. He offered Sandy his condolences and slid a piece of paper to her, along with a pen, as he explained the basic terms of the form he'd given her. It occurred to Sandy that the most consistent feature of Edith's death would be that it required her to sign things for well-groomed people. With the pen in her hand, hovering over the form, Sandy looked at the funeral director, trying to keep her eyes on his face, not his hair.

"How much will this cost?" Barely two hours since she'd struck someone for equating Edith with revenue, and now she was asking about the expense of fulfilling the old woman's last business. She felt petty and hypocritical. Still, it had also been barely two hours since she'd lost her job.

"Oh, my dear." The funeral director reached across the desk and patted Sandy's forearm. His fingernails were also immaculately manicured. "Forgive me. I'm afraid I'm so busy this morning that I haven't been as clear as I should have been. The expenses for Ms. Moser's cremation have already been paid. Some time ago, actually."

Sandy looked at the form more carefully and saw that it was an invoice, marked paid in full and dated several years before. She estimated shortly before Edith moved into the nursing home. Edith had taken care of things, leaving Sandy simply to oversee.

"Ms. Moser did, however, make arrangements only for her cremation." The funeral director leaned back into his chair and brought his fingertips together. "In fact, she left instructions that there be no service, but that's certainly not legally binding. Often family still feel the need for some sort of ceremony, and we could arrange one for you at a very reasonable cost."

"No, thank you." Sandy brought the pen down to the page and signed her name. "It's not what Edith wanted."

"Of course, Ms. Holston. What was your relation to Ms. Moser, if I may ask?"

Sandy handed the invoice and the pen back across the desk, unsure what word could ever articulate what Edith meant to her. "She was my friend."

"I didn't know her," he said. "We met only the one time, when she made her arrangements. But I'll never forget. My Uncle Wallace told me once that he worked with her at Old Dominion. Said when he was hired, he hardly knew what to make of the fact that a woman was going to be his line supervisor. And he said after he'd been there a month or so, he'd have done most anything in the world for her. She was apparently quite a character."

"She was very special," Sandy said.

He told Sandy Edith's ashes would be ready on the afternoon of the following day. She thanked him and left.

Her truck was parked underneath a tree at the back of the lot behind the funeral home, so Stink would stay cool in the shade while he waited.

Sandy walked past two other well-groomed men in dark gray suits who were lining up parking cones in the lot in preparation for the pending funeral. At the far corner of the parking lot sat the crematory, a squat, stone building, little bigger than a typical garage, with a thick cylinder of a metal chimney rising from its roof. Sandy gazed at it for only a moment as she walked to where Stink waited, his head protruding from the half-opened window. Sandy could feel a slight cooling in the air and a hint of a breeze across her skin. A few fat clouds had begun to gather off to the southwest. The rain Edith had mentioned was, perhaps, approaching.

THE laundry room off Margie's kitchen was tiny, little more than a closet. She and Sandy were folding newly laundered clothes, wedged in between the washer and dryer on one side and a single shelf on the other side that contained assorted laundry products and doubled as a folding table. Stink lay curled on the floor, just outside the laundry-room door. A small window on the back wall of the laundry room looked out into the backyard, where Margie's two sons were playing a desultory game of catch. Margie stood at the washer, Sandy behind her at the dryer. If Sandy wanted to leave the laundry room, Margie would have to exit first.

"They play nicely together," Sandy said, looking out at the boys as she folded a worn pair of jeans.

"They do," Margie said. "On those rare occasions when they do go out and play. Most times, Matthew's lost in some creepy video game and Luke's out there in those trees with his bird book. If it wasn't for baseball, I don't know they'd even be able to recognize each other."

Sandy smiled, took a pair of Margie's panties from the laundry basket, and folded them in half.

"Yes, my panties are twice the size of yours," Margie said, "but no jokes, little Miss Skinny-Butt."

"Stop it. They're not so big as that." Sandy removed a sock from the basket and pawed through the other clothes, looking for its mate.

"This is nice and all, get in a little girl talk while you help me with housework." As the washer kicked into the rinse cycle, Margie leaned against it and eyed her friend. "But I'm thinking there's something else up besides your need for womanly gossip and chit-chat. Hmm?"

"I was in town. Saw your van in the driveway and thought I'd stop by."

"I know that's bullshit. You'd have to drive half a mile from anything you'd come to town for to see that my van was in the driveway. What's up, honey?"

Sandy looked out the window again. Luke lofted the ball high in the air. Matthew camped under it, punched the palm of his glove a couple times, and watched it fall toward him. The ball glanced off the fingertips of his mitt and landed in the grass.

"Edith Moser died."

"That woman at the home you were so fond of?"

Sandy nodded, looked away from the window, and kept nodding. Margie reached her arms around Sandy and drew her tight.

"Oh, honey. I'm so sorry. There now, there now." Margie held her close and patted Sandy's back. "There now."

"I'm okay," Sandy said.

"Like hell you are," Margie said. "You loved that old gal."

Yes, she had loved her, and Sandy leaked a few stubborn tears within the arms of the only human being who had ever seen her weep.

"How'd she go?" Margie kept stroking her back and listened.

Sandy patched together a version of what had happened the day before. She told Margie about going for a picnic at Edith's special place, just as they'd done on other occasions. Sandy had to admit, though, that going yesterday had seemed more urgent to Edith this time than usual. Sandy said, though it was obviously ridiculous to think so, that it was as if Edith knew and wanted to die in that place.

"Not ridiculous at all," Margie said.

Sandy explained that by all appearances Edith had passed away easily from simple heart failure. She couldn't imagine how to explain carrying Edith's body into the river, how to explain what she'd done or why, so she said nothing of it to Margie. She told Margie she'd driven Edith's body back to the nursing home, that she hadn't called for transport, because her cell phone battery was dead.

"Figures," Margie said.

Sandy admitted she must not have been thinking clearly and related to Margie a quick version of how she had returned Edith's body to the nursing home.

"Just rolled her in the front door, right in front of everyone?" Margie said. "Holy shit."

Sandy said nothing of her night on the stoop behind her house with Stink.

She told Margie that it hadn't really come as much of a surprise that the manager had fired her that morning. She would probably have fired herself under the circumstances. What had come as a surprise was Edith listing her as next of kin and apparently making her executor of her estate, whatever that might be.

She said nothing to Margie of slapping the nursing-home manager.

"Oh, Jesus, honey." Margie hugged her again, then leaned back and looked at her, sincere concern spread across her face. "What're you going to do now?"

"Finish taking care of Edith's business. Have to pick up her ashes tomorrow. Haven't reached the lawyer yet."

"I mean, what are you going to do?" Margie said. "You know, work, a job?"

"I'll be okay for awhile." Sandy pulled more socks from the laundry basket and began pairing them. "I have some savings."

"I don't doubt it," Margie said. "You live like a goddamned monk out there. Never buy yourself clothes or anything."

"I've bought clothes."

"Oh, really?"

"Bought a new fishing vest a couple years ago."

Margie laughed and opened the lid of the washing machine as the spin cycle ran out.

Before she left, Sandy called the lawyer's office again, but still got no response. She didn't leave a second message.

Margie leaned out the screen door on the front porch and called after Sandy as she and Stink got back in the truck.

"Hey, I don't suppose you're going to be up for going to the baseball game tonight like we planned?"

Sandy helped Stink climb up onto the truck seat and closed the door. She rubbed her hands on her jeans and took her keys from her pocket. "Sure. Why not?" A wry smirk worked across Sandy's face. "Not like I have anything else to do, right? We'll meet you there."

Margie laughed again and waved as the screen door fell shut and she returned to her little laundry room.

WHEN Sandy and Stink arrived at the bungalow, Keefe's truck was there, but he wasn't. She hadn't noticed him anywhere downstream as she drove up the fire road; he would be off somewhere, further up the headwaters. Nothing out of the ordinary. In fact, it was often the case when he wasn't expecting her. Often the case when he was, for that matter. And why shouldn't it be? This was where he lived. The bungalow was his house; the headwaters were his home. Still, she found herself a little disappointed he wasn't there just then. Edith was gone. For the moment, so was Keefe. She couldn't have Edith back. She needed Keefe, to see him, to touch him, to confirm his existence. And she would need to fish. Soon.

She hadn't eaten since gorging herself on the picnic lunch she'd made for Edith. Rushing out so quickly that morning to the job she no longer had, she hadn't had time for breakfast. When she stopped back by the house on Willard Road before driving to Sherwood, she'd fed her dog but hadn't thought to feed herself. Now it was nearly midday, and she was famished.

As Stink slept in his usual spot on the sofa, undisturbed, Sandy rattled around the kitchenette. She sliced a potato and set it to fry in a cast-iron skillet. While the potato slices sizzled, she brought some water to boil in a small saucepan—Keefe had no tea kettle. Rummaging around in one of the cupboards, she located an old box of herbal tea bags she'd left here, lowered one into a cracked coffee mug, and poured the boiling water over it. In a small stainless-steel mixing bowl, she cracked three eggs and whipped them into a yellow froth with a fork. In one of the vegetable drawers in the refrigerator, she found half an onion, unwrapped. She peeled off the withered layers, chopped it up, and tossed the onion in the skillet with the potatoes, giving the mix a thorough stir. She peeled the wrapping from an unopened block of farmer's cheese, sliced off a wedge, and tightly rewrapped the remaining cheese in a piece of foil. Her tea had steeped by then, and she paused and took a few sips, stirring the potatoes and onions as she did so. As best she could with the paring knife she'd used on the onion, she shaved the cheese into the bowl of eggs, and folded the shavings into the eggs with a few strokes of the fork. After a few more sips of her tea, the potatoes looked to be done, so she poured the eggs into the skillet and stirred and scrambled the whole mess together with a little salt and pepper. Her stomach churned eagerly as she inhaled the thick scent. She dished the contents of the skillet onto a plate, picked up her mug of tea, and joined Stink on the sofa.

The potatoes should have been fried a few minutes longer, but the flaw was too minor to diminish the savory flavor or the pleasure of her stomach closing readily around the food. Stink lifted his head and stretched his neck and snout toward her plate.

"Want some?" Sandy selected an egg-caked slice of potato, blew on it to cool it some, and fed it to her dog. Stink gave the mouthful a couple of perfunctory chews, gulped it down, and extended his snout again. Sandy gave him another bite. "That's it. You already had breakfast today."

Sandy's late breakfast sat well with her, like a stone in her belly. It would last her the rest of the day. She let Stink lick her empty plate, then set it on the coffee table. From the half pack on the table, Sandy took one of Keefe's nonfilter cigarettes and lit it. Keefe smoked so infrequently that a single pack of cigarettes could last several weeks. Sandy had never been a smoker, but on rare occasions the act had a certain appeal for her. Today was such an occasion. She smoked judiciously, inhaling only a small portion of the smoke and waving her hand over Stink's head in a feeble attempt to fan the smoke away from her dog's breathing, which had settled again into a snore. Keefe's ragged, well-worn copy of *Leaves of Grass* lay on the table, open, face down, its spine wrinkled and cracked. Sandy pushed the book aside, drew the ashtray closer, and tapped the ash from her cigarette into it.

With the burning cigarette notched in her fingers, she walked to Keefe's tying bench. She ran a fingertip around a tray of newly tied flies, stopping to flick her finger through the compartment of the tray containing yellow stoneflies. The bright yellow flies infused her with a feeling of quiet simplicity, and she looked forward to the late spring, when the living yellow stoneflies would hatch from the headwaters and she might tie one of these simulated flies to the end of her line and catch a good fish with it.

Every fly in the tray under her fingertips was tied correctly.

Her gear waited on the porch. It was time to fish. She mashed out the cigarette butt in the ashtray, ran her palm along Stink's spine, and stepped out of the bungalow.

CLOSE to a couple hours after her late breakfast, maybe a quarter mile or so upstream from the bungalow, and still no sign of Keefe. Sandy began to wonder if it was really so imperative for her to see Keefe today. What special wisdom or solace had he to offer her, this man who had been so incurably mired in his own rituals of grief when she first encountered him? This man who was not yet fully free of that grief, would likely never be?

In less than the cycle of one day, she'd lost her friend and her job, yet she was at ease. The cooling pools of the headwaters had spoken in the eloquent language she knew and needed, drawing her out of the bruised creases of her head and heart, keeping her stance steady and rooted in the woven world that would outlast her. The clouds that began to roll in earlier had fully arrived, wrapping the watershed in a steely gray, shadowless light. Since leaving the bungalow, she'd caught several small fish, and three good ones.

And now four. She'd bounced the ant pattern at the end of her fly line off the downed snag angled over the back eddy. It was as if a real ant had fallen into the pool. The fly had dropped dead center atop the eddy and been struck almost immediately. The brook trout's fins flamed with orange in anticipation of the fall spawning that might have already commenced. It draped well over both sides of her hand, and the weight of it in her palm gave her a feeling of what might have been called *gratitude* in a language different from the one she spoke here. She shook the water from her hands after releasing the fish back into the pool. The word in that other language for what she felt might have been *satisfaction.*

Sandy reeled in and secured her line. Her fishing was complete for the day.

The sound came from just upstream, from the rocks above the next pool up from her position. A snap of breaking brush, a rustling of leaves, and something like a single staccato release of breath. Her eyes shifted upslope. Her gaze, accustomed for some time to the rippling surface of the water, resolved into a refreshed focus on the rocks and foliage along the stream, just in time to spy something large fleeing into the brush. In truth, she saw only the leaves and branches shaking in the wake of a large body passing through them, and a fleeting glimpse of its tail. Its impossibly long tail. She kept still, locked in place in the shallows of the pool, her breathing rapid and shallow. Her eyes scoured the slopes above her for any sign, but it had vanished utterly. Gone.

SANDY sat on a rock beside the pool across the clearing from the bungalow, her legs extended into the water up to her calves. She'd made it back to the bungalow nearly an hour before, but she still wore her vest and waders. Stink lay on the bank right behind her, his rear legs stretched out to the side, his snout resting on his front paws. He gave out a slight groan and yip as he pushed himself upright. Sandy turned at the sound and saw him move off across the clearing. Keefe had returned. He'd emerged from behind the bungalow, having come down from the fire road above, and Stink toddled across the clearing to meet him. He wore the battered fedora, as always, and his hands were sunk into the pockets of his baggy khaki pants. He carried no fishing gear. Keefe met Stink halfway across the clearing, scratched around the dog's neck and head vigorously in greeting, and continued on to where Sandy sat.

"Do any good?" Keefe settled onto the rock beside Sandy.

"Little bit." Sandy grinned briefly at Keefe, leaned to his cheek with a light kiss, and turned her eyes back to the water. "Very good."

"I wasn't expecting you till much later today. To go to the ballgame. Did I forget something?"

Sandy paused for a moment before responding, reminded of her earlier fears. "No, this was an unannounced visit. You didn't forget anything."

Stink lapped a little water from the stream and sniffed at a couple intriguing spots along the bank before circling behind Sandy and Keefe and settling back onto the ground.

"Have you been here long?"

"Awhile."

"Sorry to keep you waiting, my dear. I was walking pretty far up the fire road. Found a pit under some cut logs. Looks as though someone's been baiting bears. Not sure, but pretty sure. Hope I'm wrong."

Sandy nodded and listened, took in what he said, but kept quiet for a moment longer before speaking. She leaned forward and rested her elbows on her knees. "Doesn't a bobcat have a sort of short tail?" she asked. "I haven't seen one in quite a while. And never up close."

"Yes, pretty short," Keefe answered.

"Hmm, I thought so. Then I think I saw a mountain lion. A ways upstream. Not sure. I only saw the tail really. A very long tail."

Keefe turned his eyes upstream. His breathing grew slower, deeper, as if he were trying to inhale the distant scent, to draw into his lungs the presence of a huge cat roaming the headwaters.

"Do you think it's possible?" Sandy asked.

"Oh Lord, I hope so," Keefe said, turning back toward Sandy. "I do hope so."

Sandy sat upright again, her eyes still on the water, and waited until she could feel Keefe's eyes on her again. "Edith died."

"Oh, my dear." There was no pause, no further inquiry. While those last three syllables hung in the air around her, Keefe's arms slid smoothly around her, pulled her gently to him, and held her close. Sandy surrendered freely into his embrace, leaned into the flesh of encircling arms that knew the grammar of grief, knew its voice, its idioms, and how to form a response in fitting, intelligible language. She listened through his chest for a pulse of knowing, a throbbing articulation in the native tongue of the headwaters.

EDITH had been right. A good lot of rain coming in, she had said. It arrived that evening, in the bottom of the third inning.

Though Sandy knew nothing of the subtleties of baseball, barely knew the basic rules of play, she was disappointed when the rains came in and the game had to be postponed. She'd been enjoying herself. She found a kind of weathered beauty to the ballfield under the lights. The unseeded worn patches between home plate and the pitcher's mound touched her with a sense of what she might have called melancholy. Sherwood's baseball team, the Cougars, were a lower-level minor league team in the Appalachian League. Rookie league, J.D. had called it. The team seemed composed, according to J.D., primarily of Latin American prospects who would swing away here for a couple months, under the watchful eyes of scouts, before being shipped up the line to the next level of minor league ball or back to their native lands. Apparently, baseball at this level didn't merit the top-of-the-line groundskeeping one found on baseball diamonds at the higher levels.

Behind home plate and on down the first-base line, the stadium was a modest but relatively new structure, built of concrete and brick, with firm plastic benches for seating. An aging, covered wooden grandstand ran along the third-base line. The outfield fence was a rickety affair of wooden planks, painted with fading advertisements for Budweiser, a local hardware store, and the Old Dominion Furniture Company. At most, the stadium might have held eight or nine hundred people, and it was nearly full tonight.

Despite the dilapidated surroundings, after such a volatile day, it felt good to Sandy to be there. It pleased her to look at the precisely laid lines of white chalk demarcating the field. All the struggle that would occur here would be contained within those lines, would transpire according to clearly defined rules, and all she would be called upon to do was watch, offer an occasional cheer of support, while safely seated in the bleachers. Even the tape-recorded national anthem, played on an organ and piped through the ballpark's crackling loudspeakers, held a certain charm for her. She'd been a bit surprised and intrigued in the way Keefe carried himself during the anthem. Along with the others in attendance, he'd stood and removed his fedora. While others stood with their caps off, hands held over hearts, some singing half-heartedly, Keefe held his hat at his waist, his stony gaze moving slowly over the crowd around him.

Sandy had wondered how Keefe would carry himself in a crowd like this, a man who left his hideaway only reluctantly, perhaps once or twice a month for groceries and to tend to the unavoidable details of paying his few bills and collecting what little mail he got from a post office box. But Keefe had softened after the game got going. He seemed at ease, engaged even. He'd held forth to J.D., something about baseball and the American pastoral myth, and J.D. had listened respectfully, slipping back into the role of student in the presence of his former teacher. But Keefe had also helped Margie's oldest son, Luke, with his scorecard, showing him how to fill it out and track the game, for which Margie was vocally grateful. The two boys had been squabbling when they arrived, and Keefe served as a buffer between the two, guiding Margie's increasingly contemplative and withdrawn older son, so Margie could chat with Sandy while better managing her more rambunctious younger son, Matthew.

"Geez," Margie said, leaning toward Sandy's ear after getting another hot dog stuffed into Matthew's mouth. "One needs to be on Ritalin and the other acts like a little monk. Wonder which one takes after his mother, eh?"

Sandy had been a little surprised at the good feeling produced by being at the ballgame, and a little less surprised by her disappointment when the game was called because of the rain. Her day had begun in grief, agitation, and anger, leveled off into sadness and resignation, and resolved into a passing serenity with a good fish at the end of her line in the pools of the upper Ripshin. She and Keefe had sat in silence by the stream for another several minutes that afternoon before going back inside the bungalow. He'd made Sandy a cup of tea, and while he slowly munched at a sandwich, they sat on the sofa as she sipped at the tea and told him everything that had happened since Edith's death—she left nothing out. When she tried to relate the details and motivation of her impromptu ceremony with Edith's body in the river, Keefe said nothing. He swallowed the bite he was chewing, wiped his mouth with his fingers, and pressed his lips to her forehead for a long moment. Her narration of striking the nursing-home manager caused Keefe to stop chewing and sit upright, his eyes wide, a hint of a grin twitching at one side of his mouth. She begged a promise from Keefe not to mention the mountain lion to J.D., a promise to which he gladly swore. The preceding twenty-four hours had left her drained, depleted, at the end of one life she thought she understood and at the beginning of another that offered only uncertainty. At the baseball game she had begun to sense the first steps toward replenishment. She had wanted to linger, grateful for the simple, sustaining fare, and felt the disappointment settle in as they all scurried through the rain, Margie's family to J.D.'s government SUV, Sandy and Keefe to her truck.

They drove back to the headwaters in relative quiet, neither speaking much, focused on the wet pavement before them. South from Sherwood, through Damascus, along the river road, around Willard Lake on the access road to the fire-road gate, the rain remained a steady, persistent downpour. Raindrops flared through the headlight beams as they turned into the entrance to the fire road and trees drew in close around them. Sandy rolled the truck to a stop at the pipe-rail gate, about fifty feet in from the access road.

"I'll get it." Keefe fished his keys from his pocket, tugged his fedora down snug on his head, and got out of the truck to open the padlock.

Rain spattered off the brim of Keefe's fedora and began to soak into his shirt as he worked the key back and forth in the tricky old lock. Sandy watched from behind the steering wheel. An old hand with the quirky padlock, Keefe usually got it open after two or three attempts, but tonight he appeared to be struggling. Suddenly, Keefe's body seemed to quake all over and from the way his arms thrust and shook, it looked as if he were trying to throttle the old lock. The back of his shirt had grown so damp with rain that it clung to his skin.

"Goddamn this old thing. Why won't it open?" Keefe rarely cursed. He never got angry.

Sandy stepped from the truck into the rain and walked to his side. She slid her hands over his. His breathing had grown rapid. In the glare of the headlights, she could see outrage and confusion in his eyes as rain ran off the brim of his hat. At the touch of her hands, he turned a startled face to her. For a moment it seemed to Sandy that he did battle with something other than the padlock. She held her hands more firmly around his.

"James." Her voice whispered through the rain.

His breathing began to settle, the confusion slid from his face. "Forgive me, my dear."

With her hands on his, they both began to work the key around in the lock. One try. Two. Three, four, five. They were both fairly well soaked but breathing evenly when the lock finally gave on that fifth try. Keefe smiled, somewhat sheepishly, Sandy returned his smile, and the space around them exploded with a massive influx of light. The white beams of the truck's headlights instantly doubled in intensity, mixed with a manic flashing of blue light. Sandy and Keefe turned abruptly to the sudden surge of light. A patrol car from the county sheriff's office had pulled in behind them.

With all the lights in their eyes, the deputy was little more than a vague shadow when he got out of his car. Sandy and Keefe couldn't actually see him at all once he trained his flashlight on them.

"What's going on here?" the deputy asked.

"Oh, just having the usual fight with this old padlock," Keefe answered. "But we finally got it. We're fine, officer." Keefe lifted the lock from the latch and began to walk the gate open.

"Stop right there, please. Pull that gate closed. I asked what's going on here."

The angle of the deputy's flashlight beam shifted, and Sandy thought she saw his hand move to what must have been a pistol holstered on his hip.

Keefe eased the gate gently closed and shielded his eyes from the blaze of lights. "It's all right, officer. Just getting the gate open. We live up there."

We. He'd said it with casual ease, with no more special emphasis than if he'd said the brook trout were hitting on yellow stoneflies. A simple statement of fact. *We live up there*. Sandy's eyes slid from the deputy's flashlight beam to Keefe, and a ripple of liquid warmth ran through her, neutralizing the chill of the rain on her skin.

"I'll need to see some ID. Let me see your driver's licenses, please."

Keefe dug his wallet from his hip pocket, removed his license, and stepped around the truck toward the deputy, extending his arm to the deputy, who took the license from his fingers. Sandy walked immediately to the side of Keefe.

"Mine's in my purse," she said. "In the truck."

The deputy stepped back and to the side, training his flashlight beam on the interior of the truck cab. "Okay. And shut off the engine while you're in there."

Sandy switched off the ignition, retrieved her license, and handed it to the deputy.

"Been living up here for years, officer," Keefe said. "I'm sure you'll find everything in order."

"Wait right there," the deputy said, and began to walk back to his patrol car.

"Might we at least wait in the truck? Out of this rain?" Keefe asked.

The deputy's flashlight beam turned back on them. "All right." His voice issued from pure shadow. "Stay right there."

They sat, dripping wet, in the truck cab, surrounded by the storm of light raging from the deputy's car. Rain drummed on the roof.

"Most in the sheriff's office know about this place," Keefe said. "He must be new."

"Must be," Sandy said. She rubbed at her wet, bare arms, trying to revive the warmth of the word *we*.

After a few interminable minutes, Sandy saw the deputy's flashlight beam bouncing toward them in her side-view mirror. She rolled her window down to receive their returned licenses, now that their identities had been confirmed. Now that it had been confirmed that *they lived there*.

"Here's your license, Mr. Keefe." The deputy's hand emerged from behind his flashlight beam. Sandy took the license, passed it to Keefe, and held out her hand for her own license. The deputy opened her door and took a step back.

"Miss Holston, I'm afraid I'll have to ask you to step out of the truck."

Sandy's eyes flashed quickly at Keefe, then back in the direction of the deputy. "What? Why?" she asked.

"Step out of the truck, please," the deputy said. "There's an open warrant for your arrest."

"That's preposterous." Keefe leaned forward in the truck cab. "There must be some mistake, officer."

"Stay where you are, sir." The light from the patrol car's headlights left no doubt. Sandy could see the deputy's free hand rise to the butt of the pistol in his holster. "Out of the car, ma'am. Arrest warrant was issued this morning. Charge of battery. You struck a coworker."

Sandy's eyes locked for a moment on Keefe's as she stepped slowly from the truck cab and back into the rain. They looked at each other with shared, furtive recognition. She'd told Keefe everything about the morning, and they both realized the situation at the same instant. The manager at the nursing home. She'd filed a complaint.

"Place your hands on the truck and spread your feet, please." The deputy's detached, professional demeanor struck Sandy as curious, considering the emotional fervor of her action that morning, which had brought her to this point.

The deputy shut off his flashlight and holstered it on his belt. Light from headlights and his flashers remained more than adequate. He patted Sandy down quickly, his hands never lingering long on any one part of her body.

"Really, officer," Keefe complained. "Is this necessary?"

"Quiet, sir. Don't move. I won't say it again."

The deputy produced a set of plastic handcuffs, pulled Sandy's arms behind her, and affixed the restraints while intoning the terms of her arrest and her rights in the same cold, mechanical voice he'd employed throughout the encounter. Sandy gazed through the windshield at the shadow of worry on Keefe's face. *We live up there.*

"It's all right, James." It looked to her as if his breathing was again becoming agitated. "Really, I'll be all right. Edith's lawyer's name is on a sheet of paper in my purse. I guess, call him."

"Of course, my dear," Keefe said. "Immediately."

"No," Sandy said. "Stink's shut in the cabin. Take care of Stink first."

Keefe's eyes glanced past the headlights to the blackness of the fire road leading up to the bungalow.

"Promise. Take care of Stink first," Sandy said.

"I promise. Of course." Keefe sighed audibly, angrily as the deputy began to lead Sandy back to the patrol car. "Outrageous."

The deputy paused at the open door of the truck, his grip firm on Sandy's upper arm. "Stay right where you are, Mr. Keefe, until I've left with Miss Holston. Then you're free to go."

"Outrageous," Keefe muttered again as the deputy led Sandy to the patrol car and tucked her into the rear seat.

Despite the deputy's warning, Keefe emerged from the cab and moved slowly around the far end of Sandy's truck. He stopped at the driver's-side door and watched through the rain, his movements apparently not sufficiently threatening to further incite the deputy.

While the deputy radioed in his situation, Sandy looked past the shadow of his flat-brimmed hat to where Keefe stood at the gate to the headwaters, upright under his drenched fedora in the roar of headlight beams and blue flashers. She had come to the Ripshin River Valley five years before to escape a criminal, and now she had become one, handcuffed in the back seat of a patrol car. She had sought solitude and been ambushed by love.

We live up there.

Autumn

11

KEEFE HAD BEEN QUIET AND WITHDRAWN MOST OF THE morning. He worked slowly, methodically, bent over his fly-tying bench, his eyes zeroed into his magnifying loop, focused on the tiny fly taking shape in the vise. The cold dregs of his second cup of coffee sat in a white mug at the edge of the bench. A cigarette butt lay bent and mashed in the ashtray. He'd been in the same position since Sandy woke three hours earlier, barely moving, except for the skilled motion of his hands around the vise. He hadn't really spoken at all.

Most times, in the past, she wouldn't have given much thought to Keefe pulling away into some private distance. She'd seen it often enough. And understood it well enough. From the very first time she'd found her way inside this place, she'd had a sense that the bungalow was an arena of sorts, in which Keefe engaged in some form of personal, interior combat. After her presence here had become a fairly regular feature, there had still been times when that presence appeared to be inconsequential, perhaps even unmarked by Keefe. If anyone could understand the occasional need to recede within a shell of solitude, it was Sandy Holston. Even love, if it was love, need not, could not, demand the constant presence and attention of the beloved.

Stink lay in his usual spot on the sofa, snoring vaguely, and Sandy sat beside him, sipping another cup of tea and aimlessly scratching behind his ear. Before the night of her arrest, she had often sat contently in the bungalow while Keefe remained silently intent on his work at the bench. Why now did his back turned toward her, positioned that way simply due to an arrangement of furniture, feel like a barricade? Had she become greedy? *We live up there.* He had spoken the words casually. Had he meant them just as casually? A practical configuration of words intended merely to offer a reasonable explanation for both of them being there at the fire-road gate that night when the deputy appeared? Had she taken his words too literally? She had, during the two weeks since her arrest, spent most of her days and nearly all her nights here at Keefe's bungalow. Had she overplayed it? Had she pushed it too far, that rush of warmth in the rainy night? Had one loss led her to some unreasonable fear of another, so much so that she was reluctant to allow what she loved out of her sight for long? She'd been a daughter, a wife, an ex-wife, even a widow of sorts. Yet she was still a fledgling, so new to this business of loving.

Or perhaps it was just the rain. Perhaps it had just driven human life too far indoors, had confined bodies within quarters too close for too long, for the sake of shelter. The rains had arrived in the bottom of the third inning of what turned out to be the last home game for the Sherwood Cougars that season. Since that evening when it left Keefe doused, standing alone in the glare of headlights while Sandy was carted off to the sheriff's office, the rain had been general throughout the Ripshin River Valley, throughout the entirety of the Rogers Ridge watershed. Until just the day before, there had not been a day without rain. The web of runs and washes coming down the slopes had swollen and churned up the lower Ripshin, already flowing above its usual levels due to the increased release of water from Willard Lake through the hydroelectric dam. Word was making the rounds of the valley that if these rains kept up much longer, they'd have no choice but to open the floodgates above the spillway of the dam, which would guarantee one hell of a downstream mess. And more rain was in the forecast. One bit of local gossip had it that the leader of the commune that owned and operated the Damascus Diner had identified in the relentless rains—along with a modest earthquake in northern Virginia and television coverage of a series of tornadoes ripping through the Great Plains—confirmation of the approach of the end of days. One version of the story said he had settled on a specific date and ordered his followers to begin preparation for the final rapture, but most valley residents said you could never tell about those folks back there off Wilson Hollow Road. The upper Ripshin was up and surging, far too deep and forceful for wading, for fishing, but still running fairly clear, only slightly muddied, more of a source for the threat of flooding downstream than for any dangerous flooding here on the slopes of the headwaters themselves.

Keefe glanced only briefly over his shoulder when Sandy opened the front door of the bungalow. She held the door open a moment and looked at her dog to see if he wanted to go out, but Stink displayed no interest in leaving the sofa. Sandy sat on the top step of the porch. Through the seat of her jeans she could feel a chill damp from all the recent rain. Even from her side of the clearing, the roar of the current through the pool was loud. The sun, so rarely seen of late, had just cut through a scattering of clouds above the ravine, painting a bright band through the treetops up the slopes around the clearing. In the sudden spray of light the forest looked washed clean. The dark green of the rhododendron, pine, and hemlock shone, wavering in the breeze, above the spongy ground. Some of the earlier hardwoods had begun the transformation to the dull browns and the reds and yellows of the season; other species would later commence the ebb into dormancy charted by the gaudy explosion of color.

The sound of a vehicle rumbling up the fire road cut down the slope through the trees to Sandy's ears. That would be Margie and J.D. and the boys, right on time. A couple more minutes and they would bump and wind their way down the gravel drive and into the clearing. Sandy wondered if Keefe would emerge from his remote shadows when they arrived.

Once locked into the back seat of the deputy's patrol car that night, Sandy had settled against her forearms and wrists, pinned and cuffed behind her back. As the deputy backed away from the fire-road gate, she'd watched Keefe recede out of the headlight beams, fading into the rainy night, and it all seemed fitting to her somehow. Perhaps inevitable. Certainly familiar. The deputy signed off his radio and accelerated out onto the access road, and Sandy's private history began to cohere, to encircle her and snap into place like the handcuffs around her wrists. An arc had been completed as she once again left a man marooned and confused, a man whose puzzled gaze tracked her departing figure, wondering just exactly what it was his eyes trailed after. In the befuddled, stunned look on Keefe's face as the patrol car backed away she recognized a matured twin of the shock on Vernon's face when she abandoned him to the prison guards and fled the clearing along Dismal Creek so many years before. Vernon had sought to possess her, had called it love, and had been destroyed by her refusal to be contained within his version of her. Keefe had sought only to be left alone in his headwater hideout, yet she had pushed her way into his life, had further entrenched herself there, for something she had yet to fully understand but for now called love. The result appeared the same—a baffled man standing alone and wet on the edge of a wild place. The handcuffs were appropriate. She was a criminal. She was guilty, though of precisely what crime, she could not be quite certain.

And yet Keefe had come through, had risen to the occasion, slipped free of that confusion she recognized, and stirred into action. There had, of course, been no answer at the lawyer's office at that hour of the evening, but Keefe had left a message, emphasizing the urgency of the situation. Before he'd gotten Stink up into his own truck for the drive to the sheriff's office in Sherwood, he'd had the good sense to call Margie and J.D., who lived in town and might get there more quickly. As he said to her later, "certainly a time to rally the troops."

ONCE they'd arrived at the sheriff's office that night, the deputy maintained his detached, professional demeanor, leading her into the office by a strictly ceremonial, light touch applied to her pinned arms. Most startling to Sandy was the brightness of the light inside the sheriff's office.

Her eyes long adapted to the night and the darkness in the rear seat of the patrol car, she blinked, nearly blinded by the panels of fluorescent lights in the ceiling of the office. The glare was then multiplied by the shine from the beige linoleum of the floor. A female deputy, probably close to Sandy in age, with her hair pulled tightly into a ponytail, sat behind a microphone on a stand at the dispatcher's counter. The deputy escorting Sandy looked at the dispatcher and nodded toward his prisoner. Behind the dispatcher's counter were four identical desks, and the deputy led Sandy through the room to a desk near the far wall. He pointed to a straight-backed chair beside the desk that faced toward the wall. "Have you a seat there, ma'am," he said.

The deputy removed his hat, and in the blazing light of the office Sandy could see his face clearly for the first time. His hair was red and closely cropped, his cheeks deeply ruddy. As Keefe had speculated, he was probably new on the job. He couldn't have been older than his mid-twenties.

He stepped away, peeling off his raincoat, then shook off the last drops of water and hung it on a hook on the back wall. To his left was a small holding cell, no more than a large cage made of chain link. On the single bench inside the cage a man in wet denim lay sprawled along the bench, flat on his back, one arm dangling to the floor, his mouth wide open. The deputy walked to the dispatcher's counter, collected a couple sheets of paper, and exchanged a few words with her. He walked around a corner and out of view for a moment, then reappeared, carrying a towel, and returned to the desk where Sandy waited.

"Here." The deputy dropped the towel into Sandy's lap, reached behind her, and freed her from the plastic handcuffs. "You can dry off a bit with that." Sandy looked down at the towel and realized she was still soaked from standing in the rain at the fire-road gate.

While the deputy filled out the arrest report, Sandy ran the towel over her arms and hair as her eyes wandered from the deputy at the desk to a small bulletin board hanging from the wall behind him. A crumpled sheaf of old FBI wanted flyers stapled to the bulletin board looked to be old enough that the grainy photos would be of little use in identifying any of the criminals still at large in the world. Tacked up beside the wanted flyers hung another flyer, newly printed on crisp green paper, announcing the pancake breakfast sponsored by the Sherwood Kiwanis club scheduled for the coming weekend. From beneath it peeked another old, crumpled flyer. Sandy recognized it. One of the flyers about the disappearance of Randy Mullins that began to show up all over the Ripshin Valley that spring. Sandy looked back at the deputy, hunched over the forms on his desk, and wondered how many different versions of her encounter with the nursing-home manager that morning had by this time been unleashed by Joyce Malden.

"Sandy, my God. What the hell?" Margie's voice flowed through her like warm honey.

Sandy turned to see her friend charging past the dispatcher's counter toward Sandy, with J.D. quickly closing behind her.

"Ma'am, stop right there." The dispatcher's warning coincided with J.D. catching his wife's arm.

Margie's eyes, darting back and forth from Sandy to her husband, flickered with a combination of fear and outrage. J.D. shook his head at her and motioned for her to sit on one of the molded plastic chairs across from the dispatch counter. Margie sat, but Sandy could see her friend's agitation. J.D. raised his hand to greet the deputy. "Ronnie," he said. Of course J.D. would know him. As a regional game warden, he would have come to know local law enforcement officers in the course of his job.

"J.D." The deputy nodded almost imperceptibly.

"Could I have a word?" J.D. asked.

"Be right with you." The deputy continued filling out the arrest report for another minute. "Remain where you are, Miss Holston," he said before getting up from his seat at the desk and walking over to J.D., the arrest report fluttering from his fingertips.

The deputy and J.D. huddled together, speaking quietly, and Margie rose to join the huddle. Margie's arm rose, pointing toward the hallway that disappeared around the corner, and J.D. lowered his wife's arm gently. Another deputy appeared from around the corner and walked to the dispatcher. He'd begun to speak to her when she turned away to take a radio call, and the other deputy walked to the back of the room, collected his hat and rain slicker from a hook on the wall. He returned to the dispatcher, took a slip of paper from her, and left. Margie began to march down the hallway, but J.D. restrained her, clearly imploring her to stay calm and wait in the chair where she'd been sitting. She looked about to explode, but she sat nonetheless. J.D. nodded to the deputy, shook hands with him, and walked around the corner after eliciting one more promise from his wife that she'd stay put.

Sandy turned away, staring blankly at the bulletin board. She wished the holding cell where the drunk lay were empty, that the deputy had locked her inside that cage instead of leaving her parked in a chair. The chain-link cage would confirm her criminal status, clarifying her vague position as a woman left alone, in damp clothing, clutching a soggy towel, under glaring lights. If she were locked in the cage, the isolation she felt would have a tangible, visible form. The cage would corroborate her guilt, provide a physical structure for how she had been removed from the negotiations of her life while others were left to clean up the consequences of her actions.

"Oh, there you are. They won't let us even talk to her." Margie's voice indicated the arrival of Keefe, but suddenly a wave of shame ran through Sandy. She remained facing the bulletin board and closed her eyes.

"Professor Keefe." The voice of the dispatcher rose to a high, girlish pitch. "I don't suppose you remember me. It's been a long time, but I was in one of your classes at the community college."

"Yes, of course." Keefe's response was low, barely audible to Sandy. What he said next rang in her ears like a bell. "I'm with her."

Sandy opened her eyes and turned to catch the gaze of an aging man in a wet fedora who was being forced to navigate channels for which he had no chart. And yet he had come for her. Love and shame rose in her throat simultaneously, nearly choking her. Edith was dead. Margie was here. Keefe was here. *I'm with her. We live up there.* The words ran through her like a braided current flowing into the same pool from two streams.

Sandy carried love and shame like a stone on her tongue as she was led through the remainder of the process she'd initiated when she slapped a well-groomed woman that morning. The arresting deputy remained reserved and professional as he filed the arrest report and led her around the corner and down the hallway to the office of the magistrate on duty that night. Margie and Keefe followed close behind. J.D. stepped out of the magistrate's office when they arrived. She was officially charged with simple battery, a misdemeanor, she was informed. Thanks to J.D.'s intervention, the magistrate agreed to release Sandy on her own recognizance. Thanks to that and, according to J.D., the sheriff's office being as understaffed as his own, there was no one available to transport her to county lockup. Her driver's license was returned to her, and she was told not to leave the county. An official summons for what the magistrate referred to as a bench trial would be forthcoming. After articulating the serious consequences of any failure on her part to appear for that trial at the appointed date and time, the magistrate released Sandy to the arms of the small group of people waiting for her in the hallway outside the office.

Rain drummed on the vinyl awning above the entry doors. The awning was just big enough to cover the four of them as they stood on the wet street. Keefe unfurled the rain jacket he had brought and slipped it around Sandy's shoulders. "Thought you might need this," he said.

"Thank you, James." Sandy pulled the jacket closed and looked into the faces around her. The isolation she'd felt earlier—weeping for Edith on the stoop behind her house on Willard Road, bound in the dark rear seat of the patrol car, left alone on the chair beside the deputy's desk while the action of others whirled around her—that isolation crumbled into dust. "Thank you. Thank you all. And you especially, J.D. I'm so sorry."

"Jesus H. Christ, what an unholy clusterfuck of a day, honey." Margie's arms reached out and encircled Sandy. Over Margie's shoulder Sandy could see a faint grimace cross J.D.'s face. He could still be shocked by his wife's salty tongue. "What are you gonna do now?"

Sandy shook her head slowly, looked out into the night rain, and pulled the jacket tighter around her. "I just want to go home and go to sleep." *Home.* Sandy couldn't say what the word *home* conjured in the minds of the three people around her, but she knew with instant certainty that for her it meant the bungalow. "Try to get my head around it all tomorrow."

"No answer at the lawyer's," Keefe said. "Which is to be expected at this hour, I'd assume. I left a message, but we'll try to catch him again tomorrow."

"Magistrate said it'd be a month or two before the trial date," J.D. said. "Pretty good bit of time to figure things out."

"You go get some rest, sweetie," Margie said. "I can't believe this bullshit."

"Outrageous," Keefe muttered.

"Stink. Was Stink okay?" Sandy looked up at Keefe's face in the shadow of his hat brim.

He nodded toward his truck, parked in the lot across the street. The truck sat under one of the mercury vapor lamps lighting the lot, and in the shower of light from the lamp Sandy saw her purple-tongued dog panting in the truck cab.

"Certainly a time to rally the troops, it seemed," Keefe said. "Including him."

Sandy reached for Keefe's hand and squeezed it.

"You get some rest, honey," Margie said, "and we'd best get home before those boys burn down the house or something."

"Oh god, Margie," Sandy said. "You had to leave the boys alone to come down here for me? I'm so sorry."

"Nonsense," Margie said. "They're fine. Luke is perfectly able to keep an eye on Matthew. Since he took up this bird-watching thing, he's become quite the little *watcher*." Margie's eyes shot over to J.D., who'd given Luke the field guide. J.D. shrugged, a sheepishly guilty grin on his face. "It's getting a bit obsessive, actually. Keeps harping on needing to spot that damned woodpecker. What is it again, a pixilated woodpecker or some such?"

"Pileated woodpecker," J.D. offered, his grin widening.

"I think we can help with that," Keefe said. "Bring him up to the place sometime. I know a spot where we've a good chance to put him onto that elusive bird of his."

"It's a date," Margie said. "But now I need to go pack those boys off to bed, and you need to do the same thing."

Handshakes and embraces were passed around the group gathered in front of the sheriff's office. Sandy took J.D. into an especially tight embrace and thanked him again. Even in the dim, damp light under the awning, she could see him blushing.

"I'll call you," Margie said as she and J.D. trotted off toward his SUV.

"Come, my dear." Keefe slid his arm around Sandy's shoulder. "Let's get you home."

Home. We live up there. I'm with her.

She leaned into Keefe's side, suddenly more exhausted than she'd ever been, and knew, as they stepped out into the rain, that *home*, at least that night, would be the bungalow along the headwaters.

MARGIE extracted a cigarette and a plastic disposable lighter from the vinyl snap-pouch where she kept them. Her lips pursed firmly around the filter tip of the cigarette as she clicked the lighter and cupped her hand around it to block the breeze. It flared into a small blue flame on the fourth try. Margie inhaled a deep draft of smoke and held it in her lungs while she tucked the lighter back into the pouch. When she exhaled, the breeze caught the smoke and carried it upstream, away from where the two of them sat on the riverbank.

"Want one?" Margie held the pouch out to Sandy, who declined with a shake of her head. Margie put the pouch into a small day pack on the ground by the rock where they sat, discharged another long plume of smoke through her lips, and turned back to Sandy.

"I know of at least two nurses at the hospital who are pregnant and going on maternity leave soon. One of them, hell, she looks ready to pop any day now." Margie seemed more concerned about Sandy's lack of employment than did Sandy herself. Sandy wondered if she was perhaps being too lackadaisical about it. Since the night of her arrest, she'd hardly given it a moment's thought. "It'd be easier if you had your RN. They don't take on LPNs that much these days, but I could look into it if you want me to."

"Thanks," Sandy said, "but I've got enough saved. I'll be fine for a while yet." Not that Sandy had ever been obsessively frugal. Her job had provided more than adequately for her modest financial needs. In truth, most of what she needed in the world didn't present itself with a price tag or bar code. She hadn't done any actual accounting, but Sandy guessed she could last without a job well into the next year before things started to get tight. "Probably best not to even start looking till after the trial."

Margie shrugged with resigned agreement.

The summons had been sitting in her mailbox on Willard Road when Sandy left the headwaters to collect her mail three days ago. Her court date wasn't scheduled until the very end of October.

"Wouldn't exactly put me in good standing with a new employer to ask for time off to go to jail."

Margie exhaled and mashed her cigarette in the damp dirt between her feet. "You're not going to jail. They just couldn't really do that."

"Sure they could. I'm guilty. I hit her."

"Bitch deserved it."

Sandy grinned and patted Margie on the knee. "Much as I'd like it, you won't be the judge in my case."

"If I was, she'd be the one heading to jail. Ought to be against the law to be that much of a bitch."

Sandy chuckled silently as Margie fished out another cigarette and lit it.

"Seriously," Margie said. A thread of smoke spun in front of her face before the breeze swept it away. "Not like you're a real criminal or anything."

Sandy could no longer be so sure about that as her friend. She'd hit that well-groomed woman. Hit her hard. She felt no regrets and knew that, given the occasion to replay the situation, she'd hit her again, just as deliberately, just as hard. Legally, it was simple—she had struck another person, and you didn't get to do that without consequences. She was a criminal—a fact of law. She was coming to recognize the undiluted core of what was designated as crime. One desire (to slap the lipstick off that well-groomed woman's face) trumped an opposing desire (the well-groomed woman's desire and presumed right not to be slapped). One need fulfilled at the expense of another. Self-interest pursued and gratified without regard to the broader interests of others. Want greater than provision. When Sandy forced it all through this tiny opening, it kept coming up the same. She was a criminal. The nursing-home manager had reduced her beloved Edith Moser to a cipher on a balance sheet, and for that she had hit her. And she'd do so again. But had her angry, violent response been instigated as much by the possibility that someone else dared to have a say over the old woman's life? The love and wonder she found in Edith, had she wanted it all to herself? And Keefe. She'd done nothing short of invade his sanctuary. *We live up there.* Yes, he'd said it, but did his remark carry the weight she'd accorded it? What part of the terse sentence did she feed most fervently on, *we* or *there?* And what of Vernon? He had killed a man. A fact. By all reasonable accounts of their final episode, he had been coming to kill her, to kill her and Margie both. But just as certainly as he sought to kill her, she had led him into the precise position where the encroaching wall of water would be most deadly. Self-defense, legally speaking. Still, had she just as much desired to erase from this new landscape in which she'd been reborn the burdensome past Vernon dragged behind him? Guilty as charged? Despite what Margie said, she had to wonder.

"What's the lawyer think?" Margie asked.

"Doesn't seem all that concerned," Sandy answered. "Said he plays poker with most of the judges around here, so not to worry much."

"Nothing like the good-old-boy network," Margie said. "At least when it's on your side."

WHEN Sandy had finally been able to meet with the attorney last week, he hadn't been much concerned at all with the battery charge. He'd spent the majority of the time talking about Edith Moser.

The attorney's office was above a furniture-rental store in downtown Sherwood. A deep voice bellowed "Entrez" when Sandy rapped on the translucent pebble glass of the office door. A small outer office was unoccupied, containing a tidy desk, a few chairs, but no person. She passed through it to the inner office, a cluttered, one-room affair, dominated by a large, heavy man with steel-gray hair seated behind a desk stacked with files and papers, his shirtsleeves rolled to the elbows over beefy forearms, his necktie loosened at his thick throat.

"I'm Sandy Holston. We spoke on the phone," she said.

"Yes, of course," he said. Sandy clasped the meaty hand he reached across the desk. "Jackson Stamper. You'll forgive me if I don't get up. As you can see, I'm a bit hobbled just now."

He sat sideways behind his desk, one foot propped on the seat of a straight-backed chair. The foot rested on a cushion, wrapped in tattered bandages and a walking boot. When Sandy had finally contacted him, he'd apologized for the delay in returning her calls, explaining he'd been in the hospital recovering from surgery.

"Please, have a seat," he said, motioning to a small sofa along the wall, equally covered with files and papers. "Just push that mess out of the way. I'll get to it sooner or later. My secretary is off this week."

"What happened?" Sandy nodded at the bandaged foot.

"Oh, nothing. They lopped off three toes." Jackson Stamper huffed, a wry grin spreading over his jowled face. "Seems I find life's pleasures far more interesting than my diabetes. Guess I'll just let them hack away at me bit by bit till there's nothing left. It won't be pretty, but I'll leave with a full belly and a smile on my face."

"Looks as though you could use a new dressing," Sandy said.

The attorney waved his hand at his foot as if swatting at a fly. "Enough about me. Let's get to your business. So, you're Edith Moser's heir."

"Well, yes, I suppose," Sandy said. "But I was thinking more about the charge of battery just now."

"Get to that soon enough." Stamper swatted the air again. "Edith Moser was a true character. Wonderful old gal. I didn't think she had any family left. Were you related?"

"She was my friend."

"Like I said, a wonderful old gal. My daddy worked with her at Old Dominion. Shoot, the way he talked about her sometimes, I swear. For years I thought he only married my mama as a last resort because he couldn't talk Edith Moser into having him. But he never had nothing but praise for her. Tell the truth, I think he carried a torch for her right up till the end. She was my first case, you know, right out of law school. Little problem with the land title to her place out there on the river."

While Jackson Stamper reminisced about Edith, Sandy recalled the surprising weight of Edith's body in her arms as she carried her into the stream that last time. She thought about the black plastic urn sitting on her kitchen counter and wondered how long it would yet be until the waters went down enough for her to wade into the lower Ripshin with Edith one more time and feather her ashes over the current in the shadow of the big hemlock that wasn't there anymore.

SANDY and Margie barely heard it over the booming rush of high water churning through the streambed of the upper Ripshin. A single rifle shot, somewhere in the distance, well over the ridge. The percussive report of the discharge, followed by a faint, rippling echo. To hear the pop of a gun being fired most anywhere in the Ripshin River Valley was hardly an occurrence to remark upon, especially in the autumn, when hunters were getting a jump on the beginning of deer season. Neither woman acknowledged the gunfire with anything more than a momentary and involuntary shift of her eyes in the general direction of the sound. And, still wrapped in the roar of the headwaters, neither woman heard the footsteps of Margie's eldest son scuffing down the path to their spot on the bank until the boy was only a few steps away from them. He held a thick, green-backed book close to his chest, an index finger laid between the leaves.

"Hey, honey," Margie said. "Did you find your bird?"

Luke nodded, opened the field guide to the marked page, and handed it to his mother to see. When he pointed to the photograph of the pileated woodpecker, Sandy thought the boy's fingertip indicated the checkmark, carefully inked into the upper left-hand corner of the photograph, as much as the bird itself.

"Now I've seen them all," he said.

"All of them?" Margie asked, genuine amazement on her face. "You've seen all the birds listed in your book?"

Luke smirked and scoffed. "No, mom. Geez. All the tree-clinging birds. Woodpeckers and stuff. Ones that hang on the sides of trees. Well, all the ones that live around here, anyway. Black-backed, three-toed woodpeckers only live in Canada, and I've never been to Canada."

"So do we need to go to Canada now?" Margie said.

"Not yet," the boy said.

Sandy leaned toward Margie and looked at the blazing color photographs. On each of the six images printed on the open pages, she saw the same checkmark, carefully inscribed into the same corner of each photograph.

"I'm glad you got to see the woodpecker," Sandy said.

"So I guess Mr. Keefe knew the right spot to take you." Margie handed the field guide back to her son, who laid it gently on his lap and gazed down at the pictures and checkmarks.

"Uh-hunh. A big old dead tree, way back there." The boy waved his arm toward the slope rising behind them. "Had to wait there for a long time, but after a while it stuck its head right out of a big hole in the trunk. Lots of waiting in bird-watching."

Margie grinned and ran her hand over her son's hair. "So you two explorers had a good time?"

"Okay, I guess. We saw the pileated. Mr. Keefe's kind of quiet and weird." Sandy and Margie traded surreptitious glances. "But so am I, so I guess it was okay."

Margie beamed, leaned over, and kissed her son on the top of the head.

"Mom." The boy grimaced and pulled away.

"Where is Mr. Keefe?" Sandy asked.

"Said he was going back home."

"Maybe we should head back, too," Margie said. She gathered up her pack and she and Sandy rose from their seats.

"It's going to rain some more," Luke said. The boy closed his book and drew it close to his chest again.

Sandy took a few steps toward the trail back up to the fire road and turned back. She had always felt a certain indistinct pleasure in watching Margie's relaxed, easy way with her children.

"Let's go, honey. It's been a big day for you and the woodpeckers," Margie said.

The boy fell in line, in front of his mother and behind Sandy, as the three of them climbed back to the fire road.

"J.D. and your brother come back down yet?" Margie asked.

"Naw, they're still up there somewhere."

EARLIER, during the general small talk amongst the entire group as they set off on their way up the fire road in search of the pileated woodpecker, Keefe had been polite enough but remained largely quiet and withdrawn. J.D. had grumbled briefly about another purported sighting of a mountain lion, the investigation of which had revealed that someone's large yellow Labrador had been snooping around a neighbor's garbage cans.

"Don't you know it's Tommy Akers," J.D. said, "blabbing about this nonsense to any fool who'll listen. Last thing I need."

Sandy shivered at the memory of the long tail she had glimpsed up here the day after Edith's death. She shot a quick glance at Keefe, but he didn't return her gaze. J.D.'s complaint about phantom mountain lions appeared to have stirred in him a recollection other than the big cat Sandy may or may not have seen.

"Not to overburden you, son," Keefe had said, "but I think someone may have been baiting bears up here, too. Couple miles up the road, found a pit. Not my area of expertise, but my guess would be bear baiting."

"Great," J.D. had muttered.

Simply the phrase "bear baiting" provided more than ample provocation to enflame the youthful bloodlust of Margie's younger son. Matthew grew instantly animated and giddy at the prospect of gobs of blood, torn hide, perhaps even a vast pit filled with the rotting carcasses of dead bears. He leapt about frantically, pleading to be taken to the bear-baiting pit. "Oh, please. Please. It'll be so cool."

J.D. sighed and reluctantly agreed to take Matthew with him in search of the bear-baiting pit. Sandy smiled, watching the glow spread across Margie's face as she watched her husband and youngest child trek back to the bungalow, where they would pile into the government SUV for the drive up the fire road.

SANDY, Margie, and Luke arrived back at the bungalow to find Stink still curled in his spot on the sofa. Keefe wasn't there. His truck sat in the usual spot. None of his fishing gear was gone—with the headwaters as high and forceful as they were, that came as no surprise. Sandy thought, perhaps, the cave, but the high water would make fording the stream to get there nearly impossible as well.

Luke settled into the armchair and reopened his book to the checked picture of the pileated woodpecker. Margie went into the bathroom, and Sandy rousted her dog. He'd been awakened by their entrance but remained on the sofa, his neck and snout stretched out slightly to take a whiff of the boy sitting near him.

"Come on, you lazy old thing," Sandy said, roughing up his fur with her hand. "Get up. Go on out there and do your business. You've been in here for hours."

Stink slid slowly from his spot on the sofa, yawned, stretched, gave another perfunctory sniff to the boy, and waddled out the door that Sandy held open for him. She followed the dog into the clearing. She looked across the stream and peered into the shadow of the cave, confirming what she already knew. Keefe was elsewhere.

Margie stepped out the front door as Sandy and Stink came back out of the clearing and up to the porch. Stink paused to let Margie pet him, then walked back inside to continue his interrupted napping. "Sure he couldn't have gone fishing?" Margie asked.

"Not in this water."

"Where do you think he went?"

"Don't know."

And just then, as their words dissolved in the air, the sound of tires slipping on gravel rose behind them, shortly followed by the green SUV rolling down the driveway and into the clearing. A serenely beaming Matthew sat strapped in the passenger seat beside J.D. Keefe was in the back.

"Oh, there's our answer," Margie said.

The two grown men stepped from the vehicle and walked to the porch. The boy brought up the rear, walking more slowly, his hands clutched at the center of his chest, as if he carried something both precious and fragile.

"Thanks for the lift," Keefe said to J.D. as they mounted the porch. Keefe nodded to Sandy and Margie and passed on into the bungalow.

Sandy's eyes followed Keefe's passage, then turned back to J.D. "Where was he?" she asked.

"We saw him on the way back," J.D. said. "He was sitting in that clearing up there with the old cabin chimneys."

When Matthew inched his way up the steps to the porch, Margie turned to her youngest. "What you got there, sweetie?"

The boy held his hands out slowly. Clutched within his tight grip, a small black tuft. "Bear hair," the boy said. There was a breathless reverence in his voice. "And there was blood, a big blob of it."

"How lovely, dear. I see handwashing in your future," Margie said, and turned to J.D. "So I take it your quest was a success?"

"Yes, damn it all," he said. "We'd better get going. Got to get back, file a report, and figure out how to handle this one now."

"It's going to rain more." Luke had come out to the porch, his book held to his chest, his index finger still marking the woodpecker page.

The wind had picked up a bit in the last few minutes. Downslope, through the trees, they could make out a hint of darker clouds beginning to roll in over the lower valley.

"You boys go get in the car," Margie said. "And Luke, tell Mr. Keefe thank you for finding your bird for you."

"Thank you, Mr. Keefe," the boy said quietly as he descended the steps with his brother. No sound came from within the bungalow. The brothers walked to the SUV, the younger holding his wad of torn bear fur in his fists, the elder clutching his book.

"What courteous little lunatics I'm raising," Margie said. "Anyway, thanks for finding Luke his damned woodpecker. You have no idea what that's going to be worth around the house."

"Glad he got to see it. They're beautiful," Sandy said.

J.D. and Margie left the porch and walked to the SUV. As they got in, Margie called back to Sandy. "I'll call you later. Where you going to be, here or your place?"

That was the question, wasn't it, Sandy thought. Not where she was going to be, but rather, which one was *her place*. "Not sure. Probably my place." Only as she spoke it did she realize she likely spoke the truth.

"And if you need anything, honey," Margie said through her open window, "anything at all, you call me."

"I will." Sandy watched the SUV roll slowly up out of the clearing, took a long, deep breath, and walked back inside the bungalow.

Keefe had returned to his tying bench, where he sat snipping narrow strands from a wild turkey feather. As Sandy closed the door behind her and looked at Keefe's back hunched over his workbench, an unexpected sensation bubbled up in her veins, something almost alien to her in regard to Keefe. It felt like anger. Had her constant presence here lately been too much to expect of this very private man? More than likely. Did her earlier concerns about Keefe's possible disorientation merit further concern? Perhaps. Probably not. But still, being eccentric and aloof was one thing. Being rude was another. And that's what it felt like to her just now—rudeness. Realizing her teeth were tightly gritted together, she took a breath and consciously relaxed her jaw muscles.

"Are you all right?" she said to Keefe's back.

"Of course, my dear. Never better," he said, not turning away from his work.

"It was good of you to find a pileated for Matthew."

"A what?"

"The woodpecker. For Margie's son. It meant a lot to him."

Keefe paused and turned halfway toward her. "Oh yes, of course," he said.

Sandy went to the bedroom and bathroom to collect what few things of hers she had here at the moment. She stuffed them into a small duffel and walked back into the bungalow's main room. She nudged Stink from the sofa and opened the door for him.

"I think I'll go on back to my place tonight." The words *my place* rattled in Sandy's ears. "Got a few things to take care of there." She had absolutely nothing to take care of there, as far as she could recall.

"Certainly, my dear. Whatever you wish." Keefe turned in his chair and looked toward her, but Sandy couldn't be sure if he looked at her or past her, through the open door into the clearing, where the wind lifted early-fallen leaves through the air. The quaint formality in his way of addressing her sometimes, what she had usually found endearing, even charming, made her furious just now.

"Thanks again for the woodpecker," she said. "Bye."

"Goodbye, my dear."

She hadn't consciously intended it, or so she thought, but the result was undeniable. The door had slammed sharply behind her on the way out of the bungalow.

Keefe at His Workbench: Pale Morning Dun

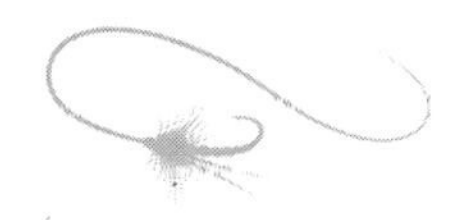

Ephemeridae. Ephemerella. A short-lived thing. Forms in the deeper water. Slips its natal skin and struggles through the current to the surface. Floats in the warming light, dries its wings, takes flight for a day, a single day. And dies, spinning down to the surface, swallowed back into the inexorable flow. And—Stop. Leave that. Turn away from the outward whirling into unraveling. Turn back to this simple core. Hold fast to the pattern. Cling to its inscribed form. Hold tight. Hold here. The comprehensible world ends beyond the ring of this light. Between here and the banks of the headwaters, a vacillating, unstable world, to be kept at bay, to be kept quiet, if possible. Follow each turn of the thread, close and tight, around the hook shank. Rule and form to the pattern. Adhere to it. The thread winds into body. Over the fattening strands, wrap the sliver of turkey feather, cut from the bands of dun between the bands of chestnut brown. A wing feather. And now, a few thin strands, synthetic, iridescent, looped onto the head of the shank, tufted into the hackle. Tighten the loop to secure it. Tighter. Tighter still. The firm fabrication that will outlast the original. The simulation more durable than the real. Grasp it. Don't let go. The safety of artifice and imitation—exactly the same, on any given day—lasting, immutable, cast onto the waters to lure the creature waiting within. Hold fast.

12

RAIN PINGED LIKE BB'S ONTO THE CANOPY OVER THE GAS pumps at the Citgo station in Damascus. It had begun as a modest shower just as Sandy jammed closed the old padlock on the fire-road gate when leaving Keefe's bungalow. By the time she reached Damascus to gas up her truck before heading to Willard Road, the rain had grown to a strong, steady downpour. Stink sat in the truck cab, his head resting on the back of the seat, his eyes staring indifferently out the rear window. The catch on the nozzle was broken, so Sandy had to hold the pump handle open. While fuel poured into her tank, she propped her elbow on the rim of the truck bed and dropped her chin into the palm of her upturned hand. As the force of the rain had increased, her anger at Keefe had diminished. The fury that slammed the bungalow door had dwindled to a dull, persistent irritation. She no longer wanted to thrash Keefe for his aloofness. She wanted only to be free of him for a few days, to go home to Willard Road until this unfamiliar aggravation fully subsided and she felt herself again.

The sound of tires spinning on wet pavement caught Sandy's ear through the thrumming of rain on the metal canopy above her. She looked up as she tightened the cap back onto her gas tank. A small hatchback scooted quickly across the road from the diner into the lot of the

Citgo and pulled up beside Sandy on the opposite side of the pump island. With the squeal of the hatchback's tires, Sandy looked up to notice the crowd around the diner. The parking lot was full to overflowing, with a few cars and pickups parked along the road to both sides of the lot. A steady stream of vehicles replaced those that pulled away, and a similarly steady stream of people hustled into and out of the diner. Those leaving carried white paper bags and stacks of styrene containers. Some even carried open plates of food, trying to shield their food from the rain as they scurried to their cars.

Small rivulets of water ran down the dark gray sides of the hatchback. The hood and roof of the car were sun-faded a lighter, mottled shade of gray. Its wiper blades screeched over the windshield until the driver cut the engine and stepped out of the car. Sandy could see a tall stack of styrene containers on the passenger seat.

"Better get over there before it's all gone." The man wore a plaid shirt and a Carhartt cap. He walked around his car to the opposite side of the gas pump from Sandy and lifted the nozzle out of its cradle.

"All what?" Sandy asked.

"All of it. Food. Everything."

Sandy glanced back at the diner. Following a group of three people carrying bags and styrene, two men waddled out, toting a long table that they carried across the lot through the rain and slid into the back of a pickup truck.

"Seems tomorrow's the big day," the man said as he began pumping gas. "And since they ain't gonna need any food in heaven, they's just giving it all away. What with all I got, I can afford to fill this thing up now. Mighty nice of 'em. Crazy, but nice. Ought to stop over and get ya some before it's too late."

"Maybe I will." Sandy recalled the rumors about the commune and its leader's prediction of the end of days. She hunched her shoulders and tucked her head against the rain and ran inside the convenience store to pay for her gas.

THE stream of cars and trucks leaving had become larger than the one arriving. Sandy found a space about thirty feet from the entrance, parked her truck, and trotted through the rain into the diner. Inside, the scene appeared to be the ruins of a storm far more formidable than the one drenching the valley outside. It looked as if half of the tables, chairs and benches usually in the diner had been removed. Those that remained were pushed askew toward the walls of the dining room. Here and there, people had found a space at a table and ate from styrene containers and drank from tall plastic glasses. A clutch of four men in muddy work clothes stood to the side of the room, talking quietly as they fisted plastic forkfuls of food into their mouths. Most of the bric-a-brac and varnished placards of Bible verses that normally adorned the diner's walls were gone.

Squarely in the middle of the restaurant, a small island of order had been maintained. An older couple, likely in their late sixties at least, sat at a table eating the last of their late lunch from mismatched plates. Farming people, Sandy surmised, from the deeply tanned face of the man beneath his startling white forehead. His John Deere cap rested on the table beside his plate. They chewed their food slowly, silently, within closed, grimly thin-lipped mouths. Their eyes darted fearfully around the room, as if to keep at bay the disorder that threatened to disrupt their luncheon.

Along one wall beyond the older couple, three tables were pushed together to form a single long one. On the tabletop, Sandy located the shambles of the diner's Judgment Day buffet. While his tongue probed for a piece of food lodged between his teeth, the farmer with the white brow watched Sandy as she stepped around the table and approached the buffet.

The long buffet table was covered from one end to the other with bowls, platters, and long stainless-steel steam-table inserts, all heavily picked over. The diner staff had clearly emptied out their larders in preparation for their departure, and the citizens of Damascus, those in the know, had responded to this final act of generosity with enthusiasm. Until two young men walked through the door as Sandy scanned the ransacked buffet, she thought she must be the last person in the valley to arrive at this last supper. She felt a bit tawdry picking over these final remains, but she was hungry and knew damn well, considering her current mood, she wouldn't feel like cooking much of anything when she got home. Not to mention, she didn't really know if she had any usable provisions to speak of at the house on Willard Road, given all the time she'd spent at Keefe's of late. She managed to scrape together the semblance of a meal she might or might not heat up back at her house—flaccid string beans flecked with bacon, brown beans coated with a congealed skin of sauce, a miraculously untouched leg of fried chicken, what she thought was a pork chop, and a crumbling hunk of cornbread. She closed her meal into one styrene container and picked up another. Into the second container she placed the last scoop of scrambled eggs and a pimiento cheese sandwich for Stink. One large bowl on the table was untouched, a full bowl of green Jell-O with tiny marshmallows suspended in it.

Sandy snapped the second container closed and moved aside for the two men who had walked in behind her.

"Told you we should've got our asses over here sooner," said one of the men.

"What the hell," said the other man as he dragged two chairs right up to the buffet table. "Get what we can. Still free."

They sat down and began to eat what they could find directly from the remains on the buffet, using the serving utensils.

"Here. You like this shit?" One of the men passed the large bowl of Jell-O to the other.

As she stepped aside, Sandy heard a low mumbling coming from the rear of the diner. Through the pass-through window between the kitchen and the restaurant, she could see the diner staff in the kitchen. All women, all dressed in varied versions of the long denim skirts with the same impossibly long hair, they stood in a circle, hands joined, eyes closed, heads bowed in softly voiced prayer. Sandy made out the word *amen* as it reverberated around the group of women when they broke their circle and walked single file out of the kitchen and through the restaurant toward the front door. Each held her clasped hands before her, each wore a vaguely serene smile on her lips as they walked straight through the diner and out the door into the rain, gladly leaving their work, their world behind for the world to come. Only one of the women, the last in the line of them, even paused to look back at the decimated diner. Her long hair was flaming red, her face freckled, and the serene smile on her face broke for a moment, revealing a twitch of worry as she gazed a final time on the world she had known, perhaps loved.

From the doorway of the diner, Sandy watched the red-haired woman close herself into a white van with the other women and drive off down the river road toward Wilson Hollow. She glanced once more into the diner. The two men were somehow still finding something to eat on the buffet table. The farmer put his John Deere cap on his head, got up from his seat, and stepped around the table to pull out his wife's chair as she rose from the table. Sandy held her two styrene containers carefully between her hands and jogged to her truck.

Stink sniffed attentively at the containers when Sandy slid into the truck cab. "I suppose you want yours now." She set the container with her meal on the floor beneath her feet. Stink's she opened and placed on the seat between them. Stink took another thorough sniff and glanced quickly at Sandy. "Go ahead. Wasn't much to choose from. Hope you like it."

While Stink scarfed his food happily, Sandy flipped on her windshield wipers and backed out of the parking space. She swung her truck to the edge of the parking lot for a closer view of the river where it flowed around the bend behind the diner. The lower Ripshin was barely contained within its channel, the water deep, churning, and muddy. Its current hammered the banks, little more than a foot or two from jumping those banks. If the rain continued much longer—and it showed no sign of abating—the floodgates on the dam would have to be opened and the feared flood would soon roll out into the Ripshin Valley. Sandy shifted into gear and headed home to Willard Road.

Home. We live up there.

Ain't Been No Mountain Lions in This Part of the Country for a Hundred Years

This cave was not right for a den. Not quite deep enough. The opening too large. Far too close to the human dwelling in the clearing on the other side of the river. But it would do for now. It would have to. She was out of the rain. She was just out of sight in the cave's scant shadow. She was safe for now. A soft layer of leaves blown into the back of the cave provided a bed on which to rest, to regain her strength, to lick the wound. Already the bloody crease along her flank had begun to sting less, but still there was pain, and she licked the wound attentively.

It had all happened seemingly in an instant, with no opportunity to recognize sequence, cause and effect, the chain of action. She'd caught the upwind human scent and turned to it as the bullet cut a shallow furrow across her rear haunch. She leapt and spun away from the sudden, searing pain. The echoing report of the rifle didn't reach her ears until her paws had reclaimed earth and she launched into wild flight. The human enemy could only be scented, not seen. No adversary to assess. No strategy to calculate. No advantage to exploit. To flee was the only option. There was no choice in it.

She ran. She ran. Downslope into the depths of the ravine, crashing through brush, leaping over deadfall, and the pain leapt with her. And she ran. Up the far slope and onto the next ridge until the scent of the human killer vanished, leaving only the moist, loamy reek of the forest floor and the drifting trace of approaching rain on the breeze. And still she ran. Along the ridge, then down the slope into the next ravine, her long tail aloft behind her, the reach of her stride expansive, stretching the pain in her thigh. And on she ran. Until she reached the surging stream cutting down through the base of the ravine, where she paused, shook her hind leg, licked briefly at the bloody stripe etched into her flank, and then loped downstream.

This occasion of her flight was contained in a single moment of time. It had a beginning, an end, and it was finished. It required no further attention or notice. The scent of human threat had long since been woven into her senses and would remain there intact, at the ready when needed. It was no longer of this moment. Still inviolate in the pulse and throb of her muscled flesh, in the ruthless crush of her fanged jaw, the blood-borne knowledge of her arrant ferocity. Without hesitation. Without doubt. Freestanding and isolate. Pure predator. The bear was larger, formidable, meriting respect, but hampered by hesitation, burdened by curiosity and thoughtful caution—it could be handled. The coyote, in itself, was no threat—what threat it posed came only in numbers. In her intractable solitude, in her stealthy stalk through the leafy shadows, she pawed her path over the forest floor, the most fearsome creature afoot within her range.

She stopped licking her wound and sat upright. The bloody seam on her thigh had begun to dry and scab over. It was not serious. She raised her snout to the scent of the rain falling beyond the mouth of the cave. The squirrel that hopped onto the ledge at the cave opening had hardly acknowledged a source of danger before the paw came down and crushed it. Now there would be a bit of food, too, along with shelter and secure solitude as the rain swelled the headwaters and pelted the ravine outside. She drew the dead squirrel closer and settled deeply onto the bed of leaves at the back of the cave.

13

STINK WAITED TILL HE STOOD SQUARELY IN THE MIDDLE OF Sandy's little kitchen before shaking off the rain soaking his coat. A brownish mist of splattered water coated the kitchen cabinets around the muddy pawprints tracked over the linoleum floor.

"Thank you, dear." Sandy decided to wait to clean up until after she had tracked in the portion of the mess that she would soon contribute. She slipped into her poncho and pulled the hood over her head.

The plain black plastic container holding Edith's ashes sat pushed to the back of the kitchen counter. She'd driven into Sherwood from the headwaters the day after her arrest to collect the old woman's remains from the funeral director. The rains had only recently begun at that point. She could have fulfilled Edith's request and disposed of her ashes right then and been done with it. The lower Ripshin was beginning to rise, but was still clear and easy enough to wade into. And she drove right by the spot. Edith's favorite spot. Sandy wondered now why she had delayed completion of the simple ritual. Had she been waiting for some sort of appropriately ceremonial moment, some set of conditions more fitting to the memory of the old woman she so revered? Truth was, she didn't want to stop for anything. She wanted to get back to the bungalow along the headwaters as soon as she could. *We live up there.*

She picked up the urn and held it for a moment, still as surprised by the heft and weight of it as she'd been when the white-haired funeral director first handed it to her with a solemn nod of his head. Densely compact there in her hands, it seemed heavier than the living woman she'd carried in her arms so many times. She set the urn back on the counter and tugged her hood closer around her face, turning to Stink, who remained beside her in the kitchen.

"I'll be right back. Just want to go look at the river." Sandy opened the screen door off the kitchen. "And stay off the furniture." Stink's bent tail wagged slowly as he sauntered into the living room and tugged himself up onto the sofa. "Good boy," Sandy said. She stepped out the kitchen door into the rain that had only rarely relented since she'd arrived back on Willard Road the afternoon before.

SANDY walked down the slope of her gravel driveway, through the stand of small pines separating her house from the road, across Willard Road and dropped onto the short path through the brush and trees to the bank of the lower Ripshin. Even as she stepped from the road onto the path, she could hear the rushing waters of the river ahead of her. Falling rain mingled with water dripping from the trees through which she walked, creating an erratic rhythm pattering against the plastic of her poncho. Through her rain gear she could feel individual drops pelting her flesh as she walked.

The weedy banks, the trees that lined the raging, coffee-colored river, maintained a striking sheen in the gray late morning light. Sandy emerged from the path and stood on the bank. The world surrounding her was drenched in a fluid, undulating glow, split by a fierce, swollen river, eager to jump its banks. Pebbled shoals that normally lined the bank at this point were invisible. Years of the river's flow had long since both nourished and exposed the roots of larger streamside trees, but those massive tangles of roots were now fully submerged beneath the seething waters that augured the looming flood. It couldn't be much longer. They'd have to open the floodgates above the dam soon. She'd keep her ears alert for the warning signal. Her house was probably far enough up the gentle slope across the road for it to be safe from the worst of the deluge, but still, the situation would merit diligent caution.

Sandy felt strangely even-tempered as she stood in the rain with the threatening river hurtling past her. The anger and irritation that had slammed the bungalow door yesterday, that had driven her in a huff away from Keefe's obstinate aloofness, her impatience to be done with the final ceremony with Edith's ashes and her nagging guilt for not having done it earlier when she could have done so easily, her inability to feel any remorse for slapping that woman—these pecking concerns washed away in the presence of the river's promised violence. It was all much simpler than she had thought. Since the rains had begun, because of the deepening, stirred-up waters, she hadn't been able to fish for more than two weeks. Edith was dead. Keefe's behavior was no different than it had ever been. The nursing-home manager was irrelevant. Her trial date was scheduled. She scoffed at herself, realizing she was a simpler creature than she had assumed. Once the flood had passed, once the waters had receded to a reasonable flow, she would cast her line into those waters and recognize herself again.

On the opposite bank of the river, perhaps twenty or thirty yards upstream, a black bear emerged from a stand of rhododendron. It extended its thick neck, pushing its snout out to test the air above the roiling waters before it. Turning its head downstream, it paused at the sight of Sandy at the riverside. Its neck seemed to extend further and its nose lifted in her direction. Confirming the scent of its sight, the bear snorted and lumbered upstream, disappearing into the brush, turning upslope in the direction of the headwaters.

Sandy recalled the bear-baiting pit up the fire road that Keefe had found, a lure for a bear like this one, treading the boundaries of its range, lurking on the fringe of a dangerous human world. She turned and disappeared back up the path to her house.

THE hydroelectric dam towered above the riverbed, a quarter mile upstream from Sandy's house. Walking the last few paces up her driveway toward the house, she could clearly hear the warning signal commence, even at that distance, as the siren blast began to roll downstream. The siren would continue to blare for a few more minutes. And then the floodgates would be opened.

As if announced by the dam's warning signal, the snarl of Tommy Akers's pickup truck ground to a lower gear as it turned into her driveway. She turned to the sound as Tommy's truck pulled through the opening in the pines and began to crawl up the slope, towing a stock trailer. The truck strained against the weight of its tow load, rear tires slipping on the wet gravel, spraying bits of rock in its wake as it lurched up the driveway. One small stone grazed Sandy's shin, and she bent to clutch at the brief, stinging pain, more out of reflex than any real need. She thought she heard Tommy calling something like "Sorry, neighbor" from within his closed truck cab as he drove on past, swerved around Sandy's truck, and pulled his rig onto the plot of nearly level ground behind the house. As he rolled past her, Sandy could see the cargo Tommy hauled inside the stock trailer—a huge, humpbacked black bull.

The tires and wheel wells, the side panels of Tommy's truck, the sides of the stock trailer—all heavily caked and splattered with mud. Tommy cut the engine and lugged himself out of the cab as Sandy reached the top of her driveway and walked toward the rig parked behind her house. Tommy flipped the hood of his rain jacket over his cap and stomped around the front end of his truck in her direction. Sandy stepped to the side of the stock trailer and looked through the slats at the bull. He wore a halter, tethered to each side of the trailer. The hump of his back rose higher than Sandy's line of sight, and his sides were every bit as mud-splattered as the truck and trailer that hauled him. The bull's black eyes were moist and wide with fear, glistening in stark contrast to the dull black of his hide. When he spotted Sandy gazing at him, he snorted and heaved his flank toward her, making the trailer jump and buck. Sandy hopped back as Tommy stormed up and pounded the butt of his fist against the side of the trailer.

"Behave, you crazy old cuss." He hammered the side of the trailer once more, and, to Sandy's mild surprise, the bull snorted again but calmed. "Still not too late to turn you into a steer."

"Sorry," Sandy said. "I didn't mean to rile him up."

"Aw, hell. He was born riled."

"He looks frightened." Sandy leaned closer for another peek.

"Well, that's kinda what I was hoping to talk to you about." Tommy cocked his head and looked past Sandy, listening to the warning siren, squinting up into the rain.

"What?" Sandy flicked rain from her cheeks with her fingertips and turned to Tommy.

"I'm sorry to come charging in on you like this without asking." Tommy scraped mud off the soles of his boots on the hitch bar of the stock trailer. The bull huffed and stomped, and Tommy slapped the side of the trailer again, not as forcefully as before. "Hush in there."

"What is it, Tommy?"

"I should've got going on this mess sooner. Seems my judgment ain't aged along with this fat old body of mine. Can't quite get things done as quick as I used to."

Sandy noticed how flushed his face was while she waited for Tommy to finish beating around this particular bush.

"Suppose I should've taken care of this guy first. After I got the cows and steers put up in the barn, I thought I'd better get some sandbags in around the doors on the barn and house. They sit far enough away from the river that they'll likely be all right, but you can't never be sure. Just took me longer than I would've thought. Once I got it all done, I couldn't think of what else to do, so I just trucked him on down here. I'm sorry."

"What? The bull?"

Tommy raised his eyebrows and smirked apologetically as he pressed the heel of one boot into the soggy ground. "Can't put him in the barn with the others. You don't know the hell that would break loose if I did. And his pen's too close to the river. Even if the water don't run out across it too much, he spooks so damned easy, he'd probably find a way to drown himself anyway."

"He seems pretty spooked now," Sandy said.

"Doesn't take much for that old fool." Tommy shot a quick glance at the trailer. "Like I said, didn't know what else to do, so I just ran him on down here. Water don't ever get up this high, even at the worst. Was hoping it'd be okay to park him up here till the flood passes."

"Of course, Tommy. It's fine."

"Good of you. I'll get unhitched and get out of your hair."

While they talked, the warning siren had become a sort of background noise. When it cut off, the silence was deafening, even with the sound of the rain. They both turned to the absence in the air.

"They're opening 'em up now," Tommy said.

Sandy and Tommy walked out from behind the house and stared down the slope to where the driveway disappeared through the pines, as if this location would afford them more precise foreknowledge of what was coming.

"It'll come up pretty fast now." Some of the red had drained from Tommy's cheeks, and he stood still and stony, staring in the direction of the river.

"You don't think the water will come up this far?" Sandy asked.

"Naw. Worst I ever saw, it should still crest a good ways down from here."

"How far down?"

"A ways." Tommy shrugged his shoulders. Rain ran in thick rivulets down the front of his rain jacket and cascaded over the round hump of his belly.

"Oh, shoot." He turned his eyes quickly toward the bull in the trailer, then back in the direction of the river. "Time I get him unhitched . . ." His voice trailed off for a moment.

Sandy followed his gaze to the trailer, then back to his face.

"Banks are a lot lower down here," Tommy said. "Road's a lot closer to the river. By the time I get unhitched . . . Oh, goddamn that government dam."

"What, Tommy?"

"Time I get unhitched and gone, the road could be underwater. Like I said, it'll come up fast now."

"You can't risk that, Tommy," Sandy said. "Just stay here."

"I was just hoping to park that fool old bull up here. I sure didn't mean to dump both of us old fools on you."

"Tommy." Sandy laid her wet hand on the wet sleeve of Tommy's rain jacket. "You're welcome here."

"Mighty good of you," he said, patting Sandy's hand. "You're a good neighbor."

"Why don't you come on inside and dry off. I'll make us some tea."

"Think I'd best stay out here a while longer," Tommy said. "Keep an eye out for just what this river's got in store for us. But I would surely appreciate a cup of that grass tea of yours."

"Okay. Tea it is."

"Besides, I'm guessing that ratty dog of yours is in the house, waiting to have a go at me."

Sandy smiled and turned toward her back door. "I'll make sure he behaves himself."

While Sandy brewed the chamomile, Tommy moved around to the little wooden deck on the front of Sandy's house. At the sound of his heavy tread thumping up the steps to the deck, Stink raised his head, let out a low, half-hearted growl, then curled back to sleep on the sofa.

"Hush, you. Behave," Sandy said from the kitchen. She pulled the hood of her poncho back up, held the two mugs of steaming chamomile close to her chest, and shouldered her way out the front door to rejoin Tommy.

The rain had let up a bit while Sandy made the tea. It still came down steadily, but more lightly now. She and Tommy stood on the deck, sipping the hot tea, shielding their mugs from the rain with cupped hands, and waited for the river to reveal itself.

"Now comes the hard part," Tommy said. He took another sip of his tea and laid his hand over the top of his mug. "Just standing here, waiting, watching, not being able to do a damn thing about any of it."

The slope on the far side of the river rose above the barricade of small pines. Leaves on some of the hardwoods had already turned brown, others beginning to hint at the shades of red, orange, and yellow to come, and all this swirled through the persistent deep greens of the hemlocks and pines. The landscape still bore that liquid shimmer, wavering, rippled, as if the rain were within the eyes and not before them.

First they only heard the water. A low, sibilant growl announced the approaching torrent of wild water that would cut its own channel, shape its own world, indifferent to what world lay in its path. Soon the growl grew into a recognizably wet sound, the sloshing, churning din of agitated water, relentlessly on the move. The rain could not be heard.

And then they began to see it. The shadows beneath the small pines began to move, to slowly brighten, first to a dark brown, then to something vaguely golden, almost shining as it flowed through the trees, rose up the trunks, and rushed on out of the pine grove, beginning its creep up the slope toward the house. Willard Road would be fully submerged.

Her eyes fixed on the rising water, Sandy clutched her mug handle tightly and sipped the lukewarm tea, oblivious to rainwater mingling with chamomile.

"Here it comes," Tommy said.

As if Tommy's words were an invitation, the flood seemed to double itself. While one strand of current continued to rush through the pine trees, a new strand split off and churned suddenly through the opening the driveway cut through the trees. It gushed out of the break in the trees, thick and heavy with flood debris, the dark, silt-laden water whirling into foamy whitecaps. For a moment, the new strand of current appeared intent on running right up the driveway to the house until, caught by its own weight and gravity, it swept in a wide curve and pushed itself alongside the other strand. Riding the new strand of current through the tree break, a large deadfall trunk crashed through the opening, rose up partially in the roiling water, and tore down two of the smaller pines in the grove, dragging them into its surging course.

"And here it is," Tommy said.

"My god." Sandy's words seemed to cling to her teeth.

And just then she noticed that something felt different.

"The rain. It stopped," Sandy said.

"It has that." Tommy's eyes turned to the sky for only an instant, then locked again on the flood before them. "Ain't gonna make a lick of difference for a while. Too much water already in the channel." Tommy glanced quickly at Sandy, as if to check that he hadn't unduly frightened her. "A step in the right direction, though."

Despite the cooler autumn temperatures, Sandy felt a stifling heat encased in the heavy plastic of her poncho. She tugged it over her head, raked her fingers through her hair, and draped the poncho over the deck railing. Tommy slid back the hood of his rain jacket and resettled his cap onto his head.

"What do we do now?" Sandy asked.

"Nothing," Tommy said. "Stand here and watch it. Maybe hope a little." He unsnapped the front of his rain jacket and laid his thick-fingered hands to the sides of his belly, patting slightly. "That grass tea of yours sure did go down nice."

"It's called chamomile, Tommy."

"Chamomile. Gotta remember that. Another cup of it sure would be nice, if it ain't too much trouble."

In the time it took Sandy to make two more cups of tea, the river crept a few more feet up the slope. The two braids of current continued to twist and swirl away from each other, only to fall back together and flow on. Sandy and Tommy leaned their elbows on the damp wood railing of the deck, held two fresh cups of chamomile in their hands, and watched the river slowly press toward them. Sandy estimated the water was still a good fifty feet down the slope from them.

"Was a lot like this the day my granddaddy died." Tommy stared straight ahead, his gaze stony and fixed on the rising water. The flush of red had left his face, except for the ruddiness of his round, stubbled cheeks, which never faded.

Tommy carried with him the history of five generations of Akers family life on the "skinniest" farm in the valley, a kind of personal history with which Sandy had no experience. And he carried it close to the skin, always. That much, that close to the surface, it couldn't help but seep out from time to time.

"Tell me about it," Sandy said.

"Nothing much to tell. The river flooded, a lot like this, and my granddaddy died that day."

Sandy took a sip of her tea and waited. She knew there would be more.

"I couldn't have been but ten years old or so. That government dam had only been built a couple years before. We weren't used to it yet, to how it changed the river. Before the dam, when the river come up, it come up more slowly. A body could get a sense of it coming and get ready. Get ready better, different, anyhow. We hadn't ever seen that big rush of water, all of a sudden, like now when they open the floodgates. Hadn't ever happened yet."

The river seemed to inch closer to them still, but the surging froth of the two currents had subsided, as if the river were settling into its new channel. Downstream to the southwest, low in the sky above the ridge, from a thin crack in the cloud cover, a hint of sunlight leaked out.

"It'd been raining pretty steady for some time, but it hadn't ever been all that heavy. No one thought much of it." Tommy slurped a mouthful of tea, a few drops of which dribbled down his chin. He wiped the drops away with the heel of his thumb. "Damn government people swear the warning signal was working that day, but I'll be damned if any of us heard it. River started coming up out of its banks, caught us flat out with our pants down. Whole lot of us running around like a flock of damn fool chickens with they heads cut off, not knowing what to do first. Mama and daddy, granddaddy and mamaw, my brother—he was still around then—and my Uncle Elias, he was there too, I think."

Sandy felt a momentary flush of something she thought might be envy for the ease with which Tommy could conjure a clan.

"What with running around getting all the cattle run into the barn, then trying to dig up a levee around the truck garden, damn, it was just too much for granddaddy. Heart give out. I can still see it. Dropped right down on his knees beside the cabbages. Slumped over on his side, still holding that shovel."

"I'm so sorry, Tommy." Sandy heard what she hoped was not the same formulaic, robotic tone of sympathy her voice carried when she was a nurse.

"Daddy called for an ambulance. Got through on the line, too. But no ambulance ever came. Road was underwater like it is now. We carried granddaddy up to the house and just sat there, watching him die, watching that river come up over the garden and wreck it, and not able to do a damn thing about either."

"How terrible for you." Sandy meant every word.

"Goddamn government dam."

Tommy downed the last of his tea and set the mug gently on the deck railing. "Well, enough of that. Seems I always end up moping or complaining about something around you. Sorry about that. You give me a safe place for that old bull of mine to ride out this flood, even make me some . . . chamomile, and all I got to offer in return is to carry on about some sorrowfulness. Not right of me."

"It's fine, Tommy. Glad to help." Sandy paused, then went ahead and said it. "It's what neighbors do."

"Well, I owe you my thanks." Tommy nodded to the thick, heavy flow of muddy water flowing before them. "Looks like it's crested. Still a hell of a mess, but it seems to have stopped rising. Be back in its banks by tomorrow sometime, I'm guessing."

"So you think we're safe up here?"

"Looks like it. Gonna go harder on some of the folks further downstream, though."

Sandy knew that, for Tommy, "the folks further downstream" signified a complicated and detailed inventory of lives and locations. Sandy thought of Edith's spot on the riverbank where the big hemlock no longer cast its shadow, of the river bending behind the Damascus Diner and the apprehensive face of the redheaded woman making her final exit from the diner yesterday.

SANDY washed the tomatoes in the sink and watched through the open kitchen window as Stink sniffed eagerly around the stock trailer, hiking his leg several times to mark this new and intriguing territory while the bull huffed and stomped inside. The tomatoes were a gift from Tommy, some of the last ones from that year's garden.

After the flood crested, Tommy had left the deck briefly to tend to the bull—to get it settled in the trailer as best he could, with a fresh flake of hay and a tub of water. He'd returned to Sandy on the deck with a brown paper bag containing ten or twelve tomatoes.

"At least I didn't barge in on you completely empty-handed," he said as he handed her the bag.

"Thank you," she said. "We may need them. Not all that much to eat here just now."

And there wasn't. What groceries she'd purchased over the past two weeks had been taken to Keefe's bungalow. Most of what little she found on hand in the refrigerator here on Willard Road had gone bad and had to be thrown out. All she'd eaten since she'd come home the day before was what she'd brought from the diner's last buffet. The pork chop remained in its container. Once she'd gotten home and started in on her meal, the pork chop no longer seemed appealing. She'd saved it as a future treat for Stink, but now it looked as though she and Tommy might have to make do with it.

She selected two of the larger tomatoes and sliced them into thick rounds. Reviewing what little food she had to offer, she chose another tomato and sliced it, too. She had some eggs she could scramble. There were a couple of English muffins that would probably do if she pinched the bits of mold off the edges. And there was that one pork chop. Not much of a meal, but at least she could feed them something.

Wiping her hands on her jeans, Sandy stepped quietly back out onto the deck to find Tommy where he'd remained for most of the afternoon. He sat in one of the two cheap plastic chairs on the deck, slumped forward, one hand dangling at his side. For one involuntary moment she thought she might check for a pulse, until she saw the round lump of his belly rise with his breathing. His snoring rumbled low and resonant. Sound asleep. Bless his heart, Margie and Joyce would have said. In the rhythmic rise and fall of his rotund paunch, in the florid, unshaven cheeks, in his heavy, slouched body, Sandy could see, almost feel, the exhaustion incurred from his flood preparations. Further, she could sense the enduring weight he bore from maintaining his small farm single-handedly at his age, the weight of his lingering grief, of this gregarious old man's life alone.

Bless his heart.

Only then did Sandy notice that Stink had come around the house to the deck and now sat on the other side of Tommy. His eyes were locked on the sleeping man, and there was a hint of a snarl in the twitch of his jowls. Her dog was not about to forgive his old adversary for the wad of birdshot still lodged in his back leg. Sandy hissed at Stink, opened the front door, and pointed firmly to the house's interior. Stink bared his teeth briefly, then relented and waddled inside.

Sandy held her hand to her forehead to shade her eyes from the glare. As if there were a cause-and-effect relation, as if some level of satisfaction had been reached, once the flood had pushed its way into the valley, the rains had ceased. The thick cloud cover that had blanketed the Ripshin

Valley for most of the preceding few weeks blew away to the northeast. It was late afternoon now, and the sun was dipping toward the ridges to the west, illuminating a disquietingly clear sky. For Sandy, something incongruous lurked in the scene before her. Down the slope from her, a murky, surging torrent, inscrutable and intractable. Above her, an alarming clarity. And reflected across the surface of the rushing current, a blinding shine. Still, in the end, Sandy thought, it was what it was—too much water pouring too quickly into too small and confined a space. Because the dam was never imagined to hold this much, and because it was all else that the water could do, the flood poured on down the valley, indifferent to human desire, effort, and explanation.

"Almost pretty, ain't it." Tommy had awakened and sat upright in the chair.

"Yes. In a way, yes, it is," Sandy said.

"Goddamn government dam," Tommy said.

For the remainder of the afternoon and evening, the floodwaters receded, at a glacial pace, back down the slope toward their customary riverbanks. At one point, while Tommy still slept on the deck, Margie had called. At first Sandy was uncertain of the sound she heard, until she realized it was her rarely used cell phone, ringing inside her little canvas purse on the kitchen counter. Sandy noticed several missed calls from Margie on the phone's display when she dug the phone out of her purse and answered. Breathlessly, Margie recounted calling the bungalow several times, never receiving an answer. Though there was nothing uncommon in Keefe being outside or, in fact, ignoring his ringing telephone. Margie said she didn't think she could get through to Sandy's cell, but gave it a shot, out of desperation, and was surprised to hear that Sandy had gone home to Willard Road just when the flood would be coming. Sandy had assured her the floodwaters had crested and that she and Tommy were safe.

"Tommy? That guy down the road that's always giving J.D. a hard time?"

Sandy took her through a condensed version of the afternoon—Tommy's arrival with his bull, getting stranded there when the floodgates opened and the road was submerged, the rising river having crested, the bag of tomatoes.

"Hell, you've got a regular party going out there," Margie said.

When Sandy asked, Margie assured her she and her family were likewise safe and sound. The river was wider through Sherwood, and though it was getting "pretty damned deep and scary," no one expected it to break out of its banks in town.

"So you're sure you're okay?" Margie asked as they wrapped up their conversation.

"Just fine. High and dry, sort of." Sandy glanced through her living room window, as if to confirm the truth of her own words. "And if we weren't? What would you do, jump in your boat and come to our rescue?"

"Point taken," Margie said.

When Sandy set their meal on the counter, it looked every bit as meager and unappealing as she'd expected, with the pale yellow of the scrambled eggs and the dull brown of each half pork chop in contrast with the bright red of the fresh tomatoes. But Tommy was more than grateful for the hospitality. As they sat to eat, Sandy was caught off guard when he closed his eyes, nodded his head, and mumbled a short grace.

"A flood at the door, that qualifies as prayin' weather if ever I seen it," Tommy said when he finished and recognized the uneasy surprise on Sandy's face.

They ate the paltry meal greedily. Given the taste of the eggs, meat, and muffins—flat and stale from long refrigeration—the flavor of the homegrown tomatoes exploded in their mouths. They passed the salt shaker back and forth and devoured them.

Tommy had seemed genuinely disappointed when he discovered that Sandy didn't own a television. Miraculously, Sandy found an old deck of playing cards in her kitchen junk drawer, unable for the life of her to remember how they had come to be there. Tommy sat on the couch, Sandy sat cross-legged on the floor on the other side of the coffee table, and they played gin rummy, the only card game for which either of them could recall the rules. From time to time, while one of them shuffled the deck for the next hand, the other would step out to the deck to monitor the flood's retreat.

At the tail end of the evening, Sandy stood on the deck. A gibbous moon had crept above the ridge. She marked its glow captured in the floodwaters, a mottled, flickering glimmer emanating from within the pine grove at the bottom of the slope. It appeared that Tommy had been right. The river should be back in its banks by morning.

When Sandy stepped back inside the house, Tommy had slumped back on the sofa, asleep again, snoring softly. Sandy gathered the cards and finished cleaning up their dinner dishes. She retrieved a blanket and draped it over Tommy, who snorted slightly during her ministrations, then slipped back into his rhythmic snoring.

For Tommy's sake, Sandy had put Stink outside for the evening, during which he'd spent the greater part of the evening pestering Tommy's bull, a hapless, captive stand-in for his owner in the dog's eyes. Sandy let her dog in the house and sternly directed him away from Tommy and down the hall to her bedroom. "And stay off the bed," she whispered. Stink pulled himself up onto the bed, pawed the covers into a mud-streaked nest, and curled up to sleep for the night. "Good boy."

Sandy left the hall light on, so Tommy could find his way if he woke during the night. "Scoot over, you," she said to Stink. She closed her bedroom door, peeled off her clothes, and climbed into bed with her dog.

When she woke at sunrise the next morning, Tommy was gone, his blanket folded and laid neatly over the back of the sofa. From the kitchen window she saw that his truck and the trailer carrying his nervous old bull were gone, too. From the deck she could see the flood had receded, leaving a sodden carpet of brush, debris, and flood wash across the bottom of the slope. Where her driveway cut into the pine trees, she saw Tommy had dragged some of the larger branches to the side, clearing a path, so he could drive on out to the road.

Bless his heart.

Already he'd returned to the skinniest farm in the valley. Aging, exhausted, alone, he'd begun the process of reclaiming his place from whatever havoc the flood had wrought. Sandy looked off in the direction of Tommy's farm and hoped the damage was slight. All the family he'd had and loved had either died or left him, and yet he persevered on his long, narrow plot of family ground, a place heavy with a history of love and loss, with that tangled weave of the hope and disappointment, of the joy and sadness that composed a life, any life. For Tommy, Sandy realized, the love he carried for the place he lived and the people who'd inhabited it over the years were one and the same. Who they were and where they were, one and the same, and to try to distinguish between the two, a pointless and foolish exercise.

The mess of flood wash across the slope before her house would take some time to clean up, but it could wait. As soon as she could get ready, she'd load Stink and her gear into the truck and drive down to Tommy's skinny farm to help him put things back together in any way she could. And when she and Tommy were finished at his farm, only then would she turn her truck out onto flood-strewn Willard Road and drive straight up to Keefe's bungalow along the headwaters.

A Country unto Himself

Both hunt and harvest had gone better than planned. With his usual steady aim, he'd calculated he might take as many as three at once. He'd taken four. Two bears pawing into the bait pit and two others several yards back, circling, waiting their turn. Before he squeezed off the first shot, he waited as his breathing evened out into a controlled, stable, rhythmic intake and exhalation of five breaths. One. Two. Three, four, five. He'd hit three of them dead center before the fourth could even make a move to flee, and he took that one, too, only a few strides into its attempted escape. So often, terror led them in exactly the wrong direction. These black bears, they offered a respectable target, providing the means and sustenance he required, but in the end they were simple, easy prey.

The hides were fleshed, cleaned, salted, and stored away to dry. All the bloodstains had come out, and the fur combed out nicely. A single bullet hole, only one, in each skin. Each bullet hole pleased him, the record of his precision and skill. Soon enough, they would be ready for tanning. His dealer would gladly wait for hides prepared the right way. He'd keep one, a rawhide, for himself, for the winter.

The meat had dressed out at nearly 140 pounds. By his estimate, one bear was easily over 300 pounds. His freezer and storage cellar were now full—more than enough for him and the dog until next summer. The bladders were large, the claws thick and long. The dealer, pleased by the abundance of the harvest, had paid handsomely.

He had acted singly, merciless and dispassionate, as any man unto himself must. And in acting singly, he had justified himself, no law to obey but his own eternal law, his isolation an elevation. He was prepared, well equipped, ready for the cold, lean season. Now he could concentrate on the cat.

The rain had subsided, but water still dripped from the surrounding trees, splatting loudly on the tarpaulin stretched over the fire pit. Two ridges over, down in the valley, the river would probably be flooding by now, but the petty struggles of the fools down there were of no concern to him. They did not belong to him, nor did he belong to them.

He sat on his haunches by the fire pit and fed another length of wood into the flames. The mongrel redbone lay on the opposite side of the fire, just within the cover of the tarpaulin, gnawing methodically on the fore-arm bone of a bear. The midday light under the forest canopy was dim and gray, yet the rain coated the surrounding foliage with a certain sheen.

He'd first caught the scent back in the spring when he stopped to collect the man collapsed on the pavement along the road north of Sherwood. At that time he hadn't known specifically what the scent heralded, only that it was something purely wild, something he might even respect. Now he knew.

It had been a casual hunt, without his usual degree of focus, driven more by whim than need. After so many days of bear meat, he sought variety, something lighter, less greasy and fat-laden. A turkey, perhaps a grouse. Safety on, the Winchester hung casually from his shoulder by its sling. Looking for birds, he'd merely stumbled onto the cat. Well over a hundred yards down the slope, partially obscured by brush, his eyes barely caught the flash of tawny hide, a slight snap of the long tail. Mountain lion—it could be nothing else.

He'd unslung the Winchester as he dropped to his knee, winding his arm firmly through the sling. His thumb flicked off the safety as he adjusted his eyeglasses and sighted through the scope. The cat pawed slowly from the brush into full view as he sighted. Feeling the wind at his back, he knew his scent would quickly arrive downwind to reveal his presence. No time to settle his breathing, he fired too quickly, and the shot veered to the right. The cat had already caught his scent and turned. By the arc of the lion's leap, he knew he had hit it. By the speed of the cat's flight, by the elongation of its stride, he knew he had merely grazed it, perhaps nicking the rear flank, but doing nothing to hurt it or slow it in any meaningful way. There would be no wounded animal to track down.

The work of the season was complete. Now that he knew for certain what his prey was and knew that it now roamed somewhere within his range, he would be ready. He would be alert, on point, unencumbered by any frivolous distraction. He would stalk this ancient prey with the vigilance and respect such a formidable predator deserved.

He breathed in the moist, cooling air and jabbed at the fire with a charred stick until new flames leapt to life. At last, predator and prey worthy of one another.

14

AFTER SANDY CLOSED THE FIRE-ROAD GATE BEHIND HER truck and latched the old padlock, she leaned on her forearms on the pipe-rail gate and rested for a moment, her breathing deep and slow. Her hands and wrists ached; she closed her hands into fists and then opened them, repeatedly, flexing her fingers. She hunched her shoulders, stretching her sore back muscles. Her jeans and boots were caked with mud. She was tired, profoundly so.

Tommy had been well along in his flood reclamation by the time Sandy got down Willard Road to his place, but Sandy joined the process nonetheless. Perched on the seat of his tractor, Tommy protested, but Sandy brushed off his protests. They threw their backs into the work, and after three hours—Tommy with his tractor, a loader on the front and a harrow on the back, Sandy with her pickup—they'd cleared and gathered the flood trash into three huge piles. Tommy insisted he'd take care of the rest of it later. Probably just burn it.

"Whenever I damn well please," he said. "Like to see the government tell me I can't. My land. Hell, they'd be lucky if I don't sue them. It's their mess in the first place."

The bull tossed his head and stomped around his pen again. The cows and steers had been let out into their pasture. Stink sat in the cab of Sandy's truck, snarling at Tommy and eyeing his cattle.

Despite her own protests to the contrary, Sandy drove her truck slowly back up Willard Road behind Tommy's tractor, where he ran the tractor's harrow over the flood debris on the slope in front of Sandy's house. In no time at all, her driveway and the slope were fully cleared, the brush deposited in a compact pile at the edge of the pine grove.

"It's what neighbors do," Tommy had said. "Remember?"

County and state road crews were already out and at work, doing the best they could, but still Sandy had to stop three times to drag flood debris out of the road on her way into Damascus. She slowed on the river road and made a quick assessment of conditions as she passed Edith's spot. The lower Ripshin still flowed furiously, deep and muddy, but it was now well back within its banks.

It was obvious once Sandy took the curve into Damascus—the flood had delivered a hard hit to the hamlet at the bend in the river. A few houses, those set farther back and farther uphill from the river, appeared to have escaped damage. A few others had clearly taken on water. People trudged here and there, in and out of dwellings, dragging water-damaged belongings outside. A man in rubber irrigation boots with disheveled hair sat on a plastic igloo cooler beside a tangled heap of carpeting, a stunned and stupefied look on his face. One mobile home had been lifted from its supports and sat tilted at a precarious angle.

Sandy hit the brakes and skidded to a stop as another pickup truck fishtailed out of the Citgo onto the road directly in front of her. The Citgo parking lot was still partially littered with flood debris and covered with a thick, slimy coating of silt, crisscrossed by tire tracks. A stack of sodden sandbags was piled in front of the store, off to the side from the entrance. Two store employees were going at the parking lot with push brooms, long-handled squeegees, and a hose. Sandy guessed they'd be at it for the remainder of the day.

The parking lot of the Damascus Diner looked much the same, except only one set of tire tracks cut through the layer of silt and debris. The tracks cut through the slimy coating, showed where the vehicle had slid when pulling in, and ended at the parked white van Sandy had seen the women leave in two days ago. A few lines of footprints led back and forth through the silt to the diner entrance and back to the van. A single track of footprints appeared to lead out of the parking lot in the direction of the Citgo. The front door of the diner was open, hanging on one hinge. Even from her spot across the lot, Sandy could see that the abandoned diner had taken on a lot of water. The flood line around the exterior looked to be at least three or four feet high. It would be a ruin inside.

Sandy had looked over her shoulder to check for oncoming traffic before pulling back out onto the river road. When she did, she saw the red-haired woman from the diner. She came out of the Citgo, smacking the top of a new pack of cigarettes against her palm as she walked back toward the diner. She wore rubber boots that came nearly to her knees. The boots flapped as she walked, clearly two or three sizes too big for her. Her long denim skirt was thickly rolled at her waist, bringing the hem of the skirt up to her knees.

Sandy's window was open, and she nodded as she caught the woman's eye when she walked past her truck. The red-haired woman paused and walked over to Sandy. She pried a cigarette from the pack, stuck it between her lips, and held the pack out to Sandy. Sandy held up her hand to decline. The red-haired woman lit the cigarette with a disposable lighter and held the smoke in her lungs for several seconds before exhaling. She took another long drag before speaking.

"Hell of a goddamn mess, ain't it?" she said.

"Looks pretty bad," Sandy said.

The red-haired woman took another long, deep pull on the cigarette. "Well, no getting around it now. Better get on in there and see if there's anything salvageable in this disaster."

"Are others coming in to help you?" Sandy asked.

"Shit, they're too busy crying and trying to figure out what didn't happen." She exhaled another long plume of smoke. "Just sitting around like a bunch of dumb clucks. Would've done better to do a lot more preparing and a lot less praying." She flicked the cigarette into the slime at her feet, where the flame hissed out. "Enough of that nonsense. Best get at it here."

"Good luck," Sandy said.

The red-haired woman nodded in gratitude, sighed, and walked through the blanket of silt to the wrecked diner. Sandy put the truck in gear, checked over her shoulder again, and pulled out onto the road, the back of her pickup fishtailing slightly.

STINK had spent more time today in the cab of the truck than he would have liked. Recognizing that they were now on the road up to the bungalow, he sat upright, his tongue out, his tail thumping lightly.

"I know. It's been a long day for you," Sandy said. "We'll be there soon."

Sandy guided the truck along the fire road more slowly, more cautiously than usual. She was distracted, one eye on the narrow, steep road and one on the stream below. The upper Ripshin was still thick and churning, but it was nearly within its regular channel. A couple more days without rain and it would recede to its usual course and flow, the silt and debris would settle and wash out, and the headwaters would be perfect for fishing again, just in time for the heart of autumn.

The other structure along the fire road, the little cinder-block dwelling that belonged to "some fellow" from North Carolina, had sat unattended, uninhabited for so long that Sandy rarely even noticed it anymore when she traveled up the fire road. Its brown paint was badly peeling, half the windows were boarded up with plywood, and weeds threatened to fully consume it. For Sandy, the ramshackle cottage had long since become an inert, neutral part of the landscape. Unremarked. Only because she was driving cautiously, her attention split between road and river, did she notice the place at all today. Only barely, from the corner of her eye, did she catch the unexpected movement in front of the place.

Something was there.

A man.

Keefe.

He stood at the door, his shoulders hunched, struggling with the doorknob.

Sandy cut the ignition, got out of her truck, and started down the overgrown path to the little house. Something in the incongruity of the situation, with Keefe, whom she saw as inextricably coupled with the cedar-roofed bungalow further up the fire road, standing there, wholly out of place, battling with this abandoned shack—she walked slowly, tentatively toward him, as if approaching a skittish wild animal or a rare and fragile plant.

"James?"

Keefe issued no response, as if he hadn't heard her. One hand shook and twisted the doorknob while the other jabbed at the deadbolt lock with a key. His brown fedora sat askew on his head. His shirt and trousers were rumpled, and, from the knees down, his pant legs and shoes were wet and muddied. His face contorted in a grimace, his mouth hung half open, and Sandy could hear his rapid, rasping breath. She spoke his name again, calmly, again a sort of question. Again no response. She moved a step closer and laid her hand softly on Keefe's forearm.

"James?"

He jerked suddenly upright and recoiled from Sandy's touch, as if he'd received an electrical shock. The face he turned to her was clearly startled and confused.

"James, what are you doing here?"

For a moment he said nothing, only stood there, his eyes darting frantically over Sandy's face, before he turned back to his battle with the locked door. "Key won't work. Can't get in." He jabbed again at the deadbolt. "Something's wrong. Don't understand."

Sandy recognized the key immediately—his key to the bungalow, exactly like her own. "James." She paused, felt her lungs fill with air, and then said it. Aloud. "We don't live here. We live up there." Her head tilted in the direction of the bungalow in the clearing a half mile farther upstream.

"Nonsense. I ought to know where I live." Keefe tried again to force his key into the lock and slapped his hand against the door.

Sandy folded her hand around his and pulled the key away from the lock, trying to draw Keefe back from the door. "James. This isn't your house. You live further up that way."

Keefe stood away from the door and stared at Sandy, as if he'd just now noticed her presence. His lips were open, moving, his tongue working against his teeth, but no sound came out.

"James?" Sandy reached and found Keefe's other hand and held both his hands firmly in her own.

"Alice?" His lips and tongue had finally found the word they sought.

Two syllables. Only two, but the wrong two. *Alice*—Keefe's long-dead wife. He didn't recognize Sandy. He had no idea who she was. Her knees buckled, as if the ground had cracked beneath her, opening a fault line that would split and swallow the headwaters.

In an instant, all the preceding clues realigned themselves. The old man alone in the clearing at the old Rasnake homestead, seemingly unsure of which direction to turn. The improperly tied yellow stoneflies on the tying bench. The persistent detachment and withdrawal. She knew these signs, knew what they could indicate. Those earlier markers she'd tried to ignore now knotted themselves irrevocably to what now stood undeniably before her.

"James, it's me. Sandy."

"Sandy?"

"Yes, James. Me. Sandy." She released his hands and gently slid one hand around his arm. "Come. Let me take you home."

Recognition remained absent from Keefe's face, but resistance drained from him. Sandy led him away from the cinder-block shack, up the path, to her truck.

Keefe sat quietly in the truck cab, his face retaining the look of resigned confusion, as Sandy drove the rest of the way up the fire road. When she pulled down the gravel drive from the fire road and parked at the bungalow, Keefe turned to Stink, who sat between them on the seat, and laid his hand on the dog's head.

"Stink, old fella. I suppose you're ready for another long nap on the sofa."

"James?" Sandy turned to him, trying to betray no emotion in her face.

"Yes?" His voice was steady, clear in its usual timbre. He knew her. He knew where he was, but a fearful light remained in his eyes. He knew, perhaps, where he was, but not how he came to be there just then.

Sandy raised her hand to where Keefe's rested on Stink's head. She wrapped his hand in her own and pressed it tightly in her grip. "Let's go inside," she said.

"Of course, my dear."

Stink's tail thumped on the seat between them.

HOW would she speak to him about this? How to communicate about something that by its very nature hampered communication? How to question him about crucial information that he might or might not be aware of, about recollections that he might or might not recall? How to propose one set of facts when she knew he would adamantly and sincerely deny those facts, the proof of which lay within his own mind? How to broach the subject of indisputable infirmity when he felt perfectly well? And he did seem well now, while she was not. Sandy was tired. Dead tired. Everything leading up to the flood and its aftermath had left her exhausted, utterly drained. She simply couldn't manage this now. She'd wait until later, tomorrow maybe, to confront him about it. She just couldn't face it yet. Not right now.

Sandy peeled off her muddy clothes and stepped into the snug shower stall in the bungalow's bathroom. She closed her eyes, leaned her head into the hot, steaming spray, and surrendered to the water washing over her. Had she worked and struggled to come to this new understanding of love that she'd recognized in Tommy and his history, this sense of love as a thing intricately interwoven with location? Or had she merely moved dumbly through the world until she stumbled upon it? She didn't know. And if the answer mattered, she didn't care. Keefe had long since stitched himself into the fabric of the headwaters. Now she had done the same, and Keefe was, for her, the loop through which her own strand secured itself within the whole cloth. Keefe and the headwaters, they were one and the same, and she could live without neither. She lifted her head and let the hot water pelt her face until it stung. If the seams of Keefe's mind were beginning to loosen, could she still hold herself, hold them both, in place within the fabric into which they'd woven themselves?

After her shower, Sandy dug a T-shirt and a pair of flannel drawstring pants out of the duffel she'd brought along. As the day had waned, the temperature had dropped a little. She took one of Keefe's old woolen sweaters from the dresser and slid it over her head. The sweater was well-worn, showing pulls and pills here and there, but still deliciously warm and comfortable. She rolled the long sleeves up and brushed her damp hair back.

"Hope you don't mind," she said, indicating the sweater as she walked out into the bungalow's living area.

"By all means," Keefe said.

While she'd been in the shower, Keefe had changed into clean, dry clothing and made coffee. He'd also brewed a cup of chamomile tea for Sandy. He sat on the sofa, sipping his coffee and reading, with Stink curled at his side. Sandy nudged her dog until he huffed and grudgingly moved to the end of the sofa. She sat down between the two of them, lifted her mug with both hands, and took a slow, luxurious drink of the hot herbal tea.

"Mmm. Thank you," she said. The muscles and tendons in her back and legs, in her hands and wrists—they all ached but now seemed to loosen and relax with the infusion of the tea's heat.

If she had intended to deliver any sort of statement when she stormed out of the bungalow two days before, it had registered only with her. Keefe marked her recent absence only by noting that he hadn't been away from home for several days but that he guessed, what with all the rains, there must have been some flooding below the lake and dam by now.

Most often, Sandy would move through any story she told quickly, laconically, presenting her tale as no more than a series of events to be delivered in the sequence in which they occurred, free of narrative detail and nuance, seeking only to move from beginning to end, to present the necessary information and be done with it. Whether her pace was determined by the soothing influence of the hot tea, the thick warmth of Keefe's sweater, or the knowledge of the other story that lay in wait for them somewhere on the other side of this one, Sandy lingered, embracing each tangent along the path of this telling.

Speaking as one devout angler to another, Sandy gave special attention and detail to the waters of the lower Ripshin, its depth, volume, color, degree of agitation, speed of current, amount of debris carried, bank erosion, and possible lasting effects on the fishing downstream. She led Keefe through the literal free-for-all at the Damascus Diner and how the scene was occasioned by the assumption at the Wilson Hollow Road commune that the pending flood indicated Judgment Day coming around the bend. Her voice faltered, clotted with a rush of sadness and sympathy, when she told him of the wreck of the diner she'd witnessed and of the red-haired woman's return earlier that day, alone, resigned to reclaim what she might from the remnants of the disaster, entirely on her own.

"That's a shame," Keefe said. "More needless destruction because of religion. Last thing anyone needs."

It took Sandy a long time to talk her way through her day and night with Tommy—the rising water, the anxious bull parked behind her house, the tale of the grandfather's death, the dazzling freshness of the tomatoes, their cleanup work that morning, the blinding shine of the released sun across the floodwaters.

"You must be hungry, my dear," Keefe said.

She was. Sandy was ravenous.

She asked, with significant trepidation, how he had been the past two days, fearful of what might arise from the conjunction of what might have actually happened and what he might recall. Standing at the counter in the little kitchen, making sandwiches, Keefe slipped easily into a brief account of the time. The days of the flood had been far less eventful here in the headwaters. He'd spent his time as he usually did—observing the waters of the upper Ripshin, reading, tying flies at his workbench. Yesterday, as the rains were letting up, he'd hiked up the fire road to check on the bear-baiting pit he'd informed J.D. about. He was glad to report that, as far as he could tell, there hadn't been any further action there since he first discovered it. And, he told Sandy, it appeared the builder of the baiting pit had not yet done irreparable damage to the bear population. On his way back to the bungalow he'd encountered a large black bear sitting in the middle of the fire road, having a long, leisurely scratch. Having to wait until the bear finally decided to move on, he hadn't made it back to the bungalow till nearly dark.

Sandy downed the last swallow of her tea and told Keefe she'd seen a bear the day before as well.

"Here. I hope this will suit you." Keefe pushed his book aside and set a plate stacked with peanut butter sandwiches on the coffee table. He handed Sandy a smaller plate and a napkin.

"You've been part of one of humankind's most elemental disasters," he said. "Flood. Forgive my whimsy. Peanut butter sandwiches seemed an appropriately elemental food for the occasion. I should have asked. Would you rather something else?"

"This is perfect, James."

Sandy tore into the sandwiches, even hungrier than she had thought. She ate two and part of another while Keefe ate only one. Stink sat to her side, his snout projected toward her sandwich, his nose twitching as she ate. She shared a couple chunks of sandwich with him, smiling as his pink-and-purple tongue slid in and out of his mouth, diligently working away at every bit of peanut butter smeared against the roof of his mouth.

After they ate, Keefe resumed his reading. Exhausted and satiated, Sandy pulled her legs up and curled into Keefe's side, with her dog curled into her own. He was Keefe this evening. He was fine. She would sleep now. It was all she could possibly do. The other would wait until tomorrow. It would have to.

MORNING light was already working its way through the bungalow windows when she woke. This much light, this deep in the ravine, the morning must be well underway, she thought. She was stretched out on the sofa, a blanket spread over her. Sliding her legs off the sofa, she sat up, pawing at her eyes and looking around the room. She was alone. As her mind rattled its way into consciousness, she thought she recalled waking briefly during the night. She had been here on the sofa. Stink had moved to the armchair. A small fire burned in the fireplace, and Keefe sat bent over the illuminated magnifying loop at his tying bench. But the image was far too distant, too hazy for Sandy to tell if it had been a dream or real. She stood from the couch and saw ash and embers in the fireplace. When she held her hand over the embers, a hint of warmth still emanated from them. Real. Or close to it.

She went to the bathroom, splashed water on her face, and quickly brushed her teeth and hair. She changed into a pair of jeans, but remained in the T-shirt and Keefe's sweater that she'd slept in.

The aroma of coffee hung heavily in the air when she walked back into the living area, and Sandy wondered that she hadn't noticed it before. At the base of the coffeemaker, the round, red light glowed, and the pot was half full. Coffee was not her normal preference, but today was not going to be, she feared, anything like a normal day. She might need an extra jolt to push her over this particular hump. She poured herself a mug, sloshed milk into it, and gave the mixture a cursory stir with her finger. As she walked to the window behind the sofa, she licked her finger and wiped it on her jeans. She raised the mug to her lips and took a sip as she looked out the window.

Keefe sat on a slab of rock by the stream, facing the water. Stink sat at his side, looking in the opposite direction, toward the bungalow. Nothing unusual in the scene before her. Keefe, watching the river; her dog, likely ready to come back inside and return to his spot on the sofa. Nothing out of the ordinary. It would be an awful day. She would have to be practical, prepared.

She drank the rest of her coffee while she waited for two slices of bread to finish toasting. Eating the toast brought her no pleasure or satisfaction; she ate it mechanically, knowing she would need something in her stomach if she were to have any chance of keeping a clear head. When she finished the toast, she poured another mug of coffee with milk, then walked to the front door, took a deep breath, and opened it.

Keefe remained at the bank of the river, but he stood now and appeared to be staring down at Stink standing beside him. Sandy watched from the doorway, coffee in hand, as Keefe and the dog held this pose for a few moments longer before turning toward the house. When Stink noticed Sandy, he increased his pace and trotted ahead toward the bungalow. The change in the dog's gait led Keefe to look up. Seeing her in the doorway, Keefe seemed to pause, as if surprised by her presence in the doorway, before proceeding across the clearing at a noticeably slower pace. Sandy fought back an involuntary chuckle at the image of genial domesticity conveyed by the scene. The woman waiting at the door as her man approached, perhaps returning from work in the fields or from a hunting trip with his dog, and she there awaiting his return, patient and steadfast, dutiful, ready to hand him the cup of coffee she held so he might refresh himself at the end of his labors. A simple man with simple needs, easily met. As if they were a more typical couple, as if they were husband and wife, as if they were from another point in time, as if they were anyone other than the two people they, in fact, were.

As Stink brushed past her on his way to the sofa, Sandy raised the coffee to her lips and wished deeply that Edith were still alive. With Keefe slowly closing the distance between them, she longed for nothing so much as to lay her head to the side of the old woman's knee, to feel Edith's gnarled hand petting her head.

"Another day or two and conditions should be ideal. Be able to get a line in the water again soon." Keefe glanced only briefly at Sandy as he reached the porch and passed on inside the bungalow, removing his hat and jacket and hanging them on the antlers tacked to the wall by the entrance, along with the old creel and waders that already hung there.

Sandy would have loved to talk fishing with him, to discuss water conditions, casting strategies, seasonal fly selection, what specific fish might be lurking in which specific pools, the brilliant orange bellies of brook trout, flush with their fall spawning colors. Yes, that she would have loved. Sandy pushed the door closed behind them and set her coffee mug on the kitchen counter.

"James?"

"Yes, my dear?" Keefe sat down at his tying bench, his back to her.

There was no good, sure way to approach it, so she took a breath and jumped in. "We have to talk about it. I know it's difficult, but we have to."

"About what?" Keefe leaned over his magnifying loop and locked a blank hook into place in the vise.

"You. These memory lapses. The disorientation. Do you know how long it's been going on?" Her words reverberated back to her with their desperate paradox. Could he remember how long he'd been having trouble remembering?

"I've no idea what you're talking about." Keefe looked at her briefly over his shoulder, then turned quickly back to his tying bench.

"James. Please. I was there yesterday. You were trying to get into that little house down the road. You didn't know where you were."

"Nonsense." Keefe's voice was hushed, a raspy whisper. His hands closed tightly around the base of the vise.

Sandy sat on the coffee table and leaned toward him, so Keefe could at least see her in his peripheral vision. "Yes, darling. You were trying to unlock that door with your key to this place."

"That's absurd." Keefe's knuckles grew visibly white as his hands clutched more tightly around the vise.

"It's not. It's true." Sandy brought her hands to her mouth, her fingertips in a peak, as if guiding the breath into her lungs. "James. You didn't know who I was. You called me *Alice*."

Keefe's back stiffened. Sandy could hear the air hiss through his teeth. "Why are you saying these things?"

"I'm so sorry, but it's the truth."

"Liar." Keefe's hands shook, as if he were trying to strangle the vise on his workbench.

"James. What's my name?"

Again Keefe hissed the word "nonsense" through his clenched teeth.

"It's not nonsense. What's my name?"

"Ridiculous question. Of course I know your name."

"Say it." Sandy watched Keefe's shoulders rise and fall as his breathing grew more rapid. "Say it. Say my name."

"No." Keefe's response was barely audible.

"Oh, James. I'm Sandy. Sandy." She stood from the coffee table and began to inch toward him. "There are things we can do to help this, and I'll be right here with you. But we need to get you to a doctor." She stepped closer, leaned in, and laid her hand gently on his left arm.

"No!" The word exploded like a roar from deep in Keefe's lungs. At the same instant, his left arm shot up and back in response to Sandy's touch, as if to fling her hand and the interrogation accompanying it away from him. Sandy's hand dropped away from his arm, but the momentum of the act kept his arm in motion. His elbow struck hard into her cheekbone, just beneath the eye, knocking Sandy over the armchair and to the floor. He pushed himself away from the bench, kicking his chair over as he leapt to his feet and turned, looking down at her.

"Liar. Liar!" he shouted, his face twisted with rage.

Aroused by the outburst, Stink lumbered off the sofa and planted himself between the two of them, barking.

Sandy scooted away from Keefe, her feet kicking at the floor, until she backed against the kitchen counter dividing the living room from the kitchen. She reached to the counter to pull herself up, her legs wobbly, her grip unsure. Her hand slipped, knocking her half-full mug of cold coffee to the floor, along with her green canvas purse, still sitting where she'd dropped it when they returned to the bungalow yesterday. The mug broke, splattering its contents on the floor, provoking Stink to bark more fervently.

"Liar," Keefe shouted again, as Sandy managed to pull herself upright. His eyes were wide and red, frantic—the eyes of a trapped animal. He grabbed the carved wooden walking stick that leaned against the wall by his bench and raised it, cocked in his grip like a baseball bat.

"James. Please," Sandy said.

"Liar. Get out. Get out." Keefe raised the club and lurched toward her.

Sandy grabbed Stink's collar, tugging him away from Keefe. Her hand on her dog, her eyes on Keefe, Sandy reached for the doorknob behind her. She found it and opened the door. As Keefe lunged at them again, she yanked hard on Stink's collar, choking him, and she and her dog tumbled through the open door onto the porch. Keefe loomed in the doorway, walking stick raised, and Sandy scrambled to right herself. She was halfway up, on one knee, her hand still on Stink's collar, when Keefe stopped. He stared down at her, his eyes red but blank.

"James. Don't," she said, her breath coming in rapid, short bursts. "It's me. Sandy."

Keefe took one step back and dropped the walking stick. It clattered against the wood floor and rolled to a stop behind the sofa as Keefe slowly closed the door in front of him.

"James. Please. It's me." Her voice was a low gasp, and over the faint sound she heard the firm click of the deadbolt being locked shut from the inside.

Sandy stood up and leaned against the porch railing, waiting for her breathing to return to a normal rate. The side of her face was tender, and she winced slightly when she touched it. Some swelling had already begun. There would be a bruise, but Keefe's elbow had struck far enough below the eye that it wouldn't likely swell into much of a black eye.

Keefe was most often a quiet man, his demeanor shifting harmlessly from withdrawn detachment to a sort of old-fashioned, even solicitous, courtesy. Though she understood how rage could erupt as a symptom of this condition, that much of it was beyond his control, she was still shocked by the ferocity of his outburst. How much of it was her fault? Had she pushed too hard, demanded too much, too soon? Certainly, she knew the sensation of her own body responding violently, nearly involuntarily, to an emotional provocation pushed to its limit. She would stand trial for it at the end of month.

Neither was she a naïve, helpless victim. More than once she'd contended with an angry, violent man, and she'd met each confrontation face to face. Vernon was dead as a result of such an encounter. Simple anger, simple violence, could be met simply—dangerous, to be sure, but the danger unfolded in simple terms, could be read easily. This was different. There would be nothing easy about it.

She walked to the door and rapped lightly on it.

"James. Let me in." She leaned her forehead against the door and waited.

After a moment, she sidestepped to the window and looked in. Her purse, containing her keys, still lay on the floor with the broken shards of the coffee mug. Keefe had righted his workbench chair and stood slumped over, leaning on it, his hands braced on the chair back. His head drooped forward. Never had he appeared so old to Sandy. She tapped the window glass with her fingertips.

"Let me in, please. I only want to help."

Keefe's back was to her, and he made no move to turn around, showed no sign he had heard her.

She would wait it out. Until Keefe regained his senses, she had no other choice. Her purse with her keys was locked in the bungalow. The bungalow sat nearly two miles up the fire road from the access road around the lake. Even if walking out in search of help were an option, Sandy knew it was out of the question. If he took a turn for the worse, she needed to be nearby. Worse came to worst, she could break the window and get in that way. She would wait right here.

Sandy looked down at her feet. Besides, she hadn't yet put her boots on that morning. She stood on the porch in her stocking feet.

With the situation appearing calm for the moment, Stink had wandered off the porch. Sandy sat on the top step, her ears alert for any sound from within the bungalow, and watched her dog sniff and snoop around the clearing. The sun would soon top the ridge, bringing full daylight into the ravine. The stream still cascaded, thick and loud, in the channel across the clearing. Autumn had nearly arrived in full muster. Brown, crisp leaves wafted across the clearing. Broad bursts of yellow, red, and orange leaves on the hardwoods were plastered throughout the deep green of the conifers. Wild rhododendrons lined the banks of the upper Ripshin, their leaves rigid and glistening.

Sandy got up and looked through the window again. Keefe sat at his bench, his back still hunched, hands again gripping the base of the vise.

Stink barked once, and Sandy turned to the sound. Her dog stood at the edge of the stream, his bent tail wagging. His head was raised and turned to the left and right as his nose scanned the air before him. He barked twice more and continued to search out the source of whatever scent had attracted his attention. Sandy looked once more through the window to the interior of the bungalow. No change. Keefe still sat stony at his workbench.

Sandy removed her socks and draped them over the porch railing. They were the only footwear she had for the moment, and she wanted to keep them dry. Barefoot, walking gingerly over the damp ground of the clearing, she joined Stink at the riverbank.

"What is it, sweetheart? Got a line on something interesting?" Sandy briefly ran her hand over her dog's head as he continued his intent sniffing.

The cave opening was nearly even with their position on the opposite bank. It seemed peaceful, inviting, a fitting place to sit for a spell and reflect on a day like this. If she'd had access to her waders, she might have risked the strong current to get over there, but she'd brought her gear inside the bungalow yesterday as well, though just now she couldn't recall why. Another day or two, Keefe had said. Soon the stream would drain off the extra water feeding into it from the glutted runs and washes upstream, and she'd be able to fish it again. Hopefully, with Keefe at her side.

"Come on," Sandy said to Stink. "Let's go back up to the house."

She checked again on Keefe. He hadn't moved but appeared to be in no immediate danger. She tapped the glass twice and softly called his name again. Again, no response. "I'm still here."

She remained seated on the top step of the porch for the rest of the morning and into the afternoon, checking occasionally on the unresponsive man inside, with Stink sleeping beside her. Except for leaving the porch once to pee in the clearing, she held her post without interruption. Once or twice she dozed off for a few minutes, her head resting against the porch railing, but she remained in place. She must have drifted off again when she was startled by the creak of the door opening behind her. She bolted awake, scurried down the porch steps, and set her legs in a firm stance, ready for what might emerge. Stink opened his eyes and raised his head at the sudden movement.

Keefe walked slowly onto the porch, his eyes downcast, avoiding Sandy's. He carried a mug of chamomile tea. His gaze still aimed at his feet, he sat down on the top step, far to the side. Leaning to the other side, he set the mug on the next step down. Sandy could see the wispy braids of steam rising from the hot tea.

"Thank you," Sandy said.

Keefe's elbows rested on his knees. His gaze remained fixed on his hands, dangling between his legs. "Most of the time, if I wait, if I can stay calm, stay still, it will come to me. What I can't remember."

Sandy reached for the mug of tea but kept the distance between them.

"Sometimes it seems so close. Right there, but just out of reach. As if I can see it. But not say it."

Only Keefe's mouth moved as he spoke. Sandy took a sip of the tea, grateful for the infusion of aromatic heat, and listened.

"It's like reading a book. The words are there on the page, clear and meaningful, right in front of me. And then I turn a page, and the words have faded, blurred. I can see them but they're too faint to decipher. Sometimes the page is blank. If I wait, hold on, the words usually appear, become clear again." Keefe sighed deeply but kept his eyes on his hands. "Sometimes I just have to turn the page, keep turning pages until I can read them again. It's something like that."

Keefe raised his head and Sandy stiffened her stance, but Keefe's eyes avoided her. He stared across the clearing, toward the river.

"You shouldn't stay here," he said. "It's not safe for you. Just leave me here. For your own sake."

Keefe's speech was slow, labored.

"You're a young and lovely woman. Beautiful. And the best fisherman I've ever seen. You deserve to have your life back." Keefe's lips began to quiver. His eyes grew moist. "Not to be trapped here with a dotty old man. Just leave."

Sandy moved cautiously up two steps toward Keefe. "I can't. It's not that simple, James."

"I'm not worth it. You deserve better."

Sandy took another step and set her tea mug aside. She settled on the top step but remained to the side, a few feet away from Keefe. His eyes swung fearfully in Sandy's direction, clearly seeking out the bruise on her face. "It's not too bad. I'll live," she said.

Keefe's eyes quickly fell back to his hands. "Unforgivable," he said. "I'm not to be forgiven."

"I don't want to forgive you, James. I want to help you. No, it won't be easy, but I'm here. Like it or not, this is my life. This is the life I deserve. The life I want. Right here. With you."

"It asks far too much of you."

Sandy slid a few inches closer to him. "Look, I'm no prize either. I'm an unemployed criminal, maybe on my way to jail. But let me, James, and we'll find a way through this."

Stink groaned loudly and stood up, shook himself, and walked inside to his spot on the sofa.

"Clearly he's had his fill of us," Keefe said.

Sandy slid the rest of the way to Keefe's side. Slowly, very softly, she laid her arm over Keefe's shoulders. "I love you." She said it. Deliberately. Out loud, without a doubt.

A hint of a shudder went through Keefe's shoulders. He raised his head but his eyes looked straight ahead, away from Sandy's face.

"And I you . . . Sandy." His shoulders seemed to loosen with the words. "Though our timing couldn't be much worse."

"It's the life we have to live, as it is. We'll live it the best we can. Together. Right here."

We live up there.

Sandy pressed gently into Keefe's side and laid her head against his shoulder.

"I'll call Margie," Sandy said. "She'll know someone, a neurologist who's good. If I know Margie, she'll be able to pull a string or two and get us in to see someone sooner."

"Margie?" Keefe said. "Who's Margie?"

Sandy pulled back and looked at Keefe's face, where a grin teased up the corners of his mouth. "You're right," Sandy said. "You're not worth it." She leaned in, pressed her lips to Keefe's temple, and held them there for a very long time.

15

FROM THE PATH, SANDY SLID DOWN THE BANK ON HER BUTT and then crawled on her belly through a thick stand of rhododendron to get to the pool. Once through the rhododendron, she continued to crawl. Here, if she rose even into a low crouch, the fish would spot her instantly and be gone just as fast. The pool was a long crescent channel bent around a low spine of rock, fed by a thick chute of water that poured into the head of the pool. Sandy crawled to the stone ridge bordering the pool and rested her back against it. The front half of the pool surged through a deeper, V-shaped trough of stone. At the bend of the crescent there would be a tangle of branches and leaves caught there, giving the fish ample cover. The tangle would likely be a bit more than usual following the recent rains and high water. Or less if the waters had been strong enough to wash out what had been lodged at the bend in the first place. The tail of the pool widened, and the current flattened out into a calmer flow. In this pool, the fish would not be particularly large—if she took one of eight or ten inches in size, she would be more than pleased. But here she would catch nothing casually. These fish, like the others in the headwaters, were purely wild, but these brook trout also had the advantage of open terrain around the pool, offering a predator no cover as it stalked its prey. They would be caught only with stealth and precision. Here, the way something was done, the means of it, was everything, far outweighing the ends. She would get one cast and one cast only.

The yellow stoneflies were long gone for the season. From her fly box she selected instead one tiny black-ant pattern with a tuft of yellow wound into the thorax and began to tie it onto the end of her line.

Margie had come through, even better than Sandy might have expected. "But are you all right, honey?" Margie had asked after Sandy explained the incident to her. "He didn't hurt you, did he? Because if he did, I don't care what—"

"I'm fine, Margie," Sandy had said, inadvertently raising her fingertip to the bruise on her cheek.

"Good. You better be. Oh, bless his heart." Sandy could hear a long exhale on the other end of the phone. Margie was likely in the hospital parking lot, in her car, having a cigarette break. "I'll get right on it, sweetie," Margie continued. "Looks as though your suspicions last spring may have been right, after all, eh?"

Two days later, Keefe had an appointment with a physician at the community hospital in Sherwood. Three days after that, he was examined by a neurologist in Roanoke. And a week after that, they met with the neurologist again to review his diagnosis. Keefe occasionally grumbled about the battery of tests and examinations but generally submitted to Sandy and the physicians, still horrified and chastened by his outburst. The neurologist's staff had initially been hesitant to allow Sandy access since she wasn't his daughter, their first assumption, or his wife, their second assumption, but when Keefe grew visibly agitated at the prospect, they relented. Finally, the neurologist urged that, if they weren't married and Sandy was to be his primary caregiver, Keefe should at least accord Sandy power of attorney. Really, he had said, it would make things go more smoothly in the future.

For the most part, symptoms and diagnoses had been delivered to Sandy, as a nurse, as information, already established and inscribed on a chart, accompanied by a set of specific guidelines and procedures. Simple enough. She was, after all, only an LPN. A world of pain, illness, injury, and aging had been distilled into a prescribed regimen. It was clinical. Now it was personal.

Mild cognitive impairment. Sandy had yet to determine if the word *mild* before the words *cognitive impairment* gave her a sense of relief—it certainly could have been much worse—or if the vagueness of the condition made her even more uneasy. When asked about the possibility of a *series of small strokes,* neither Sandy nor Keefe could answer one way or the other. Asked about any sort of *brain injury,* Sandy and Keefe looked at each other, then confirmed there had been a slight concussion about five years earlier. Neither of them offered any details of how years earlier Sandy had found Keefe collapsed in the stream where he'd fallen and struck his head on a rock, the result of a freak misstep while crossing through a strong current. Sandy, his caregiver then, said nothing to anyone of how that incident had initially given her the access to the bungalow she had so desired. *Primary caregiver. We live up there.*

Sandy conjured an image of the book-jammed living area of the bungalow, of the ever-present volume of Whitman on the coffee table, when informed that this condition was often not as detrimental to people with *higher levels of educational and intellectual development.* She wondered about *objective memory impairment* and the botched yellow stoneflies on Keefe's tying bench. *Largely intact general cognitive function*—Sandy sighed quietly. *Unusually stressful situations could trigger another episode of rage or disorientation*—Sandy slid her hand gently down Keefe's arm and closed her hand around his.

THROUGH her shirt and vest, Sandy could feel the chill of cooler autumn nights pressed into her back from the rock she leaned against. With the ant pattern securely tied in place, she fed out just enough line to make the cast over the stone outcropping and down to the surface of the head of the pool. She lifted her rod straight out from her body, remaining concealed, and flicked her wrist once, sending her fly in a wavering arc, backwards over her head onto the film of the current. The fish struck in an instant, and Sandy rose to her full height, looming freely over the pool now as she guided the brook trout into the shallows. It fought ferociously, but Sandy brought it to hand quickly and removed the hook. A fish flawlessly adapted to its surroundings, the brook trout was nearly invisible in the water. Here, carefully cupped in her hand, with its green speckled back and ivory-tipped orange fins, the fish offered a perfect complement to the colors of the autumn foliage, the leaves still hanging from the trees and those fallen and floating down the current of the stream. Sandy released the fish and reeled in her remaining line. There would be no more fish from this pool today.

Keefe was fishing somewhere nearby. She crawled back through the rhododendron, climbed up to the path, and headed downstream to find him. In the weeks since his outburst, Sandy had rarely been away from Keefe. She had, in effect, fully moved into the bungalow, a full-time resident. One morning she'd made a run into Sherwood to go to the bank and buy groceries, after which she swung by the house on Willard Road to collect a few of her things, including Edith's ashes, which still sat tucked behind the seat in the cab of her truck. With the exception of those few hours, however, she hadn't been away from the headwaters.

Keefe had, for the most part, been clearheaded during this time—*largely intact general cognitive function.* He'd struggled a few times to call up the word for some object, but Sandy had waited patiently, allowed him the time, and most often he was able to retrieve the lost word. Still, she had been hovering, regularly scrutinizing his face for any telltale signs of disorientation. Eventually, Keefe had protested, though his rebellion was a mild one. "Please, my dear." Keefe lowered his book and rested it in his lap. "I give you my solemn promise. I'll let you know if I'm having trouble."

"That's the problem, James," Sandy had said. "You may not know you're having trouble."

Keefe had sighed and raised his eyes to the book-clogged wall above the fireplace. "Don't you think it will be rather evident? Please, allow me the last few shreds of my dignity."

Sandy had apologized, said she would try. And she had, though it hadn't been easy. Today, fishing in different sections of the river, had been the longest he'd been outside her orbit, with the exception of the one trip to town for provisions. The pleasure of being back in the waters of the upper Ripshin, of the fierce tug of a brook trout on the end of her line, had seduced her, made it easier to let him be, and she'd welcomed the seduction. But now she was concerned again. In two days she was scheduled to meet with her attorney, to consult before her case came to trial next week. Previously, she'd given so little thought to her impending trial. Now it gnawed at her. Would she be sentenced to jail? If so, for how long? What might happen to Keefe while she was incarcerated? She wanted him in her sights right now.

Sandy dropped off the trail and climbed up onto a jumble of larger boulders along the stream, a perch from which she could get a longer view downstream in the direction of where she last saw Keefe fishing. She climbed to the top of the heap, stood up, and turned her eyes down the long, descending course of the stream, a string of gradient pools, stair-stepping down the slope. She spotted Keefe immediately, maybe fifty yards downstream. Her eyes locked onto a scene she'd witnessed before, more than once, and never counted as cause for concern. But now, alert as she was, on edge for any sign of possible disconnect in Keefe's mind, a shudder of alarm pulsed through her body. Keefe inched slowly, carefully around the tail of a pool, hunched forward in a half-crouch, stalking a fish. He carried his rod in position, at the ready, his old fedora on his head. And, other than the hat, he was completely naked.

Sandy scrambled down from the boulders, leapt onto the path, and bolted downstream.

By the time she reached the pool where she'd seen him, she was frantic, winded, and Keefe had caught a hefty brook trout and was bringing the fish to hand. As he released the fish, Keefe saw Sandy on the bank, her chest heaving, gasping for air after her run down the path.

A wry grin crept onto Keefe's face as he reeled in his line. "I assure you, my dear. I'm currently fully in control of my mental faculties. I'm well aware of who you are, who I am, and where we are, not to mention what a ridiculous sight I present to the natural world. A naked old man, waving a stick in the middle of a mountain trout stream. Surprised I haven't scared all the fish away."

"I don't know about the fish, but you scared the shit out of me." Sandy's breathing began to calm to a more normal rate.

Keefe smiled. "I'm sorry, my dear. I thought maybe one last time." He raised his eyes, scanning the headwaters surrounding him. "Before the weather turns too cold."

"Seems a bit cold for it to me already," Sandy said.

"Perhaps, but not too cold yet." Keefe looked directly at Sandy. His eyes were clear and keen. "Join me."

Sandy pursed her lips and tilted her head, attempting a look of stern reprimand.

"Please." Keefe raised his arm and held out his hand to her.

Sandy chuckled softly and began to shed her clothing.

Her skin grew instantly taut and prickled as her bare feet entered the water. She inched deeper into the pool, nearly up to her knees in the chilly water when she reached Keefe's side.

"What with these memory lapses and all," Sandy said, "maybe you could forget your attraction to this particular activity?"

"It appears neither of us shall be so fortunate." Keefe took her hand as she stepped to his side. "What do you have on?"

"Nothing, rather obviously," Sandy said, feigning a more exaggerated shiver than she actually felt.

Keefe chuckled and nodded to her fly rod, held at her side. "On your line, my dear."

"Ant."

"That ought to do just fine." Keefe nodded toward a back eddy, swirling under a ledge of rock, to the right of the plume of water feeding into the head of the pool. "A good one holding just to the right side of the eddy."

Keefe released her hand and eased himself a couple paces away to give her room to cast. As Sandy fed line from her rod and set herself in a casting stance, as best she could with bare feet, she heard Keefe's voice slip into a hushed chant.

"I will go to the bank by the wood and become undisguised and naked, I am mad for it to be in contact with me."

She'd heard him utter this incantation before, in this same circumstance. These were the only lines from Whitman she could recognize with certainty. And the only ones she understood perfectly, utterly.

She raised her rod, aimed one false cast toward the head of the pool, then shot her line to the target. The ant dropped gently to the surface and rode the riffled rim of the back eddy for only a moment before the fish rose to her fly.

16

JACKSON STAMPER GROANED AUDIBLY AS HE LEANED THE girth of his upper body forward and reached to massage his calf above the foot that still wore a walking boot and rested on another chair. Sandy noticed that the tattered dressing had been exchanged for a thick sock.

"As I was saying," Stamper said, "just tell your version of events as clearly and concisely as possible. Don't go into detail. Leave that to me. Just follow my lead, okay?"

Sandy nodded. She sat in a chair opposite the lawyer's desk. Keefe sat close by on the sofa. The piles of papers and files cluttering the sofa the last time Sandy was here were gone.

"I'm not all that concerned," Stamper continued. "I've still got a couple tricks up my sleeve. A bench trial is pretty simple business. The only witness the complaining witness has called is a Joyce Malden. What can you tell me about her?"

"Not much. She was there. One of the nurses I worked with at the nursing home." Joyce Malden hadn't crossed Sandy's mind since she walked out of the nursing home for the last time.

"Any bad blood between you?"

"Not that I know of."

"Was she in the office with you when it happened?" Stamper leaned forward, resting his elbow on the desk.

"No. Out in the hall, I think."

"Fine. I can handle that." Stamper flipped through a couple of sheets of paper on the desk in front of him. "To tell the truth, since you have no record, when you apologize, show your remorse for the incident, I can't imagine more than a few months' probation at the worst."

Sandy wasn't sorry. She felt no remorse. Would she, could she offer up in the courtroom a simulation of an emotion she didn't feel? She more often had trouble showing emotions that were genuine. Could she fake it? She turned to Keefe, whose eyes met hers, his brow furrowed with concern. To fake remorse. She would have to find some way to do so. If she were put in jail, Keefe would be alone, and she couldn't, wouldn't risk that. Not now.

"One other thing regarding this," Stamper said. He seemed to hesitate before speaking, his eyes running over Sandy in a way they hadn't before. "I'd suggest you dress a bit more appropriately. A little more . . . feminine. Wear a dress. It'll make a difference."

Sandy couldn't recall the last time she'd worn a dress. It had literally been years. She only owned two, and they both still hung in the bedroom closet of the house on Willard Road. Inadvertently, she gave herself the once over, assessing her attire—jeans and hiking boots, a lightweight green sweater, a fleece vest, a canvas purse fashioned from an old fishing vest. Other than the pastel scrubs she had worn to work at the nursing home, Sandy hadn't dressed much differently than she was now for quite a long time. She looked at Keefe—heavy khaki trousers, a plaid flannel shirt, an old woolen sport jacket, his battered brown fedora lying on the sofa seat beside him. Their clothing seemed perfectly appropriate, for her, for them, for the season, for life in the headwaters. She'd have to stop by Willard Road and get a dress from the closet before next week.

"Now, on to our other business." Stamper set one file aside and picked up another. "Mr. Keefe, the power of attorney document you called about, we've got that ready here." Stamper turned his face to the door to the outer office and called out. "Sherri Lynn, a minute, please."

Stamper's assistant walked in from the outer office, smiled and nodded to Sandy and Keefe, and then turned to the attorney. "That Ridpath boy is waiting out there."

Stamper leaned back and glanced toward the outer office. "We're gonna get dirty on that one. Let him wait."

Documents were circulated to be signed by Sandy and Keefe, witnessed by Stamper and his assistant. As Keefe signed the power of attorney agreement, Sandy leaned in and spoke softly to him. "Are you sure about this, James?"

"Completely, my dear. It's only reasonable, considering. Question is, are you sure about it? Taking responsibility for a doddering old coot?"

Sandy smiled, ran her fingertips along Keefe's cheek, and signed the documents.

Stamper's assistant notarized the documents while he explained how they would be promptly filed but were now fully in effect. Sandy tucked her copy into her canvas purse.

At that point, Stamper scooped up another file. "And now our last bit of business, the estate of Edith Moser."

Sandy's attorney led her through the relatively simple documents, explaining his fees and showing Sandy where to sign. She followed along, paying little attention to the actual words printed on the pages. With this set of papers finalized and in order, with an oddly grand flourish, Stamper removed an envelope from the file and handed it over the desk to Sandy.

"And this, of course, is for you. Edith Moser was one in a million. You must be, as well, Ms. Holston, for her to hold you in such high regard. May she rest in peace."

"Yes." Edith's ashes remained in their plastic urn, tucked behind the seat in Sandy's truck. Only circumstances had delayed her in spreading the ashes as Edith had wished, Sandy told herself. It had nothing to do with any unwillingness on Sandy's part to sever her final link with the old woman. Nothing. Now that the waters were down, she could finish that last business. As soon as she had the chance.

Sandy opened the envelope slowly, as if it contained something to be approached with caution. She pulled out the cashier's check drawn on a local Sherwood bank.

"Not something you can retire on," Stamper said, "but it'll certainly smooth off some of the rough edges."

The numbers blurred before Sandy's eyes, and she blinked to focus: $34,951.00. No, not something to retire on, not nearly enough to qualify Sandy Holston as an heiress. The check bore an enumerated imprint of the hard-fought legacy of a beautiful old woman who lived on her own terms. The check Sandy held in her fingers condensed that legacy to a numerical abstraction, one that would never match the value of Edith's hand patting her head as it rested on the old woman's knee.

"Thank you," Sandy said. She slipped the check back into the envelope and tucked in into her purse. Suddenly she felt an uncontrollable urge to urinate. "Is there a restroom?"

"Just down the hall, to the right," Stamper said.

Keefe remained on the sofa in Stamper's office as Sandy walked briskly through the outer office to the hallway. Stamper's assistant was back at her desk. A young man of about twenty sat slouched in a chair, his ballcap sitting backwards on his head. Sandy barely noticed either of them.

She found the restroom, locked the door behind her, peeled her jeans down, and relieved herself in a gusher. Her elbows on her thighs, she raised her hands to her face. She had slapped the nursing-home manager for referring to Edith as a revenue source, might very well go to jail for doing so, and now Edith had become just that for her. A revenue source. And the old woman's final wish was yet to be fulfilled. The ashes sat in Sandy's truck because, she now admitted to herself, she couldn't yet part with them, with the old woman. Edith had chosen her. Time now to merit that choice. The waters were fine. On the way home, they would stop at Edith's spot on the river road. Sandy would insist that Keefe stay in the truck, that she needed to do this alone. He would say, "Of course, my dear" and remain behind, his eyes averted from the river below, trying to maintain a firm grip on the present moment. Into the crystalline waters with fallen leaves dotting the surface she would wade, not bothering to don her waders. She would scoop one small handful of the ashes into her hand, feel the last silky but gritty touch of the old woman on her skin, then scatter that handful of ashes in a fan over the water as she wept softly one last time. After she watched those few ashes spread and swirl into the braided current, she would upend the remaining contents of the urn in the shadow of the giant hemlock that wasn't there any longer, returning Edith again to water where, that one day, she had floated, the most perfect she had ever felt.

Keefe and the attorney stood by the assistant's desk in the outer office when Sandy returned. Stamper leaned toward Keefe, propped up by a metal cane, a knowing look on his face, as if to punctuate whatever he had just said. Keefe appeared to be listening politely. The visual contrast between the two men was striking. Stamper—large, flabby, loquacious—and Keefe—slender, lean, contemplative. They both nodded and smiled as she walked in. Keefe handed Sandy her canvas purse.

"Thank you," Sandy said.

The young man in the ballcap squirmed upright in his seat. "Come on, dude. I been waiting, like, forever."

"Hold your horses, you little shit," Stamper said to the young man. "I'll be with you when I'm damn well ready. You don't like it, take your business elsewhere. Not like you're doing me any favors. If it wasn't for your daddy . . ."

The young man scoffed and slumped again in his chair. Stamper turned back to Sandy and Keefe. "Tuesday morning. Nine a.m. Don't be late."

"I'll be there," Sandy said. "Thank you again."

"My pleasure. It's what I do." Stamper then turned to the slouching man waiting for him. "Now you, get your butt in there."

Sandy touched Keefe's arm as they moved out into the hallway. "James, would you mind if we made a little stop on the way home?"

"Of course not, my dear."

Keefe at His Workbench: Gray Ghost

Continue to hold fast to the pattern. Don't discount vigilance. Between the ring of this light and the banks of the headwaters, still an unstable world. But less so now. With her here, and her knowing, the fear decreases. With less devoted to containment, more to devote to the knowing, to the remembering. *All is recall'd as we flit by each other, fluid, affectionate, chaste, matured.* Loosen the grip, but don't release it. Now something more daring may be pursued, something that in isolation would be too risky, would present too great a threat. Something more of whimsy than wile. Not an imitation, but rather a fabrication beyond name and designation, beyond genus and species, shaped not by mimesis but through imagined possibilities, even fancy, to construct a pattern that will enliven and articulate the unspeakable, the unknowable. To narrate a story conjured through craft. To assemble from these alien, exotic components something not of this elemental world, yet something that will speak its intelligible language, will speak its native tongue in this native place. Thread and silver tinsel wrapping the shank from bend of hook to head for the body. Tuft of yellow, fluffed, for a beard beneath the head—pure caprice. Herl of peacock and guinea for saddle wings and cheeks. Composed by artifice within the ring of this light, like nothing in the world outside this ring, yet every atom here at hand the same as every atom groaning with the heft of ages out there, out in the headwaters. This will dip and flutter through the deeper pools, startling the wiser, older ones, luring them from their secure depths, if handled well. This, worthy of her . . . of her . . . yellow stonefly. Don't press too urgently. Wait for it to come, and it will come. Worthy of her. Of Sandy.

17

SANDY WAS AS MUCH ILL AT EASE WEARING THE DRESS AS she was being in the courtroom. She had worn her black dress, with a simple strand of artificial pearls, hoping it would be appropriate for the solemnity of the situation because it was about the best her wardrobe would allow. The dress was wrinkled, and she attempted to smooth it, running her hand over her lap. Unaccustomed to wearing a dress, she crossed and uncrossed her legs, unsure what to do with them, until she finally relented, keeping her feet flat on the floor before her, the green canvas purse clutched in her lap.

"It's terrible and all, but I have to say, it's still kind of a hoot seeing you in a dress." Margie sat to Sandy's left, a few rows back from the front of the courtroom, her hand resting on Sandy's shoulder. "Don't know that the purse really matches, though."

Sandy exchanged a brief, resigned grin with Margie before turning her eyes back to the courtroom. A low-ceilinged room, with beige walls and a tile floor of the same shade, the courtroom was awash with brash fluorescent light. The judge's bench was still empty. People squirmed in their seats or milled about here and there. A dull humming sound filled the chamber. Margie had been there when Sandy and Keefe arrived, had met them in the parking lot. She assured Sandy that it was no trouble at all for her to be there, that she wouldn't have it any other way. The boys were in school, and she had arranged to have this day off as soon as she'd found out about the summons and the court date. She told Sandy and Keefe that J.D. sent his best wishes and had wanted to be there as well, but he couldn't get away from work. "Something with this damned bear business that's had him all worked up."

Keefe sat to Sandy's right. His eyes moved about the room, a hint of worry flexing through the furrows of his face. He was struggling some right now, Sandy could tell, trying to recall all the pieces composing the scene around him. He didn't appear anxious, seemed steady enough, considering the circumstances. The glaring light and din of the courtroom presented to Keefe an environment fully alien to the headwaters, so it might take him longer to draw it all into focus. But if she didn't press, if she remained close by, she thought, he'd have it sorted out soon. Sandy kept her hand firmly on his.

Seated in the row directly behind the three of them were Tommy Akers and Joyce Malden. Sandy had passed Tommy on Willard Road when she'd gone by the house to get the dress. They had chatted for a couple minutes, window-to-window, as their trucks idled, and in the course of the brief conversation, Sandy had given up a short version of why she had come by for the dress. Tommy had assured her he'd be there in her corner. Sitting in the courtroom, he kept his cap firmly on his head and grumbled about government intruding into private business.

The nursing-home manager sat alone in the front row, dressed as smartly as she had been the day Sandy slapped her. She held a black leather planner in her lap, along with a purse that matched her suit. She checked her watch and cell phone frequently. She had been there when Sandy entered the courtroom with Margie and Keefe. When her eyes met Sandy's, something between a snarl and a smirk locked onto her face. She huffed and turned away brusquely when Margie realized who she was and stuck her tongue out at her. When Joyce Malden entered, the nursing-home manager motioned for her to join her, as Joyce had been summoned as a witness for her. Joyce showed no sign of having seen the woman's gesture, located Sandy and her group, and promptly moved to her seat behind Sandy, touching Sandy on the shoulder as she settled into her seat. Tommy removed his cap and nodded to Joyce, who returned his greeting with a nod and a smile.

"Bless your heart, I'm so sorry about this." Joyce had her summons clutched in her hand and flapped it like a fan. "They sent me this." Tommy smiled, his gaze locked on Joyce.

Sandy watched as Jackson Stamper stabbed at the floor with the cane in his beefy hand as he flitted in and out of the courtroom like a massive, wounded butterfly, followed by his assistant. He'd lumbered over to Sandy and her group a short while before and leaned over them with that knowing look on his face. "We'll get this worked out. You just sit tight. Let me earn my fee." He'd then spoken with the court clerk, leaving her giggling, her hand held over her mouth, as he laughed heartily and disappeared behind the door to the judge's chambers and the commonwealth's attorney's office. When he reappeared, he nodded to the court clerk and limped to the nursing-home manager. Leaning on his cane, he still loomed over the woman. To Sandy, she looked so small just then, so utterly alone in the room. Margie's hand still lay on Sandy's shoulder. Keefe's hand was still in Sandy's, and he turned his eyes to her, an encouraging grin on his face. He returned the pressure of her hand on his. He'd pulled it all together—he was fully with her now. Behind her, Sandy glanced at Tommy and Joyce. Joyce smiled and patted Sandy's shoulder again. Tommy's eyes were still fixed on Joyce. In stark contrast to the isolation she saw in the nursing-home manager, Sandy felt the embrace of the small group around her. Something like a family. She felt anything but alone.

"What's he doing?" Margie asked.

"No idea," Sandy said.

Stamper's conversation with the nursing-home manager continued until the woman checked her watch again, then raised one hand and swatted the air. She glanced briefly over her shoulder at Sandy, then turned back to Stamper and nodded. Stamper smiled and shook the woman's hand. His assistant stood by the court clerk. He gave them a nod as he walked to the side of the courtroom, motioning for Sandy to join him.

When Sandy joined Stamper, he laid one of his large hands on her shoulder and, in a low voice, explained the situation to her. He called it an agreement of "accord and satisfaction." Sandy would issue a public apology to the woman. That apology would be accompanied by payment of court costs and a compensation payment to the woman. She'd demanded a thousand dollars. Stamper told Sandy it was a good deal and that she'd be a fool not to take it. There would be a brief statement before the court, some paperwork to sign, but that would put the matter to rest. If Sandy agreed.

"Bottom line," Stamper said to her, "the charges are dismissed and you don't have a criminal record. Trust me, it's worth it."

Sandy glanced at the nursing-home manager, then back to her little group of supporters, focusing on Keefe. He'd had a difficult morning. It could happen again. Now there would be no danger of her going to jail, of leaving him alone.

But what would Edith have thought? She'd struck the woman for reducing Edith to a cipher in a ledger book, and she wasn't sorry for it. She would pay this compensation with money inherited from the very woman whose humanity she had demanded. What would Edith have said about this? She felt the stroke of Edith's hand on her head, imagined the old woman's voice rise up in her mind. "A thousand dollars to put that little brat in her place? Oh, sweetheart, a bargain at twice the price."

"Okay," Sandy said to Stamper.

Her case was second on the docket. Sandy sat in the midst of her group, holding Keefe's hand, and watched as two sisters accused a young man of stalking them, of lurking outside their bedroom window, attempting to break in. The accused stood before the judge in shackles and denied the charge against him, claimed one of the sisters was his girlfriend, that he was only outside her window trying to get her to talk to him. He was promptly found guilty. The two sisters looked at each other, rolling their eyes and smirking, as the convicted young man was dragged from the courtroom by two bailiffs, literally kicking and screaming, his voice desperate, filled with anger and outrage, as he avowed his love for the sister in question. Love, again. A kind of love her former husband Vernon would have understood. Not love as Sandy was coming to understand it. She pressed her cheek to Margie's hand on her shoulder and squeezed Keefe's hand a bit more tightly.

Sandy's case was decidedly less dramatic. The judge asked for public confirmation that the charge of battery against one Sandra Holston, brought against her by one Stephanie Paulson, had been resolved through an agreement of accord and satisfaction. Stamper led the participants through that confirmation, culminating in Sandy's apology. She stated, very simply and directly, that she was sorry for the incident. When Stamper glared at Sandy, his eyebrows knit, as if to say her apology could sound more sincere, Sandy reiterated her regret, said she was very, very sorry. One Stephanie Paulson shrugged her shoulders, checked her watch, and said, "Whatever."

Only one problem presented itself. As the paperwork was being signed at the clerk's desk, Sandy began to write out a check for the compensation.

"Not likely," said one Stephanie Paulson. "Cash or nothing."

Sandy wrote out a check to Margie, whose bank was only a couple blocks away. Margie would run up to her bank and cash the check, while the others waited. Sandy couldn't tell if the nursing-home manager heard the "bitch" muttered under Margie's breath as she rushed out on her bank run.

Waiting for Margie to return from the bank, one Stephanie Paulson stood by herself in the lobby, visibly anxious to be done with the business, while Sandy stood with what looked now like her entourage outside the courtroom.

"Oh, thank the Lord I didn't have to testify," Joyce said. "That woman is just awful, bless her heart."

"I'm so sorry, Joyce," Sandy said. "I hope this doesn't get you in trouble at work."

"What?" Joyce said. "From her? Oh, phooey on her. They transferred her off to the facility in Winchester a couple weeks after all this. She can't touch me."

"Still, I'm sorry. And thank you," Sandy said.

"Don't give it a second thought, honey," Joyce said. "But I am in a bit of a bind. My sister drove me here. My car's in the shop. I do need to find a ride back to work now."

Tommy Akers took a step to Joyce's side, his cap still in his hands. "I'd be glad to give you a ride. Be my pleasure."

Joyce Malden looked at Tommy, then quickly back to Sandy, her eyebrows raised, an impish smile on her face. "Thank you. So kind of you."

"Thank you. For being here, Tommy." Sandy embraced him and Joyce.

"What friends and neighbors are for," Tommy said as he and Joyce Malden walked to the exit.

Stamper's assistant held up the binder of files in her hand, caught Stamper's eye, and nodded toward Keefe. "While we're waiting?" she said.

"Yes," Stamper said. "Mr. Keefe, your documents are ready for you to sign."

The assistant produced papers from one of the files, placed it on the surface of the binder, and held it before Keefe, offering him a pen. Keefe stared down at it, his eyes darting back and forth between the paper and the assistant.

"You remember, it's the—" the assistant began before Sandy held up her hand and cut her off.

"Wait. Let him. He'll get it."

Keefe looked at the papers for a few more seconds before the fog cleared. "Ah, yes. Of course," he said and signed the document. "The last will and testament of James Keefe, angler and all-round oddball."

Stamper and the assistant signed as witnesses, passing the binder between them.

"We'll have this filed before we leave today," Stamper said. "Once it's processed, we'll get a copy in the mail to you. You appear to be an heir once again, Ms. Holston."

Sandy looked from Stamper to Keefe, her eyes begging for clarification.

"Forgive me, my dear," Keefe said. "Perhaps I should have spoken with you first."

"Your will?" Sandy said.

"I'm afraid my vast estate doesn't amount to much more than an old shack in the woods. But who else could I trust? Who else might understand it as you do?"

We live up there. Sandy had fled to the Ripshin River Valley for solitude and found herself at the center of an ad hoc family, its legacy passing on to her, the weight of which she now bore on her shoulders.

"James, are you sure about this?" she asked Keefe.

Before Sandy could pursue the question further, Margie burst through the entrance, brandishing a fistful of cash. Stamper quickly hobbled toward her when he saw Margie head right for Stephanie Paulson. With an overdramatic flourish, Margie snapped each one-hundred-dollar bill as she pressed them, one at a time, into the woman's outstretched hand.

"There. Happy now?" Margie said.

"Bunch of damn rednecks," the woman said as she huffed away to the exit, her high heels clicking over the tile floor.

Margie raised her middle finger boldly and was preparing to speak again when Stamper quickly slid one of his thick arms around her and whisked her back to Sandy's group. "Don't push it," he said to Margie. "We got off easy on this one." Stamper turned again to his assistant. "That damned Ridpath boy in there?"

"With his parents. Back row," she answered.

"We have to get back to work now," Stamper said. "I'll be in touch. And try not to slug anyone anytime soon, okay?"

"I can't thank you enough," Sandy said.

"It's what I do," Stamper said. "And what you pay me for." He smiled and limped back into the courtroom with his assistant.

"Well, at least you've got that fucking bitch off your back," Margie said, sliding her arm around Sandy's shoulder. "Felt like shoving every one of those bills right down her prissy little throat."

Sandy reached to her friend's hand on her shoulder and squeezed it fiercely.

"Sorry it took me so long," Margie said. "There was a huge line at the bank, plus J.D. called my cell. All worked up. They arrested someone down in Pepper's Fork this morning, something to do with all this bear-poaching business."

"Good for him. Glad to hear it," Keefe said.

"Shit, he was giddy about it. Sounded like they'd got the big kingpin or something." Margie began poking around in her purse. "He's supposed to give tickets to people without fishing licenses, not go running around making big busts with the state police and such."

"He is a game warden," Sandy said.

"Oh, I know, honey, but this guns-a-blazing stuff scares the shit out of me. J.D.'s just not cut out for that, bless his heart."

Margie found her pack and pulled out a cigarette. "You okay now, honey?" she asked.

"Fine. Thank you," Sandy said.

Margie engulfed her in a ferocious hug. "Next time you slap some snotty bitch, well . . ."

"There won't be a next time," Sandy said.

"Well, if there is, you call me first, so I can get in on the fun."

Margie released Sandy and kissed Keefe on the cheek. "I've got to get going," she said, the unlit cigarette bouncing between her lips. "Boys are on a half day today. They'll be home at lunchtime, and you can be sure Matthew will get into some nonsense if I'm not there. Be good. I'll call you."

After Margie pushed her way out the exit, Keefe offered his arm to Sandy in that quaint, old-fashioned way that Sandy sometimes found charming. Just now the gesture presented itself to her like food for the famished.

"Rest the chuff of your hand on my hip," Keefe said. "Well, on my arm would be more precise, I suppose. Let's go home."

We live up there.

Sandy pulled the strap of her canvas purse over her shoulder, smoothed the front of her dress, and grasped Keefe's sinewy arm with both of her hands as they walked out of the courthouse.

SANDY stood on the porch of the bungalow late that afternoon, breathing in the crisp chill of the autumn air while she watched Stink waddle around the clearing. Her black dress hung in the bedroom closet of the bungalow. She was now dressed in jeans, boots, and a heavy wool sweater, clothing her body could recognize. On the drive home from the courthouse in Sherwood, Keefe had asked if she'd like to stop a moment at Edith's spot on the lower Ripshin along the river road.

"No," she had said. "That's done now. She never really liked being fussed over."

At first Sandy had thought to question Keefe further about the surprise of his will, of making her his heir. She worried that Keefe had, in some way, surrendered his world to her. But his gesture, as simple and generous as it may have been, was equally practical, sensible. If his health deteriorated, she was his chosen caretaker. There was no one else. And she was the only one who understood what the bungalow in the headwaters meant, who valued it as Keefe did. She wouldn't sully his trust with any false graciousness. And, she knew, admitted to herself fully, he had bestowed on her exactly what she had longed for all along. Sandy felt as if a door at the end of a long hallway had been opened. She would accord Keefe's choice all the respect it deserved.

Shortly after they'd arrived back at the bungalow, Keefe had taken his carved walking stick and told Sandy he was going for a little hike up the trail along the stream. He would need the time alone along the headwaters to realign himself after spending the whole morning under the glaring lights of the crowded human world of the courthouse in Sherwood. She didn't offer to accompany him. As she watched him disappear up the trail, what she felt was different from her usual concern for the clarity of his mind when she was away from him. It would take her a while longer to understand, but the shell of her solitary self had cracked open in some way, as if the result of a chemical reaction. She wasn't less. She wasn't more. She was different, other than what she was away from him, away from the headwaters. Such as it was, they were a couple, irrevocably linked within this place.

Stink toddled up the steps, and Sandy held the door open for her dog as he went inside to his post on the sofa. "I guess one of us is going to have to start looking for a job pretty soon, don't you think?" she said to the dog as he passed inside.

THE sun had slipped fully below the ridge that rose behind the bungalow, leaving the clearing in the gray light of late afternoon. Keefe had been gone for a while now. She had to trust him, to leave him his dignity, but the worry began to rise up in her despite her best efforts to resist it. Just as she was about to give in and go in search of him, Keefe appeared where the trail opened onto the clearing. He was fine.

"Can you smell it?" Keefe asked as he walked up the steps from the clearing to the porch.

"What?" Sandy raised her nose to the air.

"A hint of winter in the air." Keefe reached the porch and leaned his walking stick against the wall by the door. "The old-timers say it's going to be an early winter this year."

"What old-timers?" Sandy grinned and leaned against the porch railing.

"Well, mainly this old-timer, now that you ask."

Keefe stepped to her side and wrapped her in his arms. They stood melded together, quiet, at ease, listening to the rush of the headwaters, breathing in the promise of winter.

"It seems we should do something to commemorate your liberation from the threat of incarceration, but I haven't the slightest idea what to do."

At that moment, Sandy felt she had been given so much, more that she deserved. What more could she ask?

"I have an idea." Sandy leaned back and looked into Keefe's furrowed face. Would it be too much to ask of him, too precious a line, too guarded a border for her to ask to cross? "Teach me to tie flies?"

The line of a grin edged slowly into Keefe's weathered cheeks.

"Of course, my dear," he said. "With pleasure."

"I suppose we'd better start with something pretty simple," Sandy said.

"I know just the one." Keefe walked to the door and opened it for them. "Yellow stonefly."

Ain't Been No Mountain Lions in This Part of the Country for a Hundred Years

The wound creasing her flank had hardened into a hairless scar. There was no longer any pain, only a slight tightness. Nothing to impede her movement in any significant way. An old wound now, it merited no further attention.

She had not abandoned the cave. Once she'd dug out the leaves and debris at the rear of the cave and found the opening into the small, buried cavern, she'd settled into it as her primary den. Here on the edge of her range, the cave was secure, undisturbed. The stream provided ready access to water and a barrier. Though the human dwelling remained too close, no activity there had ever indicated any kind of legitimate threat to her. Humans withdrew at night when she most often roamed. A couple of times the dog had caught her scent, but it was an old, feeble thing, incapable of crossing the stream, not worthy of consideration.

When she'd slipped out earlier tonight, there was light in the human dwelling, but it was dim, did not come near her side of the river. She had been to her most recent cache, fed on yesterday's deer. Well covered, in the cooler air, the carcass had been preserved and undiscovered by scavengers. She had feasted. Most of a shoulder, more of the throat, and all of one hind leg. Her belly full, she stalked her way back. Prowling along the river leading upstream to the cave, she spotted the raccoon pawing in the water at the bank. Winter was in the air, the leaner season approaching. Even with a full gut, no prey could be ignored. She crouched low and approached, her belly nearly touching the ground, her footfalls slow and silent, jowls twitching. The raccoon caught sight of her only after she leapt. It raised up on its hind legs, hissing, front paws clutched together, and she mashed it into the soft, silted soil of the river bank. The tiny neck snapped easily, instantly. The fresh carcass clamped securely in her jaws, she walked back to the cave.

With the raccoon cached in the back of the den, she crawled out to the lip of the cave and sat. The human dwelling remained dimly lit, and the night revealed itself in the muted glow of light for which her eyes were made. She raised her snout into the chill night air. It carried a trace of something she recognized, coded in her blood, in the memory of seasons within the boundary of her range. She sniffed the air deeply, intently, drawing in the scent that promised snow.

The opening of the human dwelling opened, shooting a brighter beam of light into the clearing. The shadowy form of one human walked outside and disappeared into the darkness at the end of the dwelling. A moment later the form reappeared, carrying an armload of wood. One chunk of the wood slipped from the armload and clattered loudly down the steps to the dwelling.

Too much human noise and movement to suit her. She turned, dropped to her belly, and pulled herself through the slender opening into the cavern behind the cave.

Winter

Sandy at Keefe's Workbench: Yellow Stonefly

Once the fingers and eyes adjust to the scale, it's not so difficult as it appears to be. Care and precision, attention to detail, yes. But those qualities, the same as those needed to put the fly to proper use on the stream. Same attributes, different application. More at ease wrapping the hook shanks with dubbing. More comfortable with the foundation. Less so with the hackles and saddles, laid into the pattern in one direction to be fluffed and feathered in the opposite direction on the finished product. In the glaring light within the ring of the magnifying loop, the fragile, downy plumes seem always about to disintegrate under the press of fingertips. Through attempt and failure and attempt again, he's never pressed, never pushed or grown frustrated with these limitations. He has guided, pointed out the direction, led the way into waters where secure footing might be found. He has taught. Gently, quietly, patiently. And the doing of it, the teaching, seems to have done him good. At the bench, as at the river, he never shows himself to be faltering, unsure. Only occasionally, the name for some minor thing, a specific herl or type of hackle, may be slow in coming, but a few patient moments will bring it back to his tongue. Some has been lost, but most remains, if only allowed the time and space to permit the pattern to reshape itself. Pay attention now to what is at hand. Lay the bleached squirrel tail to the head of the shank, wrap it tight with dubbing, continue to hold tight in place, fluff the fur and fold it back, feather into a tuft, wrap again, again, loop and cinch, secure the base tightly at the head, snip off the excess. Complete. Not beautiful, but complete. Serviceable. Functional. It will ride the water as intended and catch a good fish in the spring.

A Country unto Himself

The mongrel redbone had become more trouble than she was worth. She would never have been of use for hunting. Too enthusiastic with the scent, unfocused and erratic. Nor had he ever intended her for the hunt. To follow the frantic path of a mongrel to his prey would be nothing short of a failure. Beneath contempt. The hunt was between him and his prey, palpable proof of his skill and attention to detail, a demonstration of his self-sufficing, self-relying soul. The dog was there merely to give the alarm, to announce an intruder. But of late she'd begun to bark at anything, from the caw of a crow to the rustle of leaves in the wind. A dog like that would do more to reveal their own presence than to announce that of an outsider. When he found her in the storage cellar, the remains of the man from the roadside half dug up, he fetched the .25 caliber pistol.

"Sit." The dog did so, her pink tongue lolling happily, her front paws caked with dark earth.

He laced his fingers through her collar and pressed the muzzle of the .25 to the top of her head. "Shhhhhh," he said, and discharged one round through the dog's brain.

He'd tracked the mountain lion carefully, methodically. The cat's range, under natural circumstances, could be vast—many miles in any direction. He had, after all, first scented the cat many miles from here, north of Sherwood, assuming it was the same creature. But circumstances beyond these wild ridges were not natural. Human encroachment, especially from the valley below, had long since cut away at the lion's native range. He was confident the cat remained within the ravines and ridges folded around the headwaters of the upper Ripshin. And his confidence grew not from wishful longing, but from determined pursuit and meticulous scrutiny of the signs.

He'd stalked the ridges in long, concentric arcs, working his way slowly, centripetally down the surrounding slopes into the ravines below. The signs were few and subtle, but to the attentive eye, they were there. Claw marks on a fallen tree trunk, gouges thinner and deeper than a bear's. Territorial scent markings, pawed up into distinctive piles. Cached and scavenged carcasses of the cat's older kills. No individual sign distracted or pushed him to feverish excitement. He remained focused, calm, knowing that knowledge of his elusive target would come not from any single piece of evidence but from the pattern cohering from the complex combination of all these discrete signs. The closer his trajectory moved toward the central ravine of the upper Ripshin, the fresher the cached kills, the more pungent the scent markings. He had paused over each sign, observing closely, drawing in the scent of each in a series of deep breaths. One. Two. Three, four, five.

On his last foray, in the saddle of the ridge above the headwaters, he'd found the remains of a doe, the cache not more than two days old. The cat was constricting its range, conserving energy, denning for the winter now in the air. It would be holed up somewhere down the ravine cut by the upper Ripshin. He was sure of it. He could now constrict his range as well, concentrate on the slopes hugging the river. The cat was close at hand, the hunt nearly complete.

He had first smelled the approach of early winter a week ago, and now it had arrived. The snow began to fall just after midnight. A fine, light snow, it would not bury the ridges or impede movement, only coat the trees and ground with a thin, delicate layer of white, an intimation of the deeper winter yet to come. He sat on his haunches by the fire ring under the tarpaulin. Laying another length of wood into the fire, he pushed his glasses up his nose and stared into the embers, waiting for the new flame to leap up. A fresh tongue of fire rose, and he turned his gaze to the dark perimeter beyond the fire light. Snow hitting the tarpaulin melted instantly. Tiny rivulets ran down the slope of the covering, dripping lightly from the hem. The dark forest surrounding him brightened to a hint of gray as the snow collected.

The Winchester was cleaned, loaded, and sheathed in its scabbard, lying at the ready on the seat of his truck. Water and bear jerky were packed in the pouch with the .25 caliber pistol and the extra ammunition he wouldn't need. The hunt well done, he would require only one shot. He would not sleep tonight. Before dawn, he would drive to the old logging road that led down to the government fire road. By first light, he would be in position. With the snow, if the cat had been on the move in the night, he could, and would, now track it easily, all the way to its den somewhere down the ravine, along the headwaters. He had stalked his prey with skill and patience, had learned to read the pattern of its movements, to take the pulse of its life. He would go upright and vital, speak the rude truth, in the shared language of peers, seeking his equal in this wild and sovereign land.

18

THE SNOW BEGAN TO FALL JUST AFTER MIDNIGHT. A FINE, light snow, it would not bury the ridges or impede movement, only coat the trees and ground with a thin, delicate layer of white, an intimation of the deeper winter yet to come. Sandy had watched from the bungalow porch for a while as the darkened clearing brightened to a hint of gray as the snow collected. Keefe sat slumped in the armchair, asleep, his copy of Whitman lying open against his chest. Sandy stirred the fire, tucked a blanket around Keefe's legs, scratched Stink behind the ears, and went to bed.

When she awoke in the morning, Keefe was at his tying bench. A half-empty cup of coffee sat on the edge of the bench, a cigarette burned in the ashtray. Keefe smoked so rarely that the pungent odor of burning tobacco startled Sandy as she walked into the living area. He greeted her with a brief glance when she emerged from the bedroom, then turned back to the view through the lighted magnifying loop, concentrating on the fly taking shape before him. He was quiet, withdrawn today, but he was aware. Sandy was learning to read the signs. A day like this, it was harder for him to hold on firmly, to retain access to the record of what he knew and didn't know, to what he recalled and what he might forget. He constricted the range of the world he inhabited, pulled inward, created a smaller world, one he could manage more confidently. Sandy would let him be. He would be fine.

The snow lay over the clearing and the slopes as she'd expected, a thin, light layer of white, no more than an inch, if that. Keefe would stay at his bench much of the day. She would fish.

SANDY cast into the agitated water beneath the chute feeding the head of the pool and let her line drift smoothly through the gentler riffles at the pool's midsection. This early chill of winter, settled so suddenly upon the headwaters, hadn't yet reached very far below the surface of the stream. Fish would still be active for a while before the changing weather spoke to their flesh, signaling them to slow down, conserve their energy, and seek secure holds in the deeper water, where they could survive the leaner season.

The fish struck as her fly drifted out of the midsection into the widening tail of the pool. It made one desperate dive for the deeper water, but Sandy set the hook and guided the brook trout swiftly into the shallows. Though it writhed fiercely, she brought it easily to hand, removed the hook of the hare's-ear nymph from the fish's bony lip, and released it. She had tied this hare's-ear pattern herself. It was a good fly for a beginner to tie, not overly complicated in construction, intended to be rather rough and ragged, to imitate the larvae of any number of insects. She had asked Keefe to teach her to tie her own flies mostly in hopes that the act of teaching her would help focus his mind. And it had helped. A little. She hadn't thought much about it beyond that. What had surprised her was how taking a fish on a fly crafted by her own hand had deepened the act of fishing for her. The fish came to her hand as a result of knowledge and skill brought into play at both ends of the line.

She'd been fishing casually but effectively for the last hour, bringing a fish out of each pool into which she cast. Now she reeled in and walked downstream, passing three or four good pools until she reached what had been her primary destination for the morning. A thick shock of water poured through the gap between two humped boulders, each the size of a small car. From the fissure between the boulders, the chute of water plummeted several feet into the head of one of the larger, deeper pools in all of the headwaters, easily thirty feet across and six feet deep at its center. Here, in the deeper holds of this pool, she would find the larger fish she sought today.

Sandy approached the head of the pool in a low crouch, keeping herself concealed behind the two boulders. The little hare's-ear pattern now on her line would be far too paltry an offering to lure this larger prey from the safer depths into which they would already be settling. She sat and leaned her back against one of the boulders. She would need a more enticing, more extravagant temptation to seduce these large, wily fish. If they were to expend their precious energy at this time of year, it would be for something that promised a return greater than the strength spent in the pursuit. She clipped off the hare's ear and tied on a gray ghost Keefe had tied for her, a pattern large enough, exotic enough to tease these crafty fish out and into play.

She rose to one knee, peered over the boulder to the pool's surface. From this vantage point, she would spot no movement in the pool, would not see the dark, drifting shadows of fish holding in current. Here she could rely only on that combination of skill and experience, of knowledge and faith that might send her line out into this wild water to induce a big fish to rise one last time before the winter fully settled in.

The dark blue-green of the pool rippled in striking contrast to the snow-coated slopes of the ravine that rose around it. Loam and dead leaves on the forest floor showed through the thin blanket of snow, giving the hillsides a speckled appearance in the waxing morning light. To Sandy's eyes, the even spread of the snow throughout the ravine seemed to draw all she saw around her into a single, connecting embrace, confirming what she knew intuitively, that the headwaters were a single, coherent entity. She wanted to slow the moment, make it last as long as possible. She laid her rod aside and sat back against the boulder. From her vest, she removed a cigarette she'd taken from Keefe's pack before she left the bungalow and lit it, blowing the gray smoke into the gray morning. The cloud cover was breaking up. In a couple hours the sun would top the ridge, spill over into the sheltered ravine, and the snow would begin to melt.

AFTER the charge against her had been dismissed and the situation resolved, she'd left the house on Willard Road behind and moved fully into the bungalow. The years of living simply had left her with little to transport. Those few things had been easily folded into the space of the bungalow without overwhelming Keefe with a sudden disruption of the hermitage he'd inhabited for so long alone. Since the rent on the house was paid up through the end of the year, Sandy left the few things she wouldn't be bringing there, in temporary storage. When the lease ran out, she figured she'd put them in storage elsewhere, or simply dispose of them. They were no longer needed. One thing Sandy had brought was the old tractor tire Stink had always been so fond of curling up inside of. She had laid it at the end of the bungalow near the woodpile. But here in the headwaters, the old tire had lost the allure it held for her dog on Willard Road. He'd never stepped into his tire once, never even appeared to notice it, much preferring his corner of the old leather sofa inside the bungalow.

Throughout the years Sandy had lived in the Ripshin Valley, the headwaters had come to epitomize for her that perfect, palpable sustenance that might satisfy her craving for solitude. And now she had full access to all she had desired. Keefe's welcome partner and legitimate, legal heir. She had found the home she had never known, that she had never known she longed for. *We live up there.* Ironically, as Sandy's dream of headwaters solitude had morphed into concrete reality, her assumption that entry into this private paradise would complete her began to be mitigated by occasional feelings of isolation. She had not stepped naked and newly formed from the mountain waters to take possession of a pristine world inhabited solely by her, Keefe, a river of ancient, native fish, and a smelly old dog. Costs had been incurred. Prices had been paid. And there were people, other people, at every step along the path, people critical to the progression she had made to this place and time. Paradise was not enough.

A day had yet to pass since Edith's death that Sandy had not thought of her or longed for the touch of the old woman's hand on her head. She could have sacrificed anything, Keefe, the headwaters, all of it, to carry Edith's withered, living body down the embankment to the river's edge one more time, to pour her one more glass of sweet tea.

When she ran into Joyce Malden while grocery shopping at the Food Lion in Sherwood, she hadn't tried to manage a brief greeting followed by a quick exit from the chatty woman. Sandy had, in fact, lingered, happily soaking up Joyce's gossip, even initiating a couple strands of the conversation herself. She was visibly pleased, even gave Joyce a sort of congratulatory embrace, when Joyce informed her that she and Tommy Akers were, as she said, "keeping company" some these days.

"He's a good man, in his way," Joyce had said. "Of course, gonna have to do something about all his 'damn government' talk, but I'm working on it."

Her attorney, Jackson Stamper, had called, allegedly to ask a couple of minor questions to wrap up a couple of minor details regarding her case. He'd informed her that one of his poker buddies was the new human resources director at the Old Dominion plant, had taken that position after the disappearance of Randy Mullins. And the nurse who staffed the plant's first aid station had given her notice, was leaving to join her husband, who was in the army and had been transferred to a base in North Carolina. Stamper gave her a name and number, and Sandy called as soon as she got off the phone with the lawyer. She made an interview appointment with the man for shortly after the Thanksgiving holiday, surprising herself that she was eager to return to work and hopeful she'd get the job.

Waiting to pull out of the Citgo in Damascus one day, she'd sat in her truck watching the activity around the wrecked diner across the road. The red-haired woman she'd spoken to the day after the flood stood outside the entrance, smoking a cigarette as she watched a crew of workmen carry a load of new sheetrock panels into the building. Her red hair was at least a foot shorter and pulled into girlish pigtails. Large gold loops dangled from her earlobes. She wore blue jeans, a flannel shirt open at the neck, and a pair of bright red cowboy boots. Sandy had wanted nothing more at that moment than to go to the woman and see if she might help her with the work, but she couldn't imagine how to word her offer without sounding like a lunatic.

Margie had called recently to invite Sandy and Keefe to join her, J.D., and the boys for Thanksgiving. Sandy had accepted readily and offered to make two pumpkin pies for the occasion. Margie had hesitated, assuring her that she had it all covered, but Sandy had persisted.

"Are you sure, honey?" Margie had said. "Pies? Why not just bring a little wine? Probably safer that way."

Sandy was fairly certain she heard Margie snickering, perhaps with her finger over the mouthpiece of the phone. Thinking, no doubt, of Sandy's disastrous attempt at making a pie for Edith.

"Please," Sandy had said. "Let me try."

Keefe had shown no sign of being disconcerted by her daily presence at the bungalow. In fact, most of the time he seemed openly relieved she was there, more at ease. True, he had the occasional bad day, as was to be expected. From time to time, he would have to grapple for a word, but it came eventually if he, if they, were calm and patient. Only once had Sandy seen that confused look in his eye as he fought to remember who she was, but it had passed quickly, punctuated with "Yes, of course, my dear."

He'd been visibly enlivened when they realized the mountain lion might have taken up residence in the cave across the river. Sandy had been on the porch one night, calling Stink back inside from the clearing, where he'd been barking, raising a bit of a fuss. She was afraid he'd reverted to his old ways and was off rousting a skunk. A half-moon hung over the ravine. In the dim light, as her dog passed by her on his way back inside, she thought she had caught a glimpse of the cat. Again, not the whole creature, just a momentary flash of what could have been that long tail vanishing into the depths of the cave. Keefe was delighted. The next morning, he had waded the shallows to the far side of the stream. He hadn't caught sight of the mountain lion, but he'd found definite pawprints in the streamside silt in front of the cave. "It well could be we have a new neighbor, my dear," he had said.

"What do we do now?" Sandy asked.

"Live together peacefully, I hope. Best keep it a secret from J.D."

"And Tommy Akers, bless his heart," Sandy said.

Keefe slid his arm around Sandy's waist, pulled her closer, and gazed back across the clearing at the cave. "I'm glad it's there. Makes me feel better, more . . . more content. Now, when I'm irrevocably demented and shipped off to the home, where I belong, you won't be alone out here. It'll be here to watch over you, to keep you company. Certainly make for a more reliable companion."

"That's not funny, James." Sandy pretended to punch him lightly on the shoulder.

"I don't know that I intended it to be, my dear," he said as he pulled her still closer. And still, a wry grin crept across his face.

Paradise, it turned out, was itself a porous thing, wrapped in another world—a wonderfully odd, flawed, and uncertain one—and this paradise took its value from the infusions of that cracked, bent, encircling outer world.

SANDY stubbed out her cigarette and dropped the butt into a vest pocket. She rose to one knee behind the boulder, turned toward the pool, and began to inch into casting position. The fish she stalked would spot her the moment she stood upright, so she scooted to the outer edge of the boulder, careful to keep herself as concealed as possible behind the rock. She would need to drop her line down into the pool, just ahead of the chute of water feeding the pool. If she hit her target, the large fish holding under the low rock shelf beneath the back eddy would see her fly drifting before them. In the deeper, swirling water at the head of the pool, she would have as many as three, maybe four casts to draw a fish out. After that, it would be clear to the fish that her fly was a dangerous intrusion to fear and avoid, not a succulent smaller fish to eat.

As she settled into position at the edge of the large rock above the pool, she thought she detected movement at the far edge of her peripheral vision. She turned in that direction, but saw nothing moving other than two crows flapping and squawking in the branches of a half-dead hemlock tree. A trick of the eye, attributed to the excitement of the hunt. Leaf-flecked, snow-covered ground rose up the slopes of the ravine around her, a sparser terrain than it had been a few months ago, newly opened around the stark trunks of leafless trees as the season slipped into its dormancy. Sandy shook off the distraction and turned all her attention back to her fishing, collecting herself through a series of steady, deep breaths. Three, four casts, at most. She was ready. She cocked her rod to her side and shot her line down into the wide, deep pool below.

On her second pass through the head of the pool her fly was hit. Hit hard. The resistance in her arm on one end and that of the fish on the other nearly bowed her rod in half. She rose from behind the boulder, held her rod high over her head, and scrambled down over mossy stones and snowy scree to the bank of the pool. The fish spun at the end of her line, fighting savagely. Judging by the force and ferocity of the struggle, she had found the prey she sought. Knowing the season was coming to a close, that this might well be the last good fish until next spring, Sandy delayed for a few moments, letting the fish run, dive, and spin a bit longer than necessary. She held her breath and luxuriated in the electric vibration pulsing from the fish, up her line and rod, on into her arm, her heart, not wanting the delicious tension to end.

She exhaled, inscribing the chill air above the pool with the long, vaporous plume of her expelled breath, and drew the fish to hand. She twisted the hook from the bone plate of the brook trout's upper lip and held the fish in the shallow water until it could regain its equilibrium. She held what she had sought, one of the deep-bellied old patriarchs of the deeper pools, his fins so orange they seemed ablaze, a slight hook to his aged lower jaw. She relaxed her grip on the fish. With a brutal slap of its tail, it was gone, disappeared back into the deeper holds of the pool. Sandy reeled in her line and stood for a moment longer on the snow-lined bank of the pool. Her hands were cold and red from the air, from the water. She cupped them together and filled the space within them with her own breath until they began to warm, then rested her rod against her shoulder, turned upstream, and headed back to the bungalow.

Rather than crossing over to the narrow trail on the opposite side, Sandy kept to the more rugged route on this side of the upper Ripshin. The upstream hike home led her over jumbles of rocks, gnarled tree roots, and downed tree trunks. By the time she'd climbed to the pool just below the wide clearing pool in front of the bungalow, she could feel the blood pulsing through her veins, heating her flesh as it burned off the last of the morning's chill. She paused to gather her breath. In the thin film of snow still coating the ground around the pool, she saw the tracks. Impressions of large padded paws, topped by the gouges of long claws, the imprints made even larger as they pressed through the snow into the soft riverbank ground. Sandy was no tracker, but these pawprints could have been the cat. The mountain lion might have been out in the night, returned to the cave well after the snow had fallen. She hoped so.

Sandy stretched to her toes and peered up to the clearing pool above her. She could just see the front of the ledge at the cave opening. She backtracked to the tail of this lower pool, crossed over, and walked up the bank from the stream into the clearing. As she walked to the bungalow, she glanced over her shoulder at the dark mouth of the cave, hoping for a glimpse of what she knew she wasn't likely to see today. Keefe rounded the end of the bungalow as she approached, carrying an armload of firewood, Stink following at his heels. He showed no sign of seeing Sandy as he mounted to the porch and entered the bungalow. Her dog spotted her, however, and waited for her, his tail wagging, until she reached the porch and scratched behind his ears.

"Hello, sweetheart," she said, tousled his head once more, and leaned her rod next to Keefe's walking stick by the door. Stink walked inside to the sofa as Keefe reappeared, his arms empty now.

"Ah," he said. "Do any good?" Sandy could see he had worked through the struggle of the morning. He was better now, clear-eyed and at his ease.

"Little bit," she said, smiling, for they both knew better.

Sandy tugged off her fishing vest and dropped it on the porch by her rod. Her hands were cold again, so she tucked them to the last knuckle into the waistband of her waders and stepped to the front of the porch. "I wonder if she's there. If she's home," she said.

"Home? Who?" Keefe asked.

"The mountain lion. I saw tracks in the snow."

Keefe gazed out across the clearing toward the cave, a kind of bottomless longing in his eyes. "Lovely," he said. After a long pause, Keefe continued. "And so, from these tracks, you've determined our new neighbor is female?"

"Smart-ass." Sandy chuckled as she spoke.

"I beg forgiveness," Keefe said.

"I know, it's silly. But, well, it just feels like she's female. I don't know. It just does."

"Suits me. Female it is. Shall we name her?"

"Oh, please no," Sandy said.

"Excellent," Keefe said. "We'll restrict ourselves to the female pronouns. I've got more than enough names to keep track of as it is." He began back down the steps from the porch. "A couple more loads should get us through the night." As he came off the steps and started back toward the woodpile, the telephone rang inside.

"I'll get it," Sandy said. Her announcement was superfluous. Keefe never broke his stride as he vanished around the corner of the bungalow.

When Sandy answered the call, the sound from the caller's end was so faint and garbled she could make out next to nothing, typical of the weak cell signal in the ravine. She couldn't be sure, but she thought the caller identified himself as J.D.

"J.D.? Hello?" she said, the receiver pressed to one ear, her finger jammed in the other. "J.D.? Is that you? Hello?"

The only word she could decipher from the other end was *padlock* before the signal deteriorated further and the line went dead.

The front door of the bungalow still stood ajar, letting in the cold air. Sandy closed it, then went to where her purse sat on the kitchen counter. Digging into the little canvas purse, she pulled out a spool of tippet and her case knife, laid them on the counter, and retrieved her cell phone. If it had been J.D. calling, she thought she might look up his number there and try to call him back, but the battery of her cell phone was utterly dead. The phone she'd taken the call on, an old touch-tone phone on the wall by the refrigerator, was useless for such things. Her own cordless phone would have at least had a display to show recent calls, but it was packed in one of the cardboard boxes still stored at the house on Willard Road. She was fairly certain the charger for her cell phone was packed in the same box.

She heard Keefe's footsteps coming up to the porch, followed by the loud clattering of an armload of firewood being dropped there. Stink raised his head, startled by the sudden, percussive thud, but quickly curled back to sleep on the sofa. "Just another load of firewood," Sandy said to her dog.

Setting her useless cell phone on the counter, Sandy just then noticed she still wore her waders. They were still wet, caked with mud and silt, bits of leaf and debris, and she'd left a trail of this river muck across the pine floor. She slipped back outside to strip off the waders. As she pulled the door shut behind her, she saw immediately Keefe's last load of wood scattered carelessly across the planks of the porch. Stepping over a split chunk of wood, she looked up and quickly saw also that Keefe was out in the snowy clearing, striding rather briskly across it toward the stream. He carried his walking stick, not as an aid to his movement, but at his side, like a club. Sandy looked beyond Keefe, in the direction of his projected course. On the far side of the river, a man crept down the rocks separating the clearing pool from the one beneath it and dropped into a crouch. He wore dun-colored coveralls, with a hood pulled over his head and heavy boots. What looked like an old ammunition belt was cinched around his waist. A heavy, dark beard and black-rimmed glasses covered his face. In his hands, at the ready, he held a rifle.

For a long time afterward, whenever she thought back to this day, Sandy marveled at how suddenly the scene before her had been reset, how quickly and decisively it had all unfolded. There had been no way to alter the arrangement or slow the tempo. Time revved to a pace at which no choices could be made, no decisions could be deliberated. She had been swept instantly into the irrevocable progression of events, as if cast into the torrent of a flood and washed relentlessly downstream. And yet she could still recall each distinct moment—each word, each movement—with precise clarity, like selecting a single card from a full deck and scrutinizing it closely and carefully. She could see Keefe striding across the snow-covered clearing as if she were examining a painting, one executed in muted but evocative watercolors, entitled something like "Winter Landscape with Man and River."

Before Sandy could even begin to move from the porch of the bungalow, Keefe had reached the riverbank. The man with the rifle, as he stalked slowly to the mouth of the cave, showed no sign of having noticed Keefe's approach. Sandy could see Keefe raise his walking stick, gesture with it. She could tell that he spoke to the man, but the sound of his voice was beyond the reach of her ears. As Sandy came down off the porch and began to move across the clearing, the man with the rifle turned toward Keefe, assessed his presence briefly, then turned his attention back to the cave, without speaking or altering his stance. Sandy was still several paces from the bank of the stream when Keefe stomped across the shallow shoal at the tail of the clearing pool and continued on toward the man with the rifle on the far side.

"You there," Keefe said as he walked to within a couple paces of the man with the rifle. "I said stop. You'll not do this here."

The man with the rifle held his stance, but looked back at Keefe. He released his grip from the rifle's trigger and held one finger out, half raised, half pointing, as if issuing a warning to a child or a dog that it was about to cross a forbidden line. "Shhhhhh," he said, and returned his gaze to the cave before him.

"You've no right." Keefe took another step toward the man with the rifle.

"I'm a country and an age. I make my own right." Though he spoke more quietly than Keefe had, Sandy could just make out the man's strange words from the opposite bank as she started across the stream.

Keefe seemed to pull up, taken aback, and gazed off upstream, beyond the man before him.

"The cat is in there, old fool. I'm taking it, and you got nothing to say about it."

Keefe paused for only a moment longer, then appeared to grow incensed. "Here? This? No."

Sandy had reached the opposite bank and walked up behind Keefe. "James?" she said softly. "Wait. Don't."

Keefe showed no awareness of Sandy's presence. The man with the rifle took one stealthy step ahead, positioning himself by the stone ledge at the cave opening. "Listen to your bitch, old man," he said.

"No." Keefe's voice rose along with the walking stick in his arm, but Sandy caught his arm on the upswing and pulled back.

"James, don't."

Keefe whirled around, tugging his arm free of her grasp, the walking stick still raised. His eyes were ablaze with fear, outrage, confusion. Sandy had seen the look before. He had no idea who she was. And she had only that one second to realize that Keefe was lost to her. He swung the walking stick in a tight, upward arc. The thick, heavy end of the staff slammed hard into the side of her head, catching her most forcefully from her jaw to the ridge of bone behind her ear. She stumbled backward, tumbling over a rock outcropping along the bank, and landed with a thud on her back behind the hump of stone. Even as she fell, she glimpsed Keefe turning back to the man with the rifle, his walking stick raised again. Stunned by the blow, Sandy struggled to rise to her feet.

"James, no." Her throat felt as though she spoke the words aloud, but she would never be certain.

The man with the rifle appeared oblivious to Keefe and Sandy, so intent was he on the cave and the prey within. Keefe's staff came down hard on the man's shoulder, knocking him off balance, loosening his grip on the rifle. He spun quickly, regaining his balance, snapped the rifle back into position before him, drew back on the barrel end, and rammed the butt of the stock into Keefe's abdomen. Keefe dropped his walking stick and collapsed to his knees, gasping for breath, leaning on one hand. The man held the rifle to his side with his left hand. With his right, he reached into one of the pouches on the ammunition belt and produced a small pistol. Sandy was never able to erase the look in his eyes. She could see, dazed as she was, the gaze behind the heavy eyeglasses—flat, emotionless, reptilian. Without haste or any sign of agitation, the man took two steps toward Keefe, brushed aside the brown fedora, pressed the muzzle of the pistol to the top of Keefe's head, and fired one round into his brain.

The dull pock of the pistol induced the sensation of a hammer blow to Sandy's chest, knocking the wind from her lungs as she fought to right herself, gripping the ridge of the stone she'd fallen over. She tried to scream, to propel her voice into the ravine in some way, but only a faint, brittle rasp of air managed to escape her lungs.

As Keefe's body crumpled into a heap, the man returned the pistol to the ammunition belt and spun back toward the cave. His movements remained precise and composed as he whipped the rifle back into position and planted himself directly before the cave opening. He pushed his eyeglasses up to the bridge of his nose. Sandy could see his chest rise and fall in a series of sharp, deep breaths. Sandy's jaw and head throbbed with pain, her gait wobbly and uncertain, but she started to move. To Keefe? To the man with the rifle? She didn't know. She made no conscious choice or decision. She only moved.

Keefe's body, a lifeless heap, lay only a few inches from Sandy's boot as she stepped past. She did not look at it. She knew what was there. She picked up the fallen walking stick, which lay in her path, steadied herself with it, and continued on toward the man with the rifle.

"Upright and vital." His voice hissed as he spoke into the cave.

"No," Sandy said. Her lungs could push out little more than a whisper, but she had made an audible sound. The man remained locked in position, but his eyes darted momentarily toward her then back to the cave opening. Again he shifted the rifle to his left hand, reached into the ammo belt with his right, raised the pistol, and turned his gaze back to Sandy as she brought the heavy end of Keefe's walking stick down hard into the middle of the man's face.

It always seemed to her later that the two sounds had occurred simultaneously, the crunch of the walking stick smashing the man's nose and the report of his pistol, but there must have been at least a brief instant separating them.

Sandy felt a searing pain in the flesh on the rim of her armpit, but the adrenaline rushing into her blood kept her in motion. The man had been knocked flat, and the rifle had fallen from his hand and landed a few feet away on the riverbank. The pistol lay a few inches from his fingers. His eyeglasses had been knocked off, and blood gushed from his nose into his beard, but he was still moving, clumsily groping for the pistol. Sandy raised the staff over her head and brought it down into the man's face with what felt like the last of her strength. Once. Twice. Three, four, five times. Blood seeped from his eye sockets, nose, mouth, and ears. A large flap of flesh was torn loose and hanging from his forehead. And he lay still, no longer moving.

Her lungs gulped greedily for air, and she pressed her arm to her side as if to contain the pain burning there. She coughed as she gasped for air, and felt a moist warmth running down the side of her torso.

Now she could turn back to Keefe, could look upon the remains of what she had lost. He had collapsed forward, one arm buckled beneath him, one flung out to his side. The wound on the crown of his head had bled profusely, painting a dark red stripe through his white hair as his blood drained into a pool on the stony ground in front of his crumpled body. The blood infused with the life and love of the headwaters, the blood rich with the world that could draw the word *love* audibly from Sandy's lips.

She let the walking stick fall away and dropped to her knees beside Keefe. Her vision was beginning to fade, and she could no longer move her left arm. With her right, she slid her hand into the collar of Keefe's jacket and pulled him up and back, leaning his head against a rock, as if resting it against a pillow. The body was beginning to stiffen, but she was able to push his legs out in front of him and drag his arms to his sides. A seam of congealing blood rimmed the top of his forehead at the hairline. His eyes were flat and cloudy, the eyes of a fish lying dead on the bank. Sandy extended the first and second fingers on her hand and pressed the eyelids shut. She fell to her side as she reached for the brown fedora, but she was able to pinch the brim in her fingertips, drag it to her, and push herself back up with her elbow. Once she had pressed the hat down onto Keefe's head, covering the wound, covering the eyes and blood-rimmed forehead, he looked like nothing more than an old man taking a stream-side nap, resting himself and the waters of the pool before having another go at the fish holding in the current there.

The sun had topped the ridge behind them. Across the clearing, its light had begun to creep down the slope behind the bungalow. The snow was already melting. Soon it would be gone. Sandy's head dropped to Keefe's rigid chest, not as a final act of affection but because she could no longer hold it up. As her vision began to fade and constrict, she thought she saw something that might have been the mountain lion slink from the cave and disappear in the dense brush up the slope. Her eyelids fluttered involuntarily as, across the clearing, J.D.'s green government SUV rolled down the driveway, the light bar across its roof flashing. The vehicle swerved around the two other trucks parked there and skidded to a stop at the fringe of the gravel apron. Through the trees more flashing lights moved along the fire road above. After that Sandy saw nothing, felt nothing, heard only the faint cry of Stink, barking inside the bungalow.

We live up there.

Epilogue

The fire was consuming itself, reduced to a few flames flickering in a bed of glowing coals. Sandy shuffled from the old leather sofa to the fireplace and laid two more lengths of wood in the grate. With the poker she pushed them into a better position to catch the flames. It was a little difficult to do with only one arm, but she managed well enough. Returning to the sofa, she took a last drag from the cigarette burning in the ashtray and stubbed it out in the ash of the other two butts there. Her tea was still warm. She took a sip, then another, and set the mug back on the coffee table. The cloth sling supporting her left arm was out of position, pushed up her forearm and rumpled. She winced only slightly as she smoothed out the sling and positioned her arm more securely. Raising her legs onto the sofa, she pulled the blanket over them and lay back, resting her head on Stink's rear haunch. Her dog emitted a faint groan at the pressure against his flank, but didn't move. She was tired again and would rest for a while now. Margie would more than likely arrive soon. And so would the snow.

IT came as no surprise to Sandy that Margie had swooped in and taken charge afterward. As obstinately precise as her memory of the morning in the clearing remained, she could recall little of the rest of that day, or the next. She had a vague, unreliable memory of a paramedic leaning over her as she was jostled in the back of a speeding ambulance. All she could recall of it, though, was a blur of dark blue, the paramedic's uniform, and the shine off his waxed bald head under the interior light of the ambulance. After that, there was nothing until she woke in her hospital room more than a day later. The first thing she recognized after her eyes fluttered open was Margie, dressed in her blue scrubs, slumped in the chair at her bedside, asleep. Sandy lay there for a few moments, trying to absorb her new surroundings—the fluorescent lighting, still glaring though it was dimmed, the light green walls, the battery of monitors and IV tubing surrounding her. An intensive care unit, for certain. She had survived. Keefe was dead, but she had lived. When Sandy tried to reach out to Margie, to tap her on the shoulder, her left arm barely moved before a bolt of pain shot from the base of her neck to her knees. The startled cry of pain she emitted wasn't loud, but it was enough. Margie stirred, opened her eyes, and saw that Sandy was finally conscious.

"Oh, honey," Margie said. "There you are. There you are." She pushed herself out of the chair, leaned over her friend, took her face gently in both hands, and pressed her cheek to Sandy's and held it there.

After holding the delicate embrace for a few moments, Margie released Sandy and sprang into action, transforming from the worried, watchful friend to the dutiful, efficient nurse. Her eyes darted from one monitor to the next, checking Sandy's vital signs. She removed the bag at the end of Sandy's catheter and replaced it with a new one. Sandy grimaced with pain as the head of her bed was raised a bit, and Margie pressed the button to release more pain medication into Sandy's veins. She trotted out of the room to call in the on-duty nurse and to tell the one at the desk to contact the doctor on call. Sandy would find out only later that Margie had been there nearly every moment, whether she was on duty or off, since Sandy was brought to Sherwood Community Hospital.

The on-duty nurse appeared and repeated the same series of checks that Margie had just done, followed shortly thereafter by the doctor, who did much of the same as he spoke softly to Sandy and checked the dressing on her incision. After they had completed their examinations, pronouncing Sandy in stable condition, they left, and Margie settled back into the bedside chair, pulled it closer, took Sandy's hand, and began the slow process of guiding her friend back into the present. Still weak, groggy from pain medication, Sandy faded in and out, but she remained awake and aware enough of the time to keep up.

The bullet had passed through the flesh of the outer edge of her armpit, tearing the muscle and shattering a piece of her shoulder blade. She would recover fully, Margie assured her, but she might have some limited movement with that arm because of the tearing of the muscle. It would all depend on how the wound healed, on the amount of scar tissue that built up.

"Don't worry," Margie said, trying to lighten the moment. "You'll still be able to fish."

Sandy turned her eyes away from Margie, up to the ceiling. "Is he dead?" she asked. Her jaw was sore and swollen, making it difficult to open her mouth much.

"Oh, honey." Margie squeezed Sandy's hand and began to stroke her arm. "I'm so sorry, but yes, he's—"

"Not James," Sandy said. "The other."

"Yes. My god, what the hell happened out there?"

Two investigators from the state police came into the room a short time later, seeking answers to the same question. When Margie took in their stern faces and close-cropped hair, she was adamant that Sandy's attorney be present and demanded that the officers wait. Their wait was brief, however, as Jackson Stamper was on the floor below Sandy's, having the remaining toes removed from his foot. Margie returned in a few minutes, rolling Stamper into the room in a wheelchair. He wore a hospital gown under a royal blue bathrobe with his initials elaborately stitched into the breast pocket, and his foot was freshly bandaged.

"Hello, gentlemen. I represent Ms. Holston." The sudden appearance of this big, affable man stuffed into a little wheelchair clearly caught the officers off guard. He shook the hand of each officer and rolled on to Sandy's bedside. Sandy looked at him, unsure if what she saw was real, but Stamper patted her hand and told her to answer their questions as best she could.

The investigators were terse and close-mouthed, not particularly forthcoming with information. They said they had pieced the crime scene together fairly well, but a couple of questions remained. Did she know this Charles Heaton? What was her relationship to him?

"Was that his name?" Sandy asked.

She recounted the scenario of that morning, a basic review of the events, stripped bare of the rush of terror and anger, of pain and loss, that had surged through her. She said nothing of the mountain lion that the bearded man with the rifle had stalked to its den. Neither did she tell them that as she was losing consciousness, she thought she saw the lion slip out of the cave and flee. She couldn't be sure if that hazy memory was real or a delusion, but she wouldn't have told them either way. The officers confirmed that her version of events seemed in keeping with their assessment. Since Sandy and Keefe had both been shot and the man had not, they deduced he had been the aggressor, the one doing the shooting.

The officers rose slowly. They each thanked Sandy and told her they'd be in touch again.

Stamper assured her this would all be wrapped up in no time and for her not to worry, that he'd come by and see her again soon if they didn't decide to lop off any more of his body in the interim. As Margie pushed him out of the room, Sandy asked him to hold on. "That job. At the furniture plant," she said.

"You don't fret about that," Stamper said. "I'll call him, tell him to sit tight, that he's got one hell of a woman coming his way."

Before Margie could get Stamper out the door, Sandy stopped her again. "Where's Stink?" she asked.

"He's fine, honey. We have him at our place. And good luck getting him back. Matthew is nuts for him."

After a few days, Sandy was transferred out of the intensive care unit. Margie not only remained in attendance but made sure Sandy was placed in a private room. The story was out. Sandy could see it in the faces of the nurses, both those caring for her and those who peeked surreptitiously through the open door of her room. She had seen the look before, the commingling of fear and awe, of revulsion and respect for the woman whose life unfolded so differently from their own. And this new story had blended into the old one from all those years earlier—not only a woman for whom men died, but now a woman who had killed one of those men herself. A woman who had survived a gunshot wound and beaten a man to death because he had killed another man, who had, they assumed, died for her. Their eyes revealed their uncertainty. Was she some sort of half-wild new heroine for them, or a cursed woman stalked by death? Should they admire her or pray for her redemption as they fled her presence?

One night Sandy woke to find Margie at her post in the chair by her bed, her forehead pressed to the edge of the mattress, crying quietly. Sandy lifted her hand and laid it on Margie's head. Margie's eyes dripped tears when she raised her head.

"Oh, honey. Goddamn it all," Margie said. "I wish we could bring that son of a bitch back to life so I could help you beat the motherfucker to death again."

Mingled with the irascible temperament and the profane tongue was a heart that cared deeply, unconditionally, for the lives she came into contact with. For Margie, love came naturally.

Margie rose from the chair, sat on the edge of the bed, and stroked Sandy's hair. Sandy grimaced with pain as she tried to sit up.

"Here," Margie said, and reached toward the button to release another dose of pain medication.

"No," Sandy said. Her lips began to quiver as she spoke. "Let me feel this. All of it."

For the first time since she'd regained consciousness, Sandy wept, with abandon, collapsed in Margie's relentlessly loving arms.

Margie had also taken charge of the arrangements for Keefe's body. Because the law required it, the county medical examiner had performed an autopsy, but it was perfunctory, given the obviousness of the bullet hole in the top of the head. Margie had contacted the Dawkins Funeral Home and Crematory, had the body sent there, and made arrangements for cremation. She'd also had Stamper contact them to assure them that Sandy had power of attorney over Keefe's affairs. The funeral director stopped by Sandy's hospital room to get her signature on the paperwork, as impeccably groomed and deferential as he had been when Sandy met with him at the end of the summer to tend to the arrangements for Edith. He took Sandy's hand as he offered his condolences and his sincere wishes that their paths wouldn't cross again anytime soon.

"Bullshit," Margie muttered after the funeral director left the room. "That hairsprayed fucker would love nothing more than to cash a few more of your checks."

J.D. had held back on visiting Sandy in the hospital, so riddled with guilt was he. He didn't make an appearance until Sandy had been moved to her new room, and Margie had insisted that this goddamn silliness had gone on long enough.

"I'm just so damned sorry." J.D. sat hunched over in the chair by Sandy's bed, staring at the floor, wringing his hands between his knees.

"It's not your fault, J.D." She patted his forearm and listened as J.D. unburdened himself of the parts of the story the state police investigators had withheld.

J.D. reminded Sandy about the dealer down in Pepper's Fork they'd arrested for bear poaching and trading illegally in bear organs and body parts, the one they arrested the same day as Sandy's trial. In order to make an already light sentence even lighter, the dealer had reached an agreement with the authorities to give up his suppliers, the most prolific of which was one Charles Heaton, who lived back in the woods somewhere on the east slope of Rogers Ridge. And if you were going after that crazy son of a bitch, the dealer had said, you damned well best go armed.

Once they'd located his camp, J.D. and two teams of deputies and a dog from the new K-9 unit of the Sherwood County sheriff's office had gone out there to serve a search warrant and cite him. When they arrived the morning after it snowed, they found the carcass of a dog that had been shot through the top of the head, a stack of bear hides, a load of poached bear meat, and a lot of ammunition, but Heaton was gone. Searching the camp, they found a storage cave dug into the hillside. When they were about to leave, to return later, their dog began to raise a fuss around a mound of recently dug earth inside the storage cave. It only took a few minutes of digging in the loose earth to reveal the decaying remains of a human body, who later turned out to be that Randy Mullins fellow who had gone missing last spring. His wallet was still in the pocket of his pants.

Once the body was found, all hell broke loose. A radio call went out to the office in Sherwood, and the state police were notified. One team of deputies followed the tire tracks in the snow and soon radioed back that they'd found what must be Heaton's pickup truck on an old logging road that connected with the fire road that ran down along the upper Ripshin. With the truck and the empty rifle scabbard they found in the cab, they knew that Heaton had to be somewhere in the ravine, hunting.

Now they were no longer dealing with an issue of broken game laws. This was murder, and J.D. was quickly out of the lead role. While the deputies prepared themselves, waiting for reinforcements and the arrival of the state police, J.D. raced down to the fire-road gate, intending to drive up to the bungalow to inform Sandy and Keefe of the threat of danger. When he got there, that damned rusted old padlock wouldn't budge. While he waited for a deputy to arrive with bolt cutters, he'd tried to call the bungalow, he had, but the cell signal was too weak and the connection failed.

"I thought that was you," Sandy said.

"God, I'm so sorry," J.D. said.

"It wasn't your fault, J.D."

His hands folded into fists and shook visibly. Margie stood behind the chair and leaned over, wrapping her arms tightly around her shaken husband.

"Why didn't I just call in to the office? Have them call you?"

"J.D." Sandy's hand on his forearm tightened. "It's not your fault."

Sandy rolled back onto her pillow and stared out the window.

When Joyce Malden and Tommy Akers stopped in to see her, Joyce sat at Sandy's bedside, patting her hand.

"Oh, poor dear. Bless your heart."

Tommy stood behind Joyce, holding his cap in his hand. The eyes in his ruddy face showed worry as his fingers fidgeted with the bill of the cap. He was clearly unsure what to say to the woman he thought he knew as a neighbor, as a friend, but who was now beyond anything he had ever known of a woman.

Joyce reached down to a tote bag by her chair, produced a small pumpkin, and set it on the table by Sandy's bed. "Get Well Soon, Sandy" was written across the pumpkin, and both Joyce and Tommy had signed it.

"That's the last pumpkin from the garden this year," Tommy said.

"It was Tommy's idea," Joyce said. "He's a big oaf, but he's got his sweet side, too."

"Thank you," Sandy said.

"Pretty sorry-ass pumpkin," Tommy said, "but it's about the best we could do. Flood made one hell of a mess of the garden. You saw that. Lucky there was anything there to harvest at all. That damned government—"

Joyce turned in her seat and swatted at Tommy's hands. "Now you just stop it. Enough of that. We're here for Sandy, not your grumbling."

Even though it made her jaw ache, Sandy couldn't restrain a slight smile at Tommy and Joyce's exchange, the good-natured, cranky banter only possible between two people who had comfortably settled into their roles as two halves of a couple. She thought someday she might tell Tommy about the mountain lion, let him know he'd been right about the big cat. But she couldn't risk it, not now.

Because of a postoperative infection, Sandy was kept in the hospital longer than originally predicted, and Margie insisted on having Thanksgiving dinner in her hospital room. She arrived on the holiday with J.D. and the boys in tow. From an array of bags and plastic containers, she produced a massive holiday feast and began to set the food out on Sandy's tray table, her bedside table, and on a gurney she'd pilfered from down the hall. Given how much time she'd spent at her side, Sandy couldn't imagine when Margie had been able to put it all together.

"Next year you can make the pies," Margie said as she set a pumpkin pie on the gurney.

J.D. and Matthew wanted to know if it would be okay with Sandy if they watched the football game on the television mounted on the wall in front of Sandy's bed.

"Thanks," said Matthew, jabbing at the buttons on the remote control.

"How's my dog?" Sandy asked Matthew.

"Stink's cool," the boy answered, "but he smells kind of funny, doesn't he?"

"True enough," Sandy said.

While J.D. and Matthew watched the game and Margie darted about setting up the meal, Sandy noticed that Luke, the older boy, held back, standing by the window, his bird book in his hands, staring at the floor. Sandy caught Margie's eye and nodded toward the boy. Margie peeled the cover off a container of stuffing, and spoke to her son.

"Go ahead, honey. Tell her what you wanted to say."

The boy walked slowly toward Sandy's bed, still looking at the floor.

"What is it?" Sandy asked.

"That Mr. Keefe. He's dead, isn't he?"

"Yes, he is, Luke."

The boy stared at the floor a moment longer, then turned his eyes first to his mother, then to Sandy.

"I'm sorry. He showed me a pileated woodpecker. Hardly anyone ever gets to see a pileated woodpecker, but he knew right where to look. That was nice of him. He was kind of weird, but he was nice, too. I'm sorry he died."

J.D. looked over his shoulder at his stepson. Margie held a green-bean casserole in one hand, her other hand over her mouth as her eyes welled up.

"Thank you, Luke," Sandy said. "I'm sorry, too. And you're right. He was kind of weird."

By the time Sandy was released from the hospital, the police had received the results of the ballistic tests done on the two guns found at the scene, confirming that the same pistol had killed both Randy Mullins and James Keefe. The bullet that wounded Sandy Holston was never found. The case had been resolved to their satisfaction. Ms. Holston had clearly acted in self-defense. No charges would be brought against her. A carved walking staff, heavily caked with dried blood, had been taken into evidence. It was never returned.

Margie's sons were back in school, and J.D. took a couple overdue days off to be home for them while Margie took a couple days off to stay with Sandy until she was sure her friend could manage for herself. Sandy protested, insisting she was fine, but Margie was having none of it.

"Don't even go there. It's not going to happen," Margie had said. "Besides, gives me a break from the endless joys of motherhood."

Sandy rode in the passenger seat of Margie's van. With her good hand, she held the black plastic urn containing Keefe's ashes in her lap. Stink sat on the floor behind them, his head protruding between the two women in the front. The fire-road gate hung open, the severed old lock not yet replaced. When the van arrived at the bungalow, though her legs were still rather weak, Sandy got out, let Stink out of the rear seat, and began walking across the clearing, headed straight for the pool.

"Wait. Where are you going?" Margie had to trot to catch up to Sandy and stop her. "What are you doing?"

"Ashes." Sandy stared straight ahead, her eyes locked on the clearing pool.

"Right now?" Margie said.

"Yes, now."

"Okay, I'm guessing you're planning on tromping right out there in the water, so at least come inside. Put your waders and something warmer on." With this promise, Margie was able to turn Sandy back to the bungalow. "Might want to remember you're convalescing from a gunshot wound, a broken scapula, and a post-op infection. Adding pneumonia to the list, not such a good idea."

After Margie helped her into her waders and draped a coat around her shoulders, Sandy retrieved the urn from the kitchen counter and headed for the door.

"Hold on a minute, you," Margie said.

Sandy stood at the front door, staring out into the clearing, while Margie found Keefe's waders hanging from the antlers behind the open door. They were too big for her, but she managed to cinch them up securely enough to walk, took Sandy by the arm, and led her out the door. Stink was sniffing around the jumble of firewood still lying on the front porch, but when Sandy and Margie left the bungalow and started across the clearing, he hobbled down the steps and trotted after them.

At the bank of the stream, Sandy stopped and looked down. A length of tattered yellow caution tape was tangled in a fallen branch. Sandy leaned and reached for it, but on her weak legs she lost her balance and nearly fell before Margie caught her by the arm again and held her upright.

"Let me, honey." Margie tore the tape out of the branch and stuffed it in the pocket of her jacket. Sandy had already begun to move down the bank into the pool, and Margie rushed to catch up. Stink sat on the bank, watching.

The current forked smoothly around their knees when they reached the middle of the pool and stopped. The water was cold and clear. A mild wind funneled down the ravine, seeming to run parallel with the river, as if they both issued from the same source, high up the slopes of the headwaters. The winter-thinned forest opened around them in various shades of brown and evergreen. The mouth of the cave on the far bank opened into a dark, vacant center.

Sandy gripped the urn in her good hand while Margie removed the lid and unfolded the opening of the plastic liner. Sandy spoke in a low whisper, barely audible. "I am mad for it to be in contact with me."

"What'd you say?" Margie asked.

Sandy didn't repeat the words. Her hand shook slightly from the weight as she upended the open urn and poured Keefe's ashes into the waters of the clearing pool. The ash fanned out, marking the course of the current that would carry them downstream, through pools bathed in blood, to paint the stones of the headwaters, settle into sediment, flow on through the lake and dam into the lower Ripshin, to blend with the ash of Edith Moser in the shade of a vanished hemlock tree and be carried on still further, inviolable, washed on to a distant sea.

Sandy stared at the swath of thinning gray film on the water. She felt Margie's arm slide around her waist to hold her up, and she was grateful for it. It had taken her a lifetime to learn to love, and so much of what she had loved had been ripped from her in the span of little more than two seasons. She thought surely she must now feel irreparably alone, but she didn't. The casing of her skin no longer marked her outer boundary. She did not end there. The water pulsing down the slopes of the headwaters bore no difference from the blood pulsing through her veins.

"Let's go inside now," she said to Margie.

"Of course. Come on, we'll make a fire." Margie pressed her arm more tightly around Sandy's waist and helped her friend walk out of the river. Stink rose and trotted after them, across the clearing, back inside the bungalow.

THE sun had set while she rested, and night had settled into the ravine. With her right hand, Sandy tugged the blanket around her shoulders and rose from the sofa. The fire was burning nicely, but she took the poker to it, for good measure, and shifted one piece of firewood. A few new flames flared up. She'd been home from the hospital for nearly a week but had yet to do more than glance at Keefe's tying bench. As she walked to it now, she saw that a fly still sat notched in the vise. For a moment, she wondered if it were one of hers or Keefe's, but she knew the answer to the question before she finished asking it of herself. She switched on the light in the magnifying loop and examined the fly. Yellow stonefly. Its shank was wrapped tightly, each thread wound with precision, the hackles swept back and fluffed perfectly. Keefe's work, most certainly. The wrapping around the head of the fly had been left unfinished, not yet tied off. The thin red strand of thread hung down, still connected to the bobbin lying at the base of the vise. When her wounds healed, when she had use of her arm and hand again, she would finish the work.

Through the kitchen window, Sandy saw the bright sweep of headlights coming down from the fire road. Margie had arrived. Sandy turned off the light on the tying bench, walked to the front door, and flipped on the porch light. Margie stomped up the steps as Sandy opened the door.

"It's already started," Margie said as she swept through the door, carrying a large tote bag. The flakes of snow peppering the shoulders of her coat began to melt immediately in the warm interior of the bungalow. Stink looked up at her from his post on the sofa, his tail thumping on the leather cushions. Margie leaned her face down to the dog and let him lick her nose. "How's my boy? Are you taking care of our girl?"

While Margie began to unload the contents of the tote bag onto the counter, Sandy stepped out onto the porch. The snow fell steadily, a thick curtain of big flakes. Already the clearing was coated with an inch or two of new snow. In the middle of the clearing, Sandy could see Keefe clearly, like a figure framed within a painting, striding toward the river bank, his walking stick gripped in his hand. If she had ever thought that memory unfolded with continuity and symmetry, like the orderly turning of pages in a book, she was no longer so naïve. Whole vast chunks of her life were tucked away in the folds of her brain, barely accessible, while others, records of a single, brief moment, leapt out loud and unbeckoned, with startling clarity. Memory would have its way with her, and she would let it.

"The snow's pretty heavy," Sandy said as she came back inside from the porch.

"Isn't it beautiful," Margie said.

"If this keeps up all night, we could get snowed in. You'll be stuck here."

"Oh, honey. That's the plan. That is the plan."

Sandy smiled and walked to the counter.

"If it's as much snow as they predict," Margie said, "the boys'll be home from school and will flat out drive me crazy. J.D.'s there. They'll be fine. I just worked five straight twelve-hour shifts and now I have two days off. I've earned a little vacation. No, this snow is just the ticket."

"What is all this?" Sandy asked, nodding at the containers piled on the counter.

"Supplies, of course. Food and drink to sustain us through the storm. Don't want to end up like one of those icky stories. You know, people trapped in a cabin during a blizzard, out in the middle of bum-fuck nowhere, with nothing to eat, and they're forced to roast and eat the dog to survive."

Margie leaned over the counter and spoke to Stink in a coddling voice. "Just kidding, sweetheart. We'd never eat you. Besides, you'd probably taste like skunk."

Sandy walked to the stove, lifted the saucepan from the burner, and turned to Margie. "Want some tea?"

"Not on your life, honey." With a flourish, Margie reached into the cavernous tote bag and produced four bottles of red wine. "As a medical professional, I pronounce you sufficiently recovered to have a party. God knows you deserve one."

There were no wine glasses in the bungalow. Sandy took two tumblers from the cupboard, and Margie poured them each a generous glass.

"Let's go toast the snow." Margie still wore her coat. She took a heavy woolen coat of Keefe's that hung by the door, wrapped it around Sandy's shoulders, and the two women walked outside. On the way out, Sandy lifted a finger free of the glass she held and flipped off the porch light.

Snow continued to fall. The ground of the clearing, the bare trunks of the trees, the broad green leaves of the surrounding rhododendron, all coated with a pristine cloak of snow. The whiteness of the snow seemed to create its own light. Sandy could see across the clearing to the stream, across the clearing pool to the faint outline of the cave.

"God, it's beautiful," Margie said. "To the snow." She raised her glass before her and downed a hearty swallow of wine. Sandy took a small sip.

"And to James Keefe." Margie raised her glass toward Sandy, who raised her own glass and tapped it against the lip of Margie's.

"To James," Sandy said, and raised her glass again to her lips.

Margie pulled a pack of cigarettes from her coat pocket, took one out, and lit it. She blew a long, lingering plume of thick smoke into the cold night air. And through the drifting vapor, Sandy saw it. Across the clearing, in the dim, snowy light on the far side of the clearing pool, the fleeting flash of the tawny flank, the impossibly long tail disappearing into the cave. It was gone before it had fully registered in Sandy's vision. She stared through the falling snow at the dark center of the cave, wondering if the tangle of her own memory and longing had painted the image onto the night. She glanced at Margie, who stood still as a stone, wine in one hand, cigarette in the other, looking across the clearing, her eyes wide with wonder.

"Honey, did I . . . did I just see what I think I saw?" Margie had seen it, too. The mountain lion had returned to her den.

"Yes," Sandy said. "Yes. She's home." And once again, barely a whisper. "She's home."

Acknowledgments

I am immeasurably indebted to the editors at Swallow Press for their skillful guidance along the path that led to a better novel than the one I originally handed them. For an understanding of the mountain lion and its way of living in our world, I drew upon Chris Bolgiano's fine book, *Mountain Lion: An Unnatural History of Pumas and People*. Robert A. Levine's *Defying Dementia* was a valuable resource for shaping the particulars of the dementia that begins to afflict Keefe in the novel. This novel could not have come into being without the support of Rosemary Guruswamy, chair of the Department of English at Radford University, who scheduled my teaching life to allow space for my writing life. My special gratitude to Dan Woods and Rick Van Noy—friends, colleagues, and fishing buddies—who were always there and selflessly ready to wade through the waters of trout streams and the early drafts of this novel along with me. And finally, my thanks to Jeff and Lisa Saperstein—to Jeff, who drove us all home through the rain that night—and to Lisa, who was first to spot that mountain lion.